A MOMENT (

"This is a brilliant book. Some bits are funny, some bits are sad, but mainly the whole of the series is packed full of action, adventure and excitement. I think that people of my age will thoroughly enjoy reading this epic."

Scott Griffiths aged 12

Barry and Angie's next book – fancy a reading on the beach in Portugal? Best Wishes!

FEB. 07.

A MOMENT COMES

Colin Foreman

Edited by Lillian King

The adventure continues.
As Malcolm the Younger hides with his people in the lonely
places, and as Dougie and Alistair await their fate in the
dungeons of Mountjoy, Tella the Mac Mar orders the alliance
to attack, using new weapons made from the light iron.

In the north, Thorgood Firebrand rebuilds the Norse army
and waits for his own moment to come. As he watches the
Picts, Welsh and Angles place Stirling Castle under siege, an
unexpected ally, Prince Ranald, makes Thorgood a promise
that will change the course of history.

In our time, Odin begins to build his empire and the world
kneels to his power. Peter is consumed by grief, as he hugs
Kylie's body, and Myroy helps him understand why he must be
the last Keeper of Amera's stone.

In the passing of a single hour, on a concrete slipway, the
world changes forever.

A Moment Comes is the third part of a five book series
titled, Keepers and Seekers.

Copyright © Colin Foreman 2006

The right of Colin Foreman to be identified as the
Author of the Work has been asserted by him in accordance
with the Copyright and Patents Act 1988

A catalogue record for this book is
available from the British Library.

Printed and bound in Poland by Polskabook

Published by Myroy Books Limited
Hillside House, Glenlomond, Kinross. KY13 9HF

ISBN – 978 0 9548949 2 4.

Acknowledgements

I would like to thank the following people.

Lillian King (Magnificent editing)

Wayne Reynolds (Drop dead gorgeous cover paintings)

Fiona Campbell (Cool black and white illustrations)

Rosie Crawford (Spot on proof reading)

Ian Donaldson, Royal Bank of Scotland, Kinross (A
bigger overdraft)

John Webb (Design, support, a bill for a laptop and
the coolest poster ever)

Robert Snuggs at Bounce (Boundless raw energy)

Martin West at Catnip (Super sourcing)

Craig Brown (Everything to do with getting the
book ready for the printer – the hard bit!)

Abi, Jonny and Scott (Rave reviews)

CONTENTS

ABOUT BOOK ONE

Seven and a half thousand years ago, as the great ice sheets begin to thaw across Scotland, four brothers, Odin, Thor, Tirani and Myroy, survive a terrible accident to become Ancient Ones. The key to their eternal lives and extraordinary powers is a living ruby.

Fearing his brother's cruel ambitions, Myroy steals the stone from Thor and destroys his invasion fleet. Odin, who is driven by anger and greed, swears vengeance for Thor's death and vows to recover the ruby, and use its power to destroy the free peoples of Scotland.

There follows a cat-and-mouse game, through the long centuries. Myroy chooses the Donald family and their descendants to live a quiet life, and hide the stone from Odin and his followers, the Seekers.

In our time, three children visit their grandparents in Scotland and get lost in a snowstorm. When they take shelter in a cottage, Myroy tells them a story about a Celtic shepherd who lived centuries ago.

Dougie of Dunfermline faces the challenges of Mountain, Island and Castle to become the first Stone Keeper. Even though Dougie survives these challenges he knows little about the stone's power, or the danger it holds for his family. Certainly, he does not know that Gora and the souls of everyone who has ever tried to steal Amera's stone, remain trapped inside the ruby, waiting for someone to give the stone away, break Thor's curse, and release them.

Storm clouds gather for Dougie's king, Malcolm the Younger, and for his people, who are surrounded by enemies' intent on their destruction. Norse warriors, led by Thorgood Firebrand, invade the north of the kingdom to escape famine in their own lands. At the same time, Tella the Mac Mar, eager for revenge after his defeat on Carn Liath, forges a secret and terrible alliance with the Welsh and the Angles.

When the old man's story is told, Peter Donald realises that he is to become the next Stone Keeper. The ruby is passed on to him, but he loses it, and not to Odin's Seekers, but to Smith, a descendant of Tella the Mac Mar. Smith tricks Peter's sister into giving him the ruby and he uses its fantastic power to invade London. During the battle of Pinner High School, Peter recaptures the stone, but at an awful price, and he flees with his grandmother to Corfu.

ABOUT BOOK TWO

Tella the Mac Mar cements his alliance, with the Angles and the Welsh, by gifting them a copy of a map. Denbara the Scribe travelled the length and breadth of the Scottish kingdom, and recorded the fast ways to travel and lonely places where armies might hide. Worse still, Tella discovers how to make a new and stronger type of iron, that will tip the balance of power in his favour.

As his evil Alliance grows in power, Alistair of Cadbol is imprisoned in the bowels of Berwick Castle, under sentence of death. His friends, Dougie, Donald and Hamish, pull off a daring rescue, which changes a number of lives. Hamish of Tain falls in love with a gypsy girl. Dougie of Dunfermline is made a member of the Younger's High Table, and Gora's spirit is finally freed from Amera's stone.

Malcolm the Younger sends the High Table to search his kingdom for clues about who is making the new light iron. Alistair suspects that the Picts are using the port of Stranraer to smuggle weapons to their allies and the search leads Dougie of Dunfermline into a vicious battle in a fort on the island of Man. The slaves of the foundry defeat the Black Kilts, but Tella escapes the island and sends his envoys to Mountjoy, to win the support of the Irish King, Patrick Three Eggs.

At the same time, the Younger realises he will face the three armies of Tella's alliance alone, and he sends Alistair and Dougie on another mission. To offer Patrick Three Eggs a gift. The hand of Murdoch's daughter in marriage. But Margaret has other ideas and falls in love with Patrick's son, Seamus.

Tella's envoys, Borak and Tumora, fear the Scots and the good relations they enjoy at the Irish court. In a bid to destroy a possible Scottish and Irish alliance, they trick Seamus into believing that Alistair and Dougie poisoned his father. They are now imprisoned and face death.

During the Second World War, Bernard recruits Peter's grandfather, Duncan Donald, into the Long Range Desert Group. But Duncan loses the stone and its incredible power threatens to turn the war in North Africa against the Eight Army.

With luck and a brilliant idea from Private Chalk, the friends escape from a prisoner of war camp, travel across the desert and steal back the stone from General Georg Grau. The General's convoy of fuel is destroyed, before it can re-supply the German tanks west of El Alemein, and the Allied forces secure a famous victory.

In our time, Odin's forces hunt Peter down on the island of Corfu. Thorgood Firebrand captures Kylie and uses her to trap Peter. Odin takes Amera's stone and the world becomes divided.

In this book, Malcolm the Younger hides with his people in the lonely places, and as Dougie and Alistair await their fate in the dungeons of Mountjoy, Tella the Mac Mar orders the alliance to attack, using new weapons made from the light iron.

In the north, Thorgood Firebrand rebuilds the Norse army and waits for his own moment to come. As he watches the Picts, Welsh and Angles place Stirling Castle under siege, an unexpected ally, Prince Ranald, makes Thorgood a promise that will change the course of history.

Now, Odin begins to build his empire and the world kneels to his power. Peter is consumed by grief, as he hugs Kylie's body, and Myroy helps him understand why he must be the last Keeper of Amera's stone. In the passing of a single hour, on a concrete slipway, the world changes forever.

PROLOGUE

ANCEVO RIDES WEST : AUTUMN 677 AD

In the Scottish war camp at Glen Shee, Malcolm the Younger looked into his friend's eyes.

"What shall I do?"

Myroy smiled to reassure him.

"There is nothing you can do, at the moment anyway. Keep your men here, in the lonely places, and rest them. Keep them safe and ready. Let the enemy come, and do not let fear overcome your judgement."

"How is Dougie?"

"He is imprisoned with Alistair, because of a killer in the dark."

"But you believed he would play an important part in the war against the Alliance."

"You do not know it yet, but he has already played a part and will do so again."

"It is Llewellyn I fear. He has Amera's stone."

"He has, and you will come to be glad of it."

Malcolm raised an eyebrow and Myroy continued quickly.

"Oh, he is using it against you now, but that might not always be so."

"How can I be sure?" asked the king.

Myroy drew a circle on the floor with his staff.

"You cannot be *sure*, you can only have hope."

"Ranald has fled. Was he a part of it?"

"It was as you suspected."

"My own son," gasped Malcolm.

"You are not the first king to have been betrayed by the ambition of his own kin."

"That is true, but this knowledge is painful for me to hold in my heart."

"You knew when the Elder died that it would not be easy to wear the crown and yet you have reigned justly, and carried the burden well. Do not lose hope or faith in those who support and love you."

Malcolm felt strengthened by his friend's words.

"Your moment *will* come," said Myroy, "wait for it."

3

Then he disappeared into the ground.

The king gave instructions for eight riders to join him and they arrived before he had a chance to add his new knowledge to the map. The warriors were mounted on tired, filthy horses and formed a semi-circle in front of his tent.

"I have a task of great importance for each of you," said Malcolm.

Some of the men loyally raised their swords and everyone felt the tension in the king's words. A cool breeze blew through the camp and one of the horses snorted, and reared up on its hind legs. Malcolm pointed to five of his warriors in turn.

"I raise my standard at Glen Shee. Go to each corner of the kingdom and tell every man who can fight to bring food and claymore there."

The riders galloped away without a word, leaving three to learn of their mission. Malcolm looked into their eyes as if measuring the impact his words would have. At last he spoke to two of them.

"Go quickly to our armies who stand before the Picts and the Welsh. Tell them to join me at Glen Shee. As they march they are to destroy everything that might give comfort to the enemy."

The two men nodded and left.

Malcolm spoke to the last messenger. Ancevo was young, tall, lean and eager, and, like Dougie, more used to life on the farm than the ways of the warrior.

"Go to Alistair at the Irish Court and tell him Scotland has fallen."

Ancevo's forehead creased with worry. You could have run a plough along its deep furrows and he wondered if the king believed there was really no hope of victory. Malcolm gestured to him to dismount and they walked alone, talking in secret, and the Younger gave him a parchment. Then they shook hands and the rider went west, on a mission that would be more dangerous and vital than those of the other messengers.

Two days' hard riding later, Ancevo sat like a statue in the half

4

light and wondered if his powerful stallion was still safely tethered. The horse always seemed to sense when he was frightened. Did it smell his fear or use a deeper, more ancient sense that man does not possess? Ancevo knew his growing unease was a trigger for the stallion to bolt for safety and, if that happened when they entered Pictish lands, he could be left lost, injured, or even dead. He had already been thrown off once since leaving the Younger's camp and once was quite enough. That bruising was a clear warning and Ancevo decided to be stronger inside. Like his father.

Very slowly he lifted his bow, drew back the cord, stared down the shaft and let it fly. Then he was up and running into the field. As he pulled his arrow from a hare, the hare's body twitched and, picking it up by the hind legs, Ancevo dropped it into a leather bag which he swung onto his back. He ran back to his horse and stared at an orange glow above far hills. For the rest of the journey, that glow at sundown would guide him westward.

He had food now, but no time to eat it. He yawned and wondered when he might get the chance to stop and sleep again.

***

A felled tree, the height of a man's waist, blocked the path at the base of the ravine. Ancevo's fear rose as he lay in hiding, weighing up going back against going on. Doubling back and finding another way through the hills into the High Glens would add a day to his journey, maybe two days, and Malcolm the Younger had ordered him to travel swiftly.

Where the ravine was at its narrowest, a lone Black Kilt stood on guard, although more of the enemy might be resting in a rough-looking heather shelter that stood behind the felled tree. After a time, the Pict lowered his spear and went inside the shelter. Then the same man came back out and walked towards Ancevo, drinking from a wooden cup. Unseen, Ancevo silently retraced his steps, swung his provisions bag onto his back and walked slowly, purposefully, to his stallion. He spoke soothing words and ran his hand along the grey muscular neck, and felt the horse's sweat. Had it sensed his unease? Had it felt his shaking hands? He tried to reassure the animal.

"We will be fine. Have trust, boy."

He jumped up onto the saddle blanket, digging his heels into the horse's flanks.

The Pict dropped his mug, glared at the charging horse and ran forward with his spear held ready. Ancevo unsheathed his claymore and urged the strong grey stallion into a gallop. Above the thundering hooves, Ancevo heard the man call out for help. He drove the horse at him and they smashed into the man at speed. Two warriors ran from the hut and one raised an axe. The horse jumped the felled tree and, as they flew through the air, Ancevo slashed out at the man who held the axe. His claymore cut deep into the enemy's arm and the Black Kilt screamed.

Ancevo leant forward as low as he dared, holding on for dear life as his horse raced away, out of control, up the ravine. Cold sweat poured down his face and merged with the intense smell of the horse's own sweat. The Highland's long mane swept back into Ancevo's face as the beast set its powerful neck and swerved between the rocks. Ancevo tried to drive his fear of falling from his mind by thinking of his father's stern face. The stallion turned sharply and the saddle blanket began to slip on its drenched back. Ancevo gripped the reins tighter than ever and pictured his father again. Heard his father's words.

"With a stallion you must show no fear."

Ancevo pushed his face close to the stallion's head and in a steady, clear voice said, "Easy, boy, easy."

The stallion ignored him.

"We are safe now," he whispered and the horse began to slow. Ancevo felt elated. They had done it and neither of them were injured. He spoke again in a clear voice.

"Easy, boy, easy."

As the tension eased, the horse's pace slowed even further and finally they stopped on a grassy slope with the ravine far behind them. Ancevo jumped down, adjusted the blanket and patted the horse's neck.

"Good, boy."

Under dark threatening clouds, hunger gnawed at Ancevo's belly so they found a sheltered place to hide up in. He pulled the bag from his back and saw a black arrow sticking out of it, the shaft buried deep in the hare's carcass. Sensing his fear and smelling blood, the stallion stepped back, tossed his mane and stamped an angry hoof on the ground.

***

By late afternoon the weather had become more pleasant and the Highland trotted contentedly along wide, dry paths. Ancevo had travelled this way once before on the king's business, but never with such a burden. The Younger had commanded him to seek out Kenneth of Blacklock and gain his help for the voyage to meet Alistair and Dougie at Mountjoy. But if the Outer Islands and the High Glens had fallen, then Oban must be in Pictish hands as well. He knew that he should leave the wide track soon and cut across the high moors, or risk running into more of the Black Kilts.

So far he had enjoyed good fortune, but he remembered the ravine and decided that from now on he would sacrifice speed for caution.

He shut out the thoughts of the enemy from his mind and urged the stallion on, but suddenly he sensed something, some hidden danger, and pulled back on the reins. He glanced anxiously back down the path they had taken. It was deserted. He felt cold now and the low position of the sun told him that nightfall would soon slow his progress, but aid his concealment. He made up his mind to ride right through the night and hide up the next day to get some blessed rest.

"Come on, boy," he said, but the stallion refused to move. It wanted rest too.

"Come on, boy," he repeated firmly and they trotted on.

Framed against an angry red sky, the dark silhouette of mountains soon loomed up in front of them with the path winding its way towards their foothills before disappearing into the mighty glens. These glens were the natural routeways through the high places to the coast and he was sure they would all be guarded. He dismounted and urged his steed up the slope, searching in the failing light for one of the sheep tracks that ran secretly west.

Ancevo began to lose hope as darkness fell but he stood, at last, on a narrow twisting path halfway between the valley floor and a high ridge. He patted his horse and remounted, and they walked on. As they rounded a bend with great rocks on one side, Ancevo's face became grim. Campfires shone in the distance, forming a glowing ribbon along the whole floor of the glen. This was either a very large Pictish camp, or the resting place of Tella's entire army.

There were bound to be warriors on guard, so Ancevo pulled back on the reins, and reassuringly stroked his horse's neck. The beast snorted and Ancevo froze. The air was still and you could have heard a pin drop. He wrapped his fears inside the smiling faces of his family and shut his eyes so that every part of his mind could only concentrate on the sounds of the mountainside. It was deadly quiet.

Ancevo searched for something to tether the horse to and found nothing of real use, and so he dismounted and tied the stallion's front legs together with rope, making sure it was slack enough to allow him to graze, but not run away. He seemed more content now, so Ancevo silently left him and, under a waning moon, he darted, crawled and rested, and then darted for cover again. Sometimes the path was visible a good way ahead. Sometimes it fell into shadow and here he moved on blindly.

Then came the faint sound of voices that spoke in the strange tongue of the Black Kilts. Ancevo climbed upwards and, hidden by rock, inched to a point where he could look down on them. Four human shapes, all armed, sitting around a single fire and no horses to be seen. He inched backwards, returned to his steed, and they retraced their steps.

Ancevo searched for a way up to the summit, hoping that he

could drop down into the next valley and continue the mission. Above him loose scree, backed by a line of high cliffs, formed a dark impenetrable wall. Worried, he sat down to think. Dawn was a while away yet, but he could not wait. In daylight he would be seen and killed.

He peered across the glowing ribbon, in the bottom of the glen, to the far slopes. The ridge there was lower than on this side of the valley and dipped down still further to his right. Ancevo took a deep breath, held the reins firmly, and silently crossed the heather towards a gap in the enemy tents. A hundred paces away from them, Ancevo stopped to listen. No sound, except the pounding of his heart in his head.

"We will be alright," he said in a strong voice.

He led the horse carefully past tents, wagons and campfires. They crossed the main path that ran along the valley floor and moved through more tents and fires. Ancevo sensed the stallion's unease and stopped again to pat the horse's neck.

"We will be fine."

The beast tossed his mane, but made no sound. He had put his trust in him.

Ancevo counted each step to control his fear and they began to climb away to safety. He glanced back at the hundreds of campfires and smiled.

"We will rest soon."

With grass underfoot, the going became easier and they rose past thick clumps of gorse, and heather, moving silently until they stood on top of the narrow ridge which divided the two glens. As the sun came up, both rider and horse were numbingly tired. Below them, hidden from prying eyes in the enemy glen, was a small stand of pines. Ancevo led the weary animal into the trees and tied him to a pine. Satisfied that he could now leave him tethered, with enough space to find food, he decided to go back to the ridge. Ancevo crawled on his belly to the summit and lay there, looking back down at the glen he had left in darkness. It was crammed full of tents and warriors.

Bright sunshine streamed down the valley and he realised just how far they had climbed. Just how lucky they had been to escape capture. As he yawned a wave of fear ran through him. A group of twenty riders were galloping along the main pathway. One rider pulled back on his reins and stopped, and cried out as he pointed at the ground. He had spotted the hoof prints that ran clearly across the path and up the grass, before disappearing at the line of heather below Ancevo.

Ancevo's heart missed a beat as the other riders turned and galloped back to join the man. One rider, who might have been their leader, pointed down the valley and shouted angrily at the Pict who had delayed them, and they all rode on. Ancevo let his breath out and returned to the shelter of the pines.

He hadn't slept long before being woken by the sound of drums from the next glen. He rolled onto his side and opened his eyes, still half asleep, but something inside his heart urged him to seek out the sound, and he rose and ran back to the top of the ridge. Once more he crawled the last few paces and peered down. Thousands of Black Kilts were marching along the glen, creating the illusion of a writhing snake. At the head of the snake were riders followed by warriors who beat drums. Behind them marched row upon row of Black Kilts armed with spears and axes.

Ancevo counted the first block of warriors. Ten abreast and thirty deep, so three hundred men in that block. Six blocks of warriors in all and, added to the horsemen, drummers and any others who sat in the wagons that followed the snake, an army of about two thousand men. All the Picts were heavily armed and the thunder of their march continued for a long while.

Ancevo's heart went out to his king as Tella's mighty army headed east to attack him. He wondered if he should go back and warn the Younger, but decided to push on immediately.

By dusk he was beginning to sleep in the saddle and he punched his chest, scolding himself. He had come so far and it would be an act of stupidity to fail now. His head started to nod as his body surrendered to hunger and exhaustion and, without his encouragement, the horse stopped. It began to rain and Ancevo, jolted from his dreams, glanced around. The lower slopes were utterly barren and dark clouds completely obscured the mountain tops.

"I cannot go on," he said.

He dismounted and led the horse off the path towards the meagre protection of a ruined cottage. Inside its low walls he tied the faithful beast to a rock, wrapped himself up in his plaid, closed his eyes, and in seconds was dead to the world.

Wild neighing and a flash of lightning woke him. An almighty *boom* followed almost at once as the heavens collided. Rain lashed down and Ancevo opened an eye, and struggled to overcome his exhaustion. The stallion reared up onto its hind legs and his front hooves thudded down close to Ancevo's head. Alert in an instant, he saw the outline of his horse jump the low cottage wall and bolt away in fear. He chased after him, calling out, but the poor beast was absolutely terrified.

The hills lit up again as the storm reached its peak and Ancevo watched the grey shadow gallop away. Another mighty *boom* and the horse turned sharply on the hillside and kicked out with its hind legs at an unknown enemy. Then it was gone and Ancevo was left with no choice but to follow, as best he could, through the torrential rain.

By morning he had climbed to the head of a valley and warm sun broke through the clouds as the weather turned. Grazing on a grassy slope, the stallion snorted at him, suspiciously, and backed away whenever he moved closer. Ancevo avoided direct eye contact and tried to approach the Highland by walking slowly towards his great shoulders. The stallion backed away a short distance, grazed some more, but never took his eyes off him.

After many attempts and speaking soothingly, Ancevo slowly won back his trust and took hold of the reins. He looked west. The Great Sea stretched out to the horizon and there, perched on the edge of the land, was the village of Oban. Ancevo patted the horse and grinned.

"You clever boy."

At noon he let the stallion run free. At first, the great beast seemed reluctant to leave Ancevo and stared at him through his big, intelligent eyes.

"Go now, friend. I could not have had a more loyal companion, but the next part of my journey is across the Great Sea."

The horse snorted, turned and galloped away, mane and tail flowing back like grey silk blowing in the wind. Ancevo watched him go and felt a deep sadness at the parting, before turning himself and secretly making his way down towards the cottages. Black Kilts were everywhere and he waited for a chance to enter the village.

One warrior sat alone by the main pathway. Ancevo crept behind the man, clapped a hand across his mouth and thrust a dirk into his back. The Pict went limp and Ancevo dragged his body into a hollow protected by ferns. Dressed in the enemy's plaid, Ancevo walked between the cottages and searched for the model of a ship on a windowsill. He did his best to remain calm, but his stomach was tied in knots and he tried to suppress his fear by picturing the face of his father again.

Two Picts stepped out from behind a cottage about two hundred paces away and one waved at him. Ancevo waved back and kept walking, praying that they would not come over to talk to him.

The Black Kilts watched him for a while and turned away. Ancevo saw a model ship and entered the white cottage without knocking. A big man stared up from a chair and snarled. Ancevo closed the door behind him and passed Kenneth of Blacklock a parchment. The sailor snarled again and then raised an eyebrow as his visitor lifted his plaid. Beneath the black cloth was the king's own tartan of light brown, green and ochre. Kenneth read Malcolm's message and nodded.

Ancevo collapsed onto the floor.

CHAPTER ONE

A MOMENT COMES

Dougie of Dunfermline stared at his hands and tried to remember what they looked like. The cell was cold, as dark as pitch and shaped like a stone bottle buried in the earth. Dougie had been forced down a ladder into the depths of the bottle with Alistair, protesting his innocence as guards prodded them with spears. Then the ladder had been lifted away and a wooden trapdoor slammed shut high above their heads. In that moment, all the colours in the world disappeared as they were abandoned without light, sound or warmth.

Dougie felt the bandage on his leg. It was dry, so the bleeding must have stopped. It was still sore though, and he guessed that he would have quite a scar to show his children when he got home. If he ever did see his home again. His heart cried out to be shepherd and to have his simple life back.

Alistair had said that there was only one penalty for killing a king. Death. Certainly, the Prince of the Irish People believed them to be guilty and was in no mood to listen. Dougie could think of no way of proving that Borak and Tumora were behind it all and he shuddered as he remembered Seamus's anger as he shouted down at them from the trap door.

"The hemlock was under your bed. The bed my father gave you!"

Dougie didn't know what hemlock was and had shaken his head.

"We know nothing of this," said Alistair calmly, "we came here in friendship and have nothing to gain from such a terrible act."

"Nothing to gain," shrieked Seamus, "you had everything to gain from stopping my father side with the Picts."

Dougie had looked up and blinked in the bright light that flooded into the bottle cell.

"Ask Margaret. She can tell you of our intentions."

Seamus shook with rage as he spat out his words.

"Don't bring Margaret into this."

Then the trapdoor had slammed shut and the prince was gone.

That felt like a lifetime ago and no news, water or food had been brought to reduce their utter misery.

Alistair's soft breathing stopped for a second and he stirred.

"Anything happening?" he asked sleepily.

"No nothing, nothing at all."

"I wonder how Hamish and Donald are getting on," and Alistair went back to sleep.

***

"You are too big and ugly to be of any use," said Donald.

Hamish dropped the large stone he was lifting and growled menacingly. A young boy ran over to them and smiled.

"Mamma says that you are to stop work and join us for supper."

Hamish looked at the wee laddie and smiled too.

"Food you say. Fine news."

"Aye, wise words, soot face," chirped Donald.

Ewan was fresh faced and clean, and his stomach bulged with food. His eyes shone with life and Hamish remembered the first time he had seem him. Emaciated ribs had poked from his chest and only rags covered his modesty. As the boy emerged from the depths of the mine, carrying the *goal* that they had taken back to Archie, his skin had been as black as night.

But now the slaves of the foundry were free and the two friends had offered to help the family rebuild their cottage, partly to fend off boredom and partly because Ewan's father had fallen in the battle. The many acts of cruelty by their captors would never be forgotten by the people of Man and, wherever they went, the friends sensed a deep-felt hatred for the Black Kilts. But Gawain, the Lord of Man, had not changed his mind about helping them. He would wait until his moment came.

They sat, cross-legged, under a sail cloth inside the shoulder-high walls of Ewan's cottage. The sail had been draped over a ship's rope, tied between the top of the ruined chimney and a peg in the ground, to form a snug shelter.

"We will have the roof on the day after tomorrow," said Donald.

Rekki offered her guests another bowl of fish stew.

"It really is good of you to help us. Now eat up, Ewan. You have a lot of growing to do to catch up with Hamish."

Donald declined the extra bowl and patted his stomach.

"He could eat forever and not be as big as him."

Hamish had another bowl and winked at Ewan.

"We'd have the roof on now if Donald worked more and spoke less."

"At least I use my brains when I am working. I think you have put the gap for the door in the wrong place."

"I'm not moving it now," growled Hamish.

"It is just where I want it," grinned Rekki, "and I will be mighty glad to sleep in my own cottage again."

Ewan lifted the edge of the sail cloth and pointed at a man who walked quickly towards them.

"Is that not your leader?"

Donald and Hamish sighed.

"Oh no," said Donald, "it's Robert. I wonder what he wants now?"

The sail cloth was lifted.

"Ah. I thought I would find you two here. When there is work to be done you sit around eating."

Ewan detected a deep growling noise from the depths of Hamish's chest.

"Keep your plaid on," said Donald.

The Thane of Inverness winced.

"We have received news from Mountjoy. King Patrick is dead."

The friends glanced at each other.

"Well, that makes Alistair and Dougie's task more difficult," said Donald.

"Do you think we should sail for Ireland and help them?" asked Robert.

"The Younger told us to come here and win Gawain's support," growled Hamish.

"But his help depends on the Irish," said Robert.

"We must stay and ensure the Picts make no more light iron."

"Wise words," said Donald.

Robert shook his head.

"But what should we do?"

"I'm going to have more stew," said Hamish.

"Alistair may need our help," insisted Robert.

"Alistair can look after himself. He and Dougie are probably sorting things out as we speak."

"But if they fail, we fail too."

Hamish got up from the floor, grasped the Thane's shirt and lifted him up to look into his face.

"Sometimes you have to accept things as they are. Sometimes you have to have faith in your friends."

***

Shaken from his dreams, Alistair sat bolt upright as the trap door was lifted open. Light burst into the bottle cell and a ladder was lowered down.

"Come up now," barked a voice.

"Well, this is it, young Dougie," mumbled Alistair and Dougie's heart sank.

They were completely blind as they crawled from the top of the ladder. Strong hands grabbed them and marched the prisoners up more stairs and they emerged onto the green. It was deserted.

"How long have we been imprisoned?" asked Dougie, but Finnegan and O'Mara refused to answer and roughly pushed him forward towards the banqueting hall.

They entered a packed hall and were led down the central aisle to stand before the raised table. Seamus was there, with Finn behind him, and so was Margaret. She smiled weakly at them and

Dougie thought that she had been crying. The Prince of Ireland's face was like granite as he spoke in a quiet, deliberate voice.

"Tell me again why you did not eat the food brought by Milligan to my father?"

"We had already eaten our fill," said Alistair bravely.

Seamus stared at Dougie.

"And why was hemlock found under your bed?"

"I do not know."

"And were you both with my father, all the time that the food was prepared?"

"We sat with Patrick on the green and were ready to leave to go on the hunt when your father fell ill," said Alistair.

"But do you have proof that you were with him the whole time whilst the food was prepared, for that is when the poison was added."

Dougie glanced at Alistair and they both shook their heads.

"Bring Marla to me," ordered Seamus.

Finn McCool left the hall by a door behind the raised platform and quickly returned with a young servant girl. It was the same girl who had waited on them and screamed when Patrick fell. She looked scared out of her wits and Seamus smiled, and beckoned her to come and stand beside him.

"Do not be frightened, Marla, just tell me again about what happened when my father was taken."

The servant girl blushed and spoke in a hesitant voice.

"I was asked by Milligan to attend to the king's needs and I waited upon him, on the green, for many hours."

"And were the Scots with him?" asked Seamus.

She pointed at Alistair and Dougie.

"Two were. Those two."

"And did they stay with my father the whole time?"

"They did, they sat together talking."

"And you are quite sure that they remained together from the time before Milligan was sent away to prepare the food, to the time that my father fell ill."

"Quite sure," she replied.

A muttering sound went around the hall.

"And we know that the poison was placed in a cauldron, in the kitchen, only a short while before my father's death. Others had eaten from it and they have not fallen ill. If the Scots were with my father on the green, they could not have poisoned the food."

Relief flooded through Dougie's body and he felt weak. He staggered a little on his feet and Alistair grabbed his arm. Seamus stared at them both. His face was hard and without any sign of feeling.

"You did not kill my father. That treachery belongs to another and we shall find him. You are free to go."

Seamus rose and left with Finn at his side. At the back of the hall Tumora glanced at his brother. Borak's face was grim and he thought he heard him say,

"They are sure to suspect us. We must be careful."

***

Alistair and Dougie were alone in their room, in the main keep, and ate like they had never eaten before. Marla had brought them trays of food, on Seamus's instructions, and Dougie had thanked her for speaking up on their behalf. The young servant girl had smiled.

"I only told the truth," she said and left them.

The friends finished off every morsel and the chamber door opened.

"Come with me," ordered Finn.

They rose and followed, half running, half walking, to keep up with the giant man.

"What's the matter?" panted Dougie.

"Seamus wants to see you both now."

Finn led them along the corridor and down the stairs to the castle gardens. Seamus stood beside Margaret, holding her hand. Behind them was a dozen armed warriors.

19

"So you are refreshed then," smiled Seamus.

"Aye, Your Majesty," replied Alistair, "and I am mighty glad to be out in sunshine again."

"And what a day this is going to be. You need to know that many things have happened during your imprisonment."

Dougie raised an eyebrow at Margaret. She had the strangest look on her face. It seemed both joyous and sad.

"Murdoch, the Protector of the Outer Islands has fallen on the field of battle and the Picts hold Mull."

Dougie's heart went out to Margaret.

"Oh, my lady, I am so sorry."

Margaret nodded at him.

"I have had time to grieve, and my father's memory will be with me forever. But Dougie, I must move on. We must all move on."

She glanced at Seamus who lifted her hand and kissed it.

"When I saw my father dying upon the green I felt an anger that I did not know I possessed. That anger became directed at you. I want to apologise for the way I treated you both."

"On behalf of the Younger, we promise our loyalty and friendship," promised Alistair.

"Thank you," said Seamus, "and you also need to know that tomorrow I shall be crowned King of the peoples of Ireland."

"It is in the most terrible of circumstances," said Alistair, "but I have no doubt that you will be a great king."

"And a great husband," added Margaret.

Dougie lifted an eyebrow again.

"You are to be married? How wonderful."

"Tomorrow," beamed Seamus, "and then the Princess of the Islands shall be my wife."

"I do like a good wedding," grinned Alistair and they shook hands.

"It is a tradition here that the bride must be given away and I would like you, Alistair, to act as Margaret's companion during the ceremony," added Seamus.

"That would be an honour and a pleasure."

"In fact the coronation and the wedding are to be combined. Columba will oversee them both."

Alistair thought about Myroy's prediction about the joining of the royal houses. Margaret was certainly descended from the Elder, but was Seamus a part of the Donald line? He doubted it and wondered what the future would hold for them. Dougie sensed Alistair's unease and thought his friend wanted to talk to Seamus about gaining his help in the war that now raged across the sea. But as Seamus talked excitedly about the wedding arrangements, Dougie knew that now was not the right time and so he kept quiet.

***

Thousands and thousands of people lined the track leading to the palace of Mountjoy. They cheered and jostled for the best position to see Prince Seamus and the wagon that was drawn by ten of the finest horses in the kingdom. The wagon was full of flowers and had brightly coloured shields hanging on the sides so that none of its six wheels could be seen. Some of the crowd sang and many threw flowers before the procession. Finn sat behind Finnegan and O'Mara, who held the reins of the team. Margaret and Seamus sat close together, on the bed of flowers and waved at the people. O'Mara beamed at his family as they passed them.

"Oh. Look at them. They might have got dressed up, on such an important day," said Finnegan.

"Get dressed up," replied O'Mara, "I would be surprised if any of your family have had the bath these past two summers."

"Oh. Bath is it? I'll give you a bath, Michael O'Mara, and what a shock to the system that will be for you."

"The only shock I'll have is if I hear about a woman mad enough to marry you, Declan Finnegan."

Seamus smiled at Margaret and nodded at Finn, who leaned forward and whispered to the two bodyguards.

"Stop that, right now."

Finnegan and O'Mara stopped arguing.

Later, as music played and courtiers sang on the green, Seamus walked around the keep and into the garden. Margaret waited for him beside an apple tree, with Alistair at her side. When she saw her husband-to-be, she ran and threw her arms around him. Dougie smiled at Margaret.

"You look beautiful."

"Thank you."

"It seems that you have been able to choose after all," he said kindly.

"I think it is even better than that, I think you just *know*."

Dougie nodded and thought about Mairi.

It was a gloriously hot day and the hundreds of Lords and Ladies, who had been invited from all corners of the kingdom, wilted in their finery. Columba came over to join the gathering, followed by two monks, walking slowly and solemnly. One monk carried a book, the other a tall iron cross. Columba smiled and the cross was thrust into the grass, its sharp spear-like point slicing down easily into the earth in front of Seamus, Margaret, Alistair, Dougie and Finn.

They waited for Columba to speak. One of the monks stepped forward and opened the book, holding its pages open for Columba to read. It was the same book that Dougie had seen when Columba nursed him back to health. Columba read a passage from the bible about a man named Jesus, who had feasted with his friends, knowing that the next day he would lose his life. Judas had betrayed Jesus, but even he would be forgiven.

"It is not easy to forgive, or to love," said Columba, "and yet there is a power in each of them. A power that is greater than any other. Seamus, rule justly. Rule with forgiveness and love for your people."

In front of the great and good of all Ireland he placed the crown upon Seamus's head. A huge cheer went up from the crowd, and Alistair and Dougie found themselves cheering too.

In a corner of the garden, Borak and Tumora turned to go. They had seen enough and knew that the Irish people would now side with the Younger. The noise of their boots on the gravel path was drowned out by the celebrations.

Columba joined Margaret's and Seamus's hands, and made them swear their allegiance to the House of God. They made their promises to each other and Columba took the book and held its open pages in front of Alistair; his signal for Alistair to place two rings onto the pages. Alistair reached into his pocket, glanced at Seamus and shrugged his shoulders. The crowd hushed and the king went white. Then Alistair searched another pocket, placed the gold rings upon the bible, and winked at Dougie.

***

Matina sensed another argument and quickly placed a bunch of cut flowers into a vase, and walked to the chamber door.

"I shan't go on a tour of the kingdom, so you can go and boil your head," shouted Margaret.

"But, my angel, it is expected of us," pleaded Seamus.

Margaret armed herself and Matina stepped silently into the corridor.

"I don't care what is expected of us. I am not going and that is that."

Seamus ducked as a plate flew past his head and smashed on the door.

"But every new king and queen have travelled the land to meet their people."

"I am not going anywhere until you make your mind up."

"I have only been a king for two days and it is too soon to make a decision like that."

In an instant her voice became warm and loving.

"My father is dead and my people will be slaves. I do not see why you will not make a decision."

23

Seamus went over and kissed her.

"Please decide," begged Margaret and she hugged him.

***

The banqueting hall was packed with people again and buzzing with excitement. Rumours had been flying around the palace all day that the king had decided to help the Younger in Scotland. Few of the courtiers were happy about it and blamed the influence of the new queen. It was not their fight, and they could see little gain from such an adventure. Indeed, there was much to lose. These thoughts were shared by Seamus, but he also knew that the problem wasn't going to go away. Deep down he knew that he could not trust Tella and, if the Mac Mar did conquer Scotland, then he might turn on him one day.

Borak, Tumora, Alistair and Dougie stood before Seamus and Finn. The king sat with his arms folded and stared at the envoys of the Picts and Scots.

"War rages across Scottish lands and Malcolm the Younger is in hiding. We are under no obligation to support him, but he is a just king who holds my confidence."

Tumora had feared these words, but they were not unexpected. Borak stepped forward.

"This cannot be an easy decision to make," he said generously. "It is not easy for, whichever way you decide, it will surely involve the fair people of Ireland in a terrible war."

A low murmur ran through the hall.

"But there is another decision that can be made. A decision that involves great courage. As we speak, the Scottish lands are being divided and a new order, a better order, is being established. My king offers you friendship and seeks to trade with you to increase the prosperity of all our peoples."

Borak turned to address the hall.

"The other decision is to do nothing and to wait for the natural victor to emerge."

There were many nodding heads amongst Seamus's people

24

and Dougie sensed their mood. He glanced at Finn who smiled at him. Dougie smiled back and Seamus saw it.

"And what do you say, young Dougie?" he asked.

"Er, I am not sure," muttered Dougie.

Someone at the back gave a short laugh. Dougie stuck his chest out.

"Borak has clever words to support his view, but this is not about words. If you were in need we would help you."

"I believe you," said Seamus.

Borak knew the king would decide in favour of his enemy. If he didn't now, then, with Margaret's counsel, he would later.

"I beg you not to join the war. I say again, wait for the natural victor to emerge. The Picts and Irish have a great future together. You can still choose."

"How can I choose?" asked Seamus.

"How many of your people might be lost in a war? A hundred? Many hundreds? A thousand?" Borak pointed angrily at Alistair. "The Scots have forced you into a position where you cannot win. Why should so many die? Why can this not be settled by the actions of just two people?"

"So he wants to fight," thought Alistair.

"A duel?" asked Seamus softly.

"A duel to decide once and for all who the natural victor might be."

Dougie gasped and Borak stared at Alistair.

"I challenge you, Alistair of Cadbol, to fight for the support of the Irish people." He spat on the floor and added, "If you are brave enough."

Seamus spoke quietly to them both.

"This decision should not rest on the outcome of a fight."

Dougie saw Alistair glance at Borak. He seemed to be sizing him up.

"I am prepared to die for my people," said Alistair.

"Then let it be so," commanded the king, "you will face each other, tomorrow at noon."

***

"Why did you choose to fight the Scot?" asked Tumora, "he is spoken of as a great warrior."

"We had no choice," replied Borak.

"You have no choice now," said Tumora in a dark voice.

"We do have a choice. What if I was to fight the other one? The shepherd. What might the result be?"

Tumora saw his brother smile.

"Certain victory," he said.

***

After supper Marla dashed into their chamber and handed Alistair a parchment.

Dougie helped the young servant girl gather some plates together.

"What does it say?"

His friend read the parchment and paced around.

"It is an urgent message from the Younger's secret rider. He has news that can only be told to me and he waits with Kenneth at Belfast."

"I will go for you," offered Dougie, "you need to rest before you enter the duel."

"I cannot let you go. The instructions are clear enough. I must go, and go alone. If I leave now then I can be back by first light. I can rest then."

"Are you sure that I cannot come with you?"

Alistair shook his head and left for the stables.

***

The *Leaping Salmon* bobbed up and down against the quay in Belfast. Kenneth was fast asleep on the deck and his dreams were broken by someone calling his name. He sat up and found himself looking at Alistair.

"I received your message," said Alistair brightly.

"What's going on?" asked a sleepy voice and Alistair turned

26

to see two more tired faces peering out of their plaids.

"Greetings, Hugh and Rory," said Alistair.

"It's the middle of the night," grumbled Kenneth, "and I sent you no message."

Alistair pulled the parchment from his pocket and handed it over. Kenneth read it and shook his head.

"I did not send this, nor did the king's messenger, Ancevo. He rode for Mountjoy not long ago and he *does* have a message for you."

Alistair's stomach tightened.

"I must have passed him on the road."

"You have been fooled," added Kenneth.

"I wonder who would do that?"

As Alistair spoke these words, he knew the answer. He ran back to his horse, and called out his goodbyes. Kenneth pulled his plaid back over his body and, in moments, was snoring again.

Alistair urged his steed on and galloped along dark twisting paths. He knew the way now and was confident about reaching the palace before dawn. But a Black Kilt waited for him.

Tumora checked the bowstring and the flights of his arrows.

"Do not kill him," Borak had warned, "if you do, then Seamus will know for certain that we were behind it and he will be sure to suspect us for the death of his father."

"He already does," Tumora had replied.

"He does, but he does not *know*."

In his place of hiding, beside the path, Tumora shivered with the cold and blew into his cupped hands. He had watched Alistair leave Mountjoy, had followed him at a distance, and chosen a lonely place, with good cover beside the path, to hide up in. Now he listened intently for the sound of Alistair's horse and smiled at the thought of the Scot wasting his time in Belfast. Then Tumora's ears caught something. A rider was coming. He placed an arrow on the bowstring and drew it back. At point blank range he shot into the horse's flank and the beast fell, throwing Alistair into the air.

The Black Kilt mounted his own horse, and rode away in the darkness.

***

Hundreds of restless people gathered outside the palace walls and formed a circle around a grass arena. Seamus sensed the crowd's agitation at the delay and gazed up at the high sun. It was noon.

"I do not know where he is," persisted Dougie.

"He is a coward, like all the Scots," said Borak angrily.

"So the natural victor is chosen," yelled Tumora and the onlookers cheered.

"It does not look good for you, Dougie, or for the Younger's cause," said Seamus coldly.

He was trying not to show favour to either of the contestants, but secretly felt glad that Alistair, a man he liked and admired, was not to do battle with Borak. Dougie glanced down the track that wound its way east. It was deserted. Then he looked at Borak, at his shield and mighty battleaxe. The Pict was bigger than he remembered.

"Can we not postpone the duel until tomorrow?" asked Dougie, "I am sure that something terrible has happened to Alistair on his journey to Belfast."

"Hear me," cried Borak, "the Scot has run away to Belfast."

Some of the crowd laughed.

"Alistair would not run away," whispered Dougie and he saw that Margaret was pointing at him.

Dougie pointed to himself.

She mouthed, "You fight."

"Me fight Borak?"

Margaret nodded and Dougie's heart sank as a sword was thrust into his hands

"I tend the flock," he mumbled.

"So Scotland does have a warrior brave enough to entertain us," mocked Tumora.

The crowd cheered again.

"To the death," shouted Borak.

The crowd chanted.

"To the death! To the death! To the death!"

Borak stepped forward.

"Prepare to die, Dougie of Dunfermline."

At these words a wave of fear ran through Dougie's body and he glanced at Finn. The king's bodyguard stood beside Seamus and held a huge spear. He smiled at him and Dougie tried to smile back, but his lips didn't seem to work anymore.

"Let the duel begin," commanded Seamus.

Borak began to swing the axe high above his head.

"Your Majesty," yelled a voice, "a messenger for the Scots."

"Hold the fighting," commanded Seamus.

Dougie's fear turned to relief as Ancevo was escorted through the crowd to stand before him.

"My name is Ancevo and, from the description given to me by Malcolm, you must be Dougie of Dunfermline, the Shepherd Warrior. What is going on?"

"It is a duel and much depends on it. Have you seen Alistair?"

"I have not. Dougie I *must* give you a message from the Younger."

Borak was listening in, everyone in the crowd was listening in, and so Ancevo whispered.

"Malcolm needs you to lead Patrick's army to the castle at Stirling. His forces will meet you there."

"Patrick is dead and Seamus rules," said Dougie, "and this duel will decide our fate."

"Dougie, the Younger says that Llewellyn, the Welsh king, has Amera's stone."

"I thought it was safe," stammered Dougie.

"It has been taken from its place of rest in the loch."

Deep down, Dougie felt that things were utterly hopeless. The Younger's rider put an arm around his drooping shoulders.

"And I have the worst of news for you, Dougie of Dunfermline."

The shepherd knew something bad was coming. He felt sick.

"Malcolm has asked me to speak to you at the first opportunity and I would have chosen any other place than this. Your cottage has been put to the torch by the Black Kilts. I am so sorry, Dougie. Your family is lost."

Tears welled up in Dougie's eyes and he fell to his knees, sobbing.

"Can we get on with it?" yelled Borak.

Seamus glanced anxiously at the distraught figure who wept openly in the space surrounded by the crowd. The king nodded at Ancevo to leave the arena. He felt powerless to stop the duel and now feared for Dougie, for he knew he was no challenge to Borak.

"You have delivered your message. Go in peace."

Dougie felt completely empty and stood to face the enemy. The Pict grinned at him and began to wave his axe again. In that moment, Dougie was not looking at Borak. He was looking at the man who had killed Mairi and his children. Uncontrollable anger welled up inside him and he reached down to pick up the sword. As Dougie slowly lifted his head, Borak found that he was no longer looking into the eyes of a shepherd. He was looking into the red eyes of a fearless warrior. They were intense and full of hatred and rage.

And they were staring at him.

***

Tirani sat at a table, legs dangling, playing with a group of small toy warriors. One of the toys had a painted face that looked like the Younger. The other faces looked like Tella, Llewellyn, Cuthbert, Seamus and Thorgood Firebrand. Tirani positioned them so that the King of the Scots stood defiantly before the others. Llewellyn ignored his play and stared into the heart of Amera's stone. The ruby pulsed a deep red and, for a moment, he was blinded. As his sight returned, he turned to face Tirani.

"Something has happened. The stone's power is being used."

"It is."

Tirani the Wise smiled at a toy warrior with a Black Kilt. He gently placed his finger onto the warrior's head and tipped it over. Then he moved Seamus to stand beside the Younger.

***

Dougie screamed and charged. His sword smashed down onto the Pict's shield and Borak slipped and fell backwards. Another blow crashed down, then another and another. Borak regained his balance and cut downwards with his axe. It hit Dougie's sword and they stood, eyes locked together. Dougie smashed his fist into Borak's face and the Black Kilt fell onto one knee. Dougie raised his sword and brought it down onto Borak's shield again. The shield began to split. Dougie's sword smashed down, again and again. As Borak's shield arm tired, he lifted his axe and Dougie lashed out, severing the man's hand. The crowd gasped. Borak weakly raised the split shield to protect his face. Dougie's stood above him, white foam around his mouth, hitting what was left of it like a madman. The crowd were deadly silent.

Seamus nodded at Finnegan and O'Mara to go and stop Dougie.

"I have seen enough," he said.

They got within an arm's length of him. Dougie kicked O'Mara out of the way and picked Finnegan up, held him above his head and threw him into the sea of onlookers. Then he ran back to Borak and hacked with his sword at his shield.

"Dougie, please stop," yelled Margaret.

But Dougie did not hear. A red light burnt in his eyes and, with an incredible strength, he kicked and punched the guards who ran at him from all directions. A monk stepped out of the crowd and calmly stood beside the wild man.

"Remember, Dougie, that next to love, it is forgiveness that is the greatest of all powers."

Through the red mist Dougie saw Columba. Something in him, something he had never before experienced, something that should not have been there, left him. He looked down at Borak's battered shield and face, and his severed hand. Covered in blood, the Pict was crawling away like a dog.

Dougie dropped his sword and fell to his knees, and Columba placed a comforting hand on his shoulder. Behind them Tumora raised his own sword and lunged at Dougie. A spear cut through the air and plunged deep into the Pict's chest. He was knocked off his feet by the terrible impact and breathed no more. The crowd gasped again.

Seamus glanced across at Finn's grim face and took hold of Margaret's shaking hands. Tenderly, he kissed her fingers and then released them, and stood to address his people.

"So it is decided," he said. "We go to help the Younger."

CHAPTER TWO

ANCEVO SAILS EAST

"How is he?" asked Ancevo.

"Dougie needs his own company for a while longer," replied Alistair.

"Will you ask him to go with you?"

"I will, tonight. Seamus plans to lead his army to Belfast at dawn and I can see no point in leaving Dougie behind."

"You are a true friend, Alistair."

Two days had passed since the duel and Ancevo had told Alistair about Dougie's victory, Borak's departure and the gathering of the Irish army before his late return from the *Leaping Salmon*. At first, Alistair had not believed his friend could fight with such ferocity. Then he had stayed close to Dougie, shared his grief, and taken him on long walks around the shores of Lough Neagh. When he sensed that his friend wanted to be alone he left him to sit in their chamber. Outside the chamber, he often heard Dougie crying and he told himself there wasn't anything else he could do to help him. But he felt useless.

Borak had been tended by Columba and escorted by guards to the stables in the circular courtyard where Seamus gave him a clear warning.

"Borak One Hand. Go and find Tella. Tell him I am coming."

Borak was helped up onto a horse, and another horse was led into the courtyard and tied behind it. Tumora's body was roped to the second horse, sitting upright with Finn's spear still running right through his chest.

Borak glanced at his brother and then at the bandaged stump on the end of his arm.

"I swear vengeance on you, Seamus."

"If you were not a king's envoy, you would not be leaving Mountjoy alive."

"If I have to practise with the sword in my left hand a thousand times, I will do it to be ready for our next meeting."

"I look forward to that meeting, Borak One Hand. We both have a reason to kill each other."

Seamus nodded at a guard to open the gates and smacked Borak's horse. The horse stepped forward and, as Borak led his brother away, the new king watched the spear tip sticking out of Tumora's back. He called after Borak.

"That's for my father."

"I must leave too," continued Ancevo, "I can reach Kenneth before the evening tide and arrive on Man in two days. Is the message the same?"

"Aye, it is," said Alistair. "Ask Gawain to join us. His army is small, but he has ships. Ask him to destroy the Welsh and Pictish fleets."

"He will be outnumbered."

"We will all be outnumbered."

"And Hamish and Donald?" asked Ancevo.

"When their work is done, tell them to join the High Table at Stirling Castle."

"And when you land at Stranraer, you will send word to the Younger?"

"I will."

"And you told Finnegan how to get to Glen Shee."

Ancevo nodded.

"And how to avoid the Picts in the High Glens. He sailed from Belfast yesterday with Seamus's promise."

The two men shook hands and Ancevo left for the stables.

"Good fortune to you, Alistair," he called back.

"Good fortune to you, Ancevo," called Alistair and, more quietly, "we are all going to need it."

***

Ancevo, Rory, Hugh and Kenneth of Blacklock enjoyed good weather on the voyage to Man. The *Leaping Salmon* raced through the waves and Ancevo told the skipper about Dougie. Like Alistair, he couldn't quite believe that his friend had become a great warrior, but he did know about grief and what he must be going through. He remembered the king's rider who had told him about Helden's death. He and his brother had lived apart for many years but that counted for nothing. Even now he thought about him often and felt the loss as keenly as he ever did.

"Where do you think the enemy fleets will be?" asked Ancevo softly.

"My guess is they will provision at Glasgow and Oban. From there they can control the Great Sea and bring supplies to both armies when needed. Oban is a good port to aid Tella's army who march east through the High Glens. Llewellyn's army have already taken Glasgow."

"And where would be the best place to attack them?"

"Not on the ocean," warned Kenneth, "they have too many ships, even for Gawain."

"So you would attack when they lay at anchor."

"Aye. When they are trapped on a lee shore."

"Shall we join Gawain on the hunt for the Picts?"

"No. I will return my ship to Oban."

Ancevo thought about his family and his adventures, pictured the arrow in the hare that had saved his life, and decided that he wanted no further part in the war.

"May I sail with you?"

Kenneth smiled.

"Aye."

A thin lad sprinted across the deck.

"Rory has sighted Man," he said.

"We have made good time," barked Kenneth. "Shorten the sail."

Hugh ran off to do as he was told and Kenneth stared across the Great Sea.

"Never had a better crew, and I can think of no one better to leave the ship to."

"That sounds a little final," said Ancevo.

"You have to think of these things," replied Kenneth. "My brother did."

***

Ewan raced up the path from the harbour and called out to two men who were placing slate tiles onto his roof.

"What's up with you, soot face?" asked Donald.

The wide-eyed boy grinned mischievously.

"Your leader commands you to come to the harbour."

"Our leader?" growled Hamish.

"Robert, the Thane of Inverness, says that a sail approaches."

Hamish pushed a tile into position on the roof.

"Does he now? We will finish this and join him."

"He says you are to join him without delay."

"Tell him to keep his plaid on," said Donald.

Ewan grinned again, and skipped off.

***

Hugh lowered the gangplank onto the quay at Douglas, and Kenneth of Blacklock stepped ashore, followed by Ancevo.

"Greetings, Kenneth," said Robert.

"Greetings to you. Ancevo here has a message for Gawain of Man."

"Well, what is it?" ordered Robert.

"It is a message for Gawain," repeated Kenneth crossly, "do you not have ears?"

At that moment Hamish and Donald arrived, and Donald stuck his fingers behind his ears and began to squeak like a mouse.

"Do not forget that the Younger himself placed me in charge," yelled Robert.

"We are never allowed to forget it," said Donald.

"Hello, Kenneth," boomed Hamish, "any news of Alistair and Dougie?"

"Aye, important news, but you must wait until Ancevo speaks with Gawain."

Hamish strode away up the narrow path that led to the king's house.

"Come on then, follow me."

37

"Yes, follow us," commanded Robert.

Ancevo glanced at Kenneth. He was shaking his head.

The Lord of Man was reading a parchment when the friends were led in by two of his warriors.

He glanced up and smiled at Kenneth.

"Gawain, may I introduce you to Ancevo, one of Malcolm's messengers. He has journeyed with me from Belfast."

Gawain nodded and put down the parchment. Ancevo bowed politely and cleared his throat.

"My Lord, Patrick, the King of the Irish Peoples is dead and Seamus, his first born, wears the crown. Seamus has taken Margaret, the Lady of the Islands, to be his wife and agreed to help the Younger in the war that rages upon Scottish soil."

"Well, a lot has been happening," replied Gawain. "Is there news of Dougie and Alistair, the warriors who helped free us from the Picts?"

"They are well," and Ancevo hesitated.

Gawain saw his hesitation and raised an eyebrow.

"Dougie's family are lost, at the hands of the Black Kilts who have taken his lands. He grieves terribly."

"And I grieve for him. What instructions come from Alistair?"

"No instructions, my lord," replied Ancevo politely, "only a message. Seamus will land at Stranraer today and move east to meet with Malcolm at Stirling. There they will face the forces of the Picts, Angles and Welsh on the field of battle."

"And the Welsh carry Amera's Stone?"

"I do not know," replied Ancevo, "but Malcolm fears them more than the others."

"He is wise to do so."

"And Alistair asks that you join us, but not on the land. He hopes that you might destroy the enemy fleets and cut off any supplies that may reach their armies by sea."

Gawain looked kindly at Hamish and Donald.

"So, it is as you hoped."

They stood like statues and waited for Gawain's decision. The

Lord of Man began to mutter strange words, words from the ancient Welsh tongue, and he knelt upon the floor. He brushed away the earth with his hands and clasped the hilt of a sword.

"The sword is always with us," he whispered.

Ancevo watched him draw the blade from the ground, stand tall and kiss it.

"As we must be with you. We sail on the morning tide," commanded Gawain.

"Just time to get a few more tiles on," said Donald.

"Tell my people to prepare for war. Tell them we are going to kill some Picts."

***

Backed by pretty cottages of many colours, the quay at Belfast was alive with heavily armed warriors. Twenty ships were tethered to rope stones and thirty more lay at anchor, waiting for their turn to be provisioned and boarded. Seamus, Margaret, Matina and Alistair stood together at the centre of the quay, with the new Irish king giving orders to his chieftains. Columba and his followers joined them.

"Do you think Finnegan has reached the Younger yet?" asked Alistair.

Seamus shook his head.

"It is too soon even with the fastest horse."

"And is Margaret to be spared the fighting?"

"Even though the Black Kilts hold the Outer Islands, I am sure Iona remains untroubled," said Columba.

Margaret took hold of her husband's hand.

"I stay by your side, whatever happens."

Seamus kissed her.

"We need not decide now. Michael O'Mara will take our fastest ship east to Stranraer and return to the fleet with news of the enemy. If they are few, we stay together. If they are many, you go with Columba's protection."

Secretly, the king had already decided that his new bride

could not be allowed to march with his army to Stirling. No one could be sure how the battle would end.

A long narrow ship, with two masts, slipped away from the quay. Sails were raised and the wind caught them, and the prow cut through the waves at great speed. Michael O'Mara ran to the stern and waved at Seamus, who cupped his hands around his mouth.

"Good speed. We will look for your sail at noon tomorrow."

Within the hour, the Irish fleet followed O'Mara's scout ship and Columba joined Margaret at the ship's rail. She was looking at the rail on the other side of the ship where her silent maid servant sat with her arm around Dougie. On the deck between Margaret and Matina, six fine horses shifted their feet and a small herd of goats roamed around freely, looking for food. Like the other vessels, their ship was packed with excited warriors talking about the adventure. Seamus, Finn and Alistair stood at the stern.

"What do you remember about Iona?" asked Columba.

A sad look fell across Margaret's face.

"My father took me there sometimes. I grew up on Mull and it is beautiful, but Iona has a magical feel about it. The island is small and unlike any of the Outer Islands, for it is low-lying. In the summer, my father would row me across Iona Sound to play on the lovely white beaches. I always felt different there. More at peace."

"I sensed that peace too, and the decision where to build the first church on Scottish soil was made for me."

"And you are sure that the Black Kilts do not hold the island?"

Columba stared across the ocean.

"Tella leads his army to Stirling and will need every warrior for the battle. Leave some warriors on Mull, yes. But Iona? It's too small to have any consequence."

"Is the church built?"

"I had a message from my friend, Oran, one moon ago. He says the clay walls are drying out between the timber frames and, by the time of our arrival, the roof will be completed. My people can begin to worship immediately."

"And this worship is important to you?"

"It is important to everyone. What do you believe in?"

Margaret's face lit up.

"Seamus."

"Well, one day, and let us pray it is a long time away, you and Seamus may be buried on Iona. My hope is that all kings will be laid to rest there. My hope is that after the war a new peace will fall across all lands."

Before noon on the following day, an approaching sail was seen tacking against the wind. The two masts of the scout ship headed straight for Seamus and Alistair, and the two ships were soon lashed together. O'Mara jumped aboard, remembering the words he had been commanded to say. Everyone crowded around him and the ship listed to one side.

"Stranraer is held by the Picts."

"What is their number?" asked Seamus.

"More than two hundred, maybe more."

"And riders?"

"Twelve."

"Why does Tella leave such a force to guard Stranraer?"

"No idea," said O'Mara, "But we held our position two hundred paces from the shore and the beach became alive with Black Kilts."

Seamus went to stand beside Margaret.

"Then it is decided. You go with Columba."

"But I ..."

Seamus hugged her and spoke softly.

"No buts. Stay safe until I come for you."

Margaret burst into tears and Seamus kissed her. Then he stepped away and called out orders.

"O'Mara, take twelve warriors to protect Margaret and Columba. Keep them safe until my fleet arrives at Iona."

"When can we expect you?"

41

"In one moon. If we are delayed, I will send a messenger."

As Columba's followers boarded their ship, Margaret stood at the stern surrounded by goats. She waved at Seamus and he waved back, before turning to face O'Mara.

"Well done," he said.

"Oh. You know you told me to say that Stranraer was full of Picts. Well, I've got news for you. It is."

Seamus and Alistair looked worried.

"Why the devil would Tella divide his army?" asked Seamus.

"My guess is that Borak One Hand has warned him of your coming. He knows he can weaken you more as you land, than on an open field of battle. Shall we land somewhere else?"

Seamus became fierce.

"If there is any chance to face Borak and avenge my father, I shall take it."

***

Two days after Margaret had left the main Irish fleet, Michael O'Mara, Columba and a tall, gangly monk named Ethran, stared at the distant outline of Iona.

"It's not very big," said O'Mara. "Where's the best place to land?"

"Normally, on the eastern shore, but if the Picts hold Mull, they may see us. Iona Sound is no more than a thousand paces from shore to shore. They would be sure to see our sail."

"Then where?"

"On the western side of the island is a beautiful bay. We land there."

"Is it named?"

"The Bay On The Back Of The Ocean," said Ethran.

"Nice name. Let's hope no one is there to meet us."

As the sun rose to its high point in the sky and small white clouds raced in from the west, Margaret's Irish bodyguard splashed ashore onto white sand, and ran to the top of low dunes, swords and spears ready. They signalled back to show it was safe and Columba's followers grabbed ropes and dragged the ship up onto the sand. Ethran organised the beaching and Margaret smiled as she watched him lift his grey habit above his knees, wade into the surf and push the stern towards the shore. The surf subsided to reveal the monk's stick-like legs. Then a huge wave engulfed his habit and soaked him.

Matina gathered together Margaret's possessions, placed them into a leather bag and followed the queen ashore. Soon, boxes and barrels were unloaded and the goats wandered away to find food.

A warrior was left to guard the ship and Columba led them inland, up grassy slopes broken by craggy grey rocks, then up a small craggy hill that was almost totally devoid of any grass. Matina struggled to keep up.

"Give me that," said Margaret kindly and she took the leather bag off the girl's back.

"Where the devil are we going?" asked O'Mara.

Columba turned, took a deep breath and looked back down the hill at their ship and the tiny speck that was its lone guard. The feeling of peace returned to him.

"To the top of Dun I. It has clear views of the whole island and Mull itself."

"Better safe than sorry?"

Columba smiled at Matina who walked silently behind Margaret.

"Better safe than sorry."

After a short climb, the party gathered together on the summit of Dun I and stared east. A thin trail of smoke rose up from beside a small white church that stood a few hundred paces from the shore. Across the sea was the rocky shore of Mull and in a natural harbour, opposite the church, was the Pictish fleet.

O'Mara pointed at the five cottages behind the fleet.

"Is it named?"

Margaret's heart sank as she saw the invaders on her homeland.

"Fionnphort. I know the families who live there. They are good people and do not deserve this."

"Neither do we," said Columba.

"What do we do now?" asked O'Mara.

"Leave a man here to keep watch. The rest of us need to get out of sight and return to the ship."

That night they camped on the sand, without a fire, and O'Mara left them to relieve Ethran on top of Dun I.

"Any news?" asked O'Mara.

Ethran shook his head.

"The Pictish fleet remains moored."

O'Mara looked down at the church and across Iona Sound to Fionnphort. A bright Gora moon sent a silvery path across the ocean. He shivered.

"It's cold. Get some sleep. I'll keep watch until dawn."

"Do you want any company?"

"This job only needs one pair of eyes. Go to Columba."

Ethran rose and left him, and O'Mara became bored as he counted the clouds coming and going across the night sky. Then he unsheathed his sword and, silently, in shadows cast by the Gora moon, he moved down the slope, between rocks, pausing only to check for any signs of an enemy. Across at Fionnphort, the Pictish fleet was clearly outlined by fires. No sound though, except the rhythmic waves, and the occasional faint voice from over the Sound. A light in a cottage behind the ships went out.

Five hundred paces from the church, O'Mara sat like a statue, watching for any sign of movement. None came and he ran down to it, dropping like a stone to lie on his stomach to hide behind a huge wooden cross. A mound of bodies lay off to his left, dead monks in their habits, arms and legs tangled together in unnatural angles. The mound stank. The men had been dead for a long while.

Then he was up and running again, panting, sword ready, senses alive to any danger. The church door hung on a single hinge and he ran his hand across its face. It was covered with

44

deep axe marks. O'Mara held his breath and listened for the sound of sleeping warriors inside. More faint voices from across Iona Sound, but nothing inside. He tilted the door on its hinge and squeezed inside.

Later, on the sands of the Bay at the Back of the Ocean, O'Mara gently shook Ethran's shoulder.

"It cannot be morning already," yawned the monk.

"Not yet, but I need you to go back to watch from Dun I," whispered O'Mara.

"But I've just got back."

O'Mara smiled.

"I must talk with Columba. Do this for me."

Ethran yawned again and unwound himself from his blanket.

"You had better have a good reason."

"I have a good reason."

As the monk left the camp, O'Mara woke Columba and they walked along the shore.

"The church is looted and the wooden cross pulled down."

"And Oran?"

O'Mara stopped to look across the ocean towards the end of the world.

"You already know."

They were woken at dawn by shouting, and the lanky figure of Ethran, habit billowing out behind him as he ran down from the top of a low dune. By the time his pumping stick legs made the white sand, the Irish warriors had ringed Margaret, spears ready. Ethran gasped for breath before Columba.

"The black sails are raised," he panted.

"And which way do they travel?"

"South, down Iona Sound."

Columba nodded. "Some ships, or all?"

Ethran shrugged his shoulders.

"I did not wait to measure them, master. If they follow the wind, they will turn west around the southern tip of Iona and are sure to see our ship on the sand."

45

Columba turned to face the others.

"Take the ship north and hide her in the first inlet you find."

His followers ran to gather the ropes and O'Mara came to stand beside Columba and Ethran.

"It may already be too late. We cannot outrun their fastest ships."

They stared along the ribbon of white sand towards the southern tip of Iona. The orange glow of the rising sun silhouetted its low rocks and dunes.

"Move quickly," shouted Columba.

His followers and the Irish guard pushed the hull out into the waves.

"My orders are to keep you and Margaret safe. We should hide on the island. If luck turns against us the enemy will chase our sail and leave us to find peace."

Columba picked up a tall iron cross and drove its spear point into the sand. Ethran knelt before it.

"Ethran. Steer a course into the Great Sea. Return to us when the enemy leave these waters. Spare no sail and stay safe."

They shook hands and Ethran ran to the ship and splashed through the waves to be hauled onboard.

Margaret gathered their blankets together.

"Matina, collect as many things as you can. We must leave no sign of our camp on the beach."

The silent maidservant picked up her queen's leather bag and hurried inland, stumbling as she climbed a dune. Columba and Margaret followed her, and O'Mara kicked loose sand over the places where they had slept and walked. At the top of the dunes, they searched for a place to hide and, as the tip of the sun appeared in the east, they sat in a sheltered, grassy hollow, talking quietly, with Margaret cradling Matina in her arms. O'Mara crawled up to the lip of the hollow and stared south.

"Oh, you had better come and see this."

Everyone scrambled up to join him. The sails of the enemy were rounding the southern tip of Iona and they counted as their menacing numbers grew.

"Thirty one. That's the whole fleet," said Columba.

Matina pointed west. Their ship was small, but framed by the low sun in a line of burning gold. Margaret held her breath and watched to see if the Picts changed course to chase Ethran. They did.

At noon, a thin chimney of smoke rose up on the western horizon and they knew their friends were lost.

"What do we do now?" asked Margaret.

"Survive until rescued," said Columba. "We have water from the church well, goats, and whatever we carried ashore."

"Oh, I hate goat meat," said O'Mara.

Margaret smiled and hugged Matina.

"You'll get used to it," she said.

***

Alistair and Dougie stood at the prow of an Irish ship about a hundred paces away from a shingle beach near Stranraer. There was a few hours of daylight left and the mighty fleet bobbed up and down, with sails folded and oars ready. All eyes were on the Black Kilts who watched them. Arrows had rained down and fallen short, and then stopped as the ships held a safe distance from the shore.

"How many do you think there are?" asked Alistair.

Dougie ignored him and Alistair answered his own question.

"There cannot be more than two hundred. If we can take the beach we should easily defeat them."

Dougie continued to stare ahead, as though his friend did not exist.

"Well you had better pull yourself together, Dougie. It will not be long before Seamus gives the order to attack."

"I do not have anything to fight for anymore," said Dougie in a hollow voice.

"You will always have your friends," Alistair told him.

To their right, the ship at the end of the fleet raised its sail and moved further along the coast. The ship on their far left did the

47

same. They watched as the ship on their left landed out of the range of the enemy arrows. Warriors led horses into the water and they splashed ashore. In minutes the riders mounted and held their spears ready.

"Very clever," said Alistair.

Dougie heard barking and turned to see Finn McCool leap down into the sea from the other ship. The water came up to his waist and Dougie knew that if he had jumped in there he would have been completely submerged. The Picts stared at the pack who ran excitedly around their master, then stared at the horseman. One of them shouted out instructions and the army divided into three groups, one at each end who aimed their arrows at the dogs and riders, and one larger group who faced the Irish fleet.

Seamus waved his sword at the end ships and they raised their sails, breaking away from the other ships to reinforce Finn and the riders. A Pict shouted out new instructions and more Black Kilts ran from the main part of their army to join the archers who protected the ends of their line. Seamus watched as the numbers of the enemy who faced his fleet decreased.

"Attack!" he cried.

Oars were thrust into the water and the ships tore forward. The Irish horseman charged while, at the other end of the beach, Finn lifted his great spear and walked alone towards the enemy. He whistled and the pack barked wildly, following him to do battle. Arrows rained down onto the hounds, but Murphy-dog led them on, hurling himself at an archer. As the snarling beasts hit them, some of the Picts began to run and many were brought down, savaged as they tried to flee. Finn threw his spear and it passed through the bodies of three men.

The rest of the fleet landed and Alistair ran through the water beside Seamus, sword ready. Dougie watched them from his ship and didn't move. The Irish warriors screamed as they charged up the shingle and smashed into the Black Kilts. Then the enemy turned and ran, and Stranraer was taken with little loss.

Alistair listened to the crunching of shingle as Seamus's men walked from body to body to collect weapons, and claim anything of value. He wondered if Finnegan had reached the Younger and turned to look at the fleet. Dougie was still standing at the prow, rising and falling with each wave, and staring, wide-eyed, at the dead.

"Will he be alright?" asked Finn.

"I don't know," said Alistair. "I really don't know."

***

Glen Shee was full of tents and the temporary shelters of the Scottish army. Malcolm walked through the great camp and talked to his men. His message was always the same.

"Be ready. We wait for the right moment and that moment *will* come."

Secretly, he began to doubt it, for news had reached him of Patrick's death and he feared that no alliance would now be possible with the Irish people. But he kept these fears to himself and waited patiently for more news to reach him. His riders brought him messages almost every day, but the message was always the same. The enemy were making swift progress across the kingdom and were moving towards Stirling Castle to place it under siege. He prayed that it would hold.

Fraser of Abernethy rushed into the king's tent. The young lad had replaced Cameron as the Younger's bodyguard and had done much to impress his new master. As he bowed he smiled. "A rider has come into the camp. An Irish rider."

Malcolm rose quickly and they went to greet him.

The rider bowed as they approached.

"Well, from your robes, I have no doubt that you are Malcolm the King of the Scots."

The Younger saw that the wiry, eager man had cuts on his arms and bruises on his face. Finnegan grinned at him. "Oh, I met a Welshman on the way here and we had a little disagreement."

Malcolm nodded as a Scottish warrior ran over to join them. The warrior whispered something in Fraser's ear and they ran off. Finnegan watched them go and then offered his sword to the Younger.

"Seamus, the king of Ireland, sends you his warmest greetings and says that the beautiful lady you offered to his father is in good hands."

"Good hands?"

"Seamus has married her and a fine couple they make too."

Malcolm breathed a sigh of relief.

"Oh," said Finnegan, "and I nearly forgot, Seamus leads his army from Stranraer and will reach Stirling in three days."

"So soon," gasped Malcolm.

"There is no time to waste when there is the chance of a good war with the Black Kilts."

Malcolm smiled.

"Gawain leads his fleet to attack the enemy at Glasgow. They hope to stop any comfort reaching the enemy that way."

"We have so much to be thankful for."

"Seamus says that he does not know why you need our help at all. He says that when you have such fierce warriors, you should be able to sort out three armies by yourself."

"Do you speak of Alistair of Cadbol?" asked Malcolm.

"No, the other fellow, that Dougie of Dunfermline."

"Young Dougie?" questioned Malcolm.

"He threw me through the air, you know."

The Younger stared at the Irishman's muscular body.

"Dougie threw you through the air?"

"It was Dougie who defeated the Pict, Borak One Hand. That is why Seamus is here to help you."

"So it is as Myroy foretold."

"Oh, and if you have got any of those new swords, Seamus says that he could do with a few."

"We could as well," smiled Malcolm.

Fraser ran back to his master and spoke in an urgent voice.

"Your Majesty. You had better come and see this."

The bodyguard led Malcolm and Finnegan down the glen to the edge of the camp. The valley wound its way south and on the path, strung out along the valley floor, were perhaps thirty wagons drawn by oxen. The man who led the train sat backwards. Finnegan thought that he was taking instructions from a small boy who perched on his shoulder.

"Grumf," the boy shouted.

The wagons stopped and Archie bowed away from the king. Then the alchemist spoke in his eager voice.

"Ah, Your Majesty."

"What are you doing here?" asked Malcolm.

"My latest *experident* has worked out rather well,"

Instantly the king's eyes glazed over.

"Your *experident*."

Archie lifted a box from the back of the wagon and tossed it onto the floor. Swords spilled out everywhere. "It's this new light iron. We have made two thousand and I thought they might come in handy."

"Come in handy," repeated the Younger.

"Grumf," said Gangly.

"No it is not time for supper yet," replied Archie crossly.

In that moment, Malcolm the Younger, King of the Scots and Protector of the Stone of Destiny, knew that his moment had come. Fraser sensed a great energy in the King's manner and felt that he was about to be a part of something which might shape the very course of history. The Younger turned, clenched his fist into a ball and held it in front of his bodyguard's face.

"Order the High Table to march to Stirling."

Fraser nodded.

"Tell the clan leaders that Seamus's army will join us there in three days. Together we are stronger. Tell them we are going to get out our homes back."

CHAPTER THREE

TRAPPED ON IONA

A GORA MOON

Merik Ben watched the lonely figure of Borak One Hand, Master of the Fleet, and wondered why Borak was becoming more like his own brother. Torik had disappeared after the battle at Carn Liath and Merik did not know of anyone who missed him. Even he had breathed a huge sigh of relief and there were still many who feared that one day he might somehow return to do Tella's work.

It was the third day with a westerly wind trapping the fleet onto a lee shore at Fionnphort, unable to fulfil their orders to join with the Welsh fleet at Glasgow. Borak stood on a rock ledge, partly surrounded by sea, staring west, face full of anger and revenge in his heart.

Everyone had heard about Borak's challenge to Tella and Gath, demanding that they allow him to march to Stirling and face Seamus on the field of battle. He had been lucky, he had been allowed to live and had actually been promoted to Master of the Fleet. Was it because Tella needed someone he could trust to hold the Great Sea and take him back to Deros if things went against them? Was it because he had delayed the Irish joining up with the Younger?

The warriors of the fleet had all seen Borak vent his anger on the enemy. With his axe strapped to his arm and another axe in hand, he had hacked his way across Mull and Iona. The people on Iona had been unarmed and strangely dressed. They believed in an unknown god, and some had taken sanctuary in a building Borak called a church, joining the fallen soon after. Others had fled and Borak alone had hunted them down without mercy, taking the chance to strengthen his arm and blood his axes. The men of the fleet feared him as much as they had feared Torik Ben.

Merik listened to the creaking of the ships as gentle waves rolled into Fionnphort. Rhythmically, the lines, tied to rope stones, tightened and slackened as warriors rested in the sunshine waiting for the wind to change and release them. He wondered if Tella's army placed Stirling under siege and he followed Borak's stare, across Iona Sound west to the distant church. But Borak's mind was far beyond the island, in more distant lands, as he remembered his brother's speared body strapped to a horse.

***

"Oh, up she comes."

O'Mara lifted the church door and Columba squatted down to look at the broken, bottom hinge.

"It's a bit knocked about, that's all."

"Hacked to pieces more like," said Columba.

"Oh, we'll have the church like a palace in no time. Have you seen Margaret?"

"She's with Matina, gathering the herbs. Making an effort because you do not like goat meat."

"We have to catch the little devils first, and right now I could eat a horse." O'Mara glanced across Iona Sound to the far hills of Mull. "But I can think of worse places to be a prisoner. We have just about everything we need and this sun warms my heart. As long as the Black Kilts don't come back, I think we'll enjoy our stay here."

"Enjoy your time later. We need to get this door mended and raise the wooden cross."

He looked over at the large altar, an oak box, one man long and half a man high.

"We can make our beds behind the altar. If bad weather comes, as it will, these walls will protect us."

"Did you check the roof?"

"The Picts looted everything of value and ignored the roof. How about the well?"

"I can't find the rope and bucket anywhere. Bet the Black Kilts threw them in. I'll drop Matina down, to hunt around, when she gets back."

Columba smiled and stared at the twisted hinge.

"If only we had some tools."

"I haven't found anything, have you?"

"Iron nails. No hammer."

"You know, I might have a little disagreement the next time I meet a Pict. How long will it all take?"

"With good fortune, we can have everything back to normal in a couple of days."

A fluffy white cloud moved to cover the sun and a soft breeze lifted the ring of hair below Columba's bald patch on the top of his head.

"It still moves me."

"What does?"

"The feeling of peace on the island."

Margaret's loud voice came to them from the lower slopes of Dun I.

"I've spent the whole day chasing bloomin' goats and haven't got one. This island is rubbish."

O'Mara grinned.

"That'll be the girls back then."

"Why isn't the door on yet?" demanded Margaret.

"Oh. Now before you go stomping your feet again, did you gather the herbs?"

The Queen of Ireland held out her hand and showed them a small bunch of leaves.

"Give me a forest and I'll give you enough herbs to feed an army. This place is rubbish."

Columba's forehead creased.

"One day, this island will be the resting place of kings. Where is Matina?"

"Isn't she with you?"

O'Mara shook his head.

"She hasn't been here since you left with her at sunrise."

"I dived at a goat and she laughed at me. I sent her back to the church."

"Not seen Matina," said Columba, standing. "Come on. Let's go find her."

As they climbed the lower slopes of Dun I, the clouds parted and they were bathed in brilliant sunshine. O'Mara's stomach rumbled.

"Can we not forget the church and seek the fish?"

Columba's voice was stern.

"Find Matina, repair the church, then gather food."

"My belly thinks my throat has been cut."

Margaret interrupted them by pointing down at the Bay at the Back of the Ocean.

"There she is. What is she doing? Wait till I get hold of her."

"Probably making sand castles. Is that a spade she has?" asked O'Mara.

"There is plenty of work to be done, not playing on the beach," said Margaret.

They made their way down the craggy slope, crossed the dunes and walked upon the white sand.

"Have you ever heard her speak?" asked Columba.

Margaret shook her head.

"She may have been born like it. I've heard some people are."

"I wish my wife had been born like it. She talks all the time and a trouble she is to me too," said O'Mara.

Columba waved at them to stop and they watched the little girl dig a shallow trench into hard, dry sand. A bucket and a long coil of rope lay to one side. Then she was skipping down to the sea and filling the bucket, and struggling back to the hole where she emptied the load. Matina did this many times and the trench became a shallow pool.

"We must care for Matina," said Columba. "Something terrible may have happened to her."

"Wonder where she found the rope and bucket?" said O'Mara.

Margaret began to walk towards Matina.

"Who cares? We have fresh water now."

O'Mara watched as Matina skipped down to the sea with her bucket again.

"Do you think being trapped on the island has driven her mad?"

"She should be doing something useful," said Margaret, looking at the pool.

Matina came back, water spilling, and giving them a huge smile.

"And what are you up to?" demanded Margaret.

The girl pointed at the pool.

"I know it's a pool. Come on we have got work to do."

Matina didn't move.

"In case you have forgotten, you are my servant and I am not yours."

Matina smiled and pointed at the pool again. Then she pointed up at the sun and then at the back of her hand. Margaret grabbed the hand to lead her off the beach, Matina pulling back.

"If you don't come on, I'll ask O'Mara to give you a spanking."

O'Mara winked at Matina and shook his head as if to say, "I wouldn't do that."

Matina pointed back at the pool with her free hand as she was dragged up the dunes.

"It's a lovely pool," said Columba kindly. "Now come with me and we can make our beds in the church."

That evening, they sat contentedly together around a fire on the grass between the church and the calm waters of Iona Sound, and watched the sun sink slowly, sending orange fingers across the sky. Behind them, the craggy summit of Dun I protected them from any cold winds that blew off the Great Sea. Columba remembered the feeling of inner peace he had enjoyed that day and passed Matina a fish, skewered with a stick and browned by the flames.

"How did you catch them?" asked Margaret.

"Two nails on the end of a pole. I learned spear fishing from my father."

Matina ate the fish and cuddled into Margaret's shawl.

"And tomorrow, I don't want you running off again. We have goats to catch," said Margaret.

O'Mara groaned.

The girl shook her head and her hands popped out of the queen's shawl to make a small circle.

Columba pointed up at the moon. It was full, silver and bright, the kind of moon that would signal the last days of a stone keeper.

"Do you mean the moon, Matina?"

Matina made another circle.

"The sun?"

Her face beamed and she nodded vigorously.

"I told you," warned Margaret. "No playing until we have more food."

Inside her shawl, the queen felt the little girl's shoulders shrug.

Next morning, Columba woke on a bed of ferns and rubbed his eyes. O'Mara had his mouth wide open, snoring loudly, but Matina and Margaret slept peacefully, untroubled by the noise. He rose silently, tiptoed along the aisle and squatted down to look at the hinge again. It was straightened and held in place by iron nails, hammered home crudely using stones. Whatever the weather did now, they would be snug inside.

The monk smiled and made his way across the grass to kneel in front of the wooden cross, which they had all pulled upright with ropes and bedded in with stones. He prayed for forgiveness, prayed that Matina might one day speak again, and for their safety from an enemy who was sure to return. When he got back, everyone was awake and it was decided that they would split up, with Margaret and Matina to catch the goats, and O'Mara helping Columba to search the beach for anything useful and then go fishing again. As they wished each other good fortune outside the church, the sun grew in strength and warmed them.

It was going to be another glorious day.

Later, the Queen of Ireland scowled, crouched down and moved like a hunter towards a small herd of goats that grazed on the eastern slopes of Dun I.

"Now quiet," whispered Margaret.

Matina smiled and pointed up at the sun. Margaret crept on and ten paces from the goats she raced forward before diving at a kid. The herd scattered and Margaret crashed onto the grass. Matina shook her head.

"I suppose you think that's funny," she yelled.

Matina lifted her eyes up at the sun.

"Wait till I get my hands on you!"

Matina pointed at the back of her hand.

"I'll give you the back of my hand."

Below the church, on a rocky inlet beside Iona Sound, Columba stopped cleaning his fish and watched as Margaret chased Matina, the queen yelling at the top of her voice to stop. The little girl's hair flowed behind her, face beaming with delight, as she zigzagged down the slope. Then Matina put her arms out and slowly flapped them like a bird.

Columba smiled.

"So, she has found peace at last."

A HALF MOON

Columba peered into the still waters of the inlet and whispered to O'Mara.

"Aim just in front of the fish. The water deceives your eyes. The fish are not where you think they are."

O'Mara pulled the spear back so that the two nails hovered by his chin. He threw it down, the shoal scattered and the spear floated to the surface.

"Oh. It's not my day."

"Better make it your day, or we go hungry."

O'Mara waded into the water, shuddering with the cold.

"Can we not tie a line to the shaft?"

"If we had a line."

O'Mara retrieved the spear and, as he replied, his teeth chattered.

"Oh ... there must ... be something we ... can use."

Columba thought about it and took off his rope belt, sat down and unpicked the fibres. O'Mara climbed up, spear ready again.

"Do the fish always come here at this time?"

Columba rolled two strands together to make a length of string and nodded.

"At the turning of the tide. I wonder if the tide has turned for the Younger?"

"The shoal returns."

"Aim just in front of the fish."

"I know. I know." O'Mara threw the spear and it bobbed to the surface. "Still not my day. You finished the line yet?"

"Not yet."

O'Mara sighed and waded back into the sea.

"You caught anything yet?" yelled a voice.

Columba tied a knot in one end of his string.

"Not yet. How did you get on?"

Margaret sat beside him and opened her leather bag. It was full of shellfish.

"Well done. There's a meal there."

"If we had a pot to boil them in."

O'Mara's shivering, dripping body joined them.

"Cook them ... on a flat stone. My mother ... cooks shells like that all the ... time."

"Where is Matina?" asked Columba.

Margaret stood. "That naughty girl. She keeps going off on her own."

"Here we go again," said O'Mara. "Bay at the Back of the Ocean?"

"Bay at the Back of the Ocean," repeated Columba, rising.

"We have to collect driftwood, anyway," said O'Mara.

"I still think you should give her a spanking," said Margaret.

In brilliant sunshine, they climbed Dun I and passed bare rocks, grass and later gorse and dense bracken. Before they reached the dunes, they saw Matina.

"She's holding a goat," said O'Mara.

"How did she do that?" asked Margaret. "They run off whenever I go near them."

"Perhaps it's because she doesn't talk all the time."

Margaret shot O'Mara a look and Columba watched Matina, standing in the middle of the herd, stroking a kid, with goats pushing each other out of the way to lick the back of her free hand.

"I'd say that Matina has found a new job, wouldn't you?"

They walked over to her and Margaret called out.

"How do you do that?"

Matina pointed up at the sun. As they walked through the herd, which did not bolt for safety, the little girl pulled a cloth, tied with string to form a small bundle, from her shawl. She gave it to Margaret, who dipped a finger inside.

"It's salt. Where did you get that from?"

"So that's what the pool was for. Clever girl," said O'Mara. "Sea water is full of salt and when the sun makes the water disappear, the salt is left."

Matina beamed and held the back of her hand out. A goat licked it.

"Let's have goat for supper," said Margaret.

Matina's face changed and she turned to hold the kid away from them.

"What's your idea, Matina?" asked Columba.

She made a cup with her hand and pretended to drink from it.

"Milk?" asked O'Mara.

Columba smiled.

"Well, go and get the bucket from the well. You have earned yourself a new job."

Matina shook her head and pointed west.

"What's wrong?"

Matina put the kid down and made a roof with her arms.

O'Mara's face creased.

"Oh. I've got no idea what she means."

Matina pointed west at a distant line of dark clouds.

"We have fine weather and we are enjoying good fortune," said Columba. "Margaret, take Matina to the church and find a flat stone. I'll collect driftwood."

"What about me?" asked O'Mara.

"Gulls' eggs go well with shellfish."

O'Mara looked at a crag on the side of Dun I. Gulls swooped above it and white stains showed the location of their nests.

"I'll see you later, then," he said and they parted.

At the base of the crag face, O'Mara stared up at the gulls sitting on their nests, the height of four men above him. Carefully, he placed a foot onto a ledge and pulled himself up, grasping tufts of sea grass and reassured by the dry rock that gave him a sure footing. As he climbed, gulls cried out angrily and swooped at him. He ignored them and plundered one nest after another, placing the large, speckled, blue and grey eggs into his pocket, and concentrating hard on each move. He became lost in his thoughts, as he made sure that he left at least one egg in each nest. They might be on the island for a long time.

The first few drops of rain brought his mind back to the wider world. He glanced up and back at the ocean. Thick dark clouds were racing in and a distant rumble confirmed that the storm was nearly upon him. The raindrops grew larger, more frequent, and then the rain lashed onto the crag face, driven by a ferocious wind. A bolt of lighting flashed out at sea, lighting the gulls' nests and the shiny surface of the rocks. He felt drenched and afraid, and began to climb down.

Columba had built a fire in the centre of the church, hemmed in by large stones. A bigger flat stone lay across the flames with shells on it. A great *boom* sounded overhead.

"It broke quickly. I hope O'Mara is safe."

Margaret sat down with Matina beside the fire.

"I'm sure he is safe. Wet through, though. How are the shells coming along, Matina?"

Matina poked one with a stick and shook her head.

"Should be ready soon?" asked Margaret.

Matina nodded.

The door burst open and O'Mara staggered in, shivering.

"Oh. What a night it is. I got stuck on the crag and slipped most of the way down."

"Anything broken?" asked Columba.

O'Mara squatted down by the fire, warmed his hands and handed Matina seven eggs.

"One egg, no bones."

"Get yourself dry," suggested Margaret. "We can't have you falling ill with the fever."

"Never been ill in my life," laughed O'Mara and he left them, to change into a dry habit behind the altar.

As he changed, Columba walked to the door and stared out, trying to see the half moon through the cloak of angry clouds. He shut the door, shut out the noise of the storm, and peace returned to the church. Behind the altar, O'Mara sneezed.

A FEATHER MOON

O'Mara lay helpless, trapped on his back, pinned down by unseen hands. A Black Kilt, with one hand, towered over him and brought a great war axe down onto his chest. O'Mara screamed in pain and the enemy raised the axe, ready to strike again.

"He's having another nightmare," said Margaret.

Columba dipped a cloth into the bucket, wringing it out and gently mopped his patient's forehead.

"The fever grows."

"Will he live?"

"By morning we will know if he lives or dies."

"What can we do?"

"Pray."

O'Mara's hands shot up, fighting an unknown enemy, body writhing and drenched in sweat; eyes bulging in terror.

Columba walked to the door to look at the feather moon. It was thin, curved and bright in a star filled sky. From behind the altar, O'Mara screamed and Matina buried her face in Margaret's shawl.

DARKNESS

Columba woke, rolled onto his side and saw Matina kneeling beside O'Mara. She was smiling and holding his hand.

"I am so hungry," said O'Mara in a weak voice, "I could even eat a goat."

Matina released his hand and shook her head.

"Water?"

The little girl grabbed the bucket and skipped away to fetch water.

"How do you feel?" asked Columba.

O'Mara's face creased.

"Weak."

"Your strength will return."

"I had one hell of a dream."

"We know."

"Like I died a thousand times."

Columba smiled.

"Glad to have you back, friend."

Matina skipped back into the church and, as she passed her sleeping mistress, she flicked some water at her. Margaret sat up, startled.

"Huh."

"Good morning," said Columba. "We have a friend returned to us."

Margaret yawned and wrapped her shawl around her

shoulders, and rose to join them, wiping water from her eyes.

"Is the roof leaking?"

Columba nodded at Matina who knelt at O'Mara's side, trying to give him water from her small cupped hands.

"How is he?" asked Margaret.

O'Mara coughed as Matina dripped too much water into his mouth.

"Weak."

"In five days you will be strong again," promised Columba.

"Can I have something to eat?"

"When I have fished. When we have all completed our tasks."

Matina pointed at the back of her hand and at the bucket.

"Good idea, Matina. Fetch the salt and milk the goats."

She picked up the bucket and skipped to the door. As she passed Margaret, she flicked water at her again.

"That naughty girl. I'm the Queen of Ireland."

"Here you are not a queen. Here you are a prisoner. We are all prisoners."

Margaret scowled at Columba.

"When O'Mara is strong again, I'm going to ask him to give her a good spanking."

From his bed, O'Mara groaned and Columba passed the leather bag to her, and pointed at the church door.

"The berries will not gather themselves."

At the door, Margaret glared at him and tossed her hair back.

"Huh."

"Huh," repeated Columba.

Margaret slammed the door behind her.

"Huh," mumbled O'Mara, as sleep took him.

After a silent prayer for O'Mara's recovery, Columba walked to the still waters of the inlet. After checking that the nails and string were secure to the pole, he stood motionless, staring into the water. No fish. The sun came out from behind a cloud and warmed him. The sea sparkled like jewels and a gentle breeze came from the south. Fionnphort was so close and yet so far away, and he wondered how the war was going. Who now ruled the Scottish lands? He straightened his back and held the spear over his shoulder, as his father had taught him, and looked back into the sea, lost in thoughts about his mission to establish the church on Iona, about Matina and how clever she was, and about his friends, Oran and Ethran.

A single brown fish swam lazily into the inlet, but too small to make a meal from. After an age, another joined it, but not the shoal he needed before striking. The fish turned and held their position below him, waggling their tails against the waves that rolled into the inlet. At last a shoal came in with fine sized fish amongst them. Columba threw his spear and it surfaced with a flapping, shiny shape on the tip. He pulled on the line, retrieved supper and, back on the rock, he looked at the patterns made by its scales.

"There is beauty everywhere," he said.

He glanced across Iona Sound towards the five white cottages. A huge fleet lay at Fionnphort. Red and black sails sat side by side to show that the Picts and Welsh had joined together to rule the Great Ocean. A thousand paces away, a Pict with one hand stood by the shore on a rock ledge, staring west. Columba crouched down, but the warrior ran back to his ship, shouting out new orders.

The church door burst open and Columba called out.

"O'Mara."

Behind the altar, Margaret stood, berries in her hand.

"What's the matter?"

"Black Kilts and Welsh ships. Their fleet lies at Fionnphort. A ship comes here."

"Not good," whispered O'Mara.

"Not good," repeated Margaret. "What do we do?"

"Where is Matina?" asked Columba.

"She tends the goats."

"Let us pray that she sees the enemy from Dun I and hides."

"Shall we hide?"

Columba joined her at O'Mara's bedside.

"Can you walk?"

O'Mara looked up at him.

"I can try."

Columba put his arms around him and lifted him to his feet. O'Mara fell back down.

"Margaret, secure the door."

She looked around, at their bedding and meagre possessions.

"What with?"

Columba covered O'Mara's shivering body with another blanket.

"The altar."

At first, they struggled to even move the heavy altar. Then the oak scraped noisily across the stone floor, with Columba's shoulder driving hard, his legs pumping, and Margaret pulling for all her worth, before it slammed against the door.

"It will hold them for a while," said Columba.

"Your followers would have done the same and they were more than us. The enemy still got inside. What do we do now?"

"Pray."

Borak One Hand and Merik Ben jumped down and splashed ashore. Twenty warriors followed them, war axes flashing in the sun. Soon, they surrounded the small church, six men pushing at the door. Borak looked across the grass.

"Fetch the cross."

More men ran to the giant wooden cross and pulled it down.

Inside the church, Columba's forehead creased as something stirred in his memory.

"Do you recognise the voice?"

They listened as a warrior called out orders to his men in the strange tongue of the Picts. Margaret thought she recognised it too.

"In Ireland, at Mountjoy."

Columba banged his fist onto the shaking door. The blows from the cross stopped.

"Borak, envoy of the Mac Mar, hear me."

Borak's eyes opened wide and he waved his hand at his men, who made way for him.

"I am Borak," he shouted.

"It is I, Columba. The man of God who tended your injury. I demand that this place be our sanctuary."

Borak wondered if his own prayers had been answered. Was Seamus here? At his mercy?

"I give you no sanctuary. I bring you death."

"We are no threat to you."

"We?"

Silence followed and Borak stepped back as his warriors charged the door with the cross.

"We need fire," said Merik.

Matina looked proudly at the milk in her bucket and smiled. Her mistress would be pleased too, and she picked up a kid and stroked him, before picking up the bucket and skipping down the slope of Dun I. She passed an area of gorse and followed a path through dense bracken, and rose up past rocks to continue downwards across the grassy slope.

Matina stopped to look down at the church. She stood, open-mouthed, staring in horror at the wicked flames that engulfed its walls and roof. Columba and Margaret staggered out, followed by O'Mara. As they escaped the smoke and flame, O'Mara's coughing and choking turned to screams as cruel men, with cruel axes, hacked him down. Matina tried to cry out, but the invisible hand held her around the throat and no sound came. An everlasting scream echoed inside her head and she remembered hearing that scream before.

A warrior ran up from the church, right towards her and, terrified, she ran back up the slope, dropping the bucket and diving into the bracken, curling her arms around her knees, and trying to make her body as small as possible. She held her breath and peered through the green stalks of her protective den. The silence was suddenly broken by the sound of pounding feet.

A great man, in a black kilt, dashed past the den and then the pounding feet stopped. She felt sick.

Borak turned on his heels and retraced his steps. He knelt to pick up the bucket, looked at it, and gently parted the bracken with his axe. The little girl's mouth fell open again and her whole body shook. Borak's mind went back to a girl he had once spared in the High Glens. Surely this could not be her? Here on Iona? His brother had walked beside him in the High Glens and been his greatest friend. He thought about Margaret and Columba, and how he would now hold them hostage at Deros to lure Seamus to his death.

"I pray he still lives. That death *will* be by my hand," he whispered.

Borak looked into the eyes of the rocking, terrified girl and remembered giving orders to his warriors to search the island for more of the enemy.

"Stay here until morning comes," he said.

CHAPTER FOUR

ODIN'S LIE

Aboard the space station Mir, Commander Gregoriev slept like a baby, dreaming about the forests around his home. He had dreamt a lot about trees lately and his thoughts wandered from forests to the heating unit he should have repaired. Half in dream, he thought he heard someone calling his name.

"Ivor."

He pulled his thermal blanket over his shoulders.

"I will repair the heater later," he said sleepily.

Someone was shaking him.

"Ivor, get up."

He opened his eyes and smiled at a lady dressed in a green jumpsuit.

"Lesley. Is it time for the boring routine to start again?"

"Not today, Commander. Follow me immediately."

She turned her weightless body and, using the rails, pulled herself out of his cabin and floated off along the Long Corridor.

"Everything is a bloody drama to you botanists," he said, as he unclipped his harness and floated after her.

Lesley was pushing past the rest of the team who crowded around the port observation window.

"Does anyone know what it is?"

A short, eager scientist pulled his face away from the glass.

"If it is meteorological, then I've not seen anything like it before."

Commander Gregoriev moved to the window.

"My God."

Ten miles above the earth, following its curve, was an unbroken and impenetrable red shell. As the space station continued its orbit, he saw that the shell covered half of the planet, making an orange band around its edge. Further out, the orange faded to be replaced by the deep blue of the Gulf of Mexico. As Mir orbited further south west, the red shell disappeared altogether and he was looking down onto the beautiful greens of the Amazon Basin.

"The red cloud is centred on the Mediterranean Sea," said Lesley.

Commander Gregoriev pushed himself away from the window.

"Is the radio working?"

"No," she said.

Later, Lesley entered the Commander's tiny cabin. He closed his laptop and put it away into a drawer in the wall, and saw her take something from her breast pocket. Lesley gently tossed it to him and he watched it float through the air. He took the pebble between his thumb and index finger, and nodded at her to speak.

"The radio was sabotaged. We have a Seeker onboard."

***

Spiros and Bernard looked around the street café. All the other customers knelt to Odin's new authority, still as stone, amongst fallen chairs, and broken glass and plates. In the centre of the café, their waiter knelt too, the pages of his notepad turning in the gentle, cooling breeze. Everyone faced out to sea at a dot on the horizon that was the *Maid Of Norway*.

"Why does Myroy smile?" asked Spiros.

"Something has happened that we did not expect."

"Shall we go to the Keeper?"

Bernard took a sip of coffee and glanced up at the top of the old fortress, and the Ancient One shook his head at him. Then Bernard looked down onto the concrete slipway. Peter was cradling Kylie in his arms, rocking back and forth.

"We must wait until we are called for."

Spiros pointed up at the red sky.

"It is over a thousand years since Odin held the stone. The Younger and the Protector were children then. What will the Seekers do now?"

"Build their empire with Oslo at its heart. Protected by the stone and its light, half of our planet is now in Odin's hands and, as you well know, that will not be enough for him."

73

"He will try to rule everything."

Bernard nodded. "His greed will drive him."

"And how do the Free Forces stand?"

"Once the world leaders realise that a new order exists, they will quickly organise their armies and defend the orange band."

Spiros shrugged his shoulders.

"But they will be poorly armed."

"The Seekers have moved many arms factories north so that they would be covered by the stone's red sky. But even Amera's stone cannot shine through the earth. Half the world was always going to remain free of its power and Myroy guessed his brother would centre his empire on Norway. So, Australia, South Africa and South America were likely places to stockpile our own weapons."

They both looked down onto the concrete slipway. Myroy had risen up beside the rocking children. Spiros glanced at his watch. Twenty past three.

"This cannot be easy for Myroy."

"No," agreed Bernard.

Myroy stood like a statue and listened to Peter crying out.

"Don't leave me, Kylie. Don't leave me. I don't want to be alone again."

"You are sad at the passing," said the Ancient One.

Peter continued to hold the girl in his arms. After an age he tried to wipe the tears from his eyes and smeared blood across his face. When he spoke, his words were as cold as ice.

"Why are you doing this to me?"

"To help you."

Peter thought about the explosion that had destroyed his family. Then he looked into Kylie's white face and kissed her. Myroy stared up at the red sky.

"Are you ready for the next part of the story? To understand the future you ..."

"Must understand the bloody past," cut in Peter. "What a great future I have. You have taken away everyone I love. Grandpa said I would be alone as a Keeper, but I never believed it would be like this."

Myroy ignored him.

"The Younger has sent a messenger to Ireland, named Ancevo. He must travel through the High Glens, past the Black Kilts who are on the march, to reach Oban and win the help of Kenneth of Blacklock."

Peter felt as though he was beside Ancevo as Myroy told the story. As the King's Rider collapsed on the floor, Peter gasped and shook his head, trying desperately to drive the Ancient One's words from his mind.

Myroy's face creased and he raised his voice.

"Patrick Three Eggs has been murdered by the Pict, Borak. Murdoch, the Protector of the Outer Islands, has fallen in battle. The Younger hides his warriors in the lonely places as the forces of the Alliance march across Scottish soil. Tella the Mac Mar has armed the Welsh and the Angles with the light iron, and Thorgood Firebrand waits. Remember that sometimes you need to wait whilst others fight."

Uncontrollable anger rose up inside Peter and he laid Kylie onto the concrete and ran at Myroy, trying to punch and kick him. But each blow passed harmlessly through the old man's body and Peter collapsed, completely drained. It was as if every last ounce of energy had been sapped from his body and he lay, helpless, at the Ancient One's feet.

"If you have stopped thinking about yourself, then I will help you."

Myroy waved his staff at Peter, and the boy rose up to stand beside him, held up by invisible hands. The Ancient One went on with his story.

"Order the High Table to march to Stirling," said the Younger. Fraser nodded.

"Tell the clan leaders that Seamus's army will join us there in three days. Together we are stronger. Tell them we are going to get out our homes back."

Myroy smiled at Peter's floating body.

"The next lesson is in a time when Arkinew's powers were at their height. When the Scottish people lived in fear of the Elder and when his children hid the stone from him. Now, you must learn about Odin's lie."

Two brothers played hide and seek inside the Elder's palace.

"And this time count to the full fifty," said Malcolm.

Murdoch grinned, closed his eyes and turned to face the wall.

"One, two, three ...."

Malcolm ran down the corridor, past shields hung on the walls, with his brother counting and sneakily looking to see which way he went. Murdoch stopped counting at thirty and chased after him, going left into the Great Hall and bumping straight into Arkinew. Fear gripped him.

Peter tried not to listen and forced himself to think of anything except the story. Myroy's words seemed to actually take him to the Elder's palace. They were irresistible words that consumed Peter's thoughts. He bit his tongue to create something he could focus on. Myroy stopped speaking and nodded. Some force prised the boy's mouth open and he could not bite his tongue. Peter clenched his fists, digging his finger nails into his palms. Myroy nodded again and his fingers straightened out. He clenched his toes and Myroy made him rise up to hover six inches above the ground. The Ancient One's face became fierce.

"In your time, half of the world has fallen. Odin's forces are preparing to move south. They will conquer everything unless you listen."

Peter hated him and tried desperately to free himself. Myroy spoke strange words, and the boy's body became stiff, as if encased in ice. He floated with his mouth open, fingers pointing out and limbs completely rigid. Myroy began the story again.

SUMMER 637 AD

Malcolm ran down the corridor, past shields hung on the walls, with his brother counting and sneakily looking to see which way he went. Murdoch stopped counting at thirty and chased after him, going left into the Great Hall and bumping straight into Arkinew. Fear gripped him.

"I am so sorry, Arkinew."

The king's alchemist had his back to him and, when he spoke, it was in his normal cold, calculating voice.

"How many times have I asked you to watch where you are going?"

"We were only ..."

Arkinew interrupted his excuse.

"You have much to learn before the boy becomes a Protector. Do not be late for your lessons at noon. There will be extra work for you."

Murdoch's heart sank.

"I will arrive early for study," he promised.

Arkinew turned and walked away, backwards, his intense eyes staring angrily at his pupil.

"I will be talking to your father about your behaviour. He can decide if you will be beaten."

Murdoch had been beaten many times by his father.

"That doesn't scare me anymore," he thought.

Arkinew stopped in his tracks and snarled. Murdoch's head swam and blacked out, and he woke with flames all around him. The heat was incredible and he leapt up, and ran to the stairs, coughing as smoke filled his lungs. The flames chased him up the stairs to the very top of the tower. He staggered, screaming, out onto the roof, hair on fire and blisters bursting. The pain was awful, and still the flames chased him.

He climbed out onto the edge of the tower and stared down at rocks, hundreds of paces below. The heat became unbearable as his robes began to smoulder. He jumped and felt himself plummet to his death.

Then he was standing again before Arkinew in the Great Hall. The pain was gone and he felt his hair. It wasn't on fire now.

"Do not be late for your lessons," repeated Arkinew and he left him.

Murdoch shook with fear and decided to tell Malcolm about the fire.

He searched the kitchens, stables and the huts on the Palace Green, before entering the North Tower. No sign of Malcolm on the ground floor, nor the first. Surely he wasn't hiding on the top floor? Many times they had been warned not to play near the Elder's chamber, and they were totally forbidden to enter the room at the far end of the tower. Murdoch ran up the circular stairs and froze before looking along the top corridor. It was deserted and, cautiously, he edged his way down it, opening heavy oak doors and sneaking inside to search around.

At last he came to his father's chamber, where he hesitated before opening the door a fraction. He listened for any warning noise from inside and none came, so he entered. Bright sunshine shone through the large, arched window and lit up a great oak bed with forest animals carved onto its pillars. Fear gripped him as he heard voices outside. The voices grew louder and he dived under the bed.

"The last of the Donalds are rising in the North."

It was the Elder and he sounded angry.

"They are," replied Arkinew.

"But they have no heir to claim my throne."

Arkinew ignored his words.

"They gather in Glen Shee and are small in number."

"But what is your counsel?"

"Raise your army and destroy them completely. It will be an example to the other clan leaders who may doubt your authority."

Under the bed, Murdoch felt cold sweat drip down his back.

He edged away from the side of the bed and pushed his back against a wooden panel that lined the wall. The panel silently moved inwards.

"I will raise my warriors now," said the Elder.

"On your return, you should speak to your son, Murdoch. He needs to understand that obedience is expected of him."

The Elder laughed.

"I shall beat him soundly."

Murdoch heard the chamber door slam shut and pushed his hand into the space behind the wooden panel. It was too small for him to climb into and about the size of one of the stones from which the tower was made. He moved the panel in and out on its hinges and wondered why it was there. The panel gave a small click as he shut it and he decided to tell Malcolm about this as well.

He ran to the door and listened for any sound outside, but all was deadly quiet. His nerve failed him outside of the door at the far end and he ran back along the forbidden corridor, and went to see if his brother was hiding in another tower.

Just before noon, Murdoch was hot and tired of searching. He was convinced that his brother must have cheated and hidden outside the palace walls, because he had searched everywhere else.

Looking down at his tiny shadow on the Green, he remembered being chased by flames and ran to his lessons in Arkinew's chamber. Malcolm stood outside the alchemist's door.

"Wait until after study," said Malcolm. "I've got loads to tell you."

"I have loads to tell you. Where did you hide? I searched for ages."

The door opened and Arkinew beckoned them in. The room was bright and barely furnished, and in the centre were two small wooden desks with rolled parchments on them.

"What do we learn today?" asked Malcolm, secretly hoping it wasn't going to be more of the Old Norse that confused him.

Arkinew gave him a rare smile and pointed at their chairs. They sat obediently.

"Not Old Norse. There is so much you must learn if you are to one day rule. Today we are to have a special history lesson."

Deep inside the brothers groaned and Arkinew rounded on them.

"To understand the future you must understand the past."

As he said these words, the floor shimmered like moonlight on water and an ancient-looking man rose up through the floor. Arkinew knelt before him and Myroy told him to stand. Murdoch's mouth fell open and Malcolm went cold with fear.

Myroy pointed his staff at Malcolm.

"You are destined to rule as the Younger. On your father's passing you will create a long peace, unite the clans and raise a High Table to defend the Scottish people."

He pointed at Murdoch.

"And you will become the Protector of the Outer Islands. You will have a daughter. Name her Margaret. It is Margaret who will unite the houses of Donald and Elder."

The boys sat in stunned silence until Malcolm asked the question they were both thinking.

"Who are you?"

"I am Myroy and I will advise you. But first, you must come with me."

Arkinew disappeared into the ground before their very eyes and Myroy came over to stand between them. He held them tightly.

"Do not be afraid. Before you are steps that will take us to another place. Step down into the floor and I will guide you."

Murdoch glanced at Malcolm and they both stared down at the hard floor.

"All you have to do is step down," reassured Myroy.

They stepped down and, as their feet disappeared into the ground, the children shook with fear. Myroy's grip tightened.

"I am with you."

They stepped down into darkness and utter silence, and waited for some word, some sign that the journey was over. But standing without any sensation made the time pass so slowly and it seemed like an age before Myroy spoke again.

"Before you are steps leading upwards. Raise your feet and find the first step."

Nervously, they felt ahead for the step and then Myroy forced them upwards into a new world. They were standing in a cave with a high rock ceiling. On one side was a ledge with the mummified body of a woman lying on it. One wall was covered in pulsing red crystals. It felt bitterly cold, but the dull red light from the crystals reached inside the children and warmed them.

"Welcome to the Oracle of the Ancient Ones," said Arkinew.

"Where are we?" asked Malcolm.

"I have told you," snapped Arkinew and he went over to the crystals and touched them.

The wall became a weak picture that showed metal carriages moving along a road. Faint, unclear words came from the mouths of people who stepped out of the carriages beside the road.

"They are called *Alto Mobiles* and one day man will not need to use horses to travel great distances."

Murdoch glanced at Myroy.

"I do not believe what I am seeing. Is this a dream?"

"It is no dream. Now listen to my words."

The Ancient One told them about Speer's death and how his brothers had discovered that they did not die. His words gripped them and they lived the adventures in their minds. The destruction of Thor's invasion fleet, Gora trying to steal Amera's stone, Dunnerold's race to Amera's cairn to take the stone before Odin's arrival and, finally, the death of the Donalds at Kings Seat. As he told them about their father and his ruthless pursuit of power they felt ashamed.

"You should not be ashamed of your father, or fear him. His destiny is set and he will die. Fear Odin. Even now he comes to claim what was once his."

81

Myroy stared at Malcolm.

"And you have a story to tell."

Malcolm felt his leather purse and nodded.

"We were playing hide and seek, and I hid in the North Tower. I thought that the one place Murdoch would not look was the end room. We are forbidden to go there. Inside are all my father's treasures and one is a brooch with a ruby."

He took Amera's stone from his purse, its last place of hiding, and it pulsed an angry red. The crystals on the wall pulsed the same colour and stronger now.

"I was drawn to it and when I pointed it at swords and jewels they rose up if I imagined them in my mind rising up into the air."

"You used the power of the stone," said Arkinew coldly. "Then Odin will have heard its cry."

"He comes," warned Myroy, "and we must unite the clans to do battle."

Myroy went over to stand with his apprentice. As a boy, Arkinew had been schooled to become powerful, but on the Elder's death his mind would wither and the age of alchemy be gone forever.

"You sent the Elder north?"

"I did," said Arkinew.

"And the Donald clan is ready?"

"It is."

Myroy turned to face Murdoch.

"You found the hiding place I prepared for you?"

Murdoch's mouth fell open again.

"Behind my father's bed?"

"The last place he will look for a lost treasure, is under his own bed. Both of you must keep the stone hidden from the Elder. If he holds it his greed will nourish it and his terrible authority will threaten all that we know."

The boys looked at each other, not quite believing that any of this was happening.

"Thousands will die in the battle to defend the stone. Odin's forces will land in two days and Arkinew will make the Elder combine his forces with the Donalds to defeat the greater enemy."

Arkinew nodded and disappeared down into the floor.

"And both of you must hide the stone until a young shepherd fights in battle and asks to go home as his reward. Pass it on to him and him only. He will be the first Keeper."

"How will we know him?" asked Murdoch nervously.

Myroy smiled. "You will know him. Now, we go back to the palace. Hide the stone from your father and learn your lessons well."

Before they descended into the earth, the Ancient One touched them on the shoulder.

"This will help you learn," he said.

***

Odin stood at the stern of a longship. The wooden deck creaked as a strong breeze blew from the north and filled the ship's huge sail. They were making good time. He glanced back over his shoulder at the Norse fleet. Ninety sails at his command. He thought about Amera's cairn and how he had missed recapturing his stone by just one day. Maybe this would be his time? If only it would cry out near to water.

***

The brothers rose out of the ground in Arkinew's chamber with Myroy holding them as tightly as ever.

"Remember my words," he said, releasing them.

The floor began to shimmer and he descended down into the earth.

Murdoch looked at Malcolm.

"Did that really happen?" he asked.

Myroy's head came back up.

"It did," he said and then he was truly gone.

"Come on," said Malcolm, "let's go and hide the stone."

They ran across the Palace Green towards the North Tower and, like thieves, made their way up to the top floor. Outside the Elder's chamber they hesitated and listened for sounds inside. Men talked. One man shouted something out in an angry voice. "We had better come back later," said Murdoch and they ran back to the Green.

"Well, what do we do now?"

Murdoch shrugged his shoulders.

"Myroy said that the battle against Odin would not start until two days have passed. It will probably take another two days for the Elder to march back to the palace so there is no need to hurry. What shall we do to pass the time?"

"Let's go fishing," said Malcolm.

Beside the great river, the Tay, they threw out lines and caught nothing, then lay on grass and rested in the beautiful afternoon sunshine, with Malcolm's breathing becoming slower as he dozed.

"What did you think of Myroy?" asked Murdoch.

"I think he is very powerful," said Malcolm sleepily.

"And deep down, do you feel stronger knowing that he will guide us?"

"Aye."

"And did you see the picture on the crystal wall?"

"Aye."

"I wager that's where Arkinew gets his knowledge of the future."

"Aye."

"But who is his master? The Elder or Myroy?"

Malcolm rolled onto his side and put his folded arm under his head.

"They both are, I think."

"Can I see the stone?"

Lazily, Malcolm reached down and took the brooch from his purse. He tossed the stone to his brother and yawned.

84

"Now stop talking and let me sleep."

Murdoch fingered the stone. It didn't look powerful. He stared deep into the ruby and saw faces staring back at him. The faces were gaunt and they seemed to be calling out to him. He tried to turn away and yet some power held his gaze. What were the people inside the stone saying? He threw it onto the ground and it pulsed the colour of blood. Malcolm woke.

"What have you done?"

"I looked inside the ruby and saw faces," said Murdoch, his voice trembling.

Ten paces from the bank a tower of bubbles rose up and Odin towered above them.

"I have an urgent message from Myroy."

The boys stood and the hairs on the backs of their necks prickled.

"Who are you?" asked Malcolm.

"I am Tirani the Wise. My brother may have spoken of me."

Murdoch nodded.

"What is the message?"

"There is a battle about to begin to the north. There are more of the enemy than even Myroy predicted. He asks for the stone to aid him."

"But he has asked us to hide it," said Malcolm.

"He has," said Odin.

"But how can we be sure we are doing the right thing?" asked Murdoch.

"You cannot be sure. You can only trust in the wisdom of the Ancient Ones."

Malcolm nodded and Murdoch threw the stone to him.

***

As the Norse fleet approached Scottish soil, his men dropped the sails and took up arms. Odin held Amera's stone aloft and cried out.

"We are invincible. Let none of the enemy live."

Arkinew stood beside the Elder at the head of his army.

"What does he hold?"

"It looks like a brooch," said Arkinew.

"Is it powerful?"

"Can anything be as powerful as two armies who hold the advantage of the land?"

The Elder nodded and looked across at the Donald clan. They had brought about four hundred warriors to the field of battle. "One day I will destroy them," he thought.

Myroy walked through the ranks of the Donalds and stared at Odin. How could this be? He held the stone. Odin stared back and smiled. Then he pointed the stone at one of his longships. It raced forward, cutting through the waves like a knife, and scraping its way up the beach towards the enemy. He turned to use the stone's power on the whole fleet and the stone pulsed in his hand. Then it began to disappear. He roared with rage and shouted at Myroy.

"You did this!"

Myroy returned his stare and said nothing. Then he disappeared into the ground, to rise up by the banks of a great river to stand before two children.

"Tell me what happened."

"Tirani came to us and told us that you needed the brooch," said Murdoch.

"And you gave it to him?"

"We did."

"Did Tirani rise up through the earth?"

Malcolm shook his head and pointed at the water.

"He rose up there."

Myroy paced around on the grass.

"I just do not understand what has happened. The stone is in Odin's hand and the first time he uses its power, it leaves him."

"It has come back to me," said Malcolm excitedly and he took the brooch from his leather purse. "It pulsed inside my purse moments before you rose up from the ground."

Myroy smiled.

"There is so much I do not understand about its power. Still, it seems to have returned to us because of Odin's lie and returned to its last place of hiding."

The brothers smiled too.

"And you are not cross at us for giving the stone away?"

"Please. When I ask you to do something, do it. Now, go and hide the stone."

He watched as they ran back to the palace and knew the stone was safe, for a while at least. But thousands would die in the battle that raged to the north.

An hour later, Odin rose out of the sea and looked at the broken and bloody bodies of his army. The brave amongst the fallen would join him in his eternal struggle. How had the stone been taken from his hand? How had so many of the enemy gathered to face him in such a short time? He realised that this could only be Myroy's doing and anger pulsed through his veins. He swore revenge. One day his time would come. One day Myroy's luck *would* run out.

Three days later, Malcolm and Murdoch sat and waited for Arkinew to arrive for their lesson. The chamber door burst open and the alchemist walked in, backwards, holding many rolls of parchment.

"What do we study?" asked Murdoch.

"The Old Norse."

The brothers' hearts sank.

Arkinew's voice became cold.

"One day you will defend the kingdom against the warriors from the north. Do you not think that learning their tongue might give you an advantage?"

They nodded obediently and took the parchments he gave them. As they read the runes and talked about their meanings, they found that they could remember every word. The years of knowledge held by Arkinew became their knowledge and, by sundown, they could read and speak the Old Norse. As the light grew too dim to study by, Arkinew smiled, satisfied at their progress. He gathered up the parchments and nodded at the door as a sign for them to leave. Murdoch skipped out and as Malcolm made the door, the alchemist called after him.

"There is one lesson I cannot teach you. I have no answers to the many questions you are sure to ask, so do not ask them. One day you will defend the kingdom against your own son."

***

Peter felt as though he was being gripped in a vice. Myroy's story sang in his mind. He hated him. Hated all the Ancient Ones and what they had done to him. He tried to see Kylie, but her body was behind him and he pictured her deathly white face.

"That is all for now," said Myroy.

The invisible hands released Peter and he fell onto the concrete slipway. He snarled like an animal and ran past the kneeling crowd on the quay, past the giant television screen and the kneeling musicians. He looked out to sea and the *Maid Of Norway* was a tiny speck on the horizon. He snarled again and kicked over a music stand.

Further down the quay, a small motorboat bumped continually against the concrete wall, its engine purring and a man kneeling at the stern. Peter ran over, jumped in and kicked the man away from the tiller. He pushed the throttle forward, turned the boat to face the sea and steered a course out of the harbour entrance. His blood boiled and his eyes shone red with rage and tears.

"Faster," he screamed.

The engines whined as they shot forward, cutting through the low waves at an incredible speed. Peter remembered the lie Odin had told him to take the ruby.

"Let's see if the bloody story is true and find out the real power of the stone."

He kept the coastal road to Kassiopi on his left hand side and saw hundreds of kneeling sunbathers on the beach. They were completely under Odin's control, but Peter didn't care about them. He didn't care about anything anymore except revenge. He pushed the tiller over as he approached Secret Cove and, when the boat raced into the horseshoe bay, he cut the engine and dived overboard. Then he was swimming underwater towards the black tunnel, his lungs bursting for air and, at last, his head broke the surface inside the cave. He felt his way to the ledge, the stone's last place of hiding, and in the darkness searched along it. His fingers clasped the brooch and it felt his anger.

The cave became alive with cold, red flame and everything, even the darkest shadows, glowed red.

Peter pictured the concrete slipway in his mind and dived back into the water. His body shot like a bullet through the sea and he rose up to stand next to Kylie. He looked at her and complete rage gripped him. He pointed the stone out to sea and, thirty miles away, the *Maid Of Norway* exploded in a red fireball. Peter watched as tongues of flame and a tower of acrid black smoke rose up on the horizon. He turned on Myroy.

"One down. One to go," he spat.

When the beam hit him, Myroy's body exploded into a million pieces. Peter threw the brooch away and stared, in horror, at the fresh blood on the concrete.

CHAPTER FIVE

THE SCHOOL BUS

Up in the street café, Bernard and Spiros watched Peter on the slipway.

"What time is it?"

Spiros glanced at his watch.

"Four twenty."

Bernard took another sip of coffee.

"Then it is over. The price is paid."

The red concrete in front of Peter began to shimmer and Myroy rose up.

"Dougie faced three challenges to become the first Keeper. You have passed two terrible tests, to become the last Keeper, and I think that is more than enough for anyone."

He raised his staff and the boy collapsed onto the ground.

"Well done, Peter of the line of Donald," said the Ancient One.

***

Peter opened his eyes and looked at his alarm clock. It read 07:28 so he had a few more minutes before having to get up. He sat bolt upright, completely confused, and felt his pyjamas as he glanced around his bedroom. Everything was exactly as it always had been. How could this be?

His mother called out from downstairs.

"OK, kids. Breakfast is ready."

Peter's heart leapt and he jumped out of bed, and ran to the door. His phone beeped and stopped him in his tracks. A text message.

See you on the school bus. Love you. Kylie. Xxx

He dropped the phone and ran down to the kitchen, not daring to dream that his world was unchanged, his family still alive. Julie Donald poured orange juice out of a carton into a tall glass jug and smiled.

"Hungry today, are we?"

Peter threw his arms around her and she gasped.

"How can this be?" said Peter.

"How can what be, my angel?"

Peter hugged her as hard as he had ever hugged anyone.

"How can this be?" he said again.

James joined them, head down, shuffling his feet and yawning.

"Don't think I should go to school today. Got a blinding headache."

"Of course you are going to school and don't forget to find out the times for parents' evening. Your father and I are particularly keen to talk to your English Teacher, Mr Greacher. We hope your behaviour's been better this term."

"Whatever."

Peter released his mother and hugged James.

"What's up with you? You dipstick."

"I thought I'd lost you."

James twisted his body.

"Wish I'd bloody lost you."

"James!" said Julie.

"What a great way to start the day. I've got a headache and a tree-hugging dipstick of a brother."

He poured orange juice out of the jug and into a glass. Most of it spilled onto the kitchen table.

"Can we get Broadband? Seen a great deal on the net."

"You'd better talk to your father about that. He's back from Amsterdam tonight. That reminds me. We've had a nice postcard from Grandma. She's decided to spend a week on Corfu with Bernard. You might remember him, Peter. He gave you a lift after Grandpa's funeral."

A voice shouted down from upstairs.

"Mum. Have you seen my black trousers?"

Julie shouted back.

"In the ironing basket."

Peter dashed upstairs and hugged his sister. James and Julie listened as Laura shouted abuse at him.

"He's weird," said James.

"How about when you eat your breakfast, you get some of it

in your mouth and not spill most of it on the floor."

James gave her his *who me?* look, and Laura marched in holding her trousers.

"These aren't ironed. I haven't got anything to wear to school."

"If you didn't just throw your dirty washing on your bedroom floor and put it in the wash-basket, you would have plenty of clothes to wear."

"And what's up with Peter? Just kissed me. He's weird."

James grinned.

"It's hanging around with Kylie. Enough to make anyone go bonkers."

Peter came in and sat at the table. His head swimming.

"I don't know what is real and what is unreal."

Julie smiled.

"Your biology test is real. It's at eleven, isn't it?"

"Don't know."

"Oh, Peter. Have you done your revision?"

"No. I've had the most amazing dream though. Except I know it was too real to be a dream."

"And your results have been so good since you got back from Grandma's."

Julie walked over to the family notice board and looked at Peter's timetable.

"You've got history at nine, a free study-period at ten, the exam at eleven and the afternoon off for more free study. You can get some revision done at ten."

"Can I have the afternoon off?" asked James.

"No."

Julie looked at James's timetable.

"And that explains the headache. You've got PE with Mr Sweeney, first thing."

"Whatever," said James.

Laura poured milk onto a huge bowl of muesli.

"Abby's had an increase in her allowance. Can I get more too?"

"I'll check with her mum, first."

Laura looked sheepish.

"Abby's dad gave her the increase."

"I'll check anyway. Besides, we've only just given you an increase."

"But I have to buy my own lunches now. I'm getting less than I was."

James went to get his PE kit and shouted back.

"If Laura gets an increase can I get one too? I'd pay for my broadband if I got more."

Julie ignored him and nodded at Peter.

"The bus will be here in a minute. Go and pack your bag and don't forget your biology stuff."

Peter went up to his room and sat on his bed. He felt down for the shoebox he hid under the bed and took Amera's stone out.

"So, some things have definitely happened."

He put the stone in his pocket, packed his bag and ran down the stairs, praying that Kylie would be on the bus. His mum opened the front door for him.

"Let me know how you get on," she said.

Peter kissed her on the cheek.

"It's nice to be home."

Julie smiled and watched him go. Half way to their gate, Peter stopped, knelt and picked something up.

"You never know when you might need a pebble," he called back.

Julie's smile disappeared.

"Are you finding these exams a bit stressful, Peter?"

He didn't reply and, back in the kitchen, she stared at the breakfast table. Laura's bowl was half full of muesli, bits of toast swam in orange juice and James's PE kit sat in a heap on a chair.

"Just another day at the office," she said.

Peter caught up with his brother and sister at the bus stop, and looked at his watch.

"What's up with you today?" asked Laura.

"Just a bad dream," said Peter.

"There's the bus," said James. "Why can't Mr Denver be late sometimes?"

Peter's heart leapt and he tried to see if Kylie was onboard. As the doors opened, he pushed past Laura and showed Mr Denver his bus pass.

"And how are we today?" asked the driver.

"I'll be better when I have checked something."

Mr Denver smiled and nodded up at a TV screen showing the top deck.

"Kylie's upstairs."

Peter bounded up the stairs and sat next to his girlfriend.

"Hi, Peter," she said.

"Hi."

Peter kissed her.

"I know this is a bit odd, but could you lean forward?"

She leant forward and Peter pulled her shirt up over her back. No bullet wound. No blood.

"Peter!"

"Just checking."

The bus made a sharp turn and they were thrown to one side.

"Mr Denver's on a mission today," said Kylie.

The school bus lurched again as it entered New Hope Drive. A large poster by the bus stop proclaimed –

**THE BIG ONE! ENGLAND V SCOTLAND
AT THE NEW WEMBLEY
COMING SOON!**

Peter nodded and groaned as Mac and Toady came up the stairs.

"Bet they come and sit with us again," whispered Kylie, out of the corner of her mouth.

The boys came and sat in the seat in front of theirs, and swivelled round to annoy them. Toady Thompson lit a cigarette and blew smoke at Kylie.

"Fancy a new boyfriend?"

Something deep inside Peter, something that had not been there before, snapped. Anger welled up in the depths of his soul and he clenched his fists.

"You think you're tough, don't you."

Mac grinned.

"We'll see you after school."

"Why wait?" asked Peter.

His fists shot forward at an incredible speed, smashing into the boys faces. Their limp bodies slumped down onto their seat.

The bus accelerated down New Hope Drive and Mr Denver slammed on the brakes outside the gates of Pinner High School. Peter stared at them. The last time he had seen them, they had been a tangle of twisted metal beside a BBC Outside Broadcast lorry.

"I'm still not sure what is real."

"You hitting Mac and Toady was real. What's come over you?"

Peter kissed Kylie.

"Not sure. Something just snapped. We've put up with their bullying for too long."

"You're bound to get into trouble with Mrs Bold."

"Worth it, though."

They walked through the staff car park towards the main doors of the school, as Mr Denver got ready to drive away. The driver glanced into his TV screen, a final check that everyone had gone. Two boys were holding their faces and shaking their heads.

After registration, Kylie went off to her art lesson and Peter walked past The Poems of Peace and into the school library. It was as neat as a pin. The ranks of low tables and chairs in the restaurant were back to normal too, and he continued down the science corridor. Peter remembered Dougie looking in awe at the posters of space and sea exploration, and quickened his pace to pass physics, biology and chemistry. He climbed the stairs at the end of the corridor, towards his history class, and stopped in his tracks. The unmistakable, bearded figure of Mr Smith was ushering everyone inside.

Peter sat at the back of the classroom, as close to the door as he could be. Mr Smith smiled at the class and his black beard bunched up into balls on his cheeks.

"Unfortunately, Mr Crumple is ill today and will not be able to take your history lesson. My name is Mr Smith and I am here on supply to cover for Miss Grenoski, who is on maternity leave. Apparently, my job is to look after 1G, so my new timetable is in ruins as well."

Someone laughed and Peter put his hand into his pocket to check that the stone was safe.

"Can someone please tell me where you have got up to in your studies?"

A girl put her hand up and Mr Smith smiled.

"And you are?"

"Jodi McNab."

"A Scottish name. Good. Good. Where are you up to?"

"Just starting The Impact Of War. We were asked to read up on World War Two. Evacuation and rationing, the Blitz and how the Welfare State changed the lives of people in Britain after the war."

"That's quite a list, then. Did you read up on the topic?"

Jodi nodded.

"I was particularly interested in how the role and status of women changed between 1941 and 1944."

Most of the class stared blankly at their books. Mr Smith's face creased with worry.

"I'm afraid I am no expert on this topic and I certainly haven't prepared anything to help me run a good lesson on it."

He looked at the back of the class at Peter.

"Is there anything you would like to go over today, laddie?"

Peter's natural reaction would be to say nothing, or divert the conversion onto something that would not bring attention to him. Now though, he leaned forward.

"Aye, how the Picts were defeated on Carn Liath by Malcolm the Younger."

Mr Smith's face creased again.

"Is that on the curriculum?"

"No. But it should be."

"No. Can't cover that one either."

Peter looked into his teacher's eyes, and knew that this man was not the same one he had killed using the stone.

After the worst lesson Peter had ever sat through ended, he went to the library for his free study period. He started by making a list of the main topics that would come up in his Microbiology exam.

Biotechnology.
Micro-organisms.
Disease.
The immune system.
Germ theory of disease.
Industrial fermentation.
Food and drug production.
Food preservation.
Biogas/ethanol as fuel.

Then he took out his revision guide and past papers, and read them, ticking off each topic as he went. By five to eleven he knew every word and left for his exam in the school gym. It wasn't difficult at all.

Later, in the canteen, Mac watched Kylie take a yoghurt out of her lunch box.

"How did it go?" she asked Peter.

"I got lucky. The immune system and food preservation came up. I think I've done OK."

"Oh, come on. You've been getting full marks in your results all term. When do you get the time to revise all that stuff?"

Peter shrugged his shoulders.

"It's you. You inspire me."

"Yeah, that'll be right. What's happened to you this year? You seem different."

"I feel different. One day, I promise, I'll tell you why."

Mrs Bold waddled through the restaurant and came over to their table.

"Peter. Would you come and see me in my office, when you have finished lunch. In about twenty minutes?"

"Yes, Miss," he promised.

At a safe distance, Kylie whispered to Peter.

"Do you think it's about Mac and Toady on the bus?"

"Probably."

"I'll come to detention with you."

Peter smiled.

"Have you got free study time this afternoon?"

"Sure."

"How about going to the British Library? There's something I need to check out and it's a great place to revise."

"Sounds great. When do you want to go?"

"As soon as I've been told off."

Kylie held his hand.

"You'll be fine."

Peter squeezed her hand.

"You're right, I've been through much worse. See you in about fifteen minutes."

At a safe distance, Mac followed Peter out of the restaurant and saw him turn left down a cream coloured corridor towards the toilets. Mac held back and then followed him inside. Peter closed the toilet door, lowered the seat and sat down, and took his stone out. In Myroy's story, the Protector had stared deep into the ruby and seen gaunt faces staring back at him. Peter looked deep into the heart of Amera's stone too. No faces, just a warm, blood red glow.

Standing by the wash basins, Mac heard Peter say, "There is so much I do not understand."

Peter closed his eyes and thought about Odin. How he had lied to Malcolm and Murdoch and how the stone had returned to its last place of hiding when he had tried to use its terrible power.

"That's a lesson I have to remember," he said.

"You're right there, Laddie," said Grandpa's voice.

Peter smiled.

"You told Grandma about being a Keeper. When can I tell Kylie?"

"I told Maggie before we got married. I didn't think it would be fair to enter the Union of Souls without being honest about it."

"I'll tell her then," promised Peter.

"Any questions before you go off to the British Library?"

"Lots. I lost my family and girlfriend to Odin's forces. Was that a dream?"

"No. Myroy's stories are very powerful. He can make you live them, but do not doubt anything else that happened. Dougie was the first stone Keeper and he *was* imprisoned in Mountjoy castle. I did lose the stone in the desert. The Battle of Pinner High School and your adventures on Corfu could all happen if you do not learn from Myroy's words."

"It was so real."

"I felt your pain. Myroy felt your pain too. It was hard for him, but you must have anger in your heart if you are to one day face the Seekers."

"What about greed?"

"Myroy tested the early Keepers with greed. In his stories, he gave them all the money they could ever desire. But it didn't work. The Donalds make safe Keepers, because they are ordinary, quiet folk. They do not desire wealth or power over others. Myroy tested them all with terrible personal loss and that armed them with anger. Greed did not follow, though, and Myroy knows that Odin's anger is greater than his greed.

Hopefully, your anger and all the lessons from history will be enough in the final battle."

"Hopefully?"

"You must always have hope."

"And Odin can sense when the stone is being used?"

Grandpa sighed.

"What does the story tell you?"

"Murdoch threw the stone onto the ground and it pulsed. Moments later, Odin appeared in a tower of bubbles rising up out of the River Tay. I must keep the stone away from water unless I deliberately hide it beneath water. Dougie hid it in the loch and its water stopped the stone crying out."

"Protected by Gora."

"The osprey."

"Not just an osprey. Gora knows more than anyone about the stone and its moods. His soul was a prisoner inside the stone for centuries. No one suffered more than him."

"Gora was a thief."

Grandpa's voice became hard.

"Forgiveness has a power too, and Gora will be your guardian when Myroy finishes the story."

"My guardian?"

Beside the washbasins, Mac's jaw dropped and his mobile phone bleeped once. He crept towards the exit. Peter's eyes grew wide.

"Grandpa, someone's listening to us."

"It is the one you call Mackinlay. What can he understand?"

"He sided with the Seekers in the story."

"He would side with the Seekers, if given the chance. Make sure he is not given the chance."

"But, he can tell others that I am a Keeper."

Grandpa sighed again.

Before Mac made the door, Grandpa rose out of the floor like a sand coloured demon, barring his way. He lowered his rifle and placed the tip of his bayonet under the boy's throat.

"Do you believe in ghosts?"

Mac felt the hair on his neck rise up. Fear flooded through his bones. Grandpa repeated his question.

"I said, do you believe in ghosts?"

Somehow, Mac's frozen body managed to nod.

"Good. Because if you say anything about this, if you or Toady do anything to hurt my grandson, I will be speaking to you."

Grandpa disappeared down into the floor and Mackinlay fled. Peter grinned and went to see Mrs Bold, and doubted that Mac and Toady's parents would make a complaint about him.

A sign on the heavy looking door read –

Mrs Bold. Headmistress.
Please knock before entering.

Peter knocked and entered.

"Ah, Peter. Well done. Come and sit down."

"Well done?"

"We are all really pleased with your exam results and I wanted to let you know that I shall be writing a letter to your mother and father saying how pleased I am at the hard work you have put into your studies. You're turning into a model pupil. First class."

Peter glanced at the school trophy cabinet and thought about Mac and Toady.

"I'm not a model pupil. I'm afraid that on the school bus this morning, I punched Thompson and Mackinlay. Their parents may make a complaint to you soon."

"What did they do?"

"They were rude and blew smoke over my girlfriend."

"Well, let's deal with that if their parents do make a formal complaint. I don't remember you being in trouble before."

"First time, I'm afraid."

"Let's talk about your test results. Geography, English, mathematics, physics, chemistry and French all one hundred percent. Miss Tag, Deputy Head of Biology, says she has looked quickly through today's exam papers and yours looks good too. So, just history to go. Tomorrow?"

"That's right, Miss."

"We have never had a pupil who got top marks in all subjects at this stage, so well done."

"Thank you."

"If you do the same in history, I will invite a photographer in from a local paper and ask them to run an article on it. Are you up for that?"

"Yes, Miss."

"First class. Right, off you go then."

As Peter left, he knew that Myroy would not want a Keeper to draw attention to himself and he decided not to do any revision for the history exam at all. In future he would need to be more careful.

Beside the school gates, Peter put an arm around Kylie's shoulder.

"You get told off?" she asked.

"No, I got praised for my results. Told her all about Mac and Toady though."

"Honesty is the best policy."

"Come on. Let's get the tube to King's Cross."

The silent Reading Room of the British Library gave off its reassuring odour of cleaning fluid and old books. Kylie settled herself at one of the desks, switched on a reading light and got her revision notes out. Peter bent down to whisper in her ear.

"Off to get a book. See you in a minute."

He walked quietly to a desk, which stood apart from the others. A sign read –

Miss Dickson, Day Librarian, Enquiries Welcome.

"Hello, Miss Dickson. Nice to see you again."

Miss Dickson stared at Peter through a huge pair of glasses.

"I'm sorry. I don't think I've had the pleasure," she said in a squeaky voice.

"It was a while ago, right enough. I'd like to see anything on the history of Scotland during Celtic times. I'd particularly like to read about the reign of Malcolm the Younger again."

"Again?"

"Aye, *Early Celtic Writings and their Meanings* would be a good way to start."

"Not here. Hold on."

She picked up her phone. "Hello, Mike. Can you do a location search for *Early Celtic Writings and their Meanings*."

Miss Dickson picked up some paperclips and placed them into her desk tidy as she waited.

"Thank you, Mike." She put the phone down. "There is one copy in existence and it is kept in Saint Andrews."

"Bit of a way to go then," smiled Peter.

Miss Dickson did not smile back.

"That depends on how committed you are to your studies."

"You must excuse me. I'm very confused at the moment. I have lived a story and parts of it seem to be true and other parts aren't true at all."

The librarian's eyes grew as they opened wide, magnified by her glasses.

"Is there something you want to give me?"

"No."

"Well I am very busy, so if you would excuse me."

Peter walked away, then stopped and took a deep breath. He went back and placed a pebble on her desk. Miss Dickson picked it up and passed it back.

"Follow me," she squeaked.

Peter struggled to keep up as they twisted through the rows of high shelving and, in minutes, they stood in-front of a deserted section –

History/Scotland/Post-Romanic/Celts.

105

Peter felt his heart pound in his chest.

"I have been here before."

"Not with me, you haven't," said Miss Dickson.

"But ..."

"Now then, keep your voice down. We do not want to draw attention to ourselves, do we?"

They walked along the aisle, past books stacked on the floor, and stood before a door marked, PRIVATE: CLEANERS ONLY. The librarian's eyes darted around before she opened the door, ushering him inside and closing the door again. They stood inside a brightly lit broom cupboard that smelled of cleaning fluid.

"Funny place to keep books," thought Peter.

Miss Dickson threw her arms around him.

"This is a great honour. Welcome, Keeper. Welcome."

"My girlfriend's here, you know."

"Oh, don't be silly, Peter. Come on, follow me."

She released him and went over to a small, red fire-extinguisher and turned it clockwise. One wall descended silently into the floor and Peter followed her into a circular, rock-faced chamber with a wooden plinth at its centre. On top of the plinth was a glass bowl, full of pebbles. Red tiles covered the floor. Around the walls were paintings of men and women dressed in historical fashions. One young man, with thick brown hair, wore a brown, green and ochre plaid. The lady in the next painting had golden hair. The rest of the paintings seemed to show how dress had changed through the long centuries since the first Keeper. Peter stared at the last two paintings. There was Grandpa in his desert uniform and there was Peter in his school uniform. There wasn't room for any more paintings.

"Come on," she squeaked. "Put your pebble into the bowl."

Peter placed his pebble into the bowl and the chamber glowed red.

"What's happening?"

"Wait and see," she said excitedly.

A deep rumbling noise came from the bowels of the earth and Peter had a strange sensation of falling. The whole chamber seemed to be going down, with Miss Dickson smiling in the red light. The falling sensation stopped as suddenly as it had started and the room became silent. The pictures, the entire circular rock wall, rose up and away from the red tiles, and Peter was looking at a larger rock chamber with red crystals on one side. The black, mummified body of a woman lay upon a ledge.

"Well, it's not the Place of the Living or the Realm of the Dead, but it is where the history of the stone really began."

"Is this really the Chamber of the Ancient Ones?" asked Peter.

"It really is. Myroy will be here soon."

"What is the Realm of the Dead?"

"Myroy will take you there when he is ready."

Peter nodded and walked over to the crystals. He took Amera's stone from his pocket and held it out. The crystals gave off a soft glow and warmed him.

"This is where Archie saw the future."

Miss Dickson's eager voice echoed around the chamber.

"Oh, yes. Although it wasn't a very good view, was it?"

"Not with *experidents, terescopes* and *bartillery* it wasn't," smiled Peter.

The rock floor began to shimmer, like moonlight on water, and Myroy rose up to meet them.

"Welcome, Peter. Can you ever forgive me for the tests in the story?"

"I was so hurt. So very sad and angry. But I can forgive anyone who brings my family back from the dead. I'm still confused though."

"All the Keepers felt like that."

Peter remembered the pictures on the wall.

"Is the chamber at the British Library a gateway?"

"It is."

"And Miss Dickson?"

107

"Head of Research for the Keepers. One of the best we have ever had."

Miss Dickson blushed and Myroy continued in a soft voice.

"Now is not the time for questions. Now is the time to listen. An important moment is about to come and at the very heart of that moment is a young shepherd."

"Dougie," said Miss Dickson and Peter together.

CHAPTER SIX

ALL ROADS LEAD TO STIRLING

Compared to the mighty fortress at Berwick, Stirling castle was small, without decoration and any square edge. No flag flew above its round central keep, which stood inside thick circular walls. These outer protective walls were the height of two men, but were raised upon the top of an earth bank so that an enemy would need to climb twice that to reach the top of its granite face.

Cameron Campbell climbed stone steps to stand on top of the South Wall. He stared across the River Stirling towards the old ruined fortress on Heather Hill and wondered if the Black Kilts would take this high position, with its clear views, as their base. He looked left at Douglas Rock and the marshes where the river sometimes flooded, then he looked right at Burn Hill and the Old Ford. It looked so peaceful, but in a few short days the armies of Tella's alliance would surround him. He thought about the Younger's promise and wondered if he would still be alive when the High Table arrived. Would any of them live?

The muscular frame of Angus of Stirling bounded up the steps, long red hair bouncing with each stride.

"They come," he said.

"You have news?"

"One rider from the south. Llewellyn's forces have crossed the Clyde at Glasgow, which puts their foot-soldiers three days from us."

"And Tella still moves through the High Glens?"

"He does, but it is Cuthbert's army that moves the fastest. They will take Culross by sunrise tomorrow."

Cameron stared down the Glen of Sighs. The Angles would arrive that way.

"Lead the men into the village. Tell the women to take the children to safety. Tell them to head northeast towards the Younger's Palace. If they flee in any other direction they will meet an enemy."

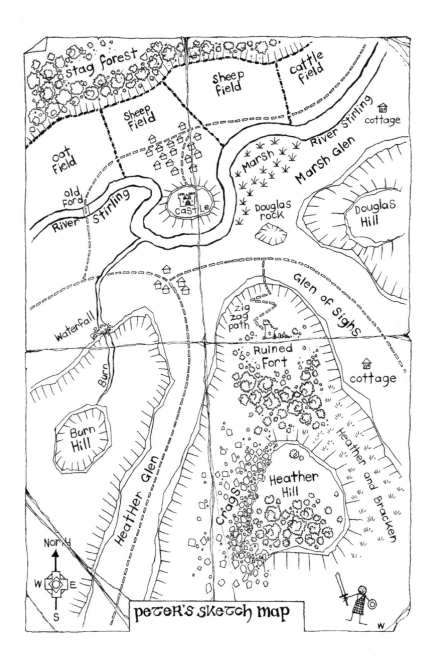

stag forest

Sheep Field

Sheep field

cattle field

cottage

River Stirling

Marsh

Marsh Glen

oat Field

old Ford

River Stirling

castle

Douglas rock

Douglas Hill

Glen of Sighs

zig zag path

Ruined Fort

cottage

Waterfall

Burn

Burn Hill

Heather Glen

Crags

Heather Hill

Heather and Bracken

North

W E

S

peter's sketch map

111

Angus nodded. "Do you expect a long siege?"

"No idea, but we must plan for one. Give the womenfolk every horse we have. We don't need them. Our war will be here, on these walls."

"Aye."

"When they are gone, tear down their cottages and bring the stones here. Burn any cottages that remain."

"Burn our houses?"

"I will give the enemy no comfort."

"And how is your surprise coming along?"

"Nearly ready."

Angus smiled.

"That was an evil idea."

"The Long Peace is over and the whole world has turned evil. Did you tell the men how to deal with the dead?"

"Throw them over the walls to lie in front of the gate. Disease follows death and bodies are hard to walk over."

"Now, take the men and help the women escape."

"And what are you going to do?"

"I'm going to round up some cattle."

***

Malcolm the Younger led the riders of the High Table east from Glen Shee towards the Great Plain in the northeast of his kingdom. The leaders of the clans in these lands were fierce and independent, and had never before sent men to strengthen the Scottish army. Malcolm knew his quest would not be easy. The families of Morgan, Munro, Ferguson, Baxter and McCreedy could provide many warriors, but the Younger needed them more than they needed him.

Morag McCreedy was the key. Her clan was the most powerful and influential of them all. He ran the words he would say to Morag through his mind and, as the sun began to fall, they crossed a winding stream and rose up a gentle grassy slope. Fifty riders on grey Highlands appeared at the top of the slope and stopped in a long line. The Younger raised his hand and the High Table pulled back on their reins.

"It looks as though we were expected."

"Do you recognise them?" asked Stuart, Thane of Coll.

The Younger glanced at Stuart, the newest member of the High Table, and remembered what Hamish had told him about his brave spirit.

"I met Morag a long time ago, at the start of the Long Peace. The others amongst them were not even born then."

"Shall we go and speak with them?"

"No, that is something I must do alone."

Fraser of Abernethy, the Younger's bodyguard, moved his horse beside the Younger.

"Let me go with you. I may be able to win you some time to escape if needed."

"No. Stay here. If things go against me, return to Glen Shee and lead the army to Stirling. Our warriors will need every member of the High Table to win against the greater enemy."

He kicked his heels into the flanks of his stallion and moved up the slope towards the leaders of the Great Plains. They looked tough and carried shields decorated with bears, crossed spears or iron fists, which meant they were Baxters, Morgans and McCreedys. The Younger smiled at an old lady who sat upright on a huge Highland, her long red hair hanging down over a chain mail vest.

"Greetings, Morag. Greetings to all of you."

The McCreedys remained stony faced.

"You know from my riders that enemies approach. I leave here to lead my army to stand before them at Stirling. Seamus, King of the Irish peoples has landed at Stranraer and moves east to aid us."

"The answer is no," said Morag in a strong voice.

"Then it is no and we all lose. When the Angles, Welsh and Picts come here, they will take your lands. Your children will be slaves."

"No one has ever taken our lands."

"Never before have three armies combined to defeat us. Even now, Thorgood Firebrand reinforces his army from their homelands across the Cold Sea. I fear the Norsemen more than the others and they are sure to wait until all sides are weakened by war."

"We will not be weakened. You will be weakened."

"Together we are stronger."

Morag spat on the ground, turned her horse, and galloped away. The other chieftains followed.

At sundown of the following day, the High Table entered the Scottish camp in Glen Shee.

"We had to try," said Stuart.

"We had to succeed," replied Malcolm. "We will need every warrior when two armies stand before three."

They dismounted and the Younger returned to his tent to rest. Morag's words troubled him and it was a long time before sleep came to him.

Cheering men woke him before dawn, and he ran from his tent towards the north of the camp to stand with a huge group of men. They stared down the glen at a long line of warriors who followed their chieftains.

"Bring my horse," said the Younger.

Later, Morag McCreedy gave him a hard stare.

"I did not believe you would come," said Malcolm.

Morag spat on the ground.

"Five hundred warriors."

The Younger smiled.

"Aye, I was asking myself that question."

"And they follow me, not you."

"A place at the High Table was offered to you a long time ago. It will always be there for you."

Morag ignored him.

"Why did you change your mind?" asked the Younger.

"Together we are stronger."

In silence, they rode side by side into the Scottish camp. Morag McCreedy sometimes glancing at the Younger and thinking about the man she had spoken to in secret, knowing that their plan would have to wait until the High Table was weakened. She admired the ambition of the king's son and would use it to seize land and power for her clan. But not yet. It was not yet time for clan to fight clan.

As they dismounted outside the royal tent, Malcolm remembered some things about her, that he had sensed when he was young. Her utter ruthlessness and coldness towards men.

***

Tella the Mac Mar dismounted and the long train of Black Kilts behind him halted.

"Camp here."

Gath's face was a picture. He had summoned all his courage for the great battle that lay ahead and now he looked like a spoilt brat who had suffered a broken promise. He glanced at his father and wondered why they should hold back, only half a day's march from Stirling.

"We promised Cuthbert and Llewellyn that we would join them," he said.

"Do you take me for a fool," snapped Tella, and his son winced. "What are we fighting for?"

"For the alliance."

"The alliance is a means to an end."

"To overthrow the Younger."

When Tella spoke, his words were soft and cruel.

"Aye, to get *our* lands back and extend our authority. Do not forget that."

"But you have pledged a share of the kingdom to the Angles and the Welsh."

Tella sneered. "A pledge is nothing. Nothing but words. As soon as Cuthbert and Llewellyn defeat the Scots, when they are at their weakest, we will kill them all."

115

Gath grinned. "You never intended to keep the alliance, did you father?"

Tella grinned too, and barked at a servant to bring supper to them.

Later, in the Mac Mar's tent, Gath and Tella studied Denbara's map and the notes made by Borak after the scribe's death. Stirling Castle could be approached along four glens. A ruined fort on the lower slopes of Heather Hill would give the best views of the area, but was too exposed and, if they were to watch the battle unseen, would be of no use to them. They settled on spying from the forest, to the north of Castle Village.

"Why did you spare Borak One Hand?" asked Gath.

"He won the time we needed to arm the Alliance."

"And the real reason?"

"Did you feel it?"

"What?"

"His hatred of Seamus."

"He *demanded* the chance to take vengeance on the Irish for the murder of his brother."

"That hatred might be useful. I can think of no one better to command the fleet and hold it ready if we need to flee to safety across the Great Sea."

"Do you fear that we might fail upon the field at Stirling?"

"No."

"Then why not have him here, fighting Seamus."

Gath sensed his father's agitation at his question.

"Because he is one man. One of our best warriors, aye. But we cannot be completely sure of victory and the main threat to our escape to Deros will be the Irish fleet. The Scottish fleet is small and Gawain's ships are no match for ours."

"Gawain's people hate us. Is he related to Llewellyn?"

"Half brothers. Descended from an ancient line of Welsh kings."

"Could Gawain turn Llewellyn against us?"

116

"Llewellyn leads his forces north from Glasgow. Gawain is on Man. I do not think so."

The Mac Mar folded the map and stood. Gath rose to his feet.

"Send riders to Llewellyn and Cuthbert. Tell them that we are fighting the Younger's army to the north, two days' march away. Tell them to expect the Irish army in two days. We will destroy the Younger's army. They must kill Seamus. Tell them not to attack the castle until we arrive."

"But we want them to be weakened. Why not encourage them to scale its walls."

Tella slapped his son's face.

"Cuthbert knows that whoever holds Stirling Castle, holds Scotland. He will attack it anyway. Now go and give the riders my orders."

As Gath hurried from the tent, Tella unfolded the map again and ran his finger along his escape route. They had marched from Oban to Stirling and that way was free of the enemy. His people held Oban and a ship was ready to sail to Fionnphort on the western side of Mull. From there it was only a short sail north, through the Outer Islands, to Deros. He had escaped death on Carn Liath with a scar on his shoulder to remind him. Borak and Tumora, with good fortune, had helped him escape from Man. This time, his escape would be planned and, satisfied that his route home was safe, he folded the map and dreamed again about the riches to be plundered from Scottish soil.

Outside the tent, Gath held his cheek and wondered if his father might be killed in battle. One stray arrow was all that was needed.

***

Grahm Deer sensed his friend's sadness and bit his lip in case he said the wrong thing. They marched side by side in a block of one hundred warriors, about one hundred paces behind Cuthbert and his riders. They had marched for four days, through the borderland, taking Melrose with little loss and otherwise seeing no sign of the enemy. Rumours had gone around the campfires that they would soon reach a great river, the Forth, and it would be there, as they tried to cross, that the Scots would attack. Grahm Deer glanced at Belus. His eyes were wide, staring forward at Cuthbert's back, knuckles white as they gripped the spear he carried over his shoulder. Grahm Deer bit his lip no longer.

"Do you want to talk about it?"

Belus continued to stare forward.

"We have been friends since we were children and you know I would do anything to help you."

Belus snapped, "Then hold your tongue and march."

Grahm Deer took a leather bottle from his belt, drank some water and offered the bottle to his friend. Belus took it, drank, and handed it back.

"The sun will soon fall. Do you think we will make the river tomorrow?"

"Who cares?" said Belus.

"I care if the Scots wait for us there. I want to return home and see my family. I have decided that I should spend less time in the fields and more time with my children."

Instantly Grahm Deer regretted his words and Belus hissed at him.

"Cuthbert need not fear the Scots. He should fear me."

"You must hold back from revenge. He will kill you and punish our village."

"The final blow, the blow that brings him death and avenges my children, will be from my hand."

"And how are you inside?"

"Angry. Empty. Without any fear of consequences afterwards."

"You must wait."

"Why not tonight?"

"His tent is well guarded."

"One guard. Maybe two?"

"Wait."

"Cuthbert did not wait when he dropped Stoyalu's cage into the water to entertain his guests."

Grahm Deer smiled weakly.

"Don't think about it."

"I see it in dreams."

"Think about killing the Scots."

"Why are they my enemy?"

"They have always been our enemy."

"They did not kill my family."

"It's just the way it is."

"It doesn't need to be like this."

"Hold back, friend."

As they marched past a ruined cottage, Belus whispered to himself.

"It doesn't need to be like this."

Two days later, Cuthbert the Cautious looked upon the village of Culross. Two of his ships had sailed north from Berwick to aid his crossing and it had taken only one night to ferry his army across the Forth, and only a small part of the morning to unload their supplies. Food, weapons, tents and many long ladders had now been divided amongst his men. The hardest part of the march was now over. The Younger must be weak, not sending an army to fight him here, where his followers would be at their most vulnerable.

Beside the north bank of the mighty river, a sail was furled and men splashed ashore, leading fine horses and carrying shields with Saxon crosses, hung across their backs. In moments, twenty more riders surrounded Cuthbert.

"Is everyone across?"

Harold of Berwick and John Standforth kicked the flanks of their steeds and steered a course through the riders. They passed a sign that read, RING THE BELL, but there was no sign of the ferry or its owner.

"Our army is across and safe, and no swords to blood as we expected," said Harold.

"Which path shall we take?" asked John.

Cuthbert nodded at the leaders of his bodyguard and unfolded his copy of Denbara's map.

"We head north towards a line of hills overlooking a loch. Then we turn northwest to march along the Glen of Sighs to Stirling. We will camp in a ruined fort that overlooks the castle."

Harold and John glanced at each other, and their horses became uneasy.

"Glen of Sighs?" asked John.

"A good path follows the floor of the glen and it is the part of the journey I have worried most about. One side of the valley is forest, one side is named Heather Hill."

"And you suspect an ambush?"

Cuthbert waved the map at them.

"We are armed with this. It is where I would ambush an enemy. Take my guard and scout the path ahead. Ride back to the army at the first sign of trouble. Remember, we carry the light iron and will crush our enemies."

Cuthbert watched as his riders went north and shouted orders. A thousand warriors formed into a line and marched after them. Amongst the warriors, a farmer remembered Cuthbert's example. Remembered the cages of shame and how his children, Cateya and Stoyalu, had been drowned for the entertainment of a Pict with a black beard. Even now, the high-pitched shrill of the chain, and the splashes as the cages plummeted deep into the moat, haunted him. Belus fingered his spear and, head down, marched beside his friends, thinking of vengeance and how he could get close enough to his master during the battle.

At one end of their ladder, Grahm Deer sensed his anger.

"Hold back, friend."

At the other end of the ladder a voice said, "It doesn't have to be like this."

Half a day's ride later, John and Harold rested their horses on the shores of a loch, their eyes searching the hillside for any sign of the enemy. They hadn't seen anyone so far and believed that the Scots were in hiding in the high places.

"It is a beautiful place," said Harold.

"It is," said John. "And it feels powerful. Do you think we should press on?"

"The gap between us and the foot soldiers has grown. We have time to kill."

John pointed up at a white cottage on the hillside. Someone had just gone inside and closed the door. A dog barked.

"We may have an enemy to fight," he said.

***

Mairi looked out of the cottage door and cried out in terror.

"Dougie."

Myroy's head shot up off the mummified body of his mother. He ran to the far wall of his eternal chamber and, as he dived into the weak pulsing crystals, a single, terrible thought went through his mind.

"I am not going to make it."

***

"Follow me!" yelled Harold of Berwick.

The warriors mounted, held their spears ready and thundered up the slope towards the three standing stones, up on the high pastures.

"Look at the sheep," called back Harold. "The army shall feast tonight."

"Let's kill some Scots," shouted John.

As they approached the cottage, a sheepdog barked and ran at them. John threw his spear and it pinned the dog to the grass. The riders jumped down, drew their swords and ran to the door, pausing before Harold kicked it in. They stood still, scared, staring at the floor. It was shimmering like moonlight on water.

"There is bad magic here," warned John. "Burn it down."

121

"We must attack before the Welsh do," commanded Cuthbert the Cautious and the leaders of his guard bowed in agreement. "Stirling is at the very heart of the Scottish kingdom and whoever holds it wields great power."

"How long do we have?" asked John Standforth.

"Llewellyn will be here tomorrow."

"So we attack now."

"How many Scots man the walls?" asked Harold of Berwick.

"My men have counted no more than two hundred and fifty warriors," replied John.

"By nightfall, I want to stand inside the walls of Stirling Castle," ordered Cuthbert, "go and prepare the army."

Harold and John bowed again and left their master's tent, pitched within the ruined walls of the fort on Heather Hill.

The Baron chuckled to himself.

"We can gain an advantage over all of them, and negotiate a bigger slice of the cake."

***

Cameron ran to the top of the wall to peer down upon the advancing army.

"Prepare for war!" he shouted and he urged his men to take their positions.

The inside of the castle looked like a building site. They had practised what they should do many times and now the weakest parts of the defences were protected by large piles of stones that had been robbed from every cottage in the village. It had been back-breaking work, carrying stones up to the battlements, and Cameron knew that they would soon find out if their labours had been in vain.

"What is their measure?" he asked.

A young warrior named Gregor came to stand beside him.

"The enemy is divided in two and each half is five hundred strong."

"And their intention?"

"It is as you expected, they march towards the main gate and the East Wall."

"Divide the men to face them," ordered Cameron.

Gregor ran off, calling out orders and grabbing a long wooden fork.

A tremendous roar went up from the Angles as they raced forward. All were armed with weapons made from the light iron and many carried ladders. Thirty walked forward, slow and determined, with the trunk of a tree held between them. Like an unstoppable beast they headed straight for the main gate. Terror gripped Gregor and he glanced anxiously across at Cameron. There were so many of the enemy. So few of them.

Cameron shouted across to the east battlement.

"Not yet, Gregor. Wait for my signal."

Arrows sliced through the air above their heads and the Scots ducked behind the walls. Cameron glanced down at the ranks of the advancing Angles. They were only twenty paces away from the base of the walls.

"Not yet," he screamed.

The tops of hundreds of ladders thudded against the battlements and then shook as they bore the weight of the men below.

"Not yet."

The first of the enemy began to appear. Gregor found himself staring into the eyes of a huge man armed with a sword.

"Not today, thank you," said Gregor, smashing his fist into the warrior's face.

"Now!" screamed Cameron.

The Scots rose and placed the ends of their long forks into the top rungs of the ladders and pushed forward for all they were worth. The ladders shot backwards and the screams of falling men surrounded the castle. A second wave of ladders were raised and Cameron cried out.

"The stones."

Without mercy, a rain of stones fell upon the warriors below. Cameron looked down at a group of the enemy with a huge tree trunk on their shoulders, marching along the narrow path that led to the main gate. They began to charge and the reed-covered ground collapsed beneath the front men. Screams came out of the pit they had fallen into, the pit that the Scots had lined with sharp stakes.

"Nasty," said Cameron.

The tree was abandoned and the bravest of the Angles pulled their bloody friends up, carrying them away to safety, as rocks landed around them. More Angles charged forward, grabbed the tree and, avoiding the trap, charged at the gate again. A thundering *Boom* echoed around the courtyard.

"Follow me," ordered Cameron and fifty of his strongest guards ran to the wall above the gate.

They tossed massive blocks of granite over the lip of the wall to crush the enemy who held the battering ram. Cameron glanced down at the broken bodies below and then anxiously at the top of the East Wall. Gregor was struggling to hold back the tide of Angles who swarmed over the battlements.

"Follow me," he yelled again.

His men sprinted along the top of the wall to aid him. They smashed into the enemy and hacked at them with their claymores. Many were thrown to their deaths.

Boom went the main gate again and Gregor jumped.

Cameron came to stand by him and he seemed to be counting. *Boom* five counts, *Boom* five counts. Cameron shouted down to the archers who waited anxiously inside the courtyard.

"Be ready."

Boom The main gate shook as though it was alive. Cameron counted in his mind. "One, two, three, four."

"Now," he yelled.

His men opened the gates. Thirty Angles stumbled into the courtyard, dropping the great tree trunk, and were cut down by a hail of arrows. The battering ram was brought fully inside the castle and the main gate shut again with the tree propped against it to thwart another attack.

"Push the ladders away," commanded Gregor.

An Angle's spear pierced Gregor's chest and he fell to his knees. Cameron Campbell slashed out with his claymore and drove the enemy over the wall.

"They are running from the main gate," said a voice.

Cameron looked down to see the Angles retreating from the East Wall too.

"They have had enough," said a warrior.

"Enough for now," said Cameron and he gave orders for the dead to be thrown from the wall above the gate, the wounded to be tended and more stones carried to the battlements.

Later, a young Scotsman ran to his master across the courtyard.

"How many lost?" asked Cameron.

"Sixty-eight brave souls."

"We can ill afford to lose six."

"We have food for two days if we spread the jam thin."

Cameron put his hand onto the boy's shoulder to reassure him.

"The Younger *will* come," he said.

Their attention was caught by a guard above the main gate. He was waving a bow above his head and pointing down at the field of battle.

"They march again," he yelled.

***

Grahm Deer stood with his friends and neighbours in the ranks that followed John Standforth. His master seemed anxious to take the castle quickly and Grahm Deer knew how cruel Cuthbert could be to those who failed him. He peered up at the battlements. They were lower than those at home, at Berwick, but still menacing, and defended by a determined enemy. He shuddered, reached down to pull his spear from the earth and

125

prayed that he might walk again upon the earth of his own farm.

"Here we go again," he said.

Belus ignored him, glancing around to see where Cuthbert was. Some of the men laughed and seemed to get a thrill from the excitement of battle. As they had marched forward, one boasted about killing two Scots in the first attack. Grahm Deer could only think about how scary it had been, climbing up the rungs, rocks falling around him, and the relief he felt when the retreat was called. Now he shouldered a ladder again, with Belus and five others behind him.

A thunderous roar went up from Harold's warriors as they charged the eastern defences and the farmer watched them scramble up the walls under the protection of a hail of arrows. But John gave no call for them to do the same and they halted before the main gate.

"What is he waiting for?" asked Grahm, his stomach tightening.

"What are any of us waiting for?" said Belus.

John Standforth stared at Harold's men and then at the Scots above the gate. Some were leaving their positions and running along the battlements to aid others who were throwing rocks and spears at the enemy below, and desperately trying to push the ladders away.

"The time is ours!" yelled John.

Grahm found himself thrown forward as part of the attack and separated from his friend. An arrow thudded into the chest of the man next to him and he fell. Then another and another. Fear drove Grahm on and he stabbed his end of the ladder into the ground. Strong hands swept the other end upwards and it crashed against the wall. Then Grahm was climbing and holding his sword ready for the combat that was sure to come. He glanced up. There did not seem to be any of the Scots above him. A great stone fell down the length of the ladder next to his and screams filled Grahm's mind.

Eight rungs to go, now seven, now six and he began to hope

that he might make the top unscathed. Then the ladder began to shake. It swayed and tried to leave the wall. Grahm saw the length of a wooden pole pushing out against the top rung and he slashed out with his sword to try to dislodge it. He failed and felt himself falling backwards through the air. It felt like a lifetime, a lifetime of falling, and he had all the time in the world to imagine what the impact would be like.

When it came it did not seem so bad, but to the others who saw it, the crash upon the earth was truly terrible. It would have broken the spine of any man.

Grahm Deer lay on his back and for a moment forgot where he was. Then, as he slowly opened his eyes, the scene at the top of the wall unfolded and the sounds of battle surrounded him, and yet he felt at peace. He thought about the journey home and the work that would need to be done in the fields. He thought about his wife and children, and his brothers, and this memory jolted him for his brothers were there, above him, climbing over the battlements, and fighting for all they were worth. They seemed to be winning now and there was Belus, stabbing out with his spear like a madman, venting his anger and wishing that each scream was from the lips of another man.

The booms had stopped and Grahm Deer glanced at the main gate. The Scots had opened it. Men charged the gate and then stopped in their tracks. The Angles at the front of the charge turned in terror as a herd of Highland cattle stampeded out of the castle crashing into warriors and tossing two into the air with their horns. Behind them, stepping out of the gate, was a Scottish warrior with two blazing torches, waving them to scare the cattle down the slope. Then he tossed his torches aside, ran back into the castle and the gates slammed shut.

Grahm Deer tried to sit up and realised that something was wrong. His body did not respond to his wishes and he had no feeling in his legs. He tried to move an arm. It remained out of sight. He tried to grip his fist into a ball and, whether he succeeded or not, he would never know.

Amongst the chaos, he felt strangely complete, strangely secure in his own thoughts. He was in his own island of peace in a sea of shouting and death.

The sound of rhythmic booming began again and he watched men strike the gate with another great tree trunk. The noise stopped and they were through. The tide had turned against the Scots.

A spear flew down and landed beside his foot. Grahm Deer didn't even try to get out of its way. He just lay there, still, detached, and watching the shaft swing backwards and forwards. He wondered why he was here. This war was not his war. Belus had said that. They were simply a part of Cuthbert's ambition. Why should he follow him anyway? Perhaps when all this was over he would spend more time with his children. They were so beautiful and so full of life. He smiled, as he pictured their faces, and then he glanced back at the top of the wall. Directly above him, a Scottish warrior held aloft a great stone. Then he released it and Grahm Deer watched it fall.

This stone was for him and it did not fall like any of the others. It fell slowly, just as slowly as he had fallen, and it promised an end to pain. The stone seemed to hover above his face. He smiled again.

"I really should spend more time with my children."

It was the last thing he ever said.

Before the crows had time to gather and feast on the dead, Cuthbert the Cautious, Baron of Berwick, walked excitedly around the battlements of Stirling Castle, whilst his men threw Scottish bodies over the walls. Many cheered for their victory and some searched outside the castle for their friends, praying that they had not joined the fallen. One warrior hacked at the wounded Scots. Harold of Berwick and John Standforth joined Cuthbert.

"How many?" asked Cuthbert.

"Two hundred and forty lost. Thirty wounded who will never

fight again. Thirty two who will wield a sword, given time," said Harold.

Cuthbert grinned.

"Not bad."

"The light iron made us strong. When we laid Neidpath Castle to waste, we lost four hundred men in one day."

"We are strong," said Cuthbert. "Put the carpenters to work immediately. I want the gate repaired by sundown. Tell the others to gather food and prepare for a siege. I liked the pit outside the gate. Prepare that too."

As his generals ran down the stairs to the courtyard, Cuthbert's eyes swept across the lands he had conquered, from Stirling Glen to Douglas Rock. He took Denbara's map out of his pocket and checked the details against the landscape. It was so accurate. His finger ran along a line on the parchment, through Marsh Glen and beyond. The Younger's palace was less than two days' ride that way and it would be his. He stared greedily across the marshes and up Marsh Glen. Far away, many riders were followed by a train of foot-soldiers. He couldn't make out the signs on their shields, or the colour of their plaids, but he could hear, just hear, the faint sound of bagpipes carried by the gentle breeze.

Below him, in the courtyard, a man stared up at Cuthbert's back, hatred in his heart, the voice of reason taken from his ears. Belus's knuckles turned white as he clenched his spear. John and Harold returned to stand behind Cuthbert, unknowingly protecting their leader from a spear throw.

"Not yet," Belus told himself.

CHAPTER SEVEN

THE RING OF FIRE

In a tortured dream, Peter's body twisted and turned, kicking his duvet off the bed, catching the alarm clock and a glass of water. He didn't hear them fall, his mind had taken him to sit by Grandma, beside the plane's window, hearing past voices. As the engines roared and they were forced back into their seats, he looked at Grandma's face. It had creased and gone white. He felt himself smile and hold her hand.

"Don't worry. Flying is very safe these days."

He glanced out of the window to get a last glimpse of his family. There they were, frantically waving their arms out of the front and back sunroofs. There was a blinding flash as their car was hurled skywards. Then it became a fireball and crashed down to earth. A metal tomb engulfed by flame. Peter sat up, his pyjamas drenched in sweat, confused, sad, eyes wide and staring at an old man in a dark cloak.

"You dream of things that have not been," said Myroy.

It took a moment for Peter to find his words.

"But it did happen to me. It did. Didn't it? In your story?"

"The armies of Tella's alliance are marching to do battle at Stirling. The Younger fears Llewellyn, king of all the Welsh peoples, more than any of the others. Tirani gifted Amera's stone to Llewellyn and now he uses its power to destroy his enemies."

Peter lifted his hands and his words shot out like bullets.

"Before I hear the story, I need to *know* that what you tell me is real, or just a story. I was there, with Grandma on the plane. I saw my family die. I grieved on Corfu and made a friend named Stefanos. Is he real? Does he exist at all? I lost the stone to Odin. I lost Kylie and felt her blood. Just tell me what is real and what is a warning for a Keeper?"

Myroy ignored him and stared at the veins and wrinkles on the back of his hands. Peter snapped and his voice became cold.

"If you ever put me through that again, manipulate me, I will kill you."

Myroy picked up the alarm clock and sat on the side of the bed.

"Two fifteen." His eyes became warm and full of concern. "Well, Peter of the line of Donald, let's hope that I have not created a monster."

***

Llewellyn looked back with pride at his massive and confident army. All the warriors were dressed in plaids, much like the Scottish plaids, and more than half were a washed-out red colour, which meant they were from families loyal to his ancient line. The rest of the army were with him to gain land, coins or cattle. Everyone was armed with weapons made from the new light iron.

"How much further to Glasgow?"

Tirani the Wise, leant forward and stroked his pony's mane.

"A scribe named Denbara paid with his life to give his master a map. Tella gave you a copy for good reason."

Llewellyn looked into the boy's eyes. So young and full of life, and yet they were old, commanding the authority that his small body did not possess. He shrugged his shoulders, took the map from his pocket and answered his own question.

"We continue north and, with good fortune, we will stand on the banks of the Clyde by sunset tomorrow."

"We will face the enemy before then. Their numbers are few and some will escape your men before the end of the battle. They will return to the defenders at Stirling and to the Younger, in the lonely places, and warn them of your arrival."

"Why did Myroy allow you to gift the stone to me? He advises the Scottish kings."

"My brother has his reasons."

"But he knows I will use its power against the Younger."

"He does."

Llewellyn stared at the boy who had walked beside his royal ancestors.

"You are not going to tell me, are you?"

Tirani grinned, drove his pony forward and the Welsh army followed. Later, after marching across barren moorland, broken occasionally by stands of twisted dwarf birch and deserted cottages, Llewellyn counted one hundred and twenty warriors, who formed three defensive lines, guarding the low ground between two hills. They wore the brown, green and ochre plaids of the Scots, and seemed well armed.

"According to the map, it adds a day to circle around the hills and, besides, I want to send a message to the Younger."

Tirani remained silent as he watched Llewellyn take Amera's stone from his leather purse and hold it tightly. It pulsed red. The king urged his stallion back towards his generals and other riders joined them to receive their orders. One family leader broke away and called for fifty mounted warriors to follow him, and then they were charging away to fight the enemy. They thundered towards the first line, spears held out, ready to strike.

The Scots waited and, a horse's length away, they dived aside and the Welsh drove through easily. Then the Scots jumped up and threw their spears into the riders' backs. The second line ran forward and cut down anyone who was left.

"Clever," said Tirani.

The king cried out in anger and his army followed him to do battle, foot-soldiers desperately trying to keep up with the horses. Llewellyn held out Amera's stone and a red beam shot forward to divide many times to strike the Scots in the front line. The enemy froze in their positions, held like statues by bloody fingers of light, and the riders ignored them as they galloped through the gaps in the line and attacked the second line.

Behind Llewellyn, his foot-soldiers hacked down the frozen men with swords. The remaining Scots bravely held firm fifty paces from the leading horses and Tirani watched as one of the Younger's secret riders arrived, calling out to the warriors in the third and last line. That line broke and ran away towards the north.

Llewellyn's horsemen thundered into the second line of the enemy, who were now outnumbered by the huge Welsh army, which swarmed around them like bees. They fell, and now the way was clear all the way to Stirling, at the very heart of the Scottish kingdom.

***

Thorgood Firebrand stared at five square sails on the horizon. His encampment on the headland, on the ancient coast of Sea People's Land, had grown and was more like a town than any of the settlements they might build in strange lands, for shelter during the season of storms.

It grew even stronger with each half moon, the time when more longships, warriors and supplies were expected from Oslo Fjord. He wondered if his friend, Hengist Corngrinder, was standing at the prow of the leading ship and carrying news from their village. News from home was in short supply, precious, and in complete contrast to the regular news he received from the riders he had sent to the south. They told him that the Scottish lands were in turmoil. Tain was deserted of warriors and open to him if he chose to invade. His people needed those rich lands to grow crops and raise cattle, and yet he feared the Younger and the fierce warriors who had once defeated him in Tain.

But, his time *would* come and that time was close now. Thorgood knew that many days' ride to the south of Tain, through great glens and over majestic mountains, armies gathered to do war. One rider had told him that the Scots marched southwest to meet the Angles and Picts. Another rider told him that an army of greater size had crossed the River Clyde at Glasgow. This army spoke in a strange tongue, and he did not know where they came from. It could not be a coincidence. Someone had planned this invasion and now, as the sails came closer to the headland, Thorgood knew it was nearly time to blood his sword, and take advantage of a weakened enemy.

He thought again about his beautiful daughter and how fever

had taken her from him, the failed harvests and the pain brought by hunger. Ulrika's Land was a good name for the lands they had taken to escape famine and he made up his mind to erect a stone in her memory, here, close to the waves that washed in from the Great Sea.

"I wish we had walked together for longer," he said.

Far away, as he spoke these words, Llewellyn used Amera's stone to destroy the Scots who stood in three lines on the lowland between two hills. The sea in front of Thorgood erupted. A tower of foam and bubbles rose up, and Odin was there, dressed in a black leather tunic with white fur around the collar. His intense blue eyes flashed and Thorgood fell to his knees in fear.

"The stone's power is being used at the head of an army. I have felt it."

"Yes, master."

"Take twelve warriors. Watch the army do battle. Find out who holds my stone and follow him to his home. Return to me with that knowledge."

"I obey, master."

"You will need a guide and a tongue speaker."

Walking out of the waves, holding a mighty battleaxe, was a man of Thorgood's height and appearance. Thorgood thought that he knew him from somewhere, from some distant memory, and yet could not remember a place where they had ever met. The tower of bubbles around the Ancient One subsided and, as Odin returned to the ocean, his words rang out.

"Meet your dead Grandfather. Warrior of the Valkyrie, Thorfinn of the line of Firebrand."

***

From behind Llewellyn, Tirani, and the riders who followed them, the mass of foot-soldiers ran down the grassy slope to stand on a sandy beach along the Clyde. It was a huge river and on the far shore, the Welsh fleet, with furled red sails, lay berthed. Some of the men shouted across to them, but no sailors heard their call. Tirani jumped off his pony and took a small pipe whistle from his leather purse. He skipped to the water's edge, put the pipe to his lips and plunged his head beneath the water. Then the boy's head was up, hair dripping.

"Your king is here. On the far bank. Look for him."

Immediately, men ran to the sterns of their ships and pointed at them.

As the sun sank below the western horizon, the Welsh army stood on the northern bank of the Clyde. The ships' crews finished unloading supplies and Llewellyn decided to make camp here, with warriors assigned as lookouts and a small number to tend a flock, three hundred strong. These fine animals would be his army's main source of food.

Next morning, the lookouts reported no danger and they went on, Tirani silent on his pony and Llewellyn regularly checking Denbara's map for the quickest way to Stirling Glen and the river at its base. The enemy castle stood next to that river and the king wondered if Tella and Cuthbert had already placed it under siege.

Would they turn on him when the fighting was over? Were Tella and Cuthbert in league together and against him? He did not wholly trust in the alliance and sensed Cuthbert's greed for land and power over others. That greed, more than Tella's lust for revenge against the Scots, put doubt into Llewellyn's mind. Anyway, it did not matter. He held the stone, not them. At Berwick Castle, they had doubted its power. They were fools to believe they could defeat him. His army, with Amera's stone before it, would show them that the new light iron was nothing compared to the ancient magic which exists in the land and the sea.

By nightfall, the army followed a slow, winding river. Ahead of them, old standing stones formed a line along the side of a path that hugged the river. Tirani smiled at Llewellyn.

"Would you take Scottish lands at any price?"

"The lands in the southwest of the Younger's kingdom were taken from us in my grandfather's time, by the Elder. They are mine by right."

"That does not answer my question. Any price?"

"Any price."

"Then you are a fool, like your grandfather."

Llewellyn snapped at the boy.

"I am the king. Not you."

"You are the king. Not me."

Tirani took the whistle from his purse and played two notes, over and over again. Amera's stone appeared in his hand.

"Give that back to me," demanded the king.

Tirani tossed the brooch to him, its gold flashing in the end of day sunshine.

"Remember my words. What is given to you, can easily be taken away."

"You mean the stone or my kingship?"

"No."

"Then what can be taken from me?"

"Your life."

The Ancient One jumped down and skipped beside the river. A cold wind blew into Llewellyn's face as he watched the boy pass one standing stone after another. The hairs stood up on the back of his neck. Then Tirani disappeared, the wind eased and the king knew he had been a fool. And, because of a thief, his time as a stone Keeper would soon end, and with terrible consequences for his people.

✲✲

The Younger raised his hand and the High Table of Scotland brought their Highlands to a halt, with the castle ahead of them, marshes to their right and Douglas Rock towering above them to their left. This granite outcrop stood proud above the low ground where the Glen of Sighs met Marsh Glen. During the Long Peace, this place had been one of the busiest for trade and barter anywhere in the kingdom, and now it was deserted, abandoned because of fear.

"The flag of the Saxon cross flies above Stirling," said Stuart, Thane of Coll.

Malcolm's stomach tightened and his heart went out to Cameron Campbell and his men. So, Cuthbert held the castle at the centre of their lands, Llewellyn held the stone and the Black Kilts had simply vanished. He ran his hands through his long grey hair and wondered what wise counsel Murdoch would have given him. Morag McCreedy gave him a dark look.

"We make camp here, by Douglas Rock," Malcolm said.

He urged his stallion forward and then immediately pulled back on the reins. The grass in front of the High Table began to shimmer, like moonlight on water, and Myroy rose up from the underworld, a small boy held tightly under one arm and a staff held in the other hand. The boy clutched something between his small fingers.

Fraser of Abernethy jumped from his horse, raised his claymore and stepped in front of his king. Myroy glanced at him and Fraser shot up into the sky, like Arkinew's *bartillery*, to hover a thousand paces above them.

"The Keeper must steal the stone. Odin's forces are nearby," said Myroy.

The Younger lowered his voice so that the others could not hear him.

"But Cuthbert holds Stirling Castle."

"He does."

"And we face three armies."

Myroy's words became hard.

"Has Scotland fallen? Is hope gone? Odin is the one to fear, not Cuthbert."

"I feel alone."

"Seamus comes."

"And what do I do?"

"You are the king. You will know what to do."

139

"And Cuthbert?"

Tirani the Wise stepped forward, grinned and held out the flat of his hand. A toy soldier stood upright on his palm. Tirani had never seen Cuthbert, but he knew the toy's face was his. He had heard it in a story. As he spoke, he slowly tipped the toy soldier to lie on its side.

"Cuthbert will die from his own greed and cruelty."

Myroy drew a circle above the earth with his staff and then gave the Younger an order.

"And remember, Dougie's family are lost."

After a time, Malcolm nodded in agreement, and Tirani skipped over and gave him his small pipe.

"Tell the Keeper that if he needs help from me, he can blow on this."

The Younger looked at the small boy and wondered how he might possibly help Dougie. What could one so small do?

"Help him steal something," said Tirani.

Then the Ancient Ones were gone and the king was left feeling troubled and wishing more than ever that his brother was by his side. Fraser of Abernethy crashed back down onto his horse.

"Welcome back," said Stuart.

He pointed down Heather Glen. Two riders were just emerging from behind the cottages that rested below the castle, one rider urging his horse into a gallop, the other following and holding on for dear life.

"Fine horses," said Malcolm.

Stuart nodded.

"And they are not from our lands."

Finnegan grinned.

"Oh, they are from the finest lands in the world. No offence to your lands, of course."

"And it looks as though the High Table is to be strengthened," said Malcolm.

They watched them pass the castle and the zig zag path, which ran up to the old ruined fort. As Dougie approached, bouncing unnaturally on top of his horse, Morag broke the silence.

"I know Alistair of Cadbol, but who is the other man?"

Malcolm glanced at the iron fist painted on the shield, hung across the long red hair that ran down her back, and sensed her coldness towards him.

"That's the fellow named Dougie, said Finnegan.

Malcolm frowned and spoke in an important voice.

"That is Dougie of Dunfermline, Knight of all Shepherds and hero of battles."

"Hero of battles?"

"He picked me up and threw me around," added Finnegan.

"Well, I know he doesn't look like a warrior, but he is as good as anyone at the High Table," said the Younger.

"That is a concern," she said.

Alistair jumped off his horse and knelt before his king.

"How is he?" asked Malcolm.

"Sad. Very sad. At Mountjoy, Dougie fought the Pict, Borak One Hand, and nearly killed him. Nearly killed everyone who tried to stop the duel. His anger, at the news of his family, drew upon the stone's power. Myroy says Odin did not sense it."

"And we need him to draw on that power again, but Llewellyn holds Amera's stone and the shepherd must steal it back."

Alistair turned to watch the young man who bounced up and down on his horse.

"I don't think he will. He refused to fight the Black Kilts on the beach at Stranraer."

"He must."

"But Dougie grieves. He feels alone."

"If he does not steal the stone, Scottish lands will fall and not to Llewellyn, Tella or Cuthbert. With Odin driving them on, the Norse peoples will one day capture the stone, rule here, and the world will never be the same again."

Dougie wearily dismounted and joined them. The Younger stared at him. He looked older, with dark rings around his eyes and slumped shoulders.

"Welcome back, Dougie. Alistair tells me the Irish peoples would not be here to aid us without your courage."

Dougie's sad expression remained unchanged.

"And I have a gift for you."

The Younger stepped forward and handed him the small whistle pipe.

"If ever you need help from the Ancient Ones, blow this."

Dougie took it and, without looking at it, placed the pipe inside his purse. The Younger pointed at the huge army marching towards a waterfall to make camp. A blood red light flashed before it.

"And I need you to help me again. Llewellyn, King of the Welsh peoples, holds your brooch. It is there, in Stirling Glen, and if his army marches with it, we will be destroyed."

Dougie shrugged his shoulders.

"I will grant you anything that is in my power to give you."

"I want my family back."

"Your family are lost."

"So is the brooch *and* the battle."

"Dougie, please help us one last time," pleaded Alistair.

"I don't care anymore."

Malcolm pointed at the castle.

"You must care, your family were killed by the Angles and not by the Picts as told to you by Ancevo. Even now, they hold Stirling at the heart of our lands. With the stone you could destroy them."

Intense anger pulsed inside Dougie's blood.

"And when this is over, I will gift you anything you need to rebuild your life."

"I do not want anything you can give me."

Down Heather Glen, the riders at the head of the Irish army came into view.

"Seamus has made good time," said Alistair. "Will we fight the enemy today?"

Malcolm shook his head.

"I think Tella is the key to that. Cuthbert and Llewellyn may delay war until his army joins them."

"Where is the Mac Mar?"

"No idea. He had the shortest distance to travel and I expected him to arrive here first."

"He is up to something."

"Revenge is what he is up to."

"Then the advantage is with us. Let us fight Llewellyn and Cuthbert now. Two armies against two."

"Not until Dougie holds the stone."

Alistair, Malcolm and Finnegan looked at him, sitting cross-legged and holding his head in his hands. A single rider broke away from Llewellyn's camp below Burn Hill and reached them at the same time as Seamus and Finn. The Welshman was craggy-faced and tough-looking, and wore a faded red plaid with six spears strapped across his back. When he spoke it was in the soft, ancient Welsh tongue that only the Younger could understand. Arkinew's schooling had been good.

"My king, Llewellyn, bids you greetings, Malcolm the Younger."

"And my greetings go to him."

"Llewellyn commands you surrender, or face war at first sun tomorrow."

"Llewellyn commands?"

"He told me that any king of these lands would know of the ancient power he now wields. No army, no matter how big or courageous, can stand before that power. Know this to be true."

"There are other powers that Llewellyn does not possess. Ask him why I choose to stand here before him, with the High Table at my side, if I know that Amera's stone is all-powerful."

For a moment, the messenger's eyes held a glint of worry. The Younger saw it and continued.

"Since my father's passing, we have lived in peace together. Why can we not continue to live peacefully?"

"The lands in the southeast of your kingdom are Welsh lands, stolen by the Elder. We have come to take them back."

"By force?"

"By force if necessary. Gift them to my king for all time and the coming battle need not be."

Malcolm thought about the clans of Dumfries and Galloway, and how Stranraer was sure to play an important part in the growing trade with Ireland and Man.

"I choose to fight."

"Then you will die."

"Tell Llewellyn we fight at dawn. Tell him he faces two armies."

He nodded at Seamus and smiled. Seamus smiled back and wondered what was being said.

"The Irish peoples stand beside us. Ask Llewellyn if he can be as sure of the help he may receive from Cuthbert and Tella."

"We do not need Cuthbert or Tella. No army can stand before the stone."

The rider turned his horse and galloped away.

"What the devil was that all about?" asked Seamus and Finnegan together.

"We do battle at dawn and have one night to steal the stone, and save the Scottish people."

***

With their horses hidden and safely tethered a long way below them, Thorfinn Firebrand led Odin's search party up a steep hill, darting between trees to avoid being seen. Hengist Corngrinder panted heavily.

"That was … good fortune."

"What was?" asked Thorgood.

"Spotting Tella and following him."

"Why was that good fortune?"

"We could have spent many moons searching for the army which holds the stone and …" Hengist stopped climbing to wipe sweat from his brow. "And now he leads us straight to them."

"As we rode south from Tain, we could have followed any of the warriors we have seen. Anyone who is of an age to fight is marching here. Besides, the Mac Mar is up to something."

"You still don't trust him."

"Not as far as I could throw him."

Thorfinn turned and placed a finger to his lips and all fourteen Norsemen sank to their knees; still and silent now. Thorfinn dropped onto his belly and crawled up the slope, and wriggled past the trunks of mighty oaks. The others copied him and joined him on the lip of the hill. Tella, Gath and another Pict they did not recognise, were lying upon an outcrop of rock, scanning the land below them and the castle which dominated the area. The flag of the Saxon cross flew above the castle and, off to their left, the Scottish army marched towards it, along the base of a deep valley.

"The Angles hold the Scottish castle," whispered Hengist.

Thorgood ignored him and watched Tella. What was he up to? Why did he hold back his army? Why did he wait and just watch? After a while another army arrived, and this time from a valley to their right. At the head of this army, a blood red flash signalled its arrival and the Norsemen stiffened. That was the army to follow. Its king held their master's stone and it had to be taken back to Odin. But Thorgood had clear instructions. Follow the army, find their homelands and report back. He crawled next to his grandfather.

"It was not our master's orders, but do you think we should try and steal the stone tonight?"

Thorfinn thought about it.

"You and I should try. Tell the others that if we do not return, they are to follow the army as planned."

***

At dusk, the combined Irish and Scottish war camp was swollen with people and soon muddy. Fires were lit, food prepared

145

and the Scots showed their allies the new light iron. Inside the Younger's tent, to the sound of swords clashing together outside, plans were being made.

"The new blades make a different sound," said Alistair.

"Oh, it's like singing," said Finnegan.

The Younger ignored them and walked to the tent flap. A hundred paces away in the fading light, Dougie sat alone, staring into space.

"The shepherd must sleep. The best time to enter the Welsh camp will be in the darkness before dawn."

"He's not eating, or sleeping. Give me fifty riders and I can lead a charge at Llewellyn. Fortune might ride with us."

"You would be killed. Bring Dougie to me."

Alistair bowed and left, and Malcolm returned to stand beside Seamus, Finn and Morag, who studied the copy of Denbara's map.

"Let's assume Dougie steals the stone," said Seamus, "I think we should attack Llewellyn at first light. Why wait a moment longer? Cuthbert's new castle can be his prison if we defend the outside of the main gate. A hundred good spearmen could do it and we can throw everything else at the Welsh."

Finn placed a huge finger onto the map. His voice boomed.

"We should divide our forces and attack on two sides in darkness. All our foot-soldiers attacking from this side. All our riders attacking them here."

Seamus nodded.

"Any news of Tella?"

"No," said the Younger.

"He's up to something."

"Aye. If you were him, where would you hide your army?"

"Oh, what about inside the castle? Could the Picts be with Cuthbert?" interrupted Finnegan.

The Younger shook his head.

"Three thousand is too many men to stand within its walls."

Finn pointed at the map, at the location of the Welsh army

beside the waterfall in Stirling Glen.

"You could hide an army in the woods above the castle, but you could not surprise anyone if you had to march in the open along valleys like these."

Malcolm began to pace around the tent.

"Right now, it makes no difference. We can only hope that the Black Kilts do not join with the Welsh before dawn and, if they do attack us when we are weak, we retreat to the lonely places. I think that Tella and Cuthbert will fight over our lands anyway, at some time."

A warrior entered through the flap, followed by Dougie and then Alistair. The warrior went down on one knee before his king.

"Your Majesty, the travelling people seek your permission to bring their caravans into the camp, and entertain us for coins. One amongst them, a woman named Benita, says that you know her."

Morag's face went red with anger.

"Kill her."

Malcolm returned her stare.

"Hamish of Tain is in union with Benita's daughter."

"She has a daughter?"

"She has, and her people are welcome here."

The warrior left and Dougie sat down, away from the others. Malcolm smiled at him.

"Dougie, I need you to steal the brooch I gave you, before dawn. Once you hold it in your hand, we attack the Welsh from two sides. We will be lost if you do not do this."

The shepherd's head dropped and Alistair went over to him, and roughly pulled him to his feet.

"Would you watch your friends die?"

Dougie grabbed Alistair's shoulders and threw him at the wall. The flying body became wrapped in canvas and the tent flew away, sideways, across the camp. Everyone stood on the rugs, which showed where the tent had once been, staring at Alistair, struggling to get out of a tangle of ropes and canvas, about fifty paces away.

"He did that to me too," said Finnegan.

Morag stared at Dougie and committed his face to memory. This man *was* dangerous, after all. Alistair angrily ran back and grabbed him.

"You did not answer me. Would you stand aside and watch me die?"

Suddenly, Dougie burst into tears and Alistair put his arm around his shoulders and led him away.

"Let's go and talk with Benita," said the Younger.

Ten brightly coloured caravans rested in a line along the path at the base of Marsh Glen, on the edge of the camp. A group of gypsies stood talking with guards. Benita gave the Younger and Seamus a huge smile, framed by her long black hair and dark skin.

"Your men are reluctant to let us entertain you. How can this be? Wherever there is a crowd, there is a chance for us to earn coins and put smiles onto faces, and good fortune into hearts."

"May good fortune be forever with you, Benita."

As Malcolm spoke, Morag McCreedy fingered the hilt of her sword and her chest swelled in her chain mail vest. Benita saw the sword and her words became hard.

"I have never returned to your lands, Morag. Just as you asked of me."

"Death awaits you, should you ever return."

"There are many lands for us to roam without ever having the need to return to yours."

Their eyes locked and the Younger broke the silence.

"Your people are welcome here, Benita, but know this, war will come soon and tonight we have much to prepare. Will your men stand with us?"

"We never take sides. In the future, we need things to be as they always are for us. To be able to enter any palace, castle or camp to earn coins."

Malcolm smiled.

"You could not get into my camp."

"That is, how you say? Unusual."

"Did you say that you can enter any camp?"

"Any camp."

Malcolm turned to a guard.

"Bring Alistair of Cadbol and Dougie of Dunfermline to me now."

He turned back to face Benita.

"One hundred coins is my gift to you."

"For what service?"

"Take two of my men into the war camp of Llewellyn, king of the Welsh peoples. He has something that I want back."

"What do we take from him?"

"A gold brooch with a ruby at its heart."

"How big is it?"

Malcolm held up his hand and moved his thumb and finger apart until they were the width of the brooch.

"It sounds dangerous."

"It will be dangerous."

"Two hundred coins sounds a more suitable gift."

"Agreed. Help Alistair and Dougie work out a plan."

As Malcolm, Morag and Seamus walked back, the Younger glanced at Morag and sensed her coldness towards men again.

"How do you know Benita?"

They continued in silence, until they stood outside of the royal tent. A warrior was just hitting the last tent peg into the ground and tying a rope to it. When Morag's words came, they were full of hatred, spat out of her mouth like unwanted gristle.

"She stole something of mine."

***

"I feel stupid," said Alistair.

Dougie smiled for the first time in a long time.

Alistair smiled back.

"And, by the way, you look more stupid than me."

Huddled in the back of a gypsy caravan, they stared at each other. Both were wearing bright yellow shirts, and baggy red trousers made of a material they had never seen before. Dougie's shirt was far too big for him. Benita had darkened their faces with dirt to make them appear more like her people. Their caravan lurched and Alistair lifted the curtain. Beyond the line of caravans which followed them, the fires in the Younger's camp were like bright pin pricks in the distance, the dark outline of Douglas Rock towering above it all.

"Benita seemed very sure that she could take the stone, but not sure at all about escaping with it. Llewellyn is sure to check that he still has it and, when it is gone, his anger will fall on us."

Dougie took the pipe out of his leather purse.

"Malcolm told me I can use this to summon help, but I can't see how."

"Why don't you blow it?"

"But I do not know what help I need."

"Blow it anyway."

Dougie blew it. No sound. A gypsy at the front of their caravan called back to them.

"No speak now. We approach the Welsh peoples."

The train of caravans stopped and a young boy rose up through the wooden floor to sit beside them. He was smiling.

"Tell Benita her plan is a good one, and give her this. It is an exact copy in all respects, except one. It cannot draw upon the power that lies within the land and sea. Give me my pipe."

Dougie exchanged the pipe for the brooch and stared at the ruby at its heart. Same size, same blood red colour, but the gold around it was cold and now he remembered holding it on the bitterest of winter days, yet it was always warm to his touch.

"It is not the brooch that the Younger gifted to me."

Tirani began to descend down through the floor, still smiling.

"There are many things the Ancient Ones cannot do."

Then his head was gone and Dougie looked at Alistair.

"Who was that?"

"Tirani the Wise, Myroy's brother."

"They cannot possibly be brothers?"

"They can …."

Alistair was interrupted by a loud bang, made by the gypsy's heel on the wooden panel between them. Then they heard voices in a strange tongue and the curtain was pulled back by a Welsh warrior who held a sword. He pointed the sword at Dougie and Benita's smiling face appeared beside the guard. She said something and the man walked off with her to check the next caravan.

As a cloud passed a Gora moon, the friends were thrown backwards as their caravan lurched into Llewellyn's war camp.

Dougie opened the curtain to see how many of the enemy were around them. Hundreds of campfires were each surrounded by pyramids of spears, and warriors who seemed to stare back at Dougie. Something caught his eye. Two warriors, running in darkness beside one of the caravans, glancing around, bent over and staying close to the wheels. Dougie thought they were dressed like the Norsemen he had seen on the Outer Islands. He felt sick and Alistair shut the curtain as the caravans reached a clearing, drew up in a wide circle and stopped.

"Come on," whispered Alistair, "let's give Benita the brooch."

Above them a horn sounded, the curtain shot back and a huge gypsy thrust drums into their hands. They jumped down to stand at the back of a line of brightly dressed men who began to march around the outside of the ring of caravans, beating their drums, inviting the Welsh to join them. *Bang, Bang, Bang, Bang.* Alistair joined in. *Bang, Bang, Bang.* Dougie marched along too, hitting his drum badly and at exactly the wrong moment. *Bang, Thwack, Bang, Thwack, Bang.* Some of the gathering crowd pointed at him and laughed. Llewellyn and Tirani stepped forward, smiling. The horn sounded again, blown by a gypsy standing on top of a caravan, and a man led a fine white horse on a long rope to the centre of the ring of caravans. Benita called out.

"Please follow me."

The crowd moved quickly through the gaps in the caravans and, as Benita passed Dougie, he placed something into her hand.

"It's a copy," he whispered.

The horse began to canter round and around, held back by the rope to run just an arm's length from the Welsh. A small, beautiful girl with brown eyes and long black hair sprinted across the ring and leapt onto the horse landing on her stomach. Then she was standing, bouncing up and down with each stride. She reached out and grabbed a spear from a gypsy and held it out with both hands, before jumping over the spear without letting go. She faltered and nearly lost her balance. The man holding the rope groaned, raised his eyebrows and gave her a weak smile. His word was said in a way that told his daughter that he knew she could do better.

"Tini."

She composed herself, jumped over the spear and landed perfectly on the horse's back. The crowd yelled for more. Another brightly coloured gypsy, holding six spears, joined the man with the rope, whilst other gypsies placed round wooden shields on the sides of six caravans. Dougie was handed one and did the same, except that he stood, staring at the shield, wondering what it was for. The spearman stood behind the rope man, both turning on the spot at exactly the same speed, the spearman's eyes fixed upon the bouncing girl. The crowd hushed. He threw his first spear, Tini jumped and the spear flashed under her feet to embed itself into a shield. Then another spear flew as before. Then another and a shield split in two. Another spear and straight at Dougie. As the blade passed under Tini's small feet, Alistair yanked him to one side and the spear cut through a fold in his huge yellow shirt, pinning him to the shield. The crowd roared again.

When the last spear was thrown, the horse was led away, the small girl skipped to her smiling Father, and took a bow. Gypsy men sang and played their flutes, lyres and drums, and the gypsy women joined them, dancing in brightly coloured dresses, swirling around in front of the crowd. The music stopped and an upright wooden ring, the height of a man, was wheeled into the centre of the circle. Benita walked slowly behind it, a casket in one hand and a flaming torch in the other. She cried out.

"Who is brave enough to defy the power of the eternal flame?"

No one replied and Benita set fire to the ring, which became engulfed in flame, lighting up the faces of the crowd. Someone gasped.

On top of the caravan behind Dougie and Alistair, Thorfinn and Thorgood firebrand peered onto the crowd, staying still and silent, and not quite believing how easy it had been to enter a war camp, because of a travelling show.

"Who is your Master's voice?" cried Benita.

Tirani skipped forward to stand beside her and she tossed aside the torch.

"And what possession do you most treasure?"

Tirani grinned and held up his pipe.

"Are you brave enough to test it through fire?"

Benita held up the wooden casket for everyone to see, opened the lid and held it in front of Tirani. With everyone's eyes fixed on the pipe, Tirani dropped it inside. Then Benita closed the lid and held the casket in front of her, arms locked out, and she ran at the flames and jumped through the ring. Still, with arms held out, she walked with ceremony to stand again with Tirani.

"Open the lid."

Tirani opened the lid.

"It has gone," he said excitedly. "Can I have it back?"

"Only if you place a coin into the box."

"Ancient Ones don't carry money."

Benita threw her head back in disgust.

"Well get a coin."

The boy skipped over to Llewellyn.

"May I have a coin?"

The king smiled and ordered a guard, in a faded red plaid, to give him a coin. Tirani skipped back, placed it into the casket

153

and closed the lid, and Benita ran to jump through the flames again.

"Open the lid," she cried.

Tirani took out his pipe and the crowd went mad.

"Who is your Master?" shouted Benita.

Tirani pointed at Llewellyn.

"Llewellyn, King of all the Welsh peoples."

"Come forward, mighty king."

Llewellyn smiled and joined them to the sound of more loud cheering.

"And what possession do you most treasure?"

Llewellyn held up Amera's stone.

On top of the caravan, at the edge of the light from the ring of fire, two Norsemen stared at it.

"That's it," whispered Thorgood, "and he is King of the Welsh peoples."

"Follow me," said Thorfinn and they climbed down, away from the show, darting between shadows, and searched for the biggest, grandest tent in the camp.

"We will never have a better chance than now to hide away in Llewellyn's own tent. Good fortune is with us," whispered Thorfinn.

"Are you brave enough to test it through fire?"

Llewellyn hesitated for a moment and placed his brooch inside the casket, and then the gypsy was off, running, arms held out, and jumping through the flames. Then she slowly walked back and knelt before him.

"Open the lid."

Llewellyn opened the lid. No brooch. A sickening feeling of immense loss held him.

"Place a coin into the casket."

He stared at the empty box.

"Is a single coin not a small sacrifice for the return of something so beautiful?"

The warrior in the red plaid ran over and gave his king a coin.

154

With the lid closed, Benita was running and jumping through the circle of flames.

"Open the lid," she demanded.

The king proudly held aloft the brooch and the crowd cheered wildly as the gypsy women returned, dancing gracefully to a single drum. The gypsy men went through the crowd collecting coins in small blue bags. Benita placed a small blue bag into Dougie's hand.

"Do not lose it," she said.

Later, when the line of caravans was well away from the Welsh camp, Benita sat with Dougie and Alistair.

"Tell the Younger that he owes me two hundred coins."

Dougie felt the stone's warmth. Alistair nodded.

"Malcolm told me you could have money and land if you asked for them."

The gypsy spat on the caravan floor.

"What would I do with land?"

"Then be a guest at the High Table. Your coins will be ready for you anytime, at the palace."

"Have them ready the third moon before the shortest day."

Alistair took her hand and kissed it.

"You have saved many lives today, Benita."

She pointed at the curtain.

"We move on now. Leave us and may good fortune follow you on your journey."

"Good fortune to you and your people."

As the friends jumped off of the back of the moving caravan, Alistair called back.

"By the way, why does Morag hate you so?"

"I stole something from her, a long time ago."

"What did you steal?"

Benita spoke in a soft voice.

"The man she loved."

CHAPTER EIGHT

THE FACE IN THE WATERFALL

Two shapes, half lit by fire glow and then in shadow, ran through the Welsh war camp. Thorgood Firebrand stopped and pointed at three men who sat huddled around a fire and the Norsemen dropped onto their hands and knees, and crawled back the way they had come.

"Not everyone likes a gypsy show," whispered Thorfinn, "we must be careful."

"Have you ever seen a camp so big?"

"No."

"What is their measure?"

"No idea, but over two thousand men."

Thorgood looked up at a full moon and waited for a cloud to cover it. As darkness returned, they ran in a wide circle around the Welshmen and headed for an area with fewer campfires, and a patch of broom and gorse. They hid to catch their breath and steady their nerves.

"My guess is at least twice that number," said Thorgood, his nose twitching at the heady smell of night scented broom. "Grandfather, may I ask you something? It has been on my mind since you rose up out of the sea."

"Ask."

"What is Valhalla like?"

Thorfinn stiffened.

"Do not ask that. The Valkyrie are forbidden to talk with the living about the eternal life."

They stared out of the broom, searching for a royal tent.

"How did you die?"

"With honour and as recorded in the Book of the Dead in Odin's Hall."

"But how?"

Thorfinn sighed.

"I fought with my brothers against the Irish peoples. We believed that our master's stone lay buried beneath an upright stone at Teamhair Na Ri, in the Kingdom of Meath. At the touch of a new king's hand, the stone is said to roar with the voices of his ancestors."

"Teamhair Na Ri?"

"Hill of Tara. The High Kings of Ireland have been crowned there since ancient times."

"What's it like?"

"A circular burial chamber inside a huge oval bank and ditch."

"Is your body inside one of the chambers?"

Thorfinn flinched.

"No. Ten of us were captured after the battle, chained together, led to Teamhair Na Ri and entombed in a mound. I still remember being forced along a narrow passage, lined with great stones and into a soulless dark prison. Food and water were passed to us each evening through a small hole. One of the Irish guards was a tongue speaker, like me, and he told me that Oisin, his king, had demanded a ransom for our release."

"The ransom never came, did it?"

"No."

"And the food and water stopped."

They stared at each other in the darkness.

"I promise to find this place and honour your death by spilling the blood of the enemy in the Kingdom of Meath."

"Search for a fierce people who worship an earth goddess, a white bull, and who measure their wealth with cattle."

"But where?"

"Two days' sail south from Belfast. It is the perfect shore to launch a war against Llewellyn, if we fail tonight."

"I will honour you."

"Save those thoughts for another time, Thorgood. We have our master's work to do."

"But which way?"

They stared out of the broom, searching for the outline of a royal tent, lit up by a campfire. There were hundreds of fires all around them and no clue as to which direction to take.

"We need to ask someone," replied Thorfinn.

159

Suddenly, Thorfinn fell to his knees.

"We are summoned. Follow me."

Without any fear of capture or death, he ran past fires, past huddled men and through fires with sparks and flame flying everywhere. Thorgood tried to keep up with him, zigzagging to avoid the flames. A Welshman stood as Thorfinn ran through his campfire and he pointed at him, mouth open. An instant later, Thorgood hit him before he could call out a warning. They joined a narrow path, rising upwards on the lower slopes of Burn Hill, passing more fires and hearing a small river flowing beside the path. Higher still, they left the camp, but the glow of the campfires below them remained strong. They reached a shallow pool, with the full moon rippling on its surface as waves shot across it. In front of them a silvery waterfall, the height of ten men and the width of four men, roared.

Thorfinn fell to his knees and bowed his head, and listened for Odin's voice.

"Our master is here."

Thorgood fell to his knees too and listened to the sound of the falling water. Odin's voice melted in with the roar.

"Come to me."

They rose and waded through the pool to stand in front of the towering pillar of water, the noise rising, wet air soaking their bodies and wondering if a tower of bubbles would rise up from the pool. They fell to their knees again.

"Stand."

They stood, staring into the falling water, straining to hear anything through the roar. Then the roar subsided and the giant outline of a face pushed itself out of the water made silver by the moonlight. Where there should have been skin, the water became glassy and hard, and formed to become like ice with water flowing down it. Gradually, the nose began to look more like a nose, then eye sockets formed to be the size of cart wheels, then the cheeks and ears. The eyelids opened and they were bathed in an intense blue light.

"Why are you here?" asked the face in a cold, deep voice.

"Master. The name of the king who holds your stone is Llewellyn."

"What land does he rule?"

"He is King of all the Welsh peoples."

The giant mouth in the ice opened again.

"How do you know this?"

Thorgood felt the god's cold breath whenever Odin spoke.

"Master, good fortune aided us. We entered Llewellyn's war camp and were not seen. Even now our way to Llewellyn's royal tent is clear. Most of the Welsh warriors are being entertained by the travelling people. We watched them, hidden on the top of a caravan, and a boy called out Llewellyn's name. A gypsy woman challenged the king to be part of an illusion."

"An illusion?"

"A magic trick."

"And why are you here?"

"We believe we can end our great search tonight," said Thorfinn, "and if we fail, the others know that they must follow this army, find their lands and return to you with that knowledge."

The face in the waterfall became still and Thorgood glanced at his grandfather. The giant mouth opened again.

"Go now and seek the stone. A place at my eternal table is gifted to you, Thorgood of the Line of Firebrand, if you succeed. If you fail, the place you hold, Thorfinn, will be denied to you."

They fell to their knees, the face moved backwards to be consumed by the waterfall and the roaring of plummeting water returned.

"Is Odin all-powerful?" asked Thorgood.

"No. But he is very powerful and when he holds the stone, every king will pay him tribute. He *will* rule everything."

They ran back down the path to the camp, praying that the gypsy show went on, and searching for a Welsh warrior who sat alone. Sharpening his sword beside a fire, a man sat with his back to them and Thorfinn placed a knife under his chin, the blade gently touching skin.

"Make a sound, any sound and I will send you to meet your ancestors," he whispered in the Welsh tongue.

The man shook with fear.

"Where is Llewellyn's tent?"

The man pointed to his right.

Thorfinn eased the blade a tiny way from the throat.

"How far?"

"Three hundred paces."

Thorfinn brought his fist down onto the warrior's head, knocking him out cold and his limp body fell backwards away from the fire. They ran again, counting each step, passing fires and one huge fire that lit up everything around it. In the orange glow, Llewellyn's tent seemed alive with flickering tongues of orange dancing across canvas.

"No guards," whispered Thorgood.

They lifted the flap and entered, eyes searching for somewhere to hide. The floor was covered with brightly coloured rugs with designs unknown to the Norse peoples. The walls too were covered in bright tapestries, one of which held a picture of a red beast with huge jaws and claws. A table in the centre of the tent had a map laid out upon it and Thorgood stared at its lines, symbols and words.

"What is it?"

"I do not know, but if it is laid upon a table for a king, then it has value. We will take it to show our master."

On one side of the tent, opposite an ornate bed, were two large chairs with high backs, sitting on either side of a huge oak throne. The bed and throne had flowers carved into every part of their wood. Thorgood grinned.

"Llewellyn likes his luxury."

Thorfinn ignored him.

"You can have the throne and sit behind it, or get under the bed."

Thorgood walked quickly, wriggled under the bed and, as his grandfather sat behind the throne, voices came from outside, first a man's and then a child's.

"Do you believe they will attack tonight?"

"No."

"And will I be victorious upon the field of battle?"

"You hold the stone."

"Will you ride with me tomorrow?"

"No."

"If I asked you to ride beside me, would you?"

"Not tomorrow. I have things to prepare for the future of your people."

"What preparation?"

The boy laughed.

"Nothing that concerns you. Now, you must rest and decide how you will fight the enemy."

"Rest well, Tirani."

"Rest well."

The tent flap opened and Thorgood listened to the man undress. Something metal, maybe a sword, was put onto the table and someone sat on the bed, and the furs were pulled back. After a short time, Thorgood listened to shallow breathing and he peered out. One side of the tent was lit up from outside by flickering orange firelight and the red beast on the tapestry looked as though it was alive. Then a pair of legs moved quickly to the bed and above him came the sound of a blow. *Thwack.*

Thorgood was out and up in a flash, standing beside his grandfather who held the ruby. Thorfinn placed it with reverence into his leather purse and picked up the map, folded it and placed it next to the stone. Guards would now be outside the door and, in silence, they went to the back of the tent, where Thorgood took his knife and ran it slowly down through the canvas. They stepped outside.

"Make for the waterfall," whispered Thorfinn. "Walk slowly, normally."

A weak, muffled voice came from the tent.

"Help … me."

"He must have a thick skull," said Thorgood.

Guards ran in to help their master and the Norsemen ran for their lives, past campfires and with the sound of angry men behind them. A spear landed in front of Thorgood. Warriors ahead of them drew their swords. Thorgood picked up the spear and threw it into a man's chest. Thorfinn charged at the enemy, knocking one off his feet and cutting the other with his sword. The man screamed and Thorgood yanked the spear out of the dead man's chest and threw it at the first of a hundred warriors who chased them.

They made it onto the narrow path with the sound of a small river to one side, but the cries behind them grew nearer. Then out of the camp and away from the campfires into the blessed cloak of darkness. Ahead of them, the waterfall began to form into a face, the silvery moonlight making the skin appear like water running over ice. The eyes opened and the shallow pool was bathed in blue light. Odin's deep, commanding voice boomed out.

"The stone."

Thorgood glanced at Thorfinn and stopped running.

"Throw the stone into the mouth. I stand here to hold them back."

Thorfinn called back.

"We will meet soon. In the Halls of the Gods."

Thorgood drew his sword and turned, and an arrow cut deep into his shoulder, spinning him around in agony. Another arrow missed Thorfinn by the width of a hand. He sprinted on and saw the waterfall, heard its roar, took the stone from his purse and pulled his arm back ready to throw. A spear cut him down and he fell to his knees, the stone rolling in front of him and coming to rest an arm's length from the pool. The face in the waterfall screamed in anger.

"You have failed me, Thorfinn of the line of Firebrand."

With the shaft of the spear sticking out of his back and chest,

Thorfinn crawled forward.

"Not … yet, master," he said.

He reached out a shaking hand and clasped the stone. A foot came down onto his hand and someone took the stone away from him.

Thorgood opened his eyes and felt the incredible pain in his shoulder. He sat up, eyes watering, head swimming through lack of blood. Up the path, he could just make out the Welsh warriors who were standing, rooted to the spot, staring at a silvery face in the waterfall. Odin's voice boomed out.

"A place at my eternal table is denied to you, Thorfinn."

Then Thorgood heard his grandfather's screams of agony.

Beside the pool, Llewellyn stared at the small mound of dust that had been his enemy. Blood trickled down the king's forehead, where this man had hit him. He looked at the stone and then at the giant face. The mouth opened.

"Give me the stone."

The king held it up and pointed it at the face.

"This is mine and no one can defeat my army now. Are you a spirit?"

"I am Odin. Give me the stone, or I shall destroy you and your people, Llewellyn."

Llewellyn felt his fingers begin to open around the brooch.

"Drop the stone into the water."

Suddenly, he thought about the battle he needed to win at dawn and the land it would bring him. He snapped himself out of his trance and stood defiantly in front of Odin.

"This stone will stay in my line forever."

There was a silence for a while, until the roar of the waterfall began again, and then the face melted backwards into the pillar of water.

Thorgood stood and looked at the arrow shaft and took hold of it, took a deep breath and, despite the pain he knew he would feel, pulled it from his shoulder and tossed it aside. He crawled in darkness into the river and let it carry him gently away from the enemy. As he floated downstream, he held his shoulder and looked up at the full moon. From this day, two things would scar him terribly; a Welsh arrow and the death screams of his grandfather.

Later, he felt exhausted, numbingly cold and completely unaware of how far he had travelled. As he floated, he gazed at faraway hills and wondered how long it would be before the sun rose above them. Not long. A weak glow was already growing in the east and crows gathered, flying in high circles.

The river was wider here, and he floated with his arm across an old tree trunk, looking up at the dark silhouette of high castle walls, with marshland off to his right. He thought about Odin and his grandfather, heard Thorfinn's screams and forced himself to think about something else, anything else. A stabbing pain pulsed through his shoulder.

"One adventure, two scars," he said.

He pictured his daughter's face, captured her smile and became determined to return, and erect a stone for her, beside the Great Sea in Ulrika's Land.

"I *will* honour your memory too."

Something moved in the marshes. A heron, disturbed from its rest, flew elegantly out of the reeds and crossed the river. More movement and Thorgood snapped himself out of his thoughts, felt the pain in his shoulder and the cold biting into his fingers and toes. Alive again in his mind, he slowly sank beneath the water to rise on the other side of the log, away from the marshes, and poked his head around the side. Many spearmen were picking their way through the marsh and he counted them as they swam across the river, spears tied to their backs.

On the castle battlements, men shouted and pointed down at the Scots, who ran from the bank to stand in a line before the castle gate.

Thorgood gently kicked out with his legs and guided the trunk towards the cover of rushes by the bank, lowering his feet into thick mud and struggling to push the log deep inside the rushes.

The golden tip of the sun rose above a far hill and a streak of yellow light shot down Marsh Glen, creating long shadows and signalling the start of war. More movement in the marshes. Horsemen this time, a mixture of sturdy Scottish horses, mainly Highlands, and faster-looking, more elegant horses that he did not recognise. Malcolm the Younger's stallion splashed into the river, just fifty paces from Thorgood. It carried the king safely across and over two hundred riders followed him. These riders were finely dressed and well armed, which meant they were family leaders or even members of Malcolm's High Table. The splashing across the river stopped and was followed by the thunder of hooves as the Younger led his warriors west.

Thorgood's forehead creased. Riders were sure to be followed by foot-soldiers and he lay, silently, beside the log. But none followed and he guessed that the Scots had chosen to divide their army. He peered through the reeds. The spearmen by the castle gate were taking the spears from their backs and sticking them into the earth in front of them. The Angles would struggle to break out of a single gate with that many weapons facing them. So, the Younger planned to keep them prisoner and attack the Welsh who camped back by the waterfall. But where were his foot-soldiers, the majority of his army? Thorgood did not know and he tore his shirt open, placed his hand around the roots of the reeds, grabbed a handful of mud and slapped it onto his shoulder. He felt the wound sting and liked it. He became alert and alive again.

Thorgood watched the crows circle above the marshes. They knew that all they had to do was wait for the feast of death that was coming. Suddenly, he realised why the Mac Mar held his army back from the battle, and he smiled.

"My people once fought the Younger and he spared only Hengist Corngrinder. Spared him to bring me a message. I got that message loud and clear. If I were you, Tella, I would not underestimate the Scottish people."

He placed his feet back into the mud and pushed the tree

trunk into the river. Instantly the cold returned and he did not care. There was something he had to do by the waves of the Great Sea in Ulrika's Land. Gripping the log and kicking out with his legs, he floated away from war.

CHAPTER NINE

BATTLE OF THE LIGHT IRON

Ignoring the spearmen who were forming a defensive line in front of the castle, the Younger led the High Table and Seamus's Irish guard into the village of Stirling. Every cottage was a ruin, with stones taken and roofs burnt away. He realised this was Cameron Campbell's work, a measure of how determined the man had been to deny the enemy any kind of comfort. Malcolm hated himself, for arriving too late to save the brave men who had defended his castle. He swore revenge on Cuthbert and remembered Tirani's words.

"Let his death from his own cruelty come soon," he had said.

They cantered in a line along the path to the old ford and crossed the river, without meeting any of the enemy. This surprised him. He would have made a stand here, where warriors were forced to cross, tightly packed and vulnerable. As a bright sun rose fully above far hills, the Scots and Irish riders formed a line on open ground with a clear view of Llewellyn's camp. Seamus and Finnegan kicked their horses to come alongside the Younger. Alistair joined them.

"It's going to be a beautiful day," said Seamus.

"Not for Llewellyn," said Finnegan, grinning.

"Do you think he knows that he no longer holds the stone?" continued Seamus.

"No idea, but he soon will." Malcolm looked at Alistair. "How is Dougie?"

"He still sleeps, in the camp by Douglas Rock, and seems a little better in himself. But he wants no part of this."

"Myroy told me that Dougie will change the course of history after stealing back the stone."

"Do you want me to bring him here?"

"No. Let him rest. He deserves to find peace."

"I wouldn't mind him being here," grinned Seamus. "I saw him fight Borak One Hand at Mountjoy. He is a great warrior."

"He is that," added Finnegan.

170

"He is more than a shepherd," said Alistair.

"The first Keeper," added Malcolm.

"This Keeper thing. Is it important?" asked Seamus.

A silence followed and Alistair stared down the line of riders, and his eyes fixed upon Morag McCreedy. She looked as though she was ready to do war, staring forward, a shield over one arm and a sword in the other. He wondered if she enjoyed killing people.

"Malcolm, if we had not taken the stone from Llewellyn, do you think Morag would have stayed for the fight?"

"No, and I am not sure that I would have stayed for it either."

Seamus pointed at the camp in front of the waterfall. Men were gathering arms and slowly forming into fighting groups of five hundred men. Some of the men were laughing.

"They look very confident," said Alistair.

"They should feel confident. They know that we have no chance of defeating them if they hold the stone. I do not think that they know most of us carry the new light iron."

"So Llewellyn does not know he holds a copy of the brooch," said Alistair.

Malcolm nodded.

"But he does believe in the old magic and that its power dwarfs iron."

"Can your spearmen stop Cuthbert reinforcing Llewellyn?" asked Seamus.

"They are from the Outer Islands and deadly with the spear. They know what to do and I am not even sure that Cuthbert will aid his ally. He may be content to watch and count the number of our fallen."

"And you think that is what Tella is doing?"

"Sure of it. Even now his eyes are upon us. I can feel his desire for revenge."

"Will Finn be in position now?" asked Alistair.

Seamus drew his sword and pointed it at the back of the Welsh camp.

171

"Finn, the pack, and our foot-soldiers will be there now, waiting for the sound of battle to begin."

Malcolm stared at the half-formed Welsh army. Llewellyn was riding out to lead it and waving at his men, a brooch pinned to his chest.

"Show them no mercy," he yelled. "They will show no mercy to you."

The horses charged forward, hooves thundering, and riders picking out the warriors they would strike with their swords.

***

"This is going to be good," said Gath.

On a rocky outcrop at the top of Stag Forest, Gath lay on his belly next to his father, looking across fields and the river towards the Welsh camp. On the right of the camp, horses charged towards Llewellyn's forces. On the left, a mass of foot-soldiers, led by a huge man and a pack of dogs, ran into the camp. The Mac Mar scanned the field of battle and his eyes rested upon the castle but he could not see the line of spearmen, hidden from view by the ruined village, who held his ally captive.

"Cuthbert will join them soon."

"How can you be sure?" asked Gath.

"Because they are not allies. They are rivals for power. Soon the Angles and Welsh will do our work for us."

"It is exactly as you planned."

Tella smiled and stood.

"Good fortune is with us. What did you make of the rider sent by Borak One Hand?"

"If he truly holds Margaret a prisoner, then Ireland could be yours through marriage."

"If Seamus falls to the sword."

"And Borak's thirst for revenge will make that so."

Gath smiled at his father.

"The Mac Mar of Scotland *and* Ireland, that is good fortune."

Tella nodded down at Stirling Castle.

"I have seen enough. Let us return to our army. We march to victory, down through these trees, when the sun is fully above the far hills tomorrow."

As they climbed back up and disappeared over the hillcrest, Hengist Corngrinder's head popped around the trunk of an oak tree.

"They are gone."

Eleven Norse warriors joined him and a tongue speaker explained what had been said.

"They go to fetch their army and they will return here before moving down through the forest."

"Do we follow them?" asked a tall warrior, with a thick brown beard.

Hengist shook his head and pointed to the Welsh on the field of battle.

"We follow *that* army. They hold the stone. It looks as though we have some time to kill."

He sat down on a rock and watched the Welsh prepare for battle.

***

"This is going to be good," thought Llewellyn. He waved at his men. "Prepare for war!" he cried.

His men cheered and held their swords in the air. He urged his stallion forward and touched his brooch to reassure himself that it was still there. In his mind's eye, he pictured an orange beam shooting out of the ruby, destroying his enemy, and he willed it to happen. Nothing happened. He painted the picture, as he had done in battle before, and willed the stone to do his will. No beam.

A feeling of utter dread swept through his body. Some of the soldiers who followed him stopped in their tracks, uncertain as to why they were not aided by the old magic. Llewellyn tore the brooch from his shirt and held it aloft.

"Destroy my enemy," he screamed.

The thunder of hooves in front of him and the wild barking of dogs behind him grew louder. He yanked back on the reins and stared into the ruby. It *was* his stone, but why did it not help him? He held it aloft again, urging the beam to cut down the Younger. He stared in horror at the galloping horses just fifty strides away now. He glanced back at his army. They were not fully ready for real war and coming out of his camp were hundreds upon hundreds of enemy foot-soldiers. Welshmen at the back of his army began to scream and run as huge dogs snarled, and leapt up to bite their faces. He glanced up at Stirling Castle. Cuthbert was there on the battlements, still, watching his defeat, making no effort to help him.

Llewellyn turned his horse and fled south towards the lower slopes of Burn Hill. With the cries of his desperate men and the clashing of iron upon iron ringing in his ears, he knew that Tirani had been right. He had been a fool like his grandfather.

***

The Norsemen sat on the side of Stag Hill watching the battle. Even from this distance, they could hear the cries of war, dogs barking and the clashing of swords. Scottish horses smashed into their enemy, creating lines behind them in the ranks of men. Behind them, foot-soldiers fought desperately and a huge man stabbed out with a long spear, sending many to join the fallen. It did not last long. The surrounded army broke and ran, following their leaders who rode south and who had been the first to desert them.

Hengist Corngrinder bit his lip and wondered why the defeated army had not used his master's stone. As he walked back down the hill, past the oaks, this thought nagged at his mind. Then it was forgotten.

"Get the horses and follow the Welsh," said Hengist.

***

Malcolm, Alistair, Seamus and Finn stood together, blood on their swords, surrounded by the wretched aftermath of battle. They watched Morag McCreedy walk from body to body, checking that the Welsh were truly dead and killing any who were injured. Finn turned his head away.

"She fought with courage," said Alistair.

"All her people fought bravely and we still need every one of them. Any sign of the Mac Mar?"

They scanned Stag Forest, the glens and the lands around the castle. No sign of anyone except Angles on their battlements and Welsh warriors who fled south, terrified of pursuit and glancing back for what they feared most. Riders with spears.

Malcolm turned to Seamus.

"I believe that Finn was right. The Picts are likely to attack us using surprise. That means charging out from Stag Forest. The glens offer no cover to an army."

"And his army does not hide inside the castle."

Malcolm held up his sword, and shouted at his warriors.

"Gather together the fallen. All of them. Place them as they now lie, before Douglas Rock. Make it look like a terrible battle has just ended there."

His men began to lift up the bodies and place them over their shoulders.

"What the devil is he up to?" thought Seamus.

"What the devil are you up to?" asked Finnegan.

The Younger smiled.

"Let us speak to Cuthbert."

The Scottish and Irish riders headed north to the old ford. Some of them now had two or three swords strapped to their horses, the valuable spoils of victory. They turned along the path towards Stirling Castle and Alistair brought his horse next to Malcolm.

"Now would be a good time for Cuthbert to break free. If he waits, we will stand beside the spearmen and he will be besieged."

175

"There is a well inside the walls, so he has water, and Cameron would have made sure his garrison was well provisioned. He may wait for Tella."

"But he cannot rely on Tella."

"No."

The Younger urged his stallion into a gallop and the other riders followed him quickly to reinforce the men of the Outer Islands. In front of the castle gate, just out of arrow range, Malcolm dismounted and walked along the line of spearmen. He spoke to a warrior at the end of the line.

"Any trouble?"

The man bowed.

"No trouble."

Malcolm called to Seamus and Alistair.

"Walk with me."

Leaving their weapons by their horses, they walked towards the gate and stopped before it, staring up at the archers who trained their arrows on them. In the courtyard, Belus heard the Scottish king call out in Belus's own tongue and, in that moment, he decided to avenge his children's death at the first opportunity.

"I am Malcolm the Younger. I wish to speak to Cuthbert."

An archer lowered his bow and his head disappeared from the battlements. A tense silence followed, then Cuthbert was there, smiling, looking down on his enemy.

"Your castle is taken and your lands will soon follow. My riders will return from Berwick with more warriors from throughout Northumbria. You cannot take this castle and you cannot wait."

Alistair watched his king's face change, shaped by anger and determination.

"I once told you that you would never take any part of my kingdom. You are a prisoner and a long way from home. Llewellyn is defeated, despite the new light iron he carried." He glanced at Seamus, who was wondering again what was being spoken, and then pointed at Cuthbert. "We are now all armed with new swords. Tella will not help you, just as you did not go to aid the Welsh peoples."

"The Mac Mar's thirst for revenge, his hatred of you, Malcolm, will ensure you do face him on the field of battle. When that battle comes, you will fight us both and our measure *will* be greater than yours."

"Then stay in your prison. You know in your heart that the Black Kilts are poor allies."

Cuthbert sneered.

"I like this castle. It is strong and a fitting place for me to rule your people."

"You will not rule my people. Your greed and cruelty will bring you death and not by my hand."

"Is that more of your old magic? The old magic in which Llewellyn so strongly believed. The magic that could not save him."

Cuthbert laughed and his men laughed too. But not Belus. He stared up at Cuthbert's back, fingering the shaft of his spear.

"I offer you a choice, Cuthbert. Leave this castle before the fall of the sun this day. I will not pursue you. Your way to freedom will be guaranteed by my word."

"And what is the other option?"

Malcolm chose his word carefully.

"Death."

"It is you who should fear death. I choose to wait until the Picts arrive and then we will see how the old ways stand up to a greater army who wield the light iron."

Malcolm turned and Alistair and Seamus followed him back. As they approached the spearmen, still in fear of an arrow in the back, Malcolm spoke out.

"Double the number of spearmen and the spears each holds. Keep the cage door shut. Build fires and keep your eyes on the gate throughout the dark hours. Send a flaming arrow into the sky if you need our help. I return now to Douglas Rock."

He glanced at Seamus.

"You were very quiet."

"I couldn't understand a word being said. Besides, I was thinking about Margaret. Wanting to be with her again."

"Is that all that was on your mind?"

"No. I was praying that we do fight Tella. I have good reason to hate his people and, one day, I *shall* face a man, with one hand, in battle."

***

Alistair and Malcolm sat with Denbara's map in front of them, trying to work out how long it would take for the Angle riders to reach Berwick, raise more men and return to Cuthbert. The floor of the royal tent shimmered like moonlight on water and Myroy rose up.

"Alistair of Cadbol. At dusk, take a horse and secretly bring your spearmen to the safety of this camp. Tonight the first Keeper uses the stone."

Then he was gone.

"I am not sure that I want to see this," said Alistair in a grim voice.

***

"Cuthbert has not gone, has he?" asked Seamus.

"No and we did not expect him to," replied the Younger. "Are the spearmen safe?"

Alistair nodded.

"And the Angles still believe them to be there, standing away from the fires."

Their campfire crackled and Seamus stared up at the moon, full, silver and bright. He wondered if Margaret, Matina and Columba were safe on Iona. If his bride was looking up at the same moon and thinking of him. Had he done the right thing, sending her away? Here there was danger. Here there was the fear of something he did not understand. A deep dread of

178

something magic held by a shepherd and, despite their victory, a feeling that the shadow of death was close by. If only they knew where the Picts were.

Later, the friends sat around a huge fire on the edge of the Younger's camp.

"I am sure you were right Finn. I think Tella will attack from the forest."

Finn's great mouth opened and he bit into a leg of lamb. He chewed for a while and stood.

"I go to feed the pack."

"Tella expects us to be weak," continued Seamus. "It cannot be otherwise if we have fought two armies."

"And we will use that to our advantage," said the Younger. He smiled at Dougie. "Do you want to return home?"

Dougie had been sitting quietly, gazing into the fire, listening to the tales of battle and thinking about his adventure with Alistair in the Welsh camp. With the Younger's question, his heart went out to Mairi. It was like being stabbed.

"If you do want to go, then go with my blessing, Dougie."

"But I am afraid."

"Why?"

"Afraid of what I might find."

"But it is where you were born."

"No. I do not know where I was born. My brother and I were taken there after a fever took our parents."

"I am sorry to hear that. You have a brother?"

"Alec, a twin."

Alistair grinned.

"You mean there is another, like you?"

"Lissy used to say it was like looking at a reflection in still water."

"Then go home."

"The shepherd put his head in his hands.

"To find their bodies? To find parts of their bodies?"

Alistair nodded at Malcolm.

"The Angles can be a cruel people," said the Younger.

Alistair's voice became sad.

"I hope they died quickly, Dougie, and with honour."

Dougie's head snapped up from his hands.

"What honour, or mercy, would they show them?"

Alistair nodded slowly.

"None."

"Your cottage can be rebuilt," said Malcolm.

"Can my life be rebuilt?"

"Forget it, Dougie."

Dougie's hands shook with rage.

"Forget it, Dougie," said Alistair.

Dougie held his hands out in front of his face.

"How can I ever forget that, somewhere, an Angle has the blood of my children on his hands."

Alistair pointed out past the firelight towards the dark outline of the castle.

"The man with blood on his hands is there."

Inside the shepherd's leather purse, Amera's stone pulsed, blood red. Dougie's voice was as cold as ice.

"Then let them die there."

"They are safe there, within the walls. Safe from justice," said the Younger, softly.

"Not safe from my justice."

Dougie stood and went to sit alone in the moonlight, his anger, hatred and frustration rising.

Seamus gave them a hard stare.

"What are you two up to? That was very cruel."

"It is something we have to do. Have you warned your men to stay here, in my camp?"

"Yes and Finn is not feeding the pack, he is tethering them. He hates what you are doing to Dougie, by the way."

"Then it is time for Alistair and I to go for a walk."

Painful images raced through Dougie's mind. Had his family been cut down with swords as they ran away, across the high pastures? Had they been burned inside the cottage? His anger rose.

"Oh no, I hope they weren't burnt," he whispered.

He tried to think about something else and couldn't. Even if they were taken as slaves, that would be so much better. Maybe they were still alive? Maybe, right now, they were at Berwick, or put to work in the fields under an Angle master. Dougie heard footsteps and took his dirk from his belt. Dark shapes were moving only twenty paces away and not walking from the direction of the camp. Was it the enemy? He lay on his stomach and crawled into a hollow with gnarled tree roots on one side. He pressed himself against the roots and listened, and heard voices that he knew.

"I think it is one of the most terrible secrets I keep," said the Younger.

"But we do hold it and what else can we do?" replied Alistair.

Dougie wanted to get up and tell them that he was there, but something stopped him. His ears burned.

"How did you find out?" said Alistair.

"Myroy told me. He was there, trying to save them, but he was too late. The shepherd's cottage was already on fire."

"He must never know."

"No."

"What would happen if Dougie found out?"

There was silence for a while until the Younger spoke.

"I think it would destroy him."

In a fit of rage, Dougie leapt from the hollow and charged at Alistair, knocking him down, sitting on his chest. He yelled into Alistair's face.

"What is it that I must not know?"

Malcolm punched Dougie on the side of his face. It made no difference. The shepherd did not even flinch and put his hands around Alistair's throat, squeezing hard.

"Tell me. Tell me. Tell me!"

"Stop it, Dougie, I command you," shouted the Younger. "Guards. To me now!"

"Tell me. Tell me."

Alistair's face turned red, eyes bulging, chest heaving in pain as he felt his life draining from his body. He hissed.

"I … am your … friend, Dougie."

"Tell me your secret, or you die."

"Before … killing your children, … they made them … watch Mairi … being cut down with … swords."

Alistair passed out and Dougie released his grip, and stared up at the Gora moon.

"Nooooo," he cried.

His face changed. Blood red eyes, teeth showing in a snarl and pulsing veins sticking out of his temples. He jumped up, took Amera's stone from his purse and ran towards the castle.

The Younger put his arm around Alistair and helped him up, his friend gasping for air.

"Well done," he said softly.

By the time Dougie had run a quarter of the way to the castle, the army stood in a long line in front of Douglas Rock, all eyes fixed on the man who ran across open ground in the moonlight.

Malcolm glanced at Alistair's sad face.

"What are you thinking?"

"I was thinking that this night, many men will join the fallen. Some of them deserve to die. Some are farmers, or shepherds like Dougie. Does it have to be like this?"

The Younger stared across at the castle.

"You know the answer to that."

Alistair sighed.

"Aye."

"What else is on your mind?"

"Two thoughts that tear at my heart. Should I go to help Dougie? And wondering if we are far enough away."

A flash of lightning from a cloudless sky lit up Stirling castle. The wind rose.

"I think we are about to find out," said the Younger.

"I do not want to see this," and Alistair turned away, fearing for his friend.

"What are we looking for?" asked Seamus.

Malcolm went to stand beside him.

"The old magic. For a short time, the shepherd holds a stone that has an incredible power. We are trying to hide it from an enemy who would use its power to destroy our peoples."

"Does Margaret know about this?"

"No."

"Can I tell her?"

"No. But you will soon meet a man who comes up from the underworld. He will tell you a story and you too will become a Keeper, like Alistair and I."

Seamus nodded at a bright red trail that began to appear behind Dougie. A deep thunder came from within the earth. A pyramid of spears fell over. All the pyramids of spears fell over as the ground shook.

"What is that?"

Malcolm stared at the tear in the ground, a growing red scar, where the shepherd had trod.

"The old magic," he said.

***

Cuthbert the Cautious, Baron of Berwick, sat alone in his new chamber, his table covered with food, silver goblets and plates, stacks of coins, jewellery and fine tapestries in rolls. A warrior burst into the chamber.

"Master, I think you should join us on the battlements. Something is happening to the land."

"I will join you when I am ready," he snapped.

A small tremor hit the castle and a stack of coins toppled over. They heard a rumbling noise, like ancient gods waging war beneath their feet. A shield fell off the wall and Cuthbert stood.

Five hundred paces from Dougie, the ground shimmered like the moonlight which bathed the shepherd in silvery light. Myroy rose up and gripped his staff for comfort. To his left was the castle, to his right the dark outline of Douglas Rock towering above the lights of the Younger's war camp. Between them, running, trance-like, eyes fixed upon his enemy, was Dougie of Dunfermline.

Myroy sighed and reassured himself.

"It has to be this way."

As the shepherd's feet pounded upon the ground, blood red lava rose up out of his footprints. A crack the width of an arm joined the footprints together and more lava spewed up from the earth to make a vein of molten rock.

As Dougie got closer to the people who had wronged him, his anger grew and grew, its intensity unspeakable, Amera's stone pulsing and sending tongues of light across the open ground. The length of his stride grew; two paces long, four paces long and now ten. His speed increased to a horse's gallop, then faster than a horse and then faster than anything anyone had ever seen. Behind him, the crack in the earth widened and lava shot up into the sky. On both sides of the running man, rocks shook and rose up so that the river of boiling blood was channelled forward.

Myroy put his arm across his eyes to protect them from the searing heat.

***

Belus looked up at the men on the battlements and Cuthbert's back. Everyone was staring, transfixed, by something which glowed red beyond the wall. He grabbed his spear and knew that his moment had come. Cuthbert sensed the fear around him.

"It is an illusion. What can one man do? Archers, prepare to cut him down."

Bows were drawn and pointed at Dougie. One man on the battlements turned and fled down the steps to the courtyard, passing a man with revenge in his heart. A pit outside the castle gate waited for him.

"Stand firm," yelled Cuthbert.

He stared down at the approaching channel of blood, felt its heat and watched it widen. Tall plumes of fire and rock shot hundreds of paces into the sky behind the running man. Another man ran down the stairs, desperate to reach the castle gate.

"Stand firm. Listen to my words, stand ..."

Belus thrust his spear into Cuthbert's back and pushed with all his might. He leaned forward and placed his face next to his master's.

"That, Cuthbert, is for my children."

The ground shook violently and part of the wall collapsed, men and stones falling onto the courtyard. Around Belus, the air was like a howling hot storm and everyone began to jump down from the battlements, desperate to escape the wrath of a Keeper.

***

Myroy took his arm away from his eyes and quickly glanced up at the night sky. Apart from the Gora moon, every part of the sky was blood red. Another lightning flash lit up the castle. He bent his ancient body into the wind and heard its wail. The ground shook and a mighty thunder rose up from the underworld. He held his breath as Dougie's body hit the castle.

The river of lava exploded and rose up like a volcano. Stones, horses and men were sent skyward, surrounded by the blistering heat of molten rock. Myroy covered his eyes again with his arm and huge steaming rocks landed around him. Then the heat was gone and silence returned to the earth. Myroy lowered his arm and watched the cracks in the earth close, the lava cool into strange string-like shapes upon the ground and the sky return to moonlight.

"Come to me," he said.

Steam rose up from a crater where Stirling Castle had once

stood. Out of the crater, a red bubble rose up and floated slowly towards the Ancient One. The red bubble faded to orange and Dougie's lifeless body was gently lowered onto the ground. Myroy knelt and stroked the shepherd's forehead. Then he placed his hand upon his shoulder.

"Forget this day. Forget this day."

He stood and drew a circle with his staff on the ground and descended to reappear immediately next to the Younger, Seamus and Alistair.

"The first Keeper lives. Give him aid then send him home, alone and without a horse."

Myroy spoke to Seamus.

"This is not your time."

Then the Ancient One was gone.

✳✳✳

In moonlight, the twisting snake of Black Kilts stopped in a glen on the other side of Stag Forest. Everyone stared over the hill. Stirling Castle was over that hill and now a red glow covered the skies above it, lightning flashed and a deep thundering boom echoed down the valley. Gath looked at his father.

"A good omen, or ill?"

Tella the Mac Mar turned and called out to his men.

"Even the gods are with us. Let us hope they leave some Scots alive for us to kill."

✳✳✳

Hengist Corngrinder and the Norse search party rode through the night, holding back when the riders ahead of them slowed. He glanced over his shoulder at a red glow in the northern sky.

"Have you ever seen a dawn sun like that?"

The others shook their heads.

"Well, we cannot stop to admire it, the Welsh move on again."

At high sun, the riders they pursued disappeared over the

186

crest of a hill as the Norse riders crossed a small river. A tower of bubbles shot up in between their horses, making them rear up in fear. Odin's blue eyes flashed at Hengist.

"The stone's power has been used. Incredible power. I have felt it."

"Yes, master."

"Do you still follow the king who holds my stone?"

"Yes, master."

The Ancient One felt his way into the miller's mind and knew he was telling the truth. Something made him look north, but the red glow had long gone.

"Did you see the stone's power being used?"

"No, master."

"And you are sure that the enemy you follow holds my stone."

"Yes, master."

The tower of bubbles subsided and Odin was gone, believing truly that his epic search should now be to the south in the land of the Welsh.

***

Peter stared at Myroy, sitting on the edge of his bed, rubbing his ancient hands together, as if needing to keep warm.

"You did it, didn't you. That is why you gifted Llewellyn the stone and had Dougie steal it back from him."

"We threw my brother off of the scent for centuries and we protected generations of Keepers. It was good fortune that Odin saw the copy of the brooch at the waterfall, but at some time our good fortune will run out."

"Is that why I am to be the last Keeper?"

"That is part of the reason. In your time, the world is a very different place to the one that Dougie knew. We could hide the stone in *Keeping* in a village in Scotland and Odin's forces would have to hunt for it, village by village. As long as the Keeper did not use it and attract attention to himself, it was safe. Safe

187

for generations. Now, the world itself is a village. You call it technology and the Seekers have the very latest, the very best internet technology for tracking and reporting on the line of Donald. There are thousands of Seekers now, all over the planet, waiting, watching and directly under their master's control, or the control of his Valkyrie, the living dead. One day they *will* capture one of our people and then they will know the answer they need."

"Have they ever captured one of our people?"

Myroy's face became sad.

"Yes."

Peter sensed that the Ancient One did not want to remember something and changed the subject.

"Is Bernard one of us? I mean, is he a Keeper?"

"Bernard is the head of operations in Europe and has been a key man since the war."

Peter thought back to the story.

"The day after Dougie used the stone to destroy the castle, Odin rose up beside Hengist and he did not know where the stone had been used. He only knew that it *had* been used. But when Malcolm was a child, Murdoch looked into the stone, saw faces and it pulsed. Odin felt it and rose up in a tower of bubbles beside them. He knew then where it was used, but he had no idea when Dougie used it to destroy an entire castle. Also, Odin had to wait. He felt the stone being used, but he could not talk to Hengist until high sun the next day, when they crossed a river. That means he can only talk to his people when they are close to water."

Myroy sat patiently, silently and picked up the alarm clock.

"Two fifteen."

"Did Thorgood get back to Ulrika's Land?" asked Peter.

"He did and was soon to receive a promise from Prince Ranald."

"Ranald wants to be king and kill his father, doesn't he?"

"Yes."

"And Tella is coming."

"Tella is coming."

Peter lay back on his bed, hands behind his head. He knew he was being taught something of great importance. He thought about how he had felt when Myroy had made him experience the loss of his family. Myroy had done the same thing to Dougie and he wondered if it was the anger that pulsed in the shepherd's heart that stopped Odin locating Amera's stone. He remembered Grandpa passing the brooch on to him, like a baton in a centuries-old relay race, at Edinburgh airport. He had felt the weight of the responsibility then, but now it was so much worse.

Suddenly Peter became very afraid and tried to forget what was hidden in a shoe box under his bed.

Myroy smiled, reassuringly at him.

"That weight you feel. It has a name. It is called the world."

CHAPTER TEN

DEATH IN THE CHURCH

At first light, Finn McCool sat with Murphy-dog, hiding behind rocks on the side of Stag Forest. He didn't need to scan the trees around him for the approach of Tella's army, he simply waited patiently, watching his dog's ears. Murphy-dog yawned and placed his great head onto Finn's lap and, as the sun rose above far hills, Finn stroked the dog's head and felt his warmth. Then Murphy-dog's head was up, alert, ears back, and Finn clapped his hand across the hound's mouth.

"No sound," he whispered, "lie down."

Finn crawled to peer around a rock. Black Kilts, hundreds and hundreds of them, carrying their traditional war axes, were making their way down the wooded slope that overlooked the crater where Stirling Castle had once been. Some of them were struggling to lead horses down the steep slope. The number of the enemy who passed him became fewer and fewer and, at last, he was alone. He stood and took a mirror from his leather purse and made an angle against the low sun.

***

"Let battle begin," shouted Seamus, when the flashes came.

Around him, the Irish foot-soldiers charged at the Scots. A small number of the High Table drew their swords and galloped towards five riders of the Irish guard. Alistair jumped from his horse and knocked the King of Ireland from his stallion, and they stood face to face, swords drawn and began to strike out at each other. Everywhere, the light iron sang, men cried out and some fell to the earth to join the hundreds of Welsh bodies that had been brought to this place near to Douglas Rock.

Alistair watched Finnegan, who seemed to be enjoying himself immensely.

"How long do we keep this up for?" asked Alistair.

"Until Malcolm's signal," said Seamus.

"How about you win this time?"

Seamus grinned and slashed down close to the Scotsman's shoulder. Alistair gave out a blood-curdling cry and fell to the floor.

"Don't overdo it," said Seamus.

Alistair writhed around for a while and then smiled up at Seamus, who was waving his sword above his head in victory.

"I wonder if Dougie is safe on his road home," said Alistair.

"The way he walked out of the camp, with his head down, I'd be surprised if he finds his lands at all."

"Oh, he will, and I dread what he will find when he gets there."

***

Huddling behind a waist-high wall on the edge of Stag Forest, Gath watched his father's face and wondered if the Mac Mar would be killed in battle this time. On that day, he would become king and his ambitions fulfilled. Tella's eyes were fixed upon the fight raging beyond a massive hole in the ground where a castle had once been. Wisps of steam rose out of the crater.

"What do you think happened to it?" asked Gath.

"I was thinking the same thing. Perhaps it was built above a cave that collapsed?"

"An army could not have done it, could it?"

"Not in a day, no."

"Do we attack?"

"We attack when the enemy on both sides are few." Tella put his hand on his shoulder and rubbed away the dull pain of his wound from Carn Liath. His voice became cruel. "And I pray the Younger survives. I have got plans for him."

"What shall I tell the clan leaders?"

"Tell them to count the men left standing and to come to me when that number is three hundred."

"We are two thousand strong, why wait?"

Tella jumped up and lifted his son by the hair. His army behind the wall stood too.

"It is easier to let the enemy do our work for us and I want to win the peace afterwards, as well as the battle. I need every one of my warriors to man garrisons and collect taxes." Tella let go of Gath's hair and searched his son's eyes, and spat into them. "One day you will be king, but it will not be this day."

The warriors behind the wall stared at them in silence, committing to memory the Prince's lack of courage in front of his father. Gath was not a Mac Mar. Even though few men had dared to stand up to their king, one man who *had* fought his case for revenge, was preparing to leave Fionnphort, on the western shore of the island of Mull.

∗∗∗

Margaret was chained around the neck to an iron bar the length of a man. Columba was chained to the other end of the bar.

"You told me your orders were to wait here until Tella tells you otherwise," she screeched.

"You are too valuable a prize to keep here," said Borak One Hand in a calm voice.

"Well I am not going and that is that."

"There could be danger here from Scottish ships. I will take you to the fortress at Deros and will then return to lead the fleet."

"Do we deserve to be chained?" asked Columba.

"Whether you deserve it or not, you remain in chains until a prison is found for you."

Columba looked at Borak's stump.

"I tended you once. Is this how you repay my kindness?"

Borak ignored him and shouted orders to his crew, and their sail was raised. Margaret tried to kick Borak.

"I shan't go to Deros."

A chubby Black Kilt, with a cheery face, jumped on board and ran to them.

"Has the rider returned from Tella yet?"

Borak wondered what his brother would have advised him to

do without new orders from the Mac Mar. His instincts told him to take Margaret away from this place and, besides, he could return quickly if needed.

"No, he has not returned."

"Any work to be done whilst you are away?" he asked.

Borak shook his head.

"No."

"Any orders?"

"Wait here until I return. Expect me in two days if there are kind winds. In three if the wind falls."

The young man smiled, glanced at Margaret and spoke in the Scottish tongue.

"I think our time here will be quieter than yours."

Borak did not smile back, as he once would have done.

"One day, Aglan, your tongue will get you into trouble. Now go ashore and keep an eye on things for me."

Margaret proudly held her head up, folded her arms and stared defiantly at Borak.

"I am not going to Deros."

"I would be very careful, if I were you, Queen of the Irish peoples. Your father may have lived with your tantrums, but I will not. Hunger is a terrible thing."

At the word, hunger, Margaret's head dropped, but not through any fear for herself. Her thoughts went to Iona, reaching out to a little girl who was trapped there alone.

"I suggest you two play along with my game for a while."

"But for how long, Borak?" asked Columba.

"Until Seamus arrives on Skye to rescue you."

***

A Black Kilt ran along the line of the wall and knelt before his king.

"Their measure is three hundred."

Another clan leader joined Tella and Gath.

"Three hundred now."

195

And another.

"Master, three hundred warriors still fight."

Tella the Mac Mar stood.

"Bring my horse. Tell your warriors to follow me in silence."

The clan leaders ran back to pass on his orders and Tella unfolded Denbara's map. The battle raged on open ground between Douglas Rock and the place where Stirling Castle had been. He placed his finger onto the old ford.

"We cross the river here. As long as the battle with Cuthbert and Llewellyn rages, we should be in charging distance of the Younger before he knows we are there."

Gath kicked down the wall in front of him and led his horse onto the field above the ruin of Stirling village.

**

Malcolm the Younger held aloft his sword.

"Victory!" he shouted.

The warriors who remained standing, held their weapons above their heads and cheered. Around them, the earth was covered in twisted bodies, a gruesome mix of cold, bloody bodies in faded red plaids and Scots, and Irish. Even Morag McCreedy had played her part well. She lay with her clansmen, a shield with an iron fist across her back, waiting for another chance to kill men.

Malcolm stared around. The bright morning sun threw the shadow of Douglas Rock, like a shroud, over the aftermath of battle. On either side of the path that came from the direction of the old ford, were mounds of the fallen, spears sticking out of the Welsh. The two mounds showed where the battle had split into two battles and formed a channel, two hundred paces wide, leaving the path clear, except for a few dead men.

Suddenly, the Younger's eyes filled with fear. Approaching from the west, was an army of Black Kilts, following riders and moving quickly, silently, towards his people. The Mac Mar had already passed the cottages where the paths from Stirling Glen and Heather Glen met. In no time he would be between the crater and the zig-zag path that went up to the ruined fort upon Heather Hill.

Malcolm ran back a thousand paces towards Douglas Rock, counting every step, so that he was halfway between the rocky outcrop and the field of battle. He raised his sword again.

"To me."

The men of the Outer Islands ran to join him, grabbing spears from the dead and forming a brave line, three men deep, in front of the Younger. They picked up more spears that were laid upon the ground and stuck them upright into the earth.

"On the first throw, one hundred and fifty spears will be right in your face, Tella. Come and get it," said Malcolm.

***

Ahead of the Mac Mar's army lay thousands of dead bodies, but the pathway forward to Douglas Rock was clear. He looked at the path and wondered why the battle had strangely left it free for him to pass easily. Beyond the dead, the Younger stood facing him, spearmen in ranks protecting him. Tella turned his horse and called out to his warriors.

"Today we take back our homeland around Carn Liath. Today we conquer Scotland." He pointed to the Younger. "Do you see that man? The man with long grey hair, who stands behind his warriors with fear in his heart. Look at his face and remember it. Bring him to me alive when our work is done."

The Black Kilts cheered and hit their shields with their war axes. Tella unsheathed his sword and turned his stallion to face the Scots.

"Stay with me," he said to Gath.

His son kissed his sword and lied.

"I am with you, father."

They kicked their heels into their horses' flanks and the mighty army charged forward along the path, a gap growing between the riders and those who followed on foot.

197

Lying beside Seamus and Finnegan, Alistair heard the thunder of hooves and opened an eye. Tella's horsemen were passing between the two fields of the dead. He watched the Younger raise his sword and keep it aloft. Alistair stood. Around him thousands of Irish and Scottish foot-soldiers stood and they all waited for the Younger's next signal.

***

Out of the corner of his eye, Gath thought that he saw the dead rise up. Behind him now, men were standing, holding sword and spear. Tella's eyes were fixed on the Younger, five hundred paces ahead of them, revenge in his heart. Gath stared forward, sweat pouring down his back, his stomach tied up in knots, the war screams of the other riders in his ears, horses charging and close together.

The Younger was standing motionless, sword in the air. Then Gath saw him lower the sword and he seemed to be pointing it directly at him. Gath heard the roar of men behind him and saw a large number of riders gallop out from behind Douglas Rock. The Mac Mar saw them too and hesitated for a moment. Then he cried out.

"We are still stronger than the enemy. Kill them."

***

Alistair saw the Younger's sword fall and point at Tella. The High Table and the riders of the Irish Guard appeared and galloped out to meet the enemy at the same time as the Pictish riders would be in spear range. Alistair grabbed a spear, Seamus and Finnegan did the same and they turned to look at the Black Kilts who were running towards them.

"Their foot-soldiers are a long way behind Tella," said Seamus.

"Aye. I'd say that the Mac Mar is about to be cut off from his men."

198

"Do you want to give the order?"

Alistair raised his sword and called out.

"To me!"

The Irish and Scots on both sides of the path ran to form a single army between Tella and his foot-soldiers. Alistair glanced at Seamus.

"Do you want to address your men?"

"No. They know how to deal with little disagreements."

"Good fortune to you both in battle."

Seamus and Finnegan grinned and shouldered their spears.

"If you come across a man with one hand, let me know," said Seamus.

The friends walked out to meet the enemy and their people followed them. They heard the Black Kilts' pounding feet and their war cries, and saw them whirl their axes above their heads.

"I'd say they are about fifty paces away," said Seamus.

Finnegan pointed at a short Pict who carried too much weight.

"You know, if an O'Mara had run as far as the Picts have, they would be exhausted."

Alistair began to run and he shouted out.

"It ends today. Let the light iron sing out."

***

Malcolm the Younger called out to his spearmen.

"Aim at the horses and bring them down."

The men from the Outer Islands launched their spears and they sailed through the air, thudding into the Pictish horses. Tella saw a spear strike Gath's stallion in the chest, heard screams around him and felt his own horse stumble and fall. The mass of riders behind the Mac Mar slowed and picked their way past the first line of writhing horses and smashed into the riders of the High Table and Irish Guard. Tella picked himself up, snarled, pulled a Black Kilt off his stallion and jumped up.

"Get a horse," he shouted at Gath.

The Mac Mar looked across at the Younger. He was ordering his spearmen to throw again, and Tella jumped off the horse and sheltered behind its great shoulder as a hail of spears cut the poor beast down.

"Up here," yelled Gath.

Tella grabbed his outstretched hand and climbed up behind him on a grey Highland. They galloped to join the other horsemen in battle. Tella unsheathed his sword and struck a Scottish rider down, and leapt from the back of Gath's horse onto the enemy's steed.

"Follow me!" yelled the Mac Mar.

The Picts turned their horses away from the High Table and the Irish Guard, and charged back down the path to attack Alistair and Seamus. The Scottish foot-soldiers were caught completely by surprise as swords, spears and axes hacked them down from behind.

The Younger's riders chased Tella and, as the light iron sang out and men screamed, the tables turned against the Picts. Huge numbers of them had fallen and Tella saw the Irish foot-soldiers cut a way right through his men and turn to attack them from behind.

In the heat of battle, Alistair spotted the Mac Mar and ran at him, sword ready. Tella kicked the flanks of his horse and drove at him, their swords clashing. Another Scot charged at the same time and a throwing axe spun through the air and buried itself into his stomach. Screams filled the air and Tella galloped away from Alistair to join Gath, who was fending off two Irish warriors. The Mac Mar's horse hit one warrior in the back and he swung his blade and severed the sword arm of the other. Gath pointed at the Younger. He and his spearmen were running to join the battle. He shouted at his father.

"The Younger comes."

Tella caught the flash of steel out of the corner of his eye and parried Alistair's sword away. *Clang*, another blow fended off. *Clang*, and another. The enemy seemed to be everywhere, hacking his foot-soldiers down and spearing his riders.

"Follow me to Fionnphort," he yelled to Gath.

They broke free from the fighting, abandoned their people, and galloped north towards the river and the steaming crater. Alistair saw them flee.

"Victory is ours," he cried.

He saw Malcolm, fighting beside his spearmen and ran to him, pointing at the two riders.

"The Mac Mar is there."

Malcolm stepped back from the battle and his spearmen closed ranks in a circle around them, protecting them both from the war. The Younger's face was like granite.

"Take the High Table. Hunt him down. Wherever he goes, you go."

Alistair bowed and ran back to the fierce fighting to get a horse. He called back.

"Do you want him alive?"

"No. I want him dead."

✱✱✱

Seamus called his men to him and they charged back into the ranks of Black Kilts. Throwing axes missed his head by the width of a finger but he drove on, slashing out with his sword and shield, and sending three men to join the fallen. Some of the Picts pointed north at two riders and began to run from the field of battle. The Irish chased them and stabbed them in their backs. A huge group of Black Kilts cried out in anger and charged him, and the fierce hand-to-hand fighting continued. Then spearmen were there, by Seamus's side and they threw their spears at the enemy. Malcolm appeared.

"Tella has fled with Alistair on his tail."

Seamus pointed at the bloody, writhing mess of bodies.

"And no sign anywhere of a man with one hand."

An arrow whistled through the air at the King of Ireland and

201

Finnegan held his shield out in front of Seamus's chest. The shaft thudded into it.

"Is that allowed? Shooting at a king?"

"No it is not," said the Younger.

Finnegan nodded and charged off to have a disagreement with an archer.

"Come on," said Seamus. "Let's kill some more Black Kilts."

Later, they stood with their smiling men around them. Huge numbers of the fallen, from all sides, littered the open ground, crows circling above the stench and Morag McCreedy searching amongst the dead for any of the enemy who still lived, her bloody sword ready to send them to meet their ancestors.

"Is there something wrong with her?" asked Seamus.

"Aye," said Malcolm softly.

They stared at a small group of Black Kilts who had escaped the slaughter, running beyond the river, up a slope and over a field. A tall man came out of Stag Forest and stood like a statue, with a spear in his hand, a wolf hound sitting patiently beside him. The Picts drew their swords and ran at him. A pack of snarling dogs jumped over the wall and into the field.

A worried-looking Finnegan ran over to talk to them.

"A tongue speaker has news of Margaret and Columba from a dying Black Kilt."

Seamus's heart sank.

"What news?"

"Tella sent a rider north to tell Borak One Hand to take them as prisoners to Deros."

"So, Iona was not a safe haven after all," said Malcolm.

Seamus shook with fury.

"I will kill him for two reasons. To avenge my father and rescue my wife."

"Do you need help?" asked Malcolm.

Seamus looked around at the dead Picts and up at Finn's dogs, savaging any who had got away. There could not be many Black Kilts left.

"No. I take my army back to Stranraer and then sail north to Skye."

Malcolm gestured towards his camp.

"I want to gift you the map. May it bring you good fortune."

But as he said the words, he thought about Myroy's prediction about the union of the royal houses of Donald and Elder, and wondered if good fortune would really be with the King of the Irish Peoples. He remembered the ancient Celtic blessing that Arkinew had made him and Murdoch say at the end of each lesson. He spoke it aloud to his friend.

"Deep peace of the running wave to you. Deep peace of the flowing air to you. Deep peace of the quiet earth to you. Deep peace of the shining stars to you. Deep peace of the sun of peace to you."

Seamus looked embarrassed, all his anger melting away.

"That is one hell of a blessing."

The Younger smiled.

"Aye, it is."

***

Tella drove his stallion across the Stirling River, below the steaming crater, Gath's horse splashing beside his. The steeds struggled to find their footing on the steep sandy bank on the far side, but when they were up they moved quickly past the ruined cottages on the edge of Stirling village and then they were away, galloping along Marsh Glen path. Gath glanced over his shoulder.

"Fifty riders."

His father did not need to look back.

"The Younger has sent the High Table to hunt us down. Safety in numbers lies at Fionnphort."

"It is a long time to high sun. They will not lose sight of us in daylight."

Tella snapped.

"Be silent."

They turned and rode northwest, over rolling hills covered in grass, heather and birch, keeping their sweating horses at full speed until dusk. Beside a loch they changed horses, giving orders to two Picts to take their tired horses and ride them south without rest. Under a big waning moon, the way onwards to Oban, then Mull, was well lit and with fresh stallions the gap between them and the High Table grew.

"Do you think they will follow our men?" asked Gath.

"No. I expect they will follow us, guessing that we head to Deros, or divide their party."

"Your escape route back is working well."

"Be silent."

They drove their horses hard until dawn, but their fear of capture did not reduce. Around them the mountains grew higher, the glens deeper, and occasionally a solitary eagle soared high above them.

"How far to Fionnphort?" asked Gath.

"We can make Oban by High Sun. If our ship is ready and we have fair winds, we should stand upon the western side of Mull by day's end." Tella answered. "But we have to get there first."

On a ridge behind them stood a line of horsemen, watching them and studying the lie of the land ahead. Tella pulled his stallion up and twisted round to look at them. A warrior led two horses forward from the line and stopped. He untied two bodies, strapped across the horses' backs, and tipped them onto the earth.

"They did fall for it, for a while," said Gath. "But they must know of faster ways to travel."

Tella kicked his heels into his horse's flanks.

"Be silent," he said.

But the intentions of the enemy had been made crystal clear.

***

"You shouldn't eat more than you can lift," said Donald.

Hamish lowered his breakfast leg of lamb from his mouth and steadied himself against the ship's rail.

"There are times when I hate you."

Donald wrinkled his nose and Gawain joined them at the prow to stare out to sea at the combined Scottish and Man fleet. Hamish growled.

"Not a sign of them."

"That's six days of searching and not a Black Kilt to fight anywhere," added Donald.

Gawain pointed south.

"Perhaps we should go back and search along the Clyde? Glasgow is where Llewellyn's army will be provisioned. Their fleet could be there."

"They weren't there before," said Donald.

"Even Oban was a ghost town. You would expect to find at least one Pictish ship," said Hamish.

"What about Skye?" asked Gawain.

"If Tella fights at Stirling, why would his fleet stay at home?"

The sail behind them cracked as the wind picked up and ropes tightened. Below the prow, the bow wave grew taller, curled and splashed, and made foam as Gawain's ship cut through the waves like a knife.

"Why not just run before the wind and see where it takes us?" asked Hamish.

Gawain stared to the northwest and nodded.

"Right, let's search around Mull."

Later, as even the small clouds disappeared and the sun became high and brilliant, everyone was bored. They would not make the rocky southern coastline until nightfall, but the lookouts remained silent, searching the horizon for sails. The rest of the crew sat around the decks, sharpening swords or losing themselves in their thoughts of home. Circling high above the fleet, the number of gulls increased which meant that they were getting closer to land, but not necessarily closer to the enemy. Hamish snoozed on the deck, feet out and his back upright against the rail. Donald came and sat next to him.

"I'm bored."

His friend let out a long, long-suffering breath.

"Go away."

Donald wiggled his feet and pulled a face. Hamish opened a tired eye.

"What are you doing?"

"Wiggling my feet."

"And annoying me."

"That's what you are for."

Hamish shut his eye, felt the ship rise and fall, and tried to let sleep take him.

"I said I'm bored."

Hamish let out another long breath.

"I know."

Donald stared up at the gulls and thought about getting a bow and practising his aim.

"I'm bored."

"Go away."

Donald wiggled his feet some more.

"I'm bored."

"There are times," whispered Hamish, "when I really do hate you."

"Do you want a fight?"

"No."

Donald wiggled his feet so that they tapped on the side of his friend's knee.

"Go away."

"I'm bored."

A deep growling noise came from bowels of Hamish's chest.

"You want to fight me, don't you."

"Go away."

A shadow fell over them and Robert, the Thane of Inverness, pointed an accusing finger at them.

"I thought I would find you two lazing around again. We

should be working out how to destroy Tella's fleet."

Hamish leapt to his feet, picked up Robert and threw him overboard, and sat back down again.

At the stern, sailors yelled out and tossed ropes over the rail. Moments later, a dripping shadow fell over the friends again.

"What was that for?" asked Robert. "Don't forget who the Younger has put in charge here."

Donald grinned up at him.

"Hamish can be a bit grumpy sometimes."

A man at the prow called out. The other lookouts around the fleet called out too.

"Sails."

"About time," said Donald.

Hamish glared at him.

"Just in time for you."

Their ship listed as the crew ran to the port rail, staring out at three dots on the horizon. As they gained on the dots, they became tiny black sails and, as the sun kissed the western ocean, the Scots knew they would board the enemy boats before darkness came. Gawain barked out his orders.

"Prepare ropes with grappling hooks. I want our archers to pin down the Picts behind their rail. Then we pull the ships together and board. Tell the crews on the other ships to be ready to do the same."

"Ready to fight?" asked Robert.

Donald nodded at the sea.

"I don't think I can be bothered today. Do you want to go for another swim?"

Hamish unsheathed his sword and watched as eight of the fastest Man ships divided and surrounded two of the enemy ships. Arrows rained down onto the Picts and ropes were flung aboard, men yelling and pulling the ships together for the attack. Two Black Kilts stood, spears held ready. An arrow hit one in the chest and the other man ducked back down below the rail.

"It's going rather well," said Donald.

207

Hamish ran back to the tiller to join Gawain and Robert, and pointed at the battle.

"Those two will be taken. Let's go after that one."

The third Pictish ship was tacking south, trying to evade the slower Scottish ships that chased it. Robert pushed the tiller over, the sail billowed out and they mirrored the Picts' course. Gawain's face was grim.

"They cannot outrun my ship in these winds. Soon we blood our swords."

They closed and the Picts tacked again and again, but each time they lost distance and Gawain called for his archers to stand ready. Hamish went back to Donald.

"Stay with me," he said.

"I thought you hated me."

A hail of arrows shot over their heads and thudded into the Pictish ship. Someone screamed. Grappling hooks followed the arrows, their lines tightening and the two rails closed together. The friends got ready to jump across the gap.

"Stay with me," repeated Hamish.

Donald grinned.

"Go on, say you like me."

Hamish let out a deep, booming war cry and leapt aboard the enemy ship.

Later, with the bodies of the Black Kilts abandoned to float in the Great Sea, Gawain spotted men on one of his ships waving madly at him. He pointed to them and Robert adjusted their course to come alongside. Hamish and Donald listened to the excited voices of the men of Man and wondered what they were telling their king. As they waited, they looked at the rest of the fleet. No ships lost and all three Pictish ships taken intact, and now in tow on long lines, a single sailor at each helm. Gawain came over.

"One of my warriors is a tongue speaker and a wounded Black Kilt has told us what we want to know."

Hamish and Donald both knew that the Black Kilt wasn't wounded anymore.

"The enemy fleet?" asked Donald.

"Berthed at Fionnphort."

"That's on the western shore of Mull," said Hamish.

"How long?" asked Donald.

Gawain looked at the light in the western sky. The sun was just below the horizon, but it still lit the underside of distant clouds, making them orange, gold and brilliant yellow.

"With fair winds we can be there in the darkness before dawn."

***

With another change of horses on their planned escape route, Tella and Gath believed that the gap between them and the High Table of Scotland would widen. Sometimes the enemy riders were lost from sight, as the path through the High Glens twisted, and then they would be there again, moving more quickly than riders with tired horses ever could.

The Picts rose up a steep slope, through heather and gorse, following a small stream that sparkled in the high sun. At the top of the slope, the land levelled and became bleak, devoid of grass. Only mosses grew on the sunny sides of huge boulders that crowned the hill. Tella smelled salt and drove his horse between the boulders, and then pulled back on his reins. Gath stopped beside him, panting.

Below them was the Great Sea, a small harbour and the village of Oban, with its white cottages and narrow lanes. A single ship lay at anchor. They rode on without any need to look back; the menacing sound of hooves was now with them. They slowed at the edge of the village, passing a cottage with a model ship on its windowsill, and turning sharply along narrow lanes to pick their way down towards the harbour, and safety. Six Black Kilts sat talking on the harbour wall and leapt up, grabbing spears, as their king came into sight.

"Prepare the ship," ordered Tella.

He and Gath dismounted and ran aboard, and cut the ropes

with their swords. The sail was raised and they drifted away from Oban. Fifty paces from the shore, the High Table rode up to the harbour wall and formed a line, staring at them with hard, determined faces. Gath went to stand beside a sailor at the tiller.

"Is our fleet still at Fionnphort with the Welsh fleet?"

"Our fleet is there under the command of Borak One Hand. The Welsh fleet received orders to return home two days ago."

"When might we arrive?"

The sailor felt the wind on his face and thought about its strength and direction.

"Dawn."

Gath pointed west.

"Take the fastest winds to Fionnphort."

A short while later, the winds turned against them and a Scottish ship sailed past them at speed, bound for Oban. Gath turned to his father.

"Shall we turn and deny the High Table a ship."

Tella stared at the hardened-looking sailor who steered the *Leaping Salmon* so that it ran perfectly before the wind.

"No," he said.

***

In darkness and with the wind on their backs, the fleets of Scotland and Man formed a long line, pinning the sleeping Picts into the natural harbour at Fionnphort. Firelight came through some of the cottage windows and the tops of the enemy masts rocked with each wave. Hamish growled.

"They are trapped on a lee shore."

"A lee what?" asked Robert.

Gawain gave him an impatient smile.

"A strong wind blows off of the Great Sea from the west. It blows across Oban Sound and directly into the mouth of their harbour. Without many oars and strong backs, they are trapped."

"How many ships?" asked Donald.

They peered through the dark at the shadowy outline of the

210

fleet. Hamish counted the masts as they rocked in front of the firelights of the cottages.

"About fifteen."

"So we are stronger than they are," said Gawain.

"Well, let's make it even more of an uneven fight," said Donald.

They talked about his idea and anything that would burn was loaded onto the three captured ships. Tar was poured out of barrels and, as the first rays of sun broke above Mull, they were set on fire and cut free. They watched as the flames grew and the fire-ships drifted into Fionnphort harbour, and as the Pictish ships, closest to the Sound, began to catch fire.

"You'd think someone would notice," said Donald.

A Black Kilt stood up on a deck, yawned and stretched out his arms to welcome the world. He opened his eyes and cried out. Picts leapt up from their decks, confused, grabbing spears, trying to push the fire-ships away. But the wind pinned them to their fleet. Other men grabbed buckets and tied lines to them, and dropped them into the sea, then pulling them up and emptying them onto the flames.

"Shall we go and fight them now?" asked Robert.

"And burn like them? The lee shore would hold us too," said Gawain.

"But they will escape onto Mull."

Gawain spoke in a dark voice.

"But they will not escape back to Deros. We will find a place to land and hunt them down. They must *all* join the fallen."

Donald looked at Hamish.

"Well, I'm not going to argue with him."

One after the other, the enemy ships caught fire and, at full sunrise, a tower of black smoke rose above Fionnphort. The Picts had unloaded weapons and food as quickly as they could and now every inch of the quayside, between the rope-stones, was littered with spears, shields, barrels and boxes.

"Shall we land now?" asked Robert.

Gawain stood up on the rail, holding a sail rope, and pointed his ancient sword at a small beach to the south of the burning fleet.

"We land there." He pointed his sword at two ships. "You stay here to guard Oban Sound."

Aboard the other ships, strong hands raised the sails.

"So the hunt is on," said Hamish.

He watched Gawain's people grab their swords and felt their burning desire for revenge.

"I wouldn't want to be a Pict trapped on Mull," said Donald.

***

With the southern coastline of Mull on their starboard bow, Gath looked back at a single sail. It was light brown, green and ochre, and gaining on them.

"Shall we risk landing?"

Tella snarled.

"We will turn soon into Iona Sound. Let the Scots follow us."

"I cannot make out their faces, but they are twenty in number and without horse. Their ship could not carry all their riders."

"Then we gather the fleet and destroy half of the Younger's High Table."

"Still too many for us to fight now."

They felt the rocking of the deck and the warm westerly breeze on their faces. The helmsman threw the tiller over and they tacked, going further out to sea, but ready for a long run towards Fionnphort with the wind on their port bow. At the same moment, the Scottish ship behind them tacked too. A Black Kilt came over to join them and bowed.

"Smoke on Mull."

They stared at the low, rocky, south westerly tip of Mull, jutting out into the Great Sea like a finger. Calmer waters lay beyond it in the sound and somewhere north of the finger a chimney of black smoke rose up above the rocks.

212

"Good or evil?" asked Gath.

Tella looked back at the bow wave of the enemy ship.

"We have no choice but to find out."

On a strong port tack, they were soon inside Iona Sound, with rocky inlets and the church of Iona on their left, and many ships berthed on a sandy beach to their right. On a high grassy slope, two Scots, one large and one small, chased three Black Kilts. The big one caught hold of a Pict and lifted him above his head. Below the grassy slope was Fionnphort and the charred wrecks of the Mac Mar's fleet, poking out of the shallow waters of the harbour.

Ahead of Tella, two sails were raised.

"The three legs of Man," said Gath. Fear in his voice.

"Gawain, curse him. I should have killed him when he was my prisoner."

Gath shouted at the helmsman.

"Turn back to the open sea."

Tella grabbed the tiller and steered the ship towards Iona.

"Are you blind?"

Gath looked south. The High Table was only ten ship lengths away, gaining in speed and with hard, determined warriors watching them constantly.

"What do we do?" asked Gath.

Tella slapped his face.

"You do whatever I tell you to do."

Tella undid his leather belt from his waist and retied it across his body so that his sword hung down his back. He spoke quickly to the helmsman.

"Drop me close to the Iona shore, then sail south out of the sound. Get to Deros and send every ship left there to collect me. I expect you to return in one moon."

The helmsman bowed.

"Yes, master."

Tella turned to face his son.

"Until I return, you are the Mac Mar."

Gath nodded and tried to control his emotions.

213

"Good fortune, father."

Tella slapped his face again.

"Do not wish me any kind of fortune that you do not mean."

He glanced around at the net that his ship was caught in, ducked down behind the rail and crawled across the deck to the side of the ship furthest away from enemy eyes. In one fast movement, he stood and slipped over the side, with only his fingers showing on the rail. He gasped at the cold of the ocean and twisted his body to see Iona. The helmsman brought the ship to within fifty paces of the shore and Tella's fingers disappeared. Then the tiller was thrown again and their race to the open sea began.

***

Alistair of Cadbol, Ancevo and Kenneth of Blacklock stared at the black sail of Tella's ship.

"Why do they steer for Iona and not go ashore, and then head back towards us?" asked Ancevo.

Kenneth of Blacklock aimed the *Leaping Salmon* directly at the Picts.

"Either they cannot sail, which I do not believe, or they have dropped off a passenger."

***

As Tella's head rose from the water, a black swirling mass of seaweed drifted round it. He looked as if he was wearing a salty, shiny, stinking wig. He stretched his legs out and could not feel the bottom of the inlet and he kicked out towards a rock, the seaweed rising and falling as waves rolled in. He took a deep breath and sank beneath the surface, feeling the numbing cold, and swam. His outstretched hands touched a rock and he lowered his legs, and touched the bottom. His head rose up beneath the seaweed again and he looked across the sound towards Mull.

"Curse the High Table."

Gath's ship must have turned to avoid the Scottish ship, which

214

had smashed into its side. Warriors fought on both decks and two more ships, with three legs on the sails, closed in quickly, weapons held ready to help kill his son.

"Curse them all."

Tella took his chance in the confusion and crawled up and out of the inlet. He sat up, cautiously, on one knee and stared at Iona. There was little cover up the long grassy slope, only a small building, a herd of goats and a fallen cross. He hesitated for a moment, weighing up his chances, and ran up the slope.

***

Kenneth of Blacklock ignored the battle on his deck and kept his eyes fixed upon Iona. A Black Kilt was escaping up towards the church. Could it be the Mac Mar? He shouted out to Alistair and pointed.

"Alistair, the church."

Alistair ducked as a spear flashed past his face and drove his claymore into a Pict's stomach. He followed the line of Kenneth's arm, saw a running man below the church, sheathed his sword and dived overboard.

***

Goats scattered as Tella dashed for cover behind the building. He threw himself behind it and then peered around the wall. The fighting was nearly over and bodies in black plaids were being thrown, with contempt, into the sea. Tella watched as a man swam towards the shore. In no time, he rose out of the waves, shook back his long hair and unsheathed a sword. The Mac Mar unsheathed his own sword and walked down to kill him.

***

Rory, Hugh and Ancevo tipped the last of the enemy overboard and went to stand beside Kenneth. But he didn't notice them, his eyes fixed on Alistair and the Mac Mar, their swords clashing, time and time again.

"Shall we take spears and help?" asked Ancevo.

Kenneth slowly lifted his head and closed his eyes, letting the sunshine warm his skin.

"No. Leave the laddie be. He has waited a long time for this."

***

As their arms tired from the fighting, they stepped away from each other, gasping for air. Alistair stared into Tella's eyes. They were full of hatred for him. After rubbing the sweat off his hands, onto his plaid, he gripped the hilt with both hands and lifted his sword again, to feel the full force of Tella's blade on his. The light iron sang out. Alistair returned the blow and lunged forward, their blades locking together. Alistair felt the side of his face explode as Tella's fist hit him. He jumped back, stunned, but instinctively raised his sword again. *Clang.* His blade held Tella's blade a hand's width away from his face. The Scot spun round, his sword cutting through the air at head height. Tella ducked and punched him in the face again, before running away up the slope.

Alistair shook his head to clear away the pain, spat a tooth out onto the ground and walked after him. He took his time, cautiously peering around each corner of the church and listening out for the sound of heavy breathing, but Alistair only heard the wind, waves and the bleating of goats. He moved to the church door and kicked it open. It flew in and twisted as the top hinge gave way. Inside, was half-light, but compared to the brilliant sunshine outside, it was as dark and silent as a tomb. Alistair reassured himself.

"The Mac Mar must be here, so why hurry?"

Holding his sword upright, ready to take a blow from the shadows, he stepped forward a single pace, totally alert to any sound or movement, but nothing came. Taking just one more step, his eyes began to adjust to the darkness. Still no sound.

"Where are you?" he whispered.

Another step, Alistair's eyes straining to make out the shape of a man. Something moved and he stiffened, the sound of his heart in his ears. Then another sound, but at the back of the church, like a fast tapping. The tapping stopped.

Gripping the hilt of his claymore and the strips of leather wrapped tightly around it, he listened out for anything, trying to think what could make such a noise. Fear rose in his soul and he took a small step back. The darkness seemed to grow at the far end of the church and so he stepped forward, sword held out, his mind searching for the sound he dreaded most. The swishing of a blade as it cut though the air. If that noise came, there was only one thing to do. Duck down, make his body as small as possible, and then strike out at the enemy. If he guessed wrong and Tella aimed his sword low, then the fight would be over. His life would be over. Would Tella aim low? Should he go back and get help? Should he go back and fetch a torch? This was madness.

The quick tapping noise started again and a shape, low to the ground, was moving towards him. The tapping grew even faster and the shape increased in speed. Sweat dripped off Alistair's forehead. Something was coming straight at him.

"It cannot be Tella crawling along the ground. Too fast," he told himself.

The shape veered and Alistair held his nerve. The goat ran past him and out into the sunshine.

Another shape moved off to the right. Again it was small. The leather strips around the hilt became slippery with sweat as he strained to hear any noise. None came. Taking one step to his right, the light from the door grew a little stronger here. Something, someone, was rocking backwards and forwards, the face dark and hidden in a cloak of shadow as she rocked back. Then, as the face came forward, he saw someone he had not seen since Mountjoy. He whispered to her.

"Matina, it is I, Alistair, the man who escorted your mistress to Ireland."

No reply, but something else was slowly moving at the back of the church.

"Matina, get up now. Do not be frightened. Get up now, walk past me and run down to the shore."

No reply and a movement closer to Alistair now. Matina's eyes widened and she pointed at the Mac Mar who was raising his sword. Alistair whirled round and his blade met Tella's. Sparks shot from the light iron as a huge *clang* rang around the church, making Matina jump and another goat bolt, and tap its way out through the twisted door. Tella snarled and drew his fist back to hit Alistair again. Alistair brought his head down onto the Mac Mar's face and immediately pulled his claymore back, ready to strike out. The blow sent Tella reeling backwards into the darkness and Alistair took two steps forward.

"Get out now, Matina," he shouted.

To his side a small shape moved out of the blackness by the side wall. He took another step forward and Tella struck out at him, catching him by surprise, and all he could do was parry blow after blow, praying none would get past his sword and cut him. The church became alive with white sparks and sound. *Clang, clang, clang, clang*, the new iron sang, the enemy's blade shooting out of darkness and wielded by an invisible opponent.

Alistair pretended to weaken and stepped backwards. Tella charged and came into the half-light.

"So that's where you are," said Alistair.

He jumped to one side and drove his sword into Tella's ribs. Tella screamed in pain and lashed out, his sword cutting deep into Alistair's arm. They drew apart, panting, feeling the blood ooze from their bodies. They fought again. *Clang, clang, clang*, but slower now as their strength drained. The sparks grew fewer as the force of each strike waned. Tella broke first and ran down the church towards the altar. Alistair took two steps forward and waited for his eyes to adjust again.

"Where are you?" he whispered.

Gradually, he could make out the large altar, made of wood, not stone, and about one man long and half a man high. A tall iron cross, with a sharp spear-like tip, lay to one side of it. The Mac Mar was sure to be hiding behind the altar.

Alistair listened for the sound of Tella's breathing. Nothing. He stepped forward, glancing from side to side in case he was wrong and a blade came at him from the shadows.

He squatted down and felt the floor, searching with his fingers, for something, anything that he could throw and make a noise. Nothing. He stood and felt for his dirk in his belt. He took it and tossed it onto the floor at one end of the altar. As it landed, he leapt up onto the altar, sword ready to strike a death blow. The dirk clattered loudly, but Tella did not show himself. Strong arms swept Alistair's feet from under him. He lost his sword and fell face down onto the wood. Then Tella was on his back, snarling with rage, holding his victim down and slamming Alistair's head onto the altar. Alistair used every last drop of his strength to twist round under the Mac Mar's great weight and wrapped his hands around Tella's throat. Immediately, Tella's hands went around his throat and they tried to drain the life out of each other, willing the other to die.

At the same moment, their strength left them and they collapsed together, eyes bulging, panting for breath. Tella fell off the altar and Alistair tried to remember where he was, and why he must not let himself fall into unconsciousness. Tella stood and fell back down. He stood again and shook his head. He bent and picked up Alistair's sword and slowly climbed up onto the altar to stand above his enemy. He snarled in triumph and lifted the sword, ready to drive it down into Alistair's stomach.

The snarl, and the wave of fear it brought, kicked Alistair's senses back into action. His eyes opened and he saw the Mac Mar drawing his sword behind his head, ready to strike. He also saw a small shape behind Tella, lifting one end of the long metal cross.

He kicked Tella, hard, in the knee, making him topple back. The Mac Mar tried to hold his balance, pushing his sword out in front of him to stop himself arching backwards. Alistair kicked him hard in the other knee and, at last, he fell back onto the spear-like tip at the top of the cross. The centre of his back arched, in agony, across the horizontal bar of the cross, the spear tip sticking out of his stomach.

Matina held the fine balance, and no matter how much Tella flailed out with his arms and legs, the cross remained upright, blood oozing down its shaft. The flailing became less and the Mac Mar's head drooped back, and he stared into the little girl's eyes, saw that she held the balance of his body on the spear.

Matina felt his warm blood drip down the cross onto her hands. She stared back into his eyes, watched them close and let the cross fall.

CHAPTER ELEVEN

A WHITE SNAKE ON THE DROVER'S ROAD

With each step and with absolutely no memory of how he had destroyed Stirling Castle, a sickening fear grew in Dougie's heart. Maybe Ancevo and the Younger had been wrong? Maybe, Mairi still lived and was now shouting at the boys outside their cottage. He stopped to look at the stand of pines, which marked the edge of his land. Somewhere in those trees was Torik Benn's axe.

Once he had been haunted by the death he had seen on Carn Liath and now he could only think of himself, and how life might be after the loss of his family. Had he also lost something deep inside? Had his intense anger for the enemy driven away the last of his innocence?

He walked on and, as he crossed the stile, a knot tightened in his stomach. The outline of the hills was the same and so were the colours, clumps of bright yellow gorse lighting up the spaces between the grass and heather. It was all still so beautiful, and he sensed the power that came from those hills and imagined them rising up into the air, like giant stone towers. That image had often been in his mind as a child. He knew that Alec had also sensed the power of the hills and even though the twins had exactly the same picture in their minds, they could not imagine any power strong enough to lift mountains.

Dougie put his hand into his leather purse and took out the brooch, Malcolm the Younger had gifted to him, from amongst the oats that surrounded it.

"It was you, wasn't it?"

The stone at the heart of the brooch pulsed blood red.

Dougie sighed. "I wish Alec was here."

The stone pulsed again and far away, aboard a small trading vessel sailing through the warm waters to the south of the land of the Gauls, a descendant of kings became suddenly homesick. Alec of Dunfermline's eyes scanned the sea around his ship and he decided to make one last voyage.

Dougie's eyes scanned the high pastures. No flock. His dark

fears returned and he began to run. Where were his sheep? Inside an Angle's stomach? Slaughtered to feed an army? So much work, tending them, and all gone in a single day. His family taken from him in a single day.

Now he felt betrayed by Myroy. His life had been so happy, safe and complete before marching to Carn Liath. Mairi had chosen him and danced with him, kissed him, during the Gathering at Arngask Farm. He remembered playing in the snow with Calum, Jock and wee Tanny, and walking home with them to enjoy the Winter Feast.

Where were Alistair, Hamish and Donald now, when he needed their friendship most? His mind went back to the Old Toll in Melrose and the death of the orphan boy, Iain. Then more death, on a beach near Stranraer and Robbie's body with an axe buried into his chest. So much death. It was Myroy who had done this to him, and his anger rose.

As the shepherd approached his cottage, all the fears that had haunted him became real. The roof had burned away and the stone walls were torn down. He felt lost and lonely, and emptiness gripped his heart like a vice. Where were the dead bodies of his family? Had they been taken as slaves, or dragged away to the high pastures to be slaughtered, or burned alive inside the cottage? Like a mad thing, Dougie ran around the cottage, searching, his circles becoming larger and larger, and his emptiness growing with each circle. Fifty paces from the charred walls, he picked up a length of rope that Jock and Calum had once fought over. The ground here was rutted by horses and he knelt to look at the tracks of many riders.

Dougie walked over to a broken pot and kicked it. What was the point of living now? To guard a stone and fulfil a promise to the Watcher on the hill? Lost in a nightmare, he stumbled away from the ruin and stood beside a carcass picked clean by crows. A spear pinned Dog's rib cage to the earth and Dougie grabbed it, and angrily threw it away with an incredible power. The spear whistled as it flew above the lower slopes before splashing into the distant loch. He sat down beside the body, consumed by grief and praying that his family had died as quickly as his sheepdog. As his tears came again and his body rocked, dark clouds moved in, tumbling down the hills on the far side of the loch.

As the sun set, the heavens opened and he sat cross-legged, wrapped in his wet plaid, staring, wide-eyed, at Dog's skull. He ate the last of his oats and remembered his friend as a moving bundle beneath the secret rider's shawl, and that he had unkindly thought that the messenger's stomach was too fat for his body until the man had handed him the puppy. Apart from his adventures with the Men of Tain, it was Dog who had been his constant companion on the high pastures; chasing hares, guiding the sheep onto fresh grass and being there whenever he missed Mairi and the children. He hadn't asked for much then, still didn't, but the little he craved for was no longer possible. Maybe it was time for him to move on to fresh pastures?

A far away voice called to him.

"Dougie."

The shepherd looked up from Dog's bones. A figure, a man of Dougie's years, was walking up the lower slopes towards him, waving, smiling and calling again.

"Dougie."

Stewart of Glenbowmond held out his hand, a look of deep concern on his face.

"How are you?"

"Not good."

"Let's sit and talk a while."

They sat.

"Dougie, we have known each other since you came here with Alec and Lissy. If there is anything I can do, please ask."

An awkward silence followed, until Dougie replied.

"Thank you."

"Why not join me at Arngask one evening for friendship. Grant was asking after you."

224

Dougie nodded, but gave his friend no reply. Stewart nodded at the ruined cottage.

"And you can come and stay with me, until things get sorted out here."

"Thank you."

"Then come and stay tonight."

"No. I am staying here."

Another awkward silence.

"Here, I brought you this."

Stewart took a loaf of oat bread from his shawl and handed it to his friend.

"Thank you."

Stewart's face became full of concern and he hesitated as he spoke.

"I … was so sorry to hear about your family."

Dougie snapped.

"Why are you here? To tell me things I already know and grieve over."

Stewart lifted up the palms of his hands.

"I am here because I am your friend."

More silence.

"I do have news," said Stewart, after a while. "Tella the Mac Mar's army is defeated upon the field at Stirling. The Long Peace returns."

"I do not care."

"You must care."

Dougie's voice rose again.

"Do not tell me what I need to care about."

"I am sorry."

"I do not need your sympathy."

"You have it anyway," said Stewart kindly and he stood. "Dougie, if ever you need anything, anything at all, come and see me."

Dougie gave him a small nod and watched his friend walk down to the drover's road. When he was out of sight, the shepherd threw the loaf of bread into the stand of pines, far away. Then he realised what he had done, how he had spoken to a true friend, and he sat back down beside Dog and wept.

Later, Dougie thought about his twin brother and of seeking him out. If he left now, before the winter storms, he could quickly be at the Younger's palace and then aboard a trader sailing out of the mighty Forth. But where then? North towards the homelands of the Norse peoples? South to warmer waters to places that the shepherd had only heard about in stories? Suddenly, Dougie felt trapped. He couldn't stay here with so many memories. Memories on every hillside and in every house stone. He couldn't leave either, with no chance of finding Alec in the vastness of the oceans. He sighed.

"I have nowhere to go."

Now he felt as though he had lost everything and that another moment of life was just too much to bear. He took his dirk from his belt and looked at its sharp point. His voice became weak and feeble.

"Maybe it is time to move on and be with Mairi."

He placed the dirk to his heart and rolled onto his stomach, holding his body up with his arms, with the blade between his chest and the ground.

"I love you, Mairi," he said, letting his arms relax.

Inside his leather purse, Amera's stone pulsed, blood red, and the shepherd's body rose up to hover above the dirk, which fell gently on its side. Then Dougie was gently lowered back to earth, with the feeling of warm, caring hands holding him, like a mother cradling her baby.

He sat there until darkness came, wondering why this stone, this power, had saved him. Did it care for him? Did it need him for some reason, some secret purpose that he could not understand? Was it trying to tell him something? Was the thin fur clad-man, to whom he had gifted the brooch in Berwick Castle, trying to talk to him? Dougie felt confused and useless, and his loneliness returned. So did his hunger and he untied his purse from his belt, released the string around the top and looked inside. Oats appeared from nowhere around the stone and the purse was full again, overflowing with magic food.

"Thank you."

The oats stopped pouring out and Dougie ate whilst peering into the heart of the ruby, half expecting to see faces, or the silky shadows of spirits, but there was only the round, distorted reflection of his own face. He yawned, his energy consumed by his grief for the loss of his family. The dark clouds returned and the fine, gentle rain turned into a torrent. The shepherd wrapped himself up into his plaid. His breathing became shallow and as sleep began to take him, he mumbled the words that were most on his mind.

"I wish I could talk to Alec."

The purse beside him pulsed again and translucent red flames rose up around Dog's bones. The flames danced, grew fierce, then subsided to become flickering fingers pointing up from a small circular fire. Dog's skull rose first, as though lifted by the heat of the flames. The skull twisted and spiralled down, before slowing to a stop just above the circular fire and then rising again with the rib cage following. Then the other bones rose up so that all of Dog's skeletal parts silently danced in a spiral, up and down.

Half visible, half invisible, Alec's body appeared on the other side of the dance to Dougie, who opened an eye and sat bolt upright, startled. Staring at his twin through the red flames and dancing bones, his words were full of fear.

"Alec. Is that you?"

"Aye, it is."

"Why are you here?"

Alec smiled in a kind way.

"You called me and your call was full of loneliness."

"I have lost everything."

"Everything?"

"My flock, my home, my family."

"Lissy? Is she taken from us?"

Dougie's eyes became heavy.

"Aye, but a long time ago, just after you left us to find adventure on the Great Sea."

Alec put his head in his hands.

"And I never had the chance to say a last goodbye," he whispered.

"She loved you. Loved us both. I found it hard to live alone for the two summers before I met Mairi."

"But you lived through the loneliness."

"Aye."

"Where does Lissy rest?"

"Under a stone cairn, up on the high pastures. It's a peaceful place."

"And powerful."

Dougie managed a weak smile.

"And powerful, but I still do not know why we think that."

"But if Lissy's passing was long ago, why do you grieve now?"

"The Angles marched north and took our lands, and killed my family. The Younger's messenger, Ancevo, told me."

"You received a message from a king?"

Dougie shuffled his feet and spoke in a hesitant voice.

"I am a member of the High Table."

"No?"

"Aye."

"Well, brother, it sounds as though you have had the adventures I left home to find."

"Aye, but I didn't want them. Things ..."

"Don't say it. Things just seem to happen to you."

"You can still finish what I am about to say."

"Isn't that what twins do?"

"Alec, did you have any adventures? Did you find what you were looking for?"

"I was nearly killed on a beach on Skye, when we dropped a

passenger ashore. Black Kilts rode at us and we pushed our ship away. Spears missed me, but killed the ship's master."

"Why do you sound surprised? The Picts have been at war with us since the ending of the Long Peace."

Alec's forehead creased.

"We were in their pay and Denbara is one of their best scribes. We expected a feast after our long journey around the Scottish kingdom, not danger."

"You sailed all the way around?"

"Aye. From Berwick in the east, to Anglesey in the west."

"Anglesey?"

"An island held by the Welsh peoples."

Something stirred in Dougie's memory and then left him again, the destruction of Stirling castle hidden, deep down.

"You mentioned a man named Denbara. I have heard that name spoken."

"It took two summers for Denbara to complete his work."

"His map."

"I never saw it, but he always wrote things down. Place names, the length of rivers and the size of islands. How do you know of his work?"

"It's a long story."

The bones between them continued to dance and spiral in the glow of the flames. Alec and Dougie stared at each other, their faces identical in every way in the red glow, except for Alec's darker brown skin. After a while, Alec broke the silence.

"Did you ever learn anything about our parents?"

Dougie shook his head.

"No, not a thing. No one around the loch knew about them and I guessed we must have been brought here by Lissy after the fever claimed them."

Alec smiled.

"You never know, we might be descended from kings."

Dougie smiled too.

"I hope not."

"You said that you lost your family."

Dougie's smile disappeared.

"I met a girl. A beautiful girl, at the Gathering at Arngask Farm. She kissed me and that was that. Did you ever find love?"

"I wasn't looking."

"Neither was I."

"I was too busy seeking out the wider world."

"Have you seen some wonderful places?"

"Aye."

"And will you always travel upon the sea."

"No."

"So you will come home."

"Aye. I felt terribly homesick yesterday. Just took hold of me."

"Make it soon, Alec."

"I will make it soon. It sounds as though we need to stand together to fight the Black Kilts."

"The Mac Mar's army was defeated at Stirling and the word is we now have a chance of peace if the High Table remains united."

"Will it stay united?"

"I don't care."

"You must care. We prospered during the Long Peace. Many families prospered."

"I don't care."

"You must care."

Dougie's eyes flashed with anger and Alec sat back.

"Dougie, I have never seen you look at me like that before."

"A lot has changed since you left us."

"They are hard words for a brother to hear."

The shepherd put his face in his hands and spoke through his fingers.

"I'm sorry. I am just not the same anymore."

A warming sun rose above the far hills and long shadows

crept across the slopes by the ruined cottage. Dougie took his hands from his face and found himself alone, and repeating the words he had spoken in his dream.

"I am just not the same anymore. I am just not the same anymore."

He shook his head to drive the last of the sleep away and stood to wrap his plaid around his waist, before throwing the last of the cloth over his shoulder. He stared at Dog's bones. They were just the same as they had been at dusk. He glanced up at the high pastures and saw fresh flowers placed upon Lissy's grave. He thought about the Watcher and screamed out in anger.

"You did this to me!"

Dougie ran up to the cairn and searched around it, but it was deserted. He grabbed the flowers and tore them to pieces, before falling to his knees and sobbing.

"You did this to me. If I had not been sent away I could have been here and saved my family."

No one answered his tearful words.

"You did this to me."

Silence calmed him and he finally stood, wavered on his feet, turned and walked back down the hill. Behind him, the top of the cairn shimmered, like moonlight on water, and Myroy rose up to stand upon the stones. His ancient face was lined with concern for the first Keeper, but now this part of the story could come to an end. Without speaking, he disappeared back into the earth to complete a journey that was long overdue.

Dougie went back to the shelter of his cottage walls, wrapped his plaid around his body, and shut out the morning sun and the wider world.

Next morning, Dougie sat in sunshine, waiting for his clothes to dry and ate oats that appeared from nowhere in his leather purse. Later, he placed small stones above Dog's bones to make a low cairn.

"Rest now."

He turned his back on the cairn and looked at the bigger

stones that had once held up the roof of his cottage. He sighed.

"Well, what else is there to do?"

Dougie picked up a stone and carried it to the low front wall, and smashed it down with a *thud*. He carried another and imagined himself smashing it down onto an Angle's head with the same sickening *thud*. Stone after stone after stone, he lifted and added to the wall, and each time he vented his anger onto the faces of enemies he did not know. By high sun, his cottage began to look like a cottage again, with walls shoulder height and a neat space left for the door. He stepped back to look at the result of his labour. It was more like the home he had loved and he charged at it, wildly lifting stones and throwing them away, tearing the walls down as though they were his enemy too. When the cottage was returned to a ruin, he sat down and cried again.

After a time, hunger pains came and, instinctively, he placed a hand into his purse. It became full of oats again, surrounding the Younger's brooch. Was this more of the stone's power? This stone had caused nothing but misery. Before he had first spoken to the Watcher, his life had been so happy, working simply on the high pastures to nature's routine.

He had been happy as a father then too. Dougie stared at the blue waters of the loch and took Amera's stone from his purse. It was beautiful, powerful and, as he looked into the depths of the ruby, his anger became intense, unbearable. Remembering the spear, he drew his arm behind his head and threw the stone at the loch. It flashed red, as it arched upwards, then downwards, always flashing, before a tiny splash appeared in the centre of the loch. The waters here bubbled and white foam erupted, and a huge bird-like figure rose up, mighty wings flapping. Dougie's skin itched as the air around him became heavy, like the air which signals an approaching storm. The osprey rose high into the sky and then dived at an incredible speed to guard Amera's stone. As the waters calmed, the shepherd's anger calmed too, but he was left feeling utterly lonely.

He thought about bouncing his golden haired daughter up and down on his knee and remembered her eyes. Those eyes had a wee bit of him in them and a bit of her mother too, but most of all they had sparkled with something precious and unique to Tanny herself. Once he had tried to guess if one day she might wear the Younger's brooch and now he knew the answer.

He went over to a large stone, lifted it and *thudded* it down onto the base of the wall. As Dougie rebuilt his cottage, killing Angles in his mind, a bright afternoon sun came out from behind a cloud and warmed him. The waters of the loch changed from slate grey to blue and, somewhere above him a skylark sang out beautifully to its family.

Suddenly, the shepherd's forehead creased. The drover's road below him seemed to be white and moving. He wiped his tears away and looked again. Something *was* moving slowly along the path, like a white snake.

"What's that?" he whispered.

The white snake's head appeared to stop, then fan out in all directions across the lower pastures and Dougie's mouth fell open as hundreds of sheep walked up across the grass towards him. Three riders, one small, one huge and one with long hair, left the road to drive the flock before them. Two sheepdogs ran excitedly around their Highlands and barked excitedly at the prospect of finding a new home. Still open-mouthed, frozen to the spot, Dougie waited for his friends to join him.

"Greetings, Dougie," said Alistair. "I bring you a gift from the Younger. He told me that this flock is from the land of the Welsh and three hundred strong. The sheepdogs who tend it are the finest in his kingdom."

The black and white dogs cautiously walked towards the shepherd and he knelt to tickle their ears. One jumped up onto his knees and licked his face. Hamish looked at the cottage.

"And you might like a bit of a *hand* putting the roof on, laddie."

Donald grinned. "Och, don't listen to him. He keeps putting the door in the wrong place."

Alistair dismounted and hugged Dougie.

"We cannot stay long, but we had to be here when you most needed us."

Dougie looked sad.

"And, by the way, we chased Tella west from Stirling across the sea to Iona. Wee Matina killed him, and saved me."

"Matina killed the Mac Mar?"

"She really did."

Hamish's stomach rumbled.

"I have no food to offer, not even broth," said Dougie, apologetically.

Alistair smiled and pointed at the sheep.

"I'd say you were surrounded by food."

Donald jumped down off his Highland.

"Wise words, but don't mention food, or Hamish will never get the roof on."

Inside the cottage walls, the floor began to shimmer like moonlight on water and Myroy rose up with his arms held tightly around Mairi and Tanny. They ran to Dougie and threw their arms around him, kissing his face. Then Myroy went back into the Earth, to reappear quickly with Jock and Calum.

"What a bloomin` adventure we've had," said Jock, picking up a piece of rope and waving it in his brother's face.

Dougie hugged his family and burst into tears again. Alistair watched them for a while and then his eyes fixed on Myroy. The Ancient One could be so cold sometimes. He could have reunited them days ago and had chosen not to. He had waited for the anger he needed to be inside the Keeper's heart to grow.

It was a terrible price for Myroy and Dougie to pay, and he felt a deep sadness for them both. But this was an eternal war and it could not be fought with the ways of the warrior and, one day, a stone Keeper *would* stand before Odin. That anger might just be enough to secure victory, and Alistair of Tain prayed that it would not be this shepherd who fought the final battle. They weren't ready yet, anyway. The Realm of the Dead held few warriors and had not been strengthened by generations of Keepers. Dougie was just the first and, given time, given enough time, they would grow in number and power.

These thoughts disappeared as he again shared in Dougie's joy. Beside him, the Men of Tain remained silent and awkward, until Myroy walked back to the cottage to go forward in time. Alistair winked at Hamish.

"You know, young Dougie. Does this not remind you of Donald?" growled the big man.

Dougie kept crying, hugging Tanny now.

"Aye, a giant wolf went to Donald's cottage and knocked on the door."

Jock and Calum smiled as they listened to the new story.

"Donald let him in and asked the giant wolf what he wanted, and the wolf says, "I want a ………………………………….. heather ale." And Donald says, "Why the big pause?" and the wolf stands on his back legs and holds out his front legs and says, "I've always had them.""

Jock and Calum groaned, and Donald didn't jump on Hamish. They just stood, embarrassed, as Dougie kissed Mairi.

"Will you tell me where you have been?" asked Dougie.

"Into the darkness, below the ground."

"And how did you escape the Angles?"

"Myroy rescued us."

"And you are really here?"

"We are all here, Dougie."

"You are here?"

"We are all here, now, with you."

"You are here?"

Mairi took hold of Dougie's head and kissed his eyes.

"We really are."

A huge shadow fell over them.

"Come on," growled Hamish. "Let's get the roof on."

CHAPTER TWELVE

A NORMAL DAY IN SCOTLAND

As Myroy stopped speaking and Peter's mind was released from the story, the numbers on the alarm clock clicked forward. 02:16. Every hurt and sadness felt by Dougie had tortured Peter and he remembered the look on Myroy's face as the shepherd had charged at Stirling Castle.

"It wasn't easy for you, was it."

"It was never easy, never."

"Every Keeper?"

"Every Keeper was tested and anger forced into their hearts."

"Does it ever leave them? Does it ever get less?"

The Ancient One's silence gave Peter the answer he did not want to hear. He thought about the story, about the face in the waterfall and how close Odin had been to holding the stone. Peter picked up Amera's stone, stared into the heart of the ruby and laid it down, carefully, on the bed.

"I didn't quite believe it at first, that Kylie really lives. But Odin did destroy Thorfinn Firebrand, as a Valkyrie, by the pool. Thorgood heard his grandfather's screams and, if Thorfinn died one thousand three hundred years ago, then he could not have been on the *Maid Of Norway*. That story was just not real."

Myroy nodded, slowly.

"But the *Maid Of Norway*, the *Black Slug* and the Computer Aided Rifle's, in the Seekers' hands, do exist. Learn from them."

The Ancient One stood, walked to the centre of the bedroom and waved his staff around in a circle.

"But what about Seamus at Deros?" asked Peter, quickly.

Myroy smiled and tossed Peter a pebble, about the same size as the ruby.

"You do not need the pebble you picked up in your garden. Keep this one safe. This is the last part of the story that I shall tell you. My work now lies elsewhere."

"Does he rescue Margaret from Borak One Hand? Does Alec

of Dunfermline return from his adventures? Does the Younger establish a new Long Peace?"

But Myroy had disappeared down into the earth and his words trailed after him.

"If you seek answers, Peter of the line of Donald, I suggest you go and read another book, and wait for your guardian to help you."

After four hours of broken and troubled sleep, Peter's alarm went off, and he sat up and placed his feet on the floor. He looked at Amera's stone.

"Did you feed Dougie with oats?"

The stone pulsed, blood red, and he picked it up and went to clean his teeth. In front of the mirror, Peter stopped brushing.

"And you can raise mountains into the sky?"

Another pulse and Peter brushed some more.

"I don't get it," he said with his toothbrush in his mouth.

No pulse.

"And who is my guardian?"

No pulse and Peter took his brush out of his mouth.

"One pulse. Is that 'Yes'?"

One red pulse.

"Yes?"

One pulse.

"Does Odin know where I am?"

No pulse.

"Well, that's something."

Peter looked up at the ceiling.

"Grandpa."

A deep voice boomed out.

"Aye, Laddie."

"You never told me the stone can, well, kind of talk."

"There are lots of things I haven't told you and for good reason. Now, go to school."

***

Julie Donald placed three plastic food containers onto a work-top, unloaded the fridge and talked to herself, as she tried to make sure the right things went into the right containers.

"OK, a carton of apple for Peter, pineapple for James and orange for Laura. A banana for everyone except James, a sandwich for everyone."

She put a sandwich in each lunchbox and got some crisps.

"Cheese and onion for James, salt and vinegar for Laura and Peter eats anything, so he can have the last of the Mini Cheddars."

James came in, yawning, looking like he had slept on a park bench.

"Why does Peter always get the Mini Cheddars?"

Julie sighed.

"You told me cheese and onion are your favourite."

"I want the Cheddars."

Julie swapped the crisps for the Cheddars.

"Happy now?"

"Why are we having packed lunches all of a sudden anyway?"

"Because money is a bit tight at the moment."

"Can I have some money for a chippy?"

"No."

James opened the fridge door, took out some pineapple juice and slammed the door shut.

"Don't slam the door, please, James. You'll break it."

James poured out his juice and most of it went over the work-surface.

"James!"

Laura came in, her long golden hair tied up in a towel. James grinned.

"That is so not a good look."

"Will you and Mum stop arguing all the bloomin` time." She saw the lunchboxes. "I don't want another packed lunch. Why can't we have money for a chippy?"

"One reason we are short of money is because we are saving

up to send you on a school trip, remember?"

"Why do I have to have a bloody packed lunch, when we are saving for Laura. Just make her have them and cut her allowance."

Julie folded her arms.

"Don't say, 'Bloody'."

Peter came in, kissed his mother, poured himself some muesli and put his lunchbox into his Berghaus rucksack.

"Thanks, Mum."

Laura's mobile rang, the ring-tone of someone being sick.

"Hi, Abby."

"Can you *please* change that ring-tone," said Julie.

Laura ignored her and put a *Pop Tart* into the toaster, and turned its dial to, "Full Toast."

"She's had a boy. OK, we'll make a card after biology. Has Miss Grenoski picked a name? Rooney! Rooney Grenoski, you are joking? OK, bye. See you on the bus."

"Why does she always have to call at breakfast?" asked James. "They talk all the time on the bus, anyway."

"Get lost, dipstick."

Laura's mobile was sick again.

"Hi, Abby."

"Laura, *please, please* change that ring-tone," said Julie.

Colin Donald came in and, in his mind, compared Peter's neat uniform with James's. James's shirt looked like he had played rugby in it and his tie was in shreds.

"The bus will be here in five."

James poured his pineapple juice onto a bowl of cocoa pops, ate three mouthfuls and decided he didn't like it.

Laura replied to Abby on her phone.

"OK."

"Peter," said Colin. "It's the end of term on Friday and Grandma has invited you to go up and stay. I can book a cheap flight for Saturday morning."

"Why hasn't she invited me?" asked James.

241

"I thought you wanted your friends around for a sleepover at the weekend," said Julie.

Laura broke off from her phone call.

"Can I have a sleepover too?"

"The weekend after next," said Julie.

Laura went back to speaking to Abby.

"OK."

Peter thought about his girlfriend.

"I don't want to go without Kylie."

"Well, why don't you talk to her. Grandma won't mind her going with you, even though she has another guest."

"Another guest?" asked Julie.

"OK," said Laura.

"Bernard has flown over from Corfu. I think they are getting on very well, those two."

Peter wondered if Bernard would tell him about Grandpa's adventure on Corfu.

"I'll speak to Kylie," he said.

"OK," said Laura and she turned her phone off.

"Was that, 'OK'?" asked James.

"Time for the bus," said Julie.

Colin smiled.

"See you tonight, my chickens."

As the kids collected their lunch-boxes and left the kitchen, Julie called after Laura.

"Laura."

"Chip money?" she asked, hopefully.

"No."

"I've got my bloomin' packed lunch."

"Towel."

"Don't need a towel."

Julie pointed at her head.

"Still not a good look," said James.

Laura took the towel off and threw it onto the hall floor.

"And you are *still* a dipstick."

She slammed the front door behind her and the fridge door fell off. Julie and Colin heard a glugging noise and turned to see a pool of milk growing on the floor. A black, smoking *Pop Tart* popped up out of the toaster and Colin Donald's mobile went off. The ring-tone of someone being sick.

"I think you had better go to work," said Julie.

***

Mr Denver took the bend into New Hope Drive too quickly and Peter and Kylie swayed.

"He's in a hurry again," said Kylie.

"Sure is. Hey, would you like to come to Scotland with me at the weekend? Grandma has invited me up."

"I would need to ask Mum and Dad."

"Could you ask them tonight?"

"Why the rush?"

The school bus lurched again and Peter held her hand.

"Dad always says that the flights are cheaper if you book them early."

On the back seats, Mac and Toady lit cigarettes.

Peter sighed.

"Would you excuse me for a moment."

Kylie squeezed his hand.

"Please don't say anything."

Peter walked to the back of the bus and pointed at a sign.

"This bus is no smoking."

Mac and Toady stubbed their cigarettes out and Peter went back to his seat.

"I'm going to get him," hissed Mac.

***

Colin Donald sat at his desk in the Upside Down Marketing office in Curzon Street, London. He clicked onto Google and typed in this month's address –

243

A purple screen appeared with five options –

Beginners' Crossword
Advanced Crossword
Word Association Test
Your Number's Up
Pot Luck Quiz

He clicked on the advanced crossword and looked for his call-sign, "Thirteen down."

"*Dark plaid (4, 5).* George has given me an easy one today."

He locked, "Black Kilt," into his mind and looked at the clue for, "Two across," Holly's emergency call-sign, and read it out.

"*The fish are jumping in Scotland.* Seven and six letters."

He sat back in his chair, sipped his coffee and tried to work it out.

"That's not easy, George."

The speakers of his computer *pinged*, which meant he had ten minutes to get to the basement car park. He gulped his coffee and picked up a pebble from the desk.

Colin waited, checking in the mirror above the Pay and Display ticket machine. When he was sure no one was around, he pushed the button marked, "Receipt?" The machine clicked and he placed his pebble into the receipt tray, which glowed red for two seconds. He took his pebble back and collected the ticket that popped out of a slot. He walked to the car park lift, called it, entered and put the ticket into a slot at the top of the panel, that no one else would even notice. The lift descended quickly, far below ground level, and he stepped out onto a well-lit underground platform. A neon sign on the curved wall opposite him read –

30 SECONDS

and the rush of air, from down the tunnel, told him he didn't have long to wait. He wondered how the Keepers had ordered the construction of a secret underground line, under the busy London streets, without the press or the public ever finding out. He smiled.

"As Bernard would say, it's all in the planning."

Sparks signalled the arrival of the train and it glided to a halt, the doors on its three carriages opened and he stepped inside. It still had that new smell, with a hint of expensive ladies perfume, which meant Holly had caught her normal train. He sat next to her, ignoring the glances of the other passengers.

"Morning, Miss Holly."

Holly Anderson closed her laptop and smiled a big smile.

"Morning, Mr Colin."

They waited for the first security check. A powerful looking man, with a ticket machine hung around his neck, walked down the carriage and towered above them.

"Tickets please."

They handed him their tickets and he put them into his pocket. Colin handed him his pebble.

"Morning, Mr George. An easy one today."

George put the pebble into his ticket machine, which glowed red.

"An easy one? I got stuck on today's crossword."

"What were you stuck on?" asked Colin, even though he knew the answer.

"Thirteen Down."

"It was *Black Kilt*."

George gave him back his pebble and took Holly's.

"And there was a tough clue about fish jumping in Scotland."

"*Leaping Salmon* does it for me," said Holly.

He gave her back her pebble.

"Well, your tickets seem to be in order. Enjoy your day."

"Thank you, George," they automatically said together.

After ten minutes, their tube emerged from darkness and stopped on a long, bright, deserted platform, five hundred metres below the MI5 Building at Vauxhall. TV cameras, set into the roof, followed the passengers as they left the train and computers checked their faces against the Human Resources databank.

"Are you in the ten o'clock update meeting?" asked Holly.

"Sure," said Colin.

"It all seems a bit rushed at the moment."

Colin smiled.

"And when was it any different?"

"But it does feel as though things are getting a little difficult."

"I was thinking the same thing."

They walked down a long corridor, with bare walls and more cameras in the roof, and joined a queue for the body scanner. A lady in jeans stepped inside the scanner cubicle, placed her pebble in a bowl and the cubicle glowed red. Then she collected her pebble and walked out into the smart offices on the other side of the wall. The queue stepped forward and Holly thought about the Mir Space Station project.

"Any news from our high-flying friends?"

"Yes. There is a bit of a concern around security."

She nodded and they stepped forward again.

"Oh, dear," said Holly, in a sympathetic voice.

"One of our friends told me that not everyone on the project was behaving as they should."

"Oh, dear."

Five minutes later, they were sitting with large cups of coffee at a huge oval desk on floor *Lower Level Five*. A huge photograph of the face of the full moon covered a wall at one end of the office. Bernard opened the meeting as he normally did.

"I just wanted to say what a pleasure it is to be back in London and to see you all again."

The six delegates sat up and reached out to place their pebbles into a bowl in the centre of the desk. Bernard continued his introduction.

"Please refer to the agenda in front of you."

Colin thought that Bernard was looking well for his age.

Tanned and immaculately dressed in a dark blue suit, white shirt and a tie with a small World War Two jeep on it. He smiled at the tie.

"Is something amusing you, Colin?"

"Oh, er, no, Bernard. I was just reminded of something I heard about in a story."

Everyone around the table smiled and that meant the formality, the need for secrecy, was over.

"We have some important points to cover."

Colin and Holly picked up the single sheet of A4 paper that had been placed in front of them. It read -

SKEPERE WEEKLY UPDATE
Protection of the Keeper.
Mir Project Update.
Arms Movements North.
Operation Cuckoo.
Any Other Business?

A large screen came down out of the ceiling to cover the moon. The first agenda point, "Protection of the Keeper," had a traffic light beside it. Bernard took a sip of coffee and spoke in his efficient voice.

"Point one."

The yellow traffic light came on and flashed.

"As you all know, since 2003 we have laid a false trail to make Odin believe that the Keeper is hidden in North America. The Seekers have placed nearly all of the Donald clan over there under twenty-four hour surveillance and, if they have not reached a conclusion by now, then they soon will. Their search will widen and may return to Europe. Holly, do you have an update?"

"There are approximately fourteen thousand Seekers in the USA under the command of Thorgood Firebrand. He is no fool and is thinking about redeploying half of his people to search in

Scotland, the homeland of the clan. If he moves quickly, Peter may be in danger when he visits his Grandmother."

"Recommendations?"

"We know they watch what we do. Another subtle diversion might be in order."

"What have you got in mind?"

"Two days ago, the enemy tried to kidnap Senator Dan Donald Junior of Denver Colorado. Blue squad under Jet Morrison stopped the attempt and it proves Thorgood has some reason to suspect the Senator. If he was to disappear for no reason, say on an eight-week safari in West Africa, we could leave behind a believable trail for them to follow. Could keep them out of our hair, for a short while at least. Still think we should think of something better, though."

Bernard nodded.

"Our people in Africa run an efficient operation. Please proceed, Holly. Point two."

On the screen, the traffic light moved down beside, "Mir Project Update," and turned yellow.

"The project has been green for months. Why the change in status? Colin."

"Just a suspicion. Some important components for the new stone tracking device have gone missing."

"Mislaid or missing?" asked Holly.

"Commander Gregoriev has ordered two searches, so not mislaid."

"Any delays?" asked Bernard.

"The components are hand-made. Six months."

"Do we have a Seeker onboard?"

"Too early to say, but we will keep an eye on things."

"Point three."

At Bernard's command, the traffic light moved next to, "Arms Movements North," and flashed green.

"Better news then, Aiden."

A young, scruffy man with an Irish accent smiled. Colin

thought he looked more like an artist than a member of MI5's SKEPERE team.

"No arms companies have relocated north into the hemisphere centred on Oslo. In the same time, we have opened new factories that can be switched over to arms production at short notice. They are in South Africa and Australia. The balance of power is now roughly equal."

"Point four."

Another green light.

"Interesting," said Bernard. "Operation Cuckoo has taken years to plan and we are now ready to put a spy into Odin's inner chamber."

The agenda on the screen was replaced by live television pictures of the embankment in front of the MI5 Building. A young boy skipped along beside the Thames and then he simply vanished.

"Tirani will report back when he is able."

"Will Odin recognise his brother?" asked Aiden.

"Myroy doesn't think so," said Colin. "They haven't seen each other since the end of the last ice age."

"But Odin can look into your mind."

Bernard stood and stretched his back.

"Tirani can look after himself. Point five."

The agenda returned to the screen and this time no traffic light.

"A.O.B. Anything else you want to raise?"

No one said anything.

"Very good. Meeting over. Keep me informed of any important developments."

As the screen rose to reveal the moon, everyone, except Colin and Bernard, filed out of the meeting room.

"Will you get back to Scotland before Peter arrives?" asked Colin.

"My flight's in an hour. I will be there well before he arrives. Thought I might pick him up from the airport."

"It's getting harder, isn't it?"

"It is."

"The Seekers are growing in number, getting quicker at spotting our false trails, using better technology to eliminate people from their search."

Bernard nodded.

"They are."

"So it is just a matter of time."

Bernard went to stand in front of the Gora moon.

"Peter will be the last Keeper. I am sure of it."

Colin walked over from the desk to join Bernard in front of the photograph.

"We will need to evacuate our people from London."

"From the whole of Europe."

"Can we do it?"

Bernard nodded.

"The plans are in place."

"Where would we go?"

"Anywhere not under the influence of Amera's stone. I thought I might go to New Zealand."

"What about our headquarters on Corfu? That's why you chose to live there."

"Because there is a risk. The Seekers have never found out about the Realm of the Dead, but it will be inside the red hemisphere."

Colin stared at the craters, shadows and dust deserts on the face of the moon.

"You found it, didn't you?"

"With the help of a pebble, during the war."

***

"Who is going to meet us in Edinburgh?" asked Kylie.

Peter heard the engines roar and they were forced back into their seats. He placed his hand on hers.

"Bernard, an old friend of the family. He lives on Corfu and was in the army with my grandfather. Last time I saw him he had this really cool car with seatbelts that move out to you when you sit down."

Then he wondered if he had actually met Bernard, or just experienced him at Grandpa's funeral. But Grandpa was dead and so he must have. He felt confused as he tried to work out which parts of his life were real, or part of an Ancient One's story.

"Something on your mind?" asked Kylie.

"Yep. I need to tell you something. Something that happened to me, but I can't do it here. Remind me to tell you about a story I heard, when we are out walking on the hills."

"OK. A walk on the hills sounds good."

"It is so beautiful up on the high pastures, and there are some standing stones, a waterfall and a cairn I need to show you."

"Cool."

"By the way, don't expect much excitement. Things are a bit slow in the village. Everything, is, well, so normal."

"I like the sound of, 'Normal.'"

"Kylie, How did your maths test go?"

"OK. How about your physics?"

Peter remembered deliberately messing up three questions so he didn't get top marks. Being able to remember everything you read and the attention it brought, had a price.

"OK."

"Oh, come on. You get top marks in everything."

"Not anymore. I'm finding my studies hard at the moment," he lied.

A nagging doubt ate at his mind and he stared out of the window. There was his father, waving out of his car's sunroof. Peter's stomach tied up in knots as he remembered the bomb that had blown his family up into the sky.

"Your hands are sweating," said Kylie. "Flying is very safe these days."

But he didn't hear her and his eyes never left his father until he was lost from view. He let out a long breath and came back to the reality of the EasyJet cabin.

"Aren't Mac and Toady a pain." Kylie smiled at him. "I was proud of you on the bus. Not many people stand up to them."

"I was angry at the way they bully us."

"Angry? I've seen that in you a few times lately and it really isn't like you. Has something happened?"

There was a pause as Peter thought about his answer.

"I'll tell you everything when we are up on the hills."

Kylie sensed that he didn't want to talk about Mac and Toady, and changed the subject.

"You said you were looking forward to your history lesson. Why do you like boring subjects like that, anyway?"

Peter smiled.

"To understand the future you must understand the past."

"Hmmm."

"And Mr Smith told us that no one knows why the Picts, as a people, disappeared."

"A whole people disappeared. Why?"

Peter thought about the slaughter at Stirling Castle.

"Apparently, no one knows."

They watched a pretty lady in an orange uniform get her trolley ready at the front of the plane.

"Fancy something to eat? I'm starving," said Peter.

***

"Great to see you again, Peter, and this must be Kylie."

Bernard shook Peter's hand and kissed Kylie on the cheek.

"I've got a hire car, so follow me. We're in the Short-Term car park."

They stepped out of the Arrivals Hall into brilliant morning sunshine.

"What time did you two have to get up?"

Peter smiled in the sunshine.

"It was an early start, right enough. Dad got me up at six."

"I was up at five. Really excited about coming up to Scotland," said Kylie.

"First time?" asked Bernard.

"First time."

Bernard pointed his keys at a big Mercedes. The car lights flashed and its alarm pinged.

"Well, you two have got the whole day to do whatever you like." He smiled at Peter. "Your grandmother and I are going to get some supplies in. She says you can eat for Pinner."

Peter looked at his girlfriend.

"Fancy a walk up to the waterfall?"

"Love to."

The front passenger door opened and Grandma climbed out, threw her arms around Peter and gave him a tight, warm hug. Her hair smelled of apples.

"But you never come to meet us."

She released him, kissed his face and gave Bernard a cheeky grin.

"Thought I might try something new."

Grandma repeated the bear hug on Kylie.

"Welcome to Scotland," she said.

They crossed the Forth Road Bridge and met little traffic on the motorway north. After fifteen minutes, Bernard turned off and soon they were driving along a winding country road with Loch Leven off to their left, framed by wonderful hills. Kylie pointed at an island in the loch.

"What's it called?"

"That's Saint Serf's. Used to be a monastery on it, years ago," said Grandma. "What are you two going to do when Bernard and I go shopping?"

"Peter says we should go for a walk up to the waterfall."

"Good choice." Grandma swivelled round in her seat to speak to Peter. "Better take a coat. You never know."

Kylie looked out of the car window at the clear blue sky and the hillsides bathed in sunshine.

Peter smiled.

"You never know."

"Do you want me to make you up a wee packed lunch?"

"Luckily, there is nothing *wee* about your packed lunches."

Grandma placed her hand onto Bernard's hand, on the steering wheel.

"Or the appetite of my men."

A deep voice boomed down from above the car roof.

"Stop that, Maggie."

Maggie sighed and Bernard smiled. He glanced in the mirror at Kylie's astonished face.

"Duncan's been like that since I arrived. Just ignore him."

The booming voice again.

"You won't be able to ignore me if you keep seeing my wife."

Grandma cut in.

"But you are dead, dear. I'm a widow."

"I'm not bloody dead."

"But we buried you." She placed her hand back onto Bernard's. "We sang *There is a Green Hill Far Away*."

Kylie's jaw dropped, her face full of horror. She stared at Peter who looked uncomfortable.

"Is it a trick?"

"Er, no."

"Is it a ghost?"

"No. It's a dead Stone Keeper. Don't worry, I'll tell you about it later."

Maggie hit the roof with the back of her hand.

"You are really getting on my nerves today, Duncan. I was in the bath this morning and you started talking to me. I've got to be allowed some privacy."

"We didn't bother with privacy when we were married."

"But, you're dead, dear."

"I'm not dead. I'm just in the Realm of the Dead."

"Realm of the Dead. Realm of the Dead. That's all you talk about these days."

"Alright, what do you want to talk about?" Maggie snapped.

"Let's talk about my next holiday. I thought I might go out and stay with Bernard on Corfu. You don't mind, do you, Bernard?"

Bernard winked up at the roof.

"Not at all, Maggie."

Grandpa's booming voice got louder.

"You are not going to stay with Bernard."

"Oh yes I am and, if I want, I will kiss him too."

Bernard smiled.

"Steady girl."

The Mercedes lifted half a metre off the road and suddenly dropped down. They were all thrown forward and their seat belts locked.

"Steady," repeated Bernard, in his calm voice.

"Do you think we should stop the car?" asked Kylie, nervously.

"Duncan, do you see what you have done? You have upset Peter's girlfriend," said Grandma.

"You are not going to Corfu with Bernard."

"Actually, I've already bought a ticket and renewed my passport."

"Good for you, Maggie," said Bernard.

The car lifted a metre and crashed back down. Something under the floor scrapped noisily on the tarmac and the suspension bounced them up and down three times. Maggie's face hardened.

"I am not taking my ticket back. I paid good money for it."

The booming voice grew in anger.

"How much was it?"

"That's none of your business. It's my money now."

The car rose up to a hundred metres in the air and Bernard let go of the steering wheel.

"Is this really necessary, Duncan?"

Kylie and Peter stared down. Would Grandpa drop them from

255

here? But they veered left and shot across the blue waters of the loch, and were placed gently down onto Saint Serf's island.

"Are you just going to leave us here?" asked Maggie, crossly.

"Until you tell me you are not going to Corfu."

"You, Duncan of the line of Donald, are banned from my house."

"*Your* house?"

"My house."

The car lifted a metre and crashed back down. Kylie and Peter got out quickly and walked away from the argument. They held hands and went down to stand by the sandy shore. Behind them the Mercedes rose up and crashed down again.

Kylie squeezed Peter's hand.

"Can you explain to me how a car can fly? How dead people can talk?"

Peter gave her a weak smile.

"I can, but not now."

"I thought you said it was so normal up here."

"It is, normally."

"What are we going to do? What happens if no one sees us?"

"Not see a car on the island? Someone will see us soon."

They turned to see the Mercedes flip over onto its roof and spin around, like a break-dancer, headlights flashing.

"I wonder what Grandma said this time?" said Peter.

***

Up on the high pastures, Kylie wiggled her toes in the ice cold stream that was fed by the waterfall.

"That is *soooooo* lovely. By the way, Peter, I thought the fishermen were very good about giving us a lift."

Peter felt the warm mid-day sunshine on his back and wondered if he could manage another sandwich. He tickled Dog's ear and the sheepdog got up, lazily, and drank water from the stream. Then Dog heard something and ran off to find rabbits.

"I don't know how Bernard is going to explain how his hire car got onto the island. I bet there's never been a car on Saint Serfs before."

Kylie smiled.

"I was sat in it and I can't explain it either. Are you going to tell me now?"

Peter put the plastic lid back onto a huge sandwich box, dropped it back into his rucksack and handed her a gold brooch with a ruby at its heart.

"It's all about this."

"A brooch?"

"A brooch."

Kylie turned it in her fingers to see the front and the back of the brooch. Identical on both sides.

"What is the stone?"

"A ruby. It's called Amera's stone."

"Who was Amera?"

"A warrior king. Leader of the Sea Peoples on the northern coast of Scotland. Myroy began my story with Gora, a thief who tried to steal the stone from Amera's death-bed, but he was entombed with the king's body for over a thousand years."

"Didn't his body just turn to dust?"

"I think so, but his soul, or spirit, or something, became trapped inside the stone. Myroy told me that Gora understands the stone better than anyone."

The stone pulsed, blood red, and Kylie dropped it onto the grass. She hesitated before speaking.

"Does his spirit still exist?"

Peter looked down the hill towards the distant waters of the loch.

"I think so. Would you like to meet him?"

"Not really."

"The stone calls out to Odin who would use its power to rule everything. But the stone cannot call out if it is hidden below water."

"Odin? Wasn't he some kind of Viking god?"

257

"Yep. He's a really bad guy."

Kylie picked up the stone and held it in the palm of her hand.

"And he would use the power in this brooch?"

"You saw some of the power when the car flew. But once it lifted mountains and destroyed a castle."

Peter took it back and nodded at the loch.

"Are you sure you don't want to meet Gora?"

"Is he scary?"

"No I don't think so. Watch this."

Peter threw the brooch towards the loch. It arched and pulsed every few seconds as it flew across the high pastures and lower fields before splashing into the centre of the loch.

The air around them became heavy, like an approaching storm. The waters, where the stone had landed, boiled and a huge bird-like figure rose up into the sky, flapping its incredible wings. It flew towards Peter and Kylie and hovered above them, the wind from its wings pinning them on their backs. It gave out a deafening screech and they held their ears, staring up into the bird's black, penetrating eyes. The osprey rose, turned and flew back above the loch, before tucking its wings to its sides and diving down into the bubbles.

The loch calmed and the air returned to normal. Kylie sat up.

"I don't believe what is happening to me."

"Myroy told me he will not be telling me any more about the stone's history and that I have to go and read a book."

"Where is the book?"

"Saint Andrews. I think I need to find it quickly."

"This afternoon?"

Peter smiled.

"Why not?"

"But I am so confused by it all."

"You're not the only one. Come on. I need to go and ask a question."

He called out to Dog as he shouldered his rucksack.

"Come on, boy."

Dog took his head out of a rabbit hole and bounded over, panting, tongue hanging out.

"You look hot," said Kylie.

The sheepdog put his head on one side and went to drink from the stream.

They walked past two standing stones and another, larger, stone and dropped down the grassy slope towards a small cairn. Sheep scattered as they approached. Kylie looked down at a bunch of flowers that someone had placed on the cairn.

"They are thistles, aren't they?"

"Yep."

"Is someone buried here?"

Peter nodded.

"Lissy, but I think that a shepherd, an ancestor of mine, might be buried here too."

Kylie shook her head, confused again.

"Sit down," said Peter.

They sat together in the bright sunshine and time stood still as he told her the story, all of it, everything that he had learned since becoming lost in a snowstorm. When he finished speaking about Dougie, the return of his family and how Myroy placed anger in his heart, Kylie threw her arms around Peter, her voice trembling.

"That's why you lifted up my shirt on the school bus. You thought I had been shot."

"I thought you were dead."

"And you said you had to ask a question."

Peter smiled as he hugged her.

"Thanks. I forgot about that." He released kylie and looked at the cairn. "Grandpa."

A deep booming voice came from somewhere above the cairn.

"Aye, Laddie."

"Did Tanny become the second Keeper after Dougie? Or did the stone pass to Jock or Calum?"

"None of them. Don't forget that the Keepers tend to live long lives. It is one of the gifts Myroy gives us for carrying the burden of the stone."

"So who was the second Keeper?" asked Kylie.

"Tanny had a beautiful golden-haired daughter named Eilidh. She is a thoughtful, quiet girl and quite the best runner of any of the Keepers."

"I think Eilidh is a wonderful name," said Kylie. "Did she have any adventures, like you and Dougie?"

"No. She lived here, quietly, peacefully and with no contact with the Seekers."

Peter smiled at the cairn.

"And can I speak to her, like I can speak to you, Grandpa?"

"Aye, you can. But I think you should go and read a book."

✳✳✳

They passed the famous Old Course on their left and modern university buildings on their right, and entered Saint Andrews. Bernard steered his replacement hire car past old, grey town houses and turned up a cobbled street with higgledy piggledy houses and a French restaurant. They crossed Market Street and turned right by a church into South Street, busy with cars, students, shoppers and tourists, and Bernard parked outside the Royal Bank of Scotland.

"Right, where do you want to go?"

"Like to go to the library first," said Peter.

Bernard smiled and pointed across the street.

"It's behind the church. I'll pick you up at five."

"Five is great."

Kylie opened her door.

"Thanks for the lift, Bernard."

"You are very welcome."

They watched the Mercedes drive away, crossed the road and went down a cobbled square with benches towards a large, rectangular building made of grey stone. Beside the library's black double doors were the opening times.

"It's open nine-thirty to five on a Saturday. Plenty of time," said Peter.

Kylie saw the toilets next to the library.

"I need to go."

"Well, go."

Peter looked up at the library's big Georgian sash windows and wondered what he would find in the book. He went in and saw a young man with long hair and a university T-shirt who manned the enquiry desk.

"Can I help you?"

"Yes please, can you tell me if you have a copy of *Early Celtic Writings and their Meanings*?"

"Who's the author?"

Peter searched his memory.

"Er, I don't know."

"Hmmm. I'll just go into the system."

He swivelled round on his chair and tapped something into a computer.

"Hmmm."

He tapped something else in.

"No luck I'm afraid. We don't have it here and it's not at the university library either."

"Are there any other libraries in Saint Andrews?"

"Not that I know of."

Kylie joined them and saw Peter's disappointed face.

"What's up?"

"It's not here," said Peter.

"Oh, that's a bit of a problem."

"Any ideas?"

"A second hand bookshop?"

Peter smiled at the student.

"Do you know of any bookshops near here?"

"There are loads, but a good place to start would be Simpsons. Out the main door, turn left then right and it's on the corner.

Look for a big lantern above the door."

"Thanks."

In less than a minute they looked at a pretty bookshop with a statue of a man set into the wall.

"No point in hanging around," said Kylie.

If ever a shop smelled of books it was this one. Every space had a shelf and every shelf held hundreds of old books. Four students sat quietly on the floor reading in a large section called *Chemistry* and a tall man, with grey hair, stood reading behind an ancient till. He looked like a retired lecturer, or teacher.

"Excuse me," said Peter.

The man lowered his book and smiled.

"Do you have a copy of *Early Celtic Writings and their Meanings*?"

"I know just about every book I've ever held in stock and that one has never graced my shelves." He saw their disappointed faces. "But do try Turners."

"We've not been here before," said Kylie.

"Oh, it's easy. Out the door, turn right down Church Street, cross Market Street and go down College Street. Turn right into North Street by a clock-tower and it's a bit further on, on your left."

"It doesn't sound easy," said Peter.

The man sighed and drew the route on a map that looked as though it had been photocopied a thousand times. He gave it to Kylie.

"I hope you find what you are searching for."

"Thanks," they said together.

They left and the old man's eyes never left them. Then he checked out the other people on the street and pushed a button on his mobile.

"Sandy, the Keeper is coming and there is no one on his tail."

Peter and Kylie turned right into North Street, with a huge clock-tower on their left, and after a short way, Kylie stopped.

"Do you think it's a coincidence?"

"What is?"

She pointed at a sign above a large university building –

Younger Music Centre

"Must be."

They walked on, with the two towers of the ruined cathedral always in view in the distance, and came to a shop with flower boxes, a green door and a green-edged sign –

Book and Coffee Shop

They went in and an elderly man, with traces of ginger in his white hair, came over to them.

"Would you like some coffee?"

"No. We'd like a book, please," said Kylie.

"Oh, good. Follow me."

He led them past a postcard stand into a back room lined with old books.

"What are you after?"

"*Early Celtic Writings and their Meanings.*"

"Who is the author?"

"We don't know."

"I'm sorry, I can't help you."

Peter sighed.

"Do you know of any bookshops that specialise in Celtic writing?"

"No. Not in Saint Andrews, anyway."

As they left, the man called after them.

"Isn't there something you want to show me?"

Something clicked in Peter's mind and he searched in his pocket for his pebble.

"Is this it?"

"It is. Put it on the floor and open the door."

Peter placed it on the floor and Kylie opened the door.

"I hope you find what you are searching for," said the man.

The pebble rolled out of the door and into the street, and turned left. They hurried after it and Peter called back.

"Thanks."

The man went to stand in the doorway, saw them turn the corner into North Castle Street, and searched the faces of the other people who walked around. He pushed a button on his mobile.

"The Keeper is coming and there is no one on his tail."

Peter and Kylie ran past a church and a gateway, and old cottages with uneven roofs, struggling to keep up with the pebble that accelerated down the hill. A boy, walking up the hill, stopped to watch them.

"I've lost my pebble," yelled Peter.

The boy jumped sideways and put his foot onto the stone, and gave it back to him.

"Thanks," said Peter, panting.

He put it back onto the road and the chase began again. At the bottom of the hill, the pebble raced across a road and bounced down some steps. Kylie grabbed Peter's arm and a car flashed in front of them.

"Careful."

They bounded down the steps, which twisted left and ended on a small beach, the walls of a ruined castle towering above the sand. They saw the pebble again, jumping up and down in front of a lady who sat on a flat rock. A flask, bath robe and Peter's Berghaus rucksack were laid out neatly beside her on the rock. They ran over and Peter caught his pebble in mid air.

"You took your time, didn't you?" said Miss Dickson.

They looked into her huge eyes, magnified by her glasses. Peter glanced around nervously.

"Let me introduce you. Kylie this is Miss Dickson, Head of Research for the Keepers. Miss Dickson, this is ..."

Miss Dickson cut in and patted the rock next to her.

"Come and sit here and have a cup of tea, whilst Peter reads the next part of the story."

"What's going to happen next?" asked Kylie.

"He can tell you later."

She poured out a cup of tea and gave it to her, before looking critically at Peter.

"Well?"

"Well, what?"

"Go and read the book."

"But I don't know where it is."

She sighed and pointed at the pebble in his hand.

"Oh, I see."

Miss Dickson nudged Kylie, spilling her tea.

"This is going to be fun."

Peter put his pebble onto the sand and it rolled towards the sea, where he stopped and stared out at swirling water, fifty metres from the shore. Four jet skis powered noisily past as they raced south.

"Go on," shouted Miss Dickson.

Peter shook his head, but picked up his pebble, clutched it tightly in his hand and waded into the sea.

"Like a sandwich?" asked Miss Dickson. "I've got egg and tomato today."

"Yes please. Is the book under the water?"

"It is and Peter won't be long, so eat up."

Peter felt the cold of the North Sea and walked out before diving in when the small waves bounced off his chest. Immediately, a red bubble enveloped his body and shot downwards, following the sea bed. He peered into the darkness and a blood red beam shone ahead, lighting up rocks and kelp beds. They brushed through the kelp and came out into a flat, sandy basin with a single standing stone at its centre. The bubble slowed and floated in front of the stone and Peter saw a life-like carving on its face. The deep grooves of the carving was of Amera's stone and the brooch it sat in, except that the ruby was not at the heart of the brooch, just a hole.

"What do I do now?"

The bubble moved forward and bounced off the standing stone.

"I have to do something to the carving?"

The bubble bounced off it again and Peter pushed his arm through the protective skin of the bubble and placed his pebble into the hole where the ruby should have been. Nothing happened and he pulled his pebble back inside the bubble. A red circle appeared in the sand below him and the bubble shot downwards at an incredible speed. Peter's stomach felt as though it was in his mouth and he felt sick. It was like being in a red plastic ball, falling inside a brightly lit red tube.

Without warning, the bubble stopped and Peter collapsed on the floor as the bubble disappeared.

He looked around at a rock chamber, lit by torches, and a lectern on one side of the chamber. Cautiously, he stood and went over to the lectern and read the title of a book on top of it –

Early Celtic Writings and their Meanings.

It was a beautiful book, leather-bound with gold Celtic knot edging and old-looking gold letters spelling out the title. Below the title was a picture of the brooch and, like the standing stone, the ruby at its heart was missing. He slowly opened the book to see a single blank page.

"The pebble," he said.

He closed the book, placed his pebble into the picture of the brooch and took it back out. He tried again and this time letters appeared on the single blank page –

**This is a record of the history of
Amera's stone and the war against the Seekers.
Written by Tirani the Wise.**

As Peter finished reading, the letters vanished and new ones appeared –

AMERA'S CAIRN : 1427 BC

Gora had been running since dusk, since he had first heard about the passing, and despite the cold, sweat poured down his face. The furs he wore reeked from the great effort of travelling so far, so quickly, but the promise of riches drove him on.

Exhausted, Gora paused to look at the moon. It was full, silver and bright, the kind of moon that would signal the last days for a Stone Keeper.

As his strength returned, he faced north and, through the darkness, saw the distant outline of a ribbon of pine trees, which marked the end of the land. The Stone Circle was this side of the pines and Amera's cairn lay only a short distance beyond the circle. Gora sniffed, smelled salt, and knew he was close.

Peter read and read, and every detail of the long story that he had heard so far was locked, completely, inside his memory. Then everything that Myroy had told him was over and he thought that it would end there. Two words proved him wrong -

Keeper Profiles

"I'd like to see those," he thought, and they appeared.

Dougie's first, then Eilidh and every other Stone Keeper including Grandpa. The last profile was Peter's and it showed his name, age when becoming a Keeper, height, weight, the things he liked, the things he didn't like and his address.

"That's not right," he said.

His address was somewhere in Australia and he stared at it, asking himself why it was wrong. Maybe he was going to move there? The profile dissolved on the page and Peter wondered if he had reached the end of the book. But a new chapter of the story began and the letters kept coming and coming, until two more words appeared.

The End.

He felt scared and excited, and wanted to dash back to tell Kylie what he had heard. But something stopped him.

"Can I see my profile again please, Tirani?"

His personal details appeared on the page, followed by a personal message from Tirani and suddenly he understood. Peter tore the ancient page from the book and carefully folded it.

"I will need a small bubble."

A small red bubble appeared around the paper he held in his hand.

"That'll keep you nice and dry," he said.

Back on the beach, Kylie asked Miss Dickson the question that was most on her mind.

"Why does Myroy say that Peter will be the last Keeper?"

"It is because of their advanced technology. In this modern world it is becoming easier to find than it is to hide." Miss Dickson handed her a pebble. "Keep it safe. They come in handy sometimes."

Kylie put it in her pocket, finished her tea and pointed at Peter's head poking out of the sea.

"He's back already. What's he got in his hand?"

Miss Dickson's eyes widened even further as the red ball around Peter's hand disappeared.

"I'm surprised he's not running."

Peter waded ashore and ran to them across the sand.

"Come on, we have to go."

Miss Dickson tossed him the bath robe.

"Take your clothes off and get into this."

"Go where?" asked Kylie.

"Corfu," said Miss Dickson, handing Kylie the rucksack. "Inside are your passports, flight tickets, some clothes to see you through." She paused. "You are a size twelve, aren't you, my dear?"

Kylie looked surprised.

"Well, yes."

"Good. There are toilet bags, some other stuff and one thousand euros in cash." She paused again. "Your favourite perfume *is* Anais Anais?"

"It is."

"And I heard that you are half way through your book. I popped a copy of that in too. Peter, dear, put your paper in the bag before it gets damaged."

Peter put the folded page in a side pocket and zipped it shut. He looked at his watch.

"Four-thirty. Bernard isn't picking us up until five."

A car horn sounded up on the road.

"Have a good flight," said Miss Dickson.

In the back of Bernard's car, Kylie turned away as Peter struggled to get out of his bathrobe and put dry clothes on. She became worried.

"What on earth are Mum and Dad going to say?"

Bernard rescued Peter.

"I spoke to them and they are pleased Peter has won a free holiday on Corfu. I live there, of course, and offered to keep an eye on you both."

Peter pulled his trousers on and Kylie turned her head back, held his hand and thought about everything that had happened to her since getting off the plane at Edinburgh airport.

"Well, I've heard a ghost talk, sat in a flying car, been pinned to the ground by the wings of a giant, screeching osprey, heard a story that will change my life, become a Keeper, chased a pebble and seen you disappear into the sea."

"Did you like it?" asked Peter.

She smiled.

"I loved every minute of it."

Peter smiled too and kissed her hand.

"Just another normal day in Scotland," he said.

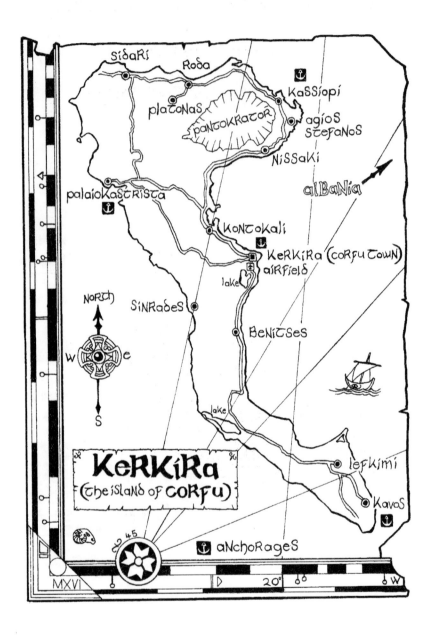

CHAPTER THIRTEEN

THE REALM OF THE DEAD

"How far is it to the airport?" asked Kylie.

Bernard glanced into his mirror.

"About an hour. Why don't you tell her about Corfu, Peter? It might pass the time."

"It hasn't done that before. Every time I hear a story, time stands still."

Kylie squeezed his hand.

"Oh, go on. I'm dying to find out what was written in *Early Celtic Writings and their Meanings.*"

"Do you want *me* to tell you about the Realm of the Dead?" asked Bernard.

"Have you been beneath the sea and read the book?"

Bernard smiled in the mirror at her.

"No, but I was there, with Peter's grandfather. We may not have time to hear all of it, but if you two are going to be partners in crime from now on, I think Kylie should know."

Peter put his arm around his girlfriend and wondered if Bernard would start with Monty meeting Aris at a secret airbase in occupied Greece.

***

General Montgomery sat with Aris Velouciotis and an interpreter, in a makeshift tent pitched beside a temporary airfield in northern Greece. Monty spoke in his clipped and eager voice.

"Will you give Mr Velouciotis my warm regards and ask him why he has called this urgent meeting."

The interpreter nodded and spoke to the leader of the Greek resistance. Aris said something and the interpreter spoke to Monty.

"He returns your warm regards. Since the defeat of the Italians and Germans in North Africa, the morale of Italian troops, who occupy Greece, has fallen dramatically. Aris believes that now is the right time to, er, make a statement."

"Please tell Mr Velouciotis, that the war in North Africa is not yet won, but that I am confident of complete victory in the near future. What does he mean by a 'statement?'"

The interpreter spoke again to the big, tough-looking man with a full black beard.

"The Greek resistance, ELAS, plans to invade Corfu by sea on the eighth of October. Aris believes it will be a signal for more men to rise up and fight the enemy. The island would then be a centre for the resistance for the rest of the war."

Monty stiffened.

"Sounds high risk and he has a problem."

Aris spoke to the interpreter, who translated.

"The Italians have many planes on Corfu. Their destruction is, er, imperative to the success of the invasion."

"Then blow up their airfield."

"They have tried, many times, but it is well guarded. He asks for your help in this matter."

"Tell Aris that, as it happens, I do have some good men on the way to the island. I will send them orders to help his people."

The interpreter told Aris, and the big, bearded man stood and hugged Monty, who looked embarrassed at the invasion of his personal space. They walked out into darkness, back to Monty's plane, and men ran to light the oil lamps along the secret airstrip. Aris said something and the interpreter smiled.

"He says, 'Safe journey and thank you.'"

Monty boarded his plane and called back.

"Tell Aris to say, 'Thank you,' when the job is done."

***

Bernard and Duncan stood by the rail on HMS *Invincible*, listening to the hum of the engines deep below their feet.

"It's a nice night," said Bernard.

"And dark. That will help us when we land. How do we get onto the island, anyway?" asked Duncan.

Bernard took a piece of paper from his pocket and unfolded it.

273

"Here, read this. Came in over the radio today from Alex. Just been decoded."

Duncan looked at the typed script –

High Priority and Strictly Confidential

FAO Captain Bernard King

28 September 1942

From Major Michael Trevellyn
Offices of the High Command
British Expeditionary Forces
Alexandria

At 01:00 hours on 8.10.1942, the National Popular Liberation Army (hereafter known as ELAS) will invade Corfu by ship.

Your mission is to destroy the Italian airbase, three miles south of Corfu Town. The airbase is reported to be heavily guarded.

The latest intelligence from ELAS is that the Italians have sixteen CANT Z506 sea planes based there.

These planes have a range of 3000 miles and a top speed of 217 miles per hour. They each carry four machine guns and a heavy payload of bombs. If you cannot destroy these planes, the invasion force will be cut to shreds on the open sea.

General Montgomery has met with Aris Velouciotis, the head of Greek Resistance, and Aris has agreed that you meet up with his top man on Corfu, Aris Agnedes. Agnedes leads a band of resistance fighters known as the Andartes. He has the reputation of being tough.

A fishing boat will pick you up tonight at 01:30 hours and drop you in a cove close to Kassiopi on the north of the island. Agnedes will meet you there. The RAF are dropping explosives to the Andartes, for your use.

The Captain of HMS Invincible will provide you with a map of the island.

Monty sends his regards. For information, the war in North Africa is nearly won.

Please destroy this paper when you have read it.

Michael.

"Got it?" asked Bernard.

"Got it."

Bernard took back the paper, tore it into small pieces and dropped them into the sea.

"Has the Captain given you the map?" asked Duncan.

Bernard gave him another sheet of folded paper.

"Kassiopi looks a long way from Corfu Town."

Duncan nodded.

"The invasion is planned for the eighth of October. It doesn't give us long."

"Ten days."

"The CANT sea planes sound impressive. Any ideas about how we get into the base?"

"No, we need local knowledge for that."

Chalky, Sandy, Lofty and SS joined them at the rail.

"Grub's good on the ship. Those navy boys sure know 'ow to live," said Chalky.

SS rubbed his belly.

"Best shepherd's pie I've had since the start of the war."

"Hope it's as good on Corfu."

SS shook his head.

"It's all that foreign stuff. Swimming in olive oil."

Lofty tried to turn the conversation away from food.

"Bernard, you said we have to go and cause mischief on the island. Any specific orders come through?"

Bernard nodded.

"Tell them, Duncan."

Duncan told them, word for word.

"This 'ain't fair," moaned Chalky. "We've only just finished fightin' in the ruddy desert."

SS frowned at Chalky's lack of respect for authority.

"Orders is orders, Private Chalk."

"Sounds a tough mission," said Sandy. "It won't be as easy as the fuel dump at Al Jaghbub."

Bernard took the map back from Duncan and gave it to SS.

"Make sure everyone memorises this, please sergeant. Then get some rest."

Three hours later, Bernard and his men sat in a lifeboat, being lowered over the side of HMS *Invicible*, their faces blackened, carrying rucksacks and weapons.

"'Ere we go again," said Chalky. "'Ere, 'ow do we know if the fishin' boat's comin'?"

Bernard pointed at his ears.

"By using these."

They drifted away from the ship, rising and falling on the choppy waves, thirty miles south of Corfu. Lofty pointed north at the dark horizon.

"Here they come."

"Cor, you've got keen eyes, 'ain't yer?"

A rhythmic thudding noise grew louder and soon the shadowy outline of a tired looking fishing boat, came alongside. Strong hands helped them aboard and Bernard shook hands with a hard-looking man dressed in a brown jumper, sleeveless sheepskin jacket and brown leather boots. The other three resistance fighters wore similar clothes.

"Good evening, gentlemen," said Bernard.

None of the Greeks replied and busied themselves by stowing their guests' rucksacks below decks. The hard-looking man came back with a huge leather bag. He pointed at it and Bernard's men put on the clothes it held to look like Greek fishermen.

"My sheepskin stinks," moaned Chalky.

Sandy struggled to pull his new boots on.

"Why don't they speak to us?"

"Maybe they can't speak English," replied Lofty. "And your German isn't going to be of much use here."

A man with a bucket on a rope joined them and pointed at their faces, and at the sea.

"Ruddy Nora. I've only just blacked up," said Chalky.

SS checked the pockets of the trousers he was pulling off.

"And with my boot polish."

Chalky took a tin from his folded jacket and gave SS back the boot polish he had stolen from him.

"Why you ..."

The man pointed at their uniforms and to the sea again. They all checked their pockets and threw their old clothes overboard, and settled on the deck for the long journey north.

Before dawn, an Andartes woke them and pointed at a string of lights which came from houses along a coastal road, about a mile away.

"Agios Stefanos," he said in a deep voice.

At dawn, they saw another, larger, string of lights and they guessed it was Kassiopi. An hour later, in brilliant sunshine, the diesel engine slowed and they floated at half speed into a sandy cove, surrounded by high limestone cliffs. A man stood alone on the beach, a long Russian rifle slung across his back. Bernard ran the words he would say to Agnedes through his mind.

"Good morning. We are here to ..."

The man cut in.

"Collect your things and follow me."

He led them inland, through olive, lemon and lime groves, and always climbing up the slopes of Pantekrator. Lofty walked beside Chalky.

"It's an extinct volcano."

"'Ope it is ruddy well extinct. 'Ere, you 'ungry? I'm starvin'." He called back. "Sarge. Any chance of a break and a cup of tea."

"Not a chance, Private Chalk."

Lofty handed Chalky a chocolate bar.

"Bless you, Lofty. 'Ere, 'av. this."

Chalky gave him back another bar.

"I nicked it off yer when you slept on the boat."

A critical voice spoke behind them.

"When the war's over, I'm going to get you locked up at Her Majesty's pleasure."

"Bless you, SS."

"That's Sergeant Sturgess to you."

Their guide turned and put his finger to his lips, and they walked on in silence, leaving the cool shade of the trees and crossing brown grass, broken by rock. They passed a herd of goats and a small white church with pots of herbs outside and, as the way became steeper, they struggled to keep up with their guide.

Their shadows shortened under the high sun and they sweated as they climbed up a dry riverbed. The riverbed narrowed, through a steep sided gorge, curved right and they stood, panting, in front of the entrance to a cave.

Bernard looked back down the slopes of Pantekrator towards the blue sea. On the top of both sides of the gorge were Andartes and he realised that, during the climb, they had been secretly watched, rifles aimed at them every step of the way. Their guide led them inside the cave, sat on a rock and drank water from a goatskin water carrier.

"It's a bit of a hike, but there is not a safer place for us on the whole island. We can see the Italians coming from miles away and their planes have never found the cave."

Bernard smiled and gestured to have some water.

"Your English is very good. Why didn't you talk to us as we walked?"

"We talk when we need to. Walk when we need to. Kill when we need to."

Despite the hard edge in the man's voice, Bernard put his arm out and they shook hands.

"Bernard King."

"Aris Agnedes." He pointed at stores at the back of the cave. "The RAF dropped them last night. One of the parachutes did not open and the explosives it carried are lost. Made a hell of a noise."

Bernard nodded at Lofty and Sandy, "Check them over." He went to sit beside Aris. "We don't know the details, but I understand you need some help."

"We do. The airbase is heavily guarded and difficult to approach without being seen. We also do not have much time."

"Ten days."

"Eight days. The invasion has been brought forward."

Later, Bernard, his men and members of the Andartes, sat together in the shade of ancient olive trees, on the lower slopes of Pantekrator.

"I don't get it, Aris," said Bernard. "How can Velouciotis assemble a fleet on the mainland when the Italians occupy it? That's one hell of a trick if he can pull it off."

"It's not a trick. It is a *crazy* plan. There are two things we are not short of; men ready to fight and fishing boats, but they are not in one place. As we speak, the entire resistance movement is walking towards small fishing villages on the western coast of Greece and Albania. At a set time, they will sail for Kassiopi. Velouciotis says it will be better for us to take Corfu and use it as a base to attack the enemy for the rest of the war."

"But why not fight them across the whole of Greece?" asked Duncan.

Aris sighed.

"This is turning into a dirty war. If we blow up a railway, kill a General or steal weapons, the Italians take revenge. They pick a village, take the men and imprison or kill them. It would be an easy step for them to do the same to the women and children. If we held Corfu, their anger would fall onto us here, and only here."

"This is a crazy plan," said Bernard.

"It is."

Suddenly, Aris's face lit up. A beautiful girl with long black hair, carrying a wicker basket, walked quickly towards them through the olive trees. When she saw Aris, her face lit up too and she put her basket down, and threw her arms around him. Duncan looked at her white blouse and white skirt, with flowers embroidered on both, and he guessed she would be about the same age as Maggie. Bernard said the obvious.

279

"You two know each other then."

Aris stopped kissing the girl.

"This is Anna, the girl I plan to marry. She risks death everyday by bringing us food and ammunition."

He said something else in Greek and Anna laughed, laid out a cloth and placed a large round loaf upon it. Cheese, tomatoes, cooked chicken and fish all followed from the basket.

Chalky glanced around at the number of men and at the amount of food.

"Blimey, that 'ain't gonna be enough. I'll nip up to the cave and get some tins."

Duncan's forehead creased.

"I don't think you should have said that, Chalky. It might be several days rations for these people."

Aris raised a hand.

"Please relax, all of you. You are our guests and everything is taken care of."

More ladies appeared with baskets and soon they were all enjoying simple, good food, feeling safe below the canopy of leaves, and trying to guess what others were saying in their different languages. Aris checked his watch and pointed up.

"It is three. Time for our Italian friends to remind us who is in charge. We stay in the trees a little longer."

A distant hum grew in strength and, after a few minutes, they saw a formation of ten sea planes through the gaps in the leaves, and high above the swifts that darted for food above the olive trees. The planes circled above Pantekrator and then headed north to check out the coastal towns of Sidari, Roda, Kassiopi and Agios Stefanos.

"Same time everyday?" asked Duncan.

"Same time and all they ever see is local people going about their honest business."

"So, if it wasn't for the planes, life would be pretty normal," said Lofty.

Aris's face became fierce.

"There are Italian troops in all the main towns. That is far from *normal*."

Bernard changed the subject.

"What do you do, Aris? I mean, before the war, for a living."

"I am a gardener, like my father and his father. I grew flowers, and Anna here," he held her hand, "will sell them for me, one day, in Kassiopi market."

"You have a farm?" asked Duncan.

"I have a small house, a very traditional house, and three fields where I grew my flowers, but now of course with the war, it is for vegetables and chickens."

Bernard found himself liking this man and wondered how a humble gardener had risen to become a tough guerrilla fighter, and leader of all the Andartes on the island.

An hour before sunset, the ladies packed away their baskets and left for their villages, and Aris led Bernard's men up the riverbed to the cave. Bernard asked Lofty and Sandy to join him.

"You checked the supplies?"

"Enough dynamite to blow up half of Corfu," said Lofty.

Sandy opened the lid of a wooden box with EXPLOSIVES stencilled in black ink on top of the lid.

"We've got eight of these and each box has twelve sticks of dynamite. The fuses are on a drum and need to be cut to length. There's black tape for holding it all together. I think bunches of six sticks, taped up and with a twelve-inch fuse, would be enough to take out a plane."

"OK. Get on the case, and ask the others if you need help."

An Andartes hurried into the cave and spoke to Aris.

"What's up?" asked Duncan.

Aris's face showed concern.

"Do you have a map of the island?"

Bernard joined them and spread out his map on a rock.

"There is a possibility that the Italians know about the invasion. If they do, then we might assume they know it will be soon and at Kassiopi. But I have no reports of the garrison at Corfu Town moving north and that makes me think they do not know where it will be. They must realise that there are only four anchorages around the coast large enough to take an invasion fleet. Kassiopi, Corfu Town, Palaiokastrista and close to Kavos in the south. Corfu Town is heavily defended and so that leaves them three places to choose from."

"What do you plan to do?" asked Duncan.

"There is only one road leading down to Kavos. It is mountainous country and if we destroy the road, they might take it as confirmation that the invasion will come from the south."

"And take their garrison as far from Kassiopi as you could hope."

"Do you need any help?" asked Bernard.

"Can you give us some dynamite?"

Bernard nodded. "We have more than we need."

Aris pointed at the map.

"I suggest you come with us, as far as the airfield. Study its defences and return here. I will take some of my men and blow up this road, here, to the west of Lefkimi."

Chalky, SS, Sandy and Lofty, finished taping bundles of dynamite together, and joined them.

"I'm bored," moaned Chalky.

Bernard smiled.

"You won't be bored for long. We are going to have a look at the airfield."

"I should keep my ruddy trap shut."

"When do we go?" asked Sandy.

They all looked at Aris, who stood and shouldered his rifle.

"That answers that then," said SS.

***

Two days of hard marching later, some of the Andartes left them in the company of Spiros and Minolas. Before heading south to Benitses, Aris told Bernard that they were two of his best men and that they knew the island like the back of their hands. As the sun fell below the hills behind them, the soldiers stared east across a large lake, towards the airbase, the calm blue sea beyond it. Bernard rested his elbows on top of a low stone wall that they hid behind.

"It's big."

"Aye," said Duncan. "Two runways forming a cross, three big hangars and eight anti-aircraft gun emplacements. They will probably have machine guns in them too. Can't see any planes. They must be inside the hangars. Have you seen the perimeter fence?"

Bernard raised his binoculars.

"It's a bit like the fences around the prison camp we stayed in. It's two fences, but they are higher and guard dogs are roaming between the fences. Hello, a lorry is pulling up at the main gate."

"Can I see?" asked Sandy.

Bernard handed him the glasses.

"I think the Italians have got wind of something. I've never seen such a thorough check."

"What are you seeing?" asked Lofty.

"About twenty guards around the lorry. There are three big stone blocks that stop the lorry driving straight in. It has to slow and zig-zag between the blocks. Three guards are standing on a walkway, a kind of bridge thing, and they are checking the roof of the lorry. The other guards are checking the driver's documents, the stuff in the back and, uh oh, they are looking underneath."

Bernard let out a long breath.

"So, even Thomas Goodfellow wouldn't get in."

"How many men on the base, Sandy?"

Sandy's binoculars swept the hangars, other buildings and machine gun posts, his lips moving as he counted.

"Hard to say. Could be over three hundred."

"Ruddy Nora," said Chalky.

"My sentiments exactly, Private Chalk," said SS.

"Any weak spots around the fence?" asked Duncan.

Sandy gave him the binoculars.

"Here, take a look. I don't think so."

"What about stealing some lorries and smashing through the main gate?" suggested SS.

Duncan focused the lenses onto the guards with machine guns at the gate.

"We might just get inside, but I don't think we would get out again."

"And it would have to be at night," said Lofty.

The sun went down and floodlights came on to bathe the base in bright light.

"So, it doesn't matter when we attack," said Bernard. "Unless we can blow up their generators."

"Got any grub?" asked Chalky.

SS handed him a rucksack and Chalky took some bread out. Spiros and Minolas remained silent as everyone tried to figure out how to get at the planes in the hangars.

"Can we ask the RAF to bomb it?" asked Lofty.

"I checked that," said Bernard. "The Hurricanes are chasing the Germans west, back in North Africa. Monty can't spare them right now."

"Ruddy Nora," mumbled Chalky, crumbs flying out of his mouth.

Duncan thought about the planned invasion and felt as though time was running out. He handed Bernard the binoculars and put his hand inside his pocket to hold his brooch. But his fingers closed around the pebble he had picked up in the desert. Behind the wall, the ground shimmered, like moonlight on water, and Myroy rose up from the underworld, looking angry.

"You nearly lost the stone and now you consider using its power again."

Minolas pointed his rifle at the Ancient One and Bernard gestured at him to lower it. Myroy spoke to the Andartes in Greek.

"After the war, you will drive a taxi and have many children. You, Spiros, will become the Head of Police. Both of you must help us protect the Keeper. Make Corfu a fortress for us." He turned to Bernard. "Later, tell them the story. They are good men and worthy of joining us." Myroy went to stand in front of Duncan. "Now, in your time, you place the stone at risk. Have you learned nothing?"

Duncan's head dropped and there was an awkward silence.

"I should never have brought it with me."

"You should not have brought it with you."

"What do I do?"

"Hide the stone for as long as war rages."

"Where?"

"You will know where."

"But I don't know where, only that it must be held below water to stop it crying out to its master."

"What gifts have you received?" asked Myroy.

"Long life, I can talk to my ancestors and remember what I read."

"Is that all?"

Duncan looked surprised.

"Aye."

Myroy's voice rose.

"Take it from your pocket."

Duncan took Amera's stone from his pocket and held the brooch in his upturned palm. Myroy slowly shook his head and Duncan took his pebble from his pocket.

"All of you, show me your pebbles."

Everyone, except Spiros and Minolas, who looked scared by the old man who had appeared from nowhere, fumbled around for their pebbles.

"Why do you carry them?"

"To identify ourselves as Keepers," said Bernard.

Myroy pointed his staff at Amera's stone and it pulsed.

"Look at them."

Their pebbles pulsed too, blood red.

"If you learn how to use the old magic, the power which exists in the land will aid you." Myroy stared hard at Duncan. "Use that power to find a safe haven for the stone. Fight your war and remember, it is nothing compared to the war that will be when Odin rules."

The vision of mountains rising up into the sky filled their minds.

"I want to do the right thing," said Duncan.

"Then hide the stone on this island."

Myroy made a circle on the ground with his staff and sank down.

"But where?"

The Ancient One stopped descending and all they could see was his head. Myroy's eyes flashed at Duncan.

"You will know where," and then the head was gone.

After a long silence, Bernard stood.

"Come on. Aris asked us to meet him back on Pantekrator. It's a long hike, so let's get going."

He walked beside Minolas and Spiros, clutching his pebble and talking for the first time in Greek, and telling them a story which spanned thousands of years. As they approached the cave, in darkness, he finished the story and asked everyone to gather round. Soon they sat in a circle on the cave floor, candles flickering around the walls. At first, he found it difficult to switch his mind, from the history of the stone to the orders sent to him by Michael Trevellyn.

"OK. I know we're tired, but has anyone got any ideas about how to destroy the airbase?"

Lofty shook his head.

"Even if we had more men, it would be a tough call."

"There must be a way," said Bernard.

"I think we just have to accept that we smash our way in, using lorries, and that we aren't going to get out alive," said Sandy.

Duncan watched the dancing candlelight and his eyes fell onto Chalky. His friend was smiling.

"How would you do it, Chalky?"

"Oh, I wouldn't bovver."

SS shook his head.

"Now then, Private Chalk. Orders is orders."

"Why wouldn't you, er, bovver, Chalky?" asked Lofty.

"Because I don't want to get myself ruddy well killed."

"What's your idea?" asked Duncan.

"I'd nick somefin'."

"What?" asked Bernard.

Chalky's smile widened.

"Their pilots."

"And how would you do that?"

"I'd invite 'em to a good night out. Everyone loves a knees up, don't they."

As the others slept, Lofty and Sandy kept watch up above the ravine, cross-legged, their guns resting across their laps.

"After the war, I think I might settle down somewhere a bit cooler," said Lofty.

Sandy nodded.

"Did I ever tell you I've always wanted to own a book shop?"

"No. I thought you would go back to boxing."

"I've had enough of fighting. Will you go back to teaching?"

"No. Actually, a bookshop sounds like a fine idea."

After four hours they woke Bernard and Duncan for their watch. Bernard looked exhausted.

"Anything to report?"

"Nothing," said Sandy. "It's deadly quiet."

"Well, get some sleep. Aris should be back around noon."

On top of the ridge, Duncan stared at the distant flat, black sea. Bernard yawned.

"What's on your mind?"

"I want to find the hiding place."

He felt something in his trouser pocket move around, and he leapt up.

"What's up?"

"Something's crawled into my trousers."

Gingerly, Duncan put his hand into his pocket and held his pebble. It tried to jump out of his hand. He showed Bernard and the pebble got away, and set off down the ridge.

"That's odd," said Bernard.

They watched it bounce down the slope, until it disappeared in the darkness. Then it bounced back and gave them a red pulse.

"It's the old magic. Can't be anything else, Duncan. Let's follow it."

The pebble bounced and rolled up the riverbed past the cave, occasionally pulsing to show them where it was. A hundred metres from the cave, the riverbed became steep and divided into two channels. They followed the pebble up the left hand channel and stood, with the stone bouncing up and down, in front of a smooth rock face.

"What now?" asked Bernard.

A narrow red beam shot out from the pebble and lit a small circle of rock, low down on the face.

They knelt to look at an ancient carving of the brooch, but with the ruby missing at the centre. The pebble leapt up into Duncan's hand.

"I think it wants you to do something."

Duncan smiled and pushed the pebble into the space where the ruby should be. Nothing happened. He pulled it out and the rock face began to shimmer, like moonlight on water.

***

Bernard glanced into his mirror.

"And Duncan and I entered into a new world."

"Let's go there," said Peter, excitedly.

Kylie sat back on the car seat and brushed her long hair away from her face.

288

"But what about the airbase?"

"There is no time in the Realm of the Dead. It felt as though we stayed for months, but when we finally left, Aris hadn't even got back from his mission at Kavos."

"Did you destroy the planes? Did the invasion happen? Did everyone get home OK?" asked Kylie.

"So many questions," continued Bernard. "I'll leave that to Peter to tell you when we arrive on Corfu."

"How far to the airport?" asked Peter.

"About twenty minutes, that's all."

"Can I finish off this part of the story?"

"Over to you, Peter. You've read it in Tirani's book and so you know it as well as anyone."

***

Bernard and Duncan gazed in awe at the shimmering blue and silver oval that appeared in the rock face. It was the height of two men and the width of three, and framed by large blocks of dark shaped stone. The design was timeless. It could have been a thousand years old, or built yesterday. Duncan hesitated.

"Shall we walk into the moonlight on water?"

"Do we have any choice? Myroy needs you to hide the stone for the rest of the war. Wherever he has chosen, it lies on the other side of this doorway. I suggest we leave our rifles here."

They took a deep breath and stepped through, momentarily feeling a blast of cold air, like entering a frozen tomb. Duncan shivered and clutched his pebble.

"It's *so* dark."

A dim red glow shone ahead and showed that they were in an oval tunnel, the same size as the entrance and lined with the same smooth, black stones.

"It looks like it goes on forever," said Bernard.

"Forever is a big word. Come on."

The tunnel went downwards for an age and the red glow lit

hundreds of paces ahead, but as soon as the friends moved on, utter blackness closed in behind them.

"I'm getting the same feeling that I had when Myroy told me about Gora going down into Amera's cairn."

"Me too," said Bernard, the hairs standing up on his arms.

At last, they stood in front of another rock face with a carving of the brooch low down.

"We could be miles under the surface," said Bernard.

Duncan held up his pebble.

"Aye. Want to try yours?"

"Why not?"

Bernard put his pebble into the centre of the carving and took it back. The second doorway shimmered and they entered the Realm of the Dead, feeling the same blast of cold air as they passed through.

"Wow," said Bernard.

They stood on a grassy slope in brilliant sunshine. A loch sparkled blue and white, and a line of distant hills surrounded the loch. A stand of pine trees marked the edge of the lands owned by the Donalds and three standing stones, close to a stone cairn, lay off to their right.

"It's just how I imagined it in my mind," said Bernard.

Duncan pointed at a tall stone tower on an island in the loch, and a rowing boat leaving the island.

"But that's different."

"And that."

Beside the shore was a small village made up of white Celtic cottages. A Great Hall stood proud at the heart of the village.

"Come on," said Duncan. "This feels like home to me."

"Can you explain to me how an ancient world can exist inside a volcano on Corfu?"

Duncan shook his head and smiled.

"No. But I wouldn't mind guessing it has something to do with the Ancient Ones."

A boy jumped out of the rowing boat and tied it to a post that was sunk into the sandy shore, close to the village. He skipped towards Bernard and Duncan.

"You took your time, didn't you?"

Bernard shook the boy's tiny hand.

"It is a great pleasure to meet you, Tirani."

The boy grinned.

"Pleasure to meet you too, Bernard. You don't know it yet, but you are going to play an important role in Keeper security. Why not buy yourself somewhere to live on Corfu after the war?"

"Would that be a good idea?"

"It would. Welcome Keeper." Tirani shook Duncan's hand. "Your grandson will be the last Keeper of the stone. Isn't there something you should do?"

Duncan took the brooch from the pocket of the trousers given to him by the Andartes. He stared at the ruby and it pulsed, once, and he felt its warmth.

"Only one place for you, laddie," and he pulled his arm back, and threw it into the loch.

Instantly, a huge bird-like figure exploded upwards from the boiling waters and flapped its mighty wings. The osprey flew around the loch, peering down at anything that moved, and then landed gracefully on top of the tower on the island.

"Gora is in a good mood today," said Tirani.

A deep *thud* came from the bowels of the earth and the waters of the loch turned red for a moment. Another *thud*, then another, and every ten seconds the waters became like blood again.

"Well, that's the stone settled, for a while at least. We're getting there."

"The stone is *settled*," repeated Bernard.

"And we have enough power now to run the Talk Tunnel, Travel Hole, Story Board and the two Location Viewers."

"What?" said Duncan.

"Just some stuff we've been getting ready for the war. I'll show you later, if you like, but I can't be bothered now. Besides, you should come and meet your ancestors, Duncan."

"Dougie? The other Keepers?" asked Duncan.

"All the Twelve are here. Eilidh suggested we lay on a feast for you in the Great Hall."

They walked into the village and, for the first time since becoming a Keeper, Duncan felt the weight of the burden he carried, dissolve away.

CHAPTER FOURTEEN

CLEOPATRA'S NEEDLE

As Peter listened to the reassuring hum of Bernard's new hire car, vivid pictures of Grandpa's wartime adventures on Corfu raced through his mind.

"Penny for your thoughts," said Kylie.

"Oh, just reliving the story. Exciting, isn't it? How many people ever get to do what we can on Corfu?"

"Do you think we will meet all of them?"

Bernard glanced in his mirror.

"You will meet The Twelve, but don't be in too much of a hurry. They are very busy right now. There is a lot of Seeker activity all around the world. How about spending a couple of days at my place? Just take in the sun and make some new friends."

Peter thought about Stefanos and wondered if he should re-read a Greek phrase book.

"Does Stefanos still clean your pool and work at Katerina's Kitchen?"

"He does."

"Bernard, this might sound like an odd question, but have you ever given me a Greek phrase book?"

"No, not that I can remember, but that is a coincidence. I asked Miss Dickson to put one in your rucksack."

"I'd like to read it."

"Learn it, you mean. You are just like your grandfather. He could remember everything he read and I guessed it was one of the powers Myroy gifts to a Keeper."

Kylie's eyes lit up.

"So that's why you have been doing so well at school."

"It is. I read a text book, remember every page and get top marks, except I have to make myself get some questions wrong so I don't draw attention to myself."

"And drawing attention to yourself is not a good idea," said Bernard.

"Is that how you made the story about the war come to life for me?" asked Kylie.

"I think so. After I read *Early Celtic Writing and their Meanings*, it, well, became a part of me."

Next to an ancient, torn-out page, Peter's mobile went off in his rucksack. He looked at the caller's name on the screen.

"Hi, Mum."

Kylie saw Peter's face change.

"What's up?"

"Hold on. No, not you, Mum. I know you're upset, but tell me what happened." Peter began to shake with anger and threw his mobile into his rucksack. "James has been beaten up by someone at school. He's in hospital and Dad's there now. Mum's in tears."

Bernard spoke in his calm voice.

"Sounds like a change of plan is in order."

He pulled the car into a lay-by and put his mobile to his ear.

"Miss Dickson, a small detour is needed. Please cancel the flights to Corfu and re-book us onto the first available flight to London Luton. I'll come back to you with further instructions when I know more."

As the sun set on Peter's normal day, he stood with Bernard and his father, in a brightly lit corridor that smelled of disinfectant. Julie had made Peter wear his school uniform to the hospital, just in case there was a chance of the doctors letting him in to see his brother.

"A good impression is everything," his mum had said.

"He's still in intensive care," said Colin Donald. "Still on the critical list, I'm afraid."

"Do you want a cup of tea?" asked Bernard.

Colin stared into the empty plastic cup he was holding.

"Drunk too much tea already. This machine stuff isn't very good, either."

Peter felt his anger rise up inside his body.

"Who did it?"

"Don't know, son. We may never know, if James doesn't come round."

"Can I see him?"

Bernard put his hand on his shoulder.

"You're too young to be a visitor. There are rules about that kind of thing."

Peter shrugged his hand away and, in a far away loch, the stone pulsed.

"I'm going to see him."

"You go and see him," repeated Bernard and Colin.

Peter walked down the corridor, following signs to the intensive care unit, and pushed open one half of a set of big double doors, and went up to a nurse who sat at a desk. She stared up at him from behind a pile of paperwork.

"You shouldn't be here. Get out at once."

"You are very busy at the moment. You have so much to do somewhere else."

"I have so much to do," she repeated, "I have to go now."

As she walked to the double doors, Peter spoke again.

"Which room is James Donald in?"

"Number six."

Peter went through another set of doors into a long narrow room with hand basins on one side and plastic bags, hanging on pegs, on the other side. A sign read –

**All Visitors Must Wash Their Hands
and Dress in the Protective Clothing Provided.**

He washed his hands and took a bag from a peg. Inside was a green disposable T-shirt, over-trousers, gloves, mask and two large elasticated bags to cover his shoes. He put them on and went to find room six.

A young doctor stood at the foot of James's bed, reading a clipboard. He stared at Peter's masked face and young eyes.

"I don't know how you got in here, but I want you to leave right away."

"I have special permission to see the patient."

"You have special permission. Please carry on."

"How is he?"

"We will know more when he wakes. Perhaps tomorrow?"

Peter looked at his brother's face. James's eyes were black and swollen and most of his face was bruised. Tubes and wires were everywhere, connecting his body to bleeping monitors and stands holding blood and clear solutions. A light unit on the wall had two X-rays clipped to it and they showed the deeper, more worrying, damage to the boy's skull.

Peter imagined himself holding Amera's stone and wished his brother would be well again. The room became bathed in a blood- red light and James's heart monitor beeped more quickly, more regularly, as his heart returned to its normal pulse-rate. He opened an eye and saw Peter's smiling face.

"Don't try and move. You have had a bit of an accident."

When he spoke, James's words were slow and weak.

"It wasn't an accident, you dipstick."

"Who did it?"

"Mac."

"Why?"

"To get at you."

Peter clutched the pebble in his hand.

"Sleep now."

"I feel so tired."

As Peter left intensive care, he tore off his protective clothing, straightened his school tie and placed his pebble onto the corridor floor.

"Find, Mac."

The pebble rolled off and Peter followed it, passing his father and Bernard.

"Where are you going?" asked Colin.

"Unfinished business."

His father stepped between Peter and the pebble. The pebble stopped rolling.

"Don't do this."

297

A hospital porter pushed a bed on wheels around the bend in the corridor behind Colin. Peter concentrated on the bed and the porter felt it pull away from his hands. Peter concentrated on his father who rose up as the bed shot under him, and the bed raced away with Colin on it.

"Tell Dad that James will be fine in the morning."

Bernard nodded and watched the bed smash into a tea machine.

"Get home as quickly as you can," he said.

Peter looked up at the ceiling and spoke.

"Grandpa, I need the stone."

"You *need* the stone?"

"I want to hold it."

"No."

"I am the Keeper, not you."

Grandpa sighed.

"You are the Keeper not me and you are making a huge mistake."

"Get me the pipe," said Peter angrily.

In the Realm of the Dead, Duncan spoke to Tirani and, a few moments later, the small pipe dropped down through the corridor roof. Peter held his hand out, and caught it. He blew the pipe and, in the loch, Amera's stone felt his anger and returned to the Keeper.

Mac was with his mates, outside a chip shop on Bridge Street in Pinner. He looked up and smiled at a lit street light.

"You should have seen that Donald kid. I gave him a right good battering."

Toady Thompson lit a cigarette.

"That'll learn him."

"Wait till Monday. I'll get his brother at school."

"Let's kick him good."

"Give us a drag."

Toady passed Mac his fag and three other boys came over to stand closer to them. One tall boy had a bag of chips.

"Can I have a drag?" asked the tall boy.

"Get lost," said Toady.

"I'll give you a chip."

"Two chips."

"OK."

"Can I have a drag?" asked another boy.

"Get lost. Go and steal some."

"What we gonna do tonight, anyway?" asked Mac.

Toady grinned and took his fag back from the boy with the chips.

"Same as normal. Muck about and get into trouble."

A small round pebble rolled along the pavement and stopped in front of Mac. He kicked it hard at a car across the street and it dented a door panel, before rolling back to him. He kicked it away again and it rolled back. Mac picked it up and turned the pebble around in his fingers.

"Did you see that?"

Toady didn't answer. He was looking at a boy, dressed in a school uniform, who had just joined them. The pocket of his dark trousers glowing red, as if he had a torch there. The pocket pulsed as Peter remembered his brother's bruised face. Fuelled with an anger that should not have been there, he took his pebble from Mac's fingers and smashed his fist into the boy's face.

***

Inside the standing stone, Odin's eyes opened and flashed, intense and blue. He waded through a salt-water pool and passed through a wall of solid rock to step out into his eternal sanctuary, deep beneath the OASV offices near Oslo. His immaculate black suit reflected in the hundreds of television screens, which surrounded a single, large LCD screen. It showed a map of the world he would one day rule and he stared at the hundreds of red dots that covered the land, pinpointing the location of the Donald clan. One dot in North London was flashing.

Peter had been too tired to get undressed and, as he slept in his school uniform, a white Ford Transit parked outside his house. From the driving seat, Olaf Adanson gave instructions to Mick Roberts, who sat in the back of the van, surrounded by electronic equipment.

"Start the first scan."

Mick put headphones on and entered instructions into a laptop.

"It'll take a few seconds."

Olaf peered through the darkness at Peter's house. It looked ordinary and that was a good sign.

"OK, scan results are back. Want a look?"

Olaf climbed into the back, sat next to Mick and lifted a black helmet off the wall, put it on and shut the visor.

"Take me in."

Mick used the arrow keys on the laptop to guide a walking cartoon figure through the plan of a house on his screen. Olaf felt himself come out of the entrance hall and into a kitchen, with a table and chairs, and into a lounge with a television in one corner.

"Deep scan," said Olaf.

Mick pushed more buttons and Olaf watched the screen on the inside of his visor change. The computer image became more detailed as a mirror and pictures appeared on the lounge wall. A pattern appeared on what had been a plain carpet and, suddenly, it was as if he was really there.

"Give me the laptop."

Olaf felt Mick place it onto his knee and he typed at great speed, feeling himself walk to a dresser, pull out a drawer and empty the contents onto the carpet. An hour later, he pulled a shoebox from under the bed of a sleeping boy and emptied its contents. He pulled the helmet off.

"Order our people to Pinner. The master's stone is here."

300

"I had the weirdest bloomin' dream," said Laura.

Julie Donald squeezed a mug into her dishwasher, shut the door and switched it on.

"Was it that someone was walking around your room?"

"How did you know that?"

"I dreamt it too. What are you going to do today?"

"Just chill. I like Sundays. No school."

Colin came in with his newspaper.

"I just called the hospital. The nurse says that James is bored and complaining about the food."

"Shall we go and get him?"

"In a while. I thought I'd read the paper first. Isn't it quiet without him?"

Peter joined them, still in his dishevelled uniform, his hair sticking out at the back.

"I've had a funny dream," he mumbled sleepily.

"That is not a good look," said Laura.

"Was someone in your room too?" asked Julie. "Want some breakfast? I've got eggs, bacon, cereals, toast."

"Bacon and eggs sounds good."

She opened her new fridge door, took out the eggs and glanced out of the kitchen window. Two men in dark suits were staring back at her. She dropped the eggs in fear.

"Colin. I think we've got company."

He came to stand next to her and shouted at his son.

"Peter, go upstairs now. Get the brooch and use it to get away. Call me when you can."

There was a loud *bang* from the front door and Peter ran up to his room. Behind him, the kitchen floor began to shimmer, like moonlight on water. Another *bang*. Peter took his mobile phone and dropped it inside his rucksack, next to the folded page from *Early Celtic Writings and their Meanings*. He shouldered the bag and tried to work out how to escape. Grandpa's voice boomed out.

"Hundreds of Seekers surround the house."

"What do I do?"

"Get away."

"But how?"

Grandpa sighed.

"Haven't you learned anything?"

With heavy footsteps on the stairs, he threw the lid off his shoebox and took the brooch in his hand and put Tirani's pipe into his pocket. The image of him lifting Stefanos and dropping the boy into Bernard's swimming pool, flashed through his mind. He tightened his grip on the stone, rose up and flew at his closed bedroom window.

"Stop," he yelled.

He stopped in mid air, dropped down, opened the window and sat, legs dangling out, on the sill. His bedroom door burst open and two men saw him. As dawn broke over Pinner, he flew out above the Donalds' wheelie bins and turned to hover above the front door. A Seeker pointed up at him.

"The Keeper is there."

Peter landed behind the white van and hundreds of Seekers chased him along the back-streets of Pinner. In the van, Mick Roberts spoke into his mobile.

"The sighting is confirmed. The Keeper's name is Peter Donald and our people chase him."

"Drive him close to water," said Thorgood Firebrand.

The line went dead and Olaf started the engine.

✳✳✳

Holly Anderson stood in front of the photo of the full moon in the Skepere office, on Lower Level Five of the MI5 building in Vauxhall.

"Screen on," she said.

The Gora moon was replaced by a large screen. Next to the first agenda item, "The Protection of the Keeper," a traffic light went red.

302

"Location of the Keeper?"

The screen changed to a map of London and the traffic light moved above Pinner.

"Zoom."

A detailed street map of Pinner came on screen and the traffic light moved slowly up Church Lane, towards the High Street.

"Location of the Seekers?"

A map of the world appeared with thousands of red dots moving slowly towards the United Kingdom. London was already a mass of red.

"Seeker numbers in London?" she asked.

The screen went black and a number appeared in the centre.

2463

"Seekers in close proximity to the Keeper?"

The street map of Pinner appeared again. Peter had just turned into the High Street and twenty dots followed him, but had not yet turned the corner out of Church Lane. Holly pushed a button on her mobile, but Peter did not reply. She watched the chase and spoke quietly to herself.

"Oh, Bernard. We are taking one hell of a risk."

***

Peter's mobile rang in his bouncing rucksack, but all he could hear was the pounding of feet behind him. He called up to Grandpa.

"I can't outrun them."

"Think about Dougie, running towards the castle."

Peter gripped the stone.

"Faster, like Dougie."

His strides increased in length and he accelerated past a pub named the Queen's Head. Panting for breath, he stopped at the end of the High Street, and stared back at his pursuers. Like the start of a marathon, the road was full of runners, except these runners were all dressed in dark suits.

"Bloody hell."

Peter stared ahead, down Chapel Lane, then left towards Pinner railway station. He chose left and sprinted for the station entrance, not caring which train he caught, just as long as there was a train at a platform right now. He gasped for breath in front of a lady in a dark grey uniform.

"Any trains leaving now?"

"There's a train just leaving platform two."

"Where's that?"

She pointed at some stairs with a sign above it –

PLATFORM TWO

"You have a ticket?"

He clutched his stone.

"I don't need a ticket."

"You don't need a ticket," she repeated. "On you go."

Her eyes widened as hundreds of men in suits ran into Pinner station.

"Tickets please," she said.

Peter took the stairs three at a time and came out onto the platform, a train already pulling away. Gripping the stone hard, he ran and leapt through the back wall of the moving train, to stand in a half-empty carriage. Most of the passengers were reading, lost in their own worlds, and no one saw him appear like magic. He stuck his head out of a window. The Seekers were swarming onto Platform Two. He breathed a huge sigh of relief and sat down in a corner, as far from anyone else as he could. Above him the tube information map showed all the stations along the mauve coloured Metropolitan Line.

"If the next is North Harrow, I'm going towards London. If I can find Miss Dickson, I can hide up at the British Museum," he thought.

Suddenly he feared for his family's safety. Had they been taken, or killed? Ignoring the other passengers, he called up to the ceiling.

"Grandpa, are Mum and Dad safe?"

"They are. Myroy collected them."

Another sigh of relief. The train slowed as it approached a station and he peered forward out of the window. A sign read –

North Harrow

"Good."

He looked up at the map again, the next stop would be Harrow on the Hill. His eyes left the map for the passengers on the platform. Every twenty paces along its entire length were men in smart dark suits. Many had blond hair and every one of them had searching eyes. Peter panicked, but as passengers got off the train, the Seekers did not move and he tried to guess why they made no attempt to board. He felt confused and slowly walked over to another seat that had a discarded newspaper on it. He lifted it and pretended to read.

The train pulled away and soon left the over-ground system to dive into the blackness of the underground. The lights came on, his panic subsided and he read the paper. A small article on page nine caught his eye –

Giant Bird Sighted Above Loch Leven.
New Species, or Stupid Hoax?
By Heida Way.

Peter read the article.

"In another ludicrous 'Nessie-type' hoax to lure tourists to the area, several local people reported seeing a giant osprey with a wingspan of over one hundred metres. Sergeant Moss at Kinross Police Station denied that the sightings were linked to the trial of longer pub opening hours."

Peter knew by the name of the reporter that the Keepers had covered up his visit to Scotland.

305

"Good job," he said.

He took Tirani's pipe from his pocket and studied it. Wooden, small and with only two blow holes on the top. The wood looked ancient. He put it into his rucksack and took out his mobile. One missed call from a number he did not recognise, so he deleted it and called Kylie. "No signal," flashed on the screen.

The tube train rocked as it rounded a bend, then it slowed to enter Harrow on the Hill. Peter picked up his paper and tried to hide behind it as passengers left their seats to stand in front of the automatic doors. They opened and Peter peered around his paper at the platform. Seekers, like statues, every twenty paces, but no one got on board. The doors shut and the train pulled away. Peter spoke to the ceiling.

"Why did they not get on, Grandpa?"

"They don't need to get on. They are stopping you getting off."

"Why?"

"Shepherding you to a place where they can attack and take the stone."

"What do I do?"

"When you can, get off and hide."

The same thing happened at the next three stations, Seekers guarding the platforms, passengers getting off, but not on, and Peter's fear growing with each stop. As the train left Finchley Road, he looked at the map and at the next station, Baker Street, with its connections to the Jubilee, Circle, Hammersmith and City, and Bakerloo lines. The station, on the map, looked like a multi coloured spider, and he decided to get off there, whatever happened, and prayed it would be busy with crowds of people that he could hide amongst.

He clutched the stone and got ready to use its power, but as the train slowed he saw that the brightly lit platform was completely deserted. He got up quickly and stepped out, looking for an exit sign. The engine revved and the train moved noisily away to leave him standing, listening to it fade into the distance. This wasn't right, even for a Sunday morning. There should be people around.

An intense blue spark down the dark tunnel and a rush of air told him another train was approaching and, fearing the Seekers it might carry, he fled into an exit tunnel and up to an information board. The board had arrows pointing to different tunnelled walkways, which led to the platforms of the other tube lines. One arrow pointed to the exit and he ran that way, and as he rounded a bend he saw twenty Seekers walking towards him. He spun around and ran back to the board.

"Which way? Which line?"

He glanced down the different tunnels, past the advertising posters and lights set into the roofs. Seekers appeared in the tunnel that went to the Jubilee Line platforms. More Seekers appeared, blocking the ways to the Circle Line and the Hammersmith and City. Peter sprinted towards the Bakerloo Line, his rucksack bouncing up and down, sweat pouring down his back. A train waited on the south-bound platform and he jumped in. His pursuers walked onto the platform and stood like statues again, staring into his eyes as the train pulled away.

"What are they up to?" he whispered.

As the train entered the darkness of the tunnel, the window became a mirror and Peter jumped as he saw two Seekers behind him, in the reflection. He whirled round and pushed his fist out, the stone pulsing in his palm. They flew back and hit the train's wall, and Peter ran down the empty carriage with more Seekers chasing and calling out to him to stop. He reached the end of the compartment and struggled to open the connecting door to the next carriage. He used the stone, it opened, and he slammed it shut behind him.

He glanced ahead towards the rear of the train and wondered why there were no passengers here either. He counted. Three more carriages to get through and then he would have nowhere to run. He looked back. The compartment he had left was now full of angry men in dark suits.

He ran again as the connecting door burst open and he heard the sound of pounding feet catching up with him. Someone grabbed his rucksack and Peter's feet kept running but he made no progress. He spun around and punched the man in the mouth. The Seeker fell and Peter made it into the next compartment, and finally into the last carriage. He glanced up and called out.

"Grandpa!"

"Aye, Laddie."

The connecting door to the last compartment burst open and Peter's stomach tightened.

"I could do with some help."

"What is their measure?"

Peter counted the men who walked confidently towards him. Their suits began to dissolve away to be replaced by the clothes of Norse warriors. They drew their swords.

"About twenty and they aren't Seekers, they are Odin's Valkyrie."

"Um. That is a worry."

"Grandpa. Now would be a good time."

The compartment floor in front of him began to shimmer, like moonlight on water, and Hamish and Donald rose up from the underworld, their plaids stinking of stale body odour. They looked at Peter and smiled. Peter pointed at the charging men behind them. Hamish growled and drew his claymore. The train rocked as it increased in speed and took a bend.

"Is that all there is?" asked Donald.

Hamish's sword thrust out and a man fell, another Valkyrie climbed over a seat to Hamish's left and Donald threw his dirk into his chest. He turned to smile at Peter, but his eyes grew wide with fear. Peter spun around and a spear smashed through the train's rear window. Amera's stone pulsed, blood-red and, as the window exploded into a thousand sharp pieces, the shards of glass missed his eyes. The spear thudded into the back of a seat.

Peter felt the rush of cold air and stared back down the tunnel.

It was lit by an orange and red glow, and a great longship chased the train, the dark silhouette of its dragon prow edging closer.

With its speed increasing, Peter's train thundered through Regents Park Station. A man, in a bowler hat and pin-striped suit, lowered his newspaper as the pages flapped violently. He saw Vikings fighting Celtic warriors with swords in the last carriage. A Norse longship, engulfed in an orange and red glow, flashed past. He shrugged his shoulders and began reading again.

In the narrow carriage, Hamish and Donald held back the Valkyrie, a growing mound of bodies protecting them. The train rocked violently.

"When is it going to stop?" thought Peter.

Oxford Circus, Piccadilly Circus and Charing Cross stations flashed by, and the train began to slow.

"Can you guys buy me some space?" asked Peter.

Donald called back, a blade cutting the air by his missing ear.

"What?"

"When the train stops, I will run out. Hold them back for me."

Hamish growled and punched a Seeker in the face, who joined the fallen on the mound.

"No problem."

Peter looked out at the station sign –

Embankment

He leapt out onto a deserted platform and ran towards an exit sign. He called back.

"Thanks."

Hamish and Donald quickly followed him and stood, side by side, guarding the pedestrian tunnel that Peter had fled down. Hundreds of men in smart suits left the train and walked towards them.

"You like me, don't you," said Donald.

309

"No," growled Hamish. "You are an annoying wee bastard."

"Go on. Say something nice."

Hamish waved his claymore above his head, practising his swing. He glared at his friend.

"Alright, I like you."

"Say it again."

"No."

"Is that all? You just *like* me."

"It's enough."

Donald grinned and pointed his sword at the enemy, who were parting to make way for a glowing longship that drifted menacingly above the platform towards them.

"Wager I kill more than you."

Hamish ignored him and roared like a wild beast, and charged.

Peter climbed up the steepest escalator he had ever seen. This station was silent and eerie. All the arched walkways and steep escalators were deserted. He came out into the main entrance and climbed over a ticket barrier, and stepped out onto Embankment Street in bright sunshine. He sniffed the dirty air. The rare green of Victoria Embankment Gardens was to his right and to his left he saw Seekers guarding a busy road that arched over a railway. He guessed it right away.

"They want me to go into the gardens."

Squeezing the stone, he ran over towards the enemy, knocking them away as they dived at him. He turned right into Northumberland Avenue, zig-zagging between shoppers and tourists, and, increasing his stride, he followed a black cab up towards Trafalgar Square.

A deep sense of fear gripped him and Peter turned to see that the road was full of running men, car horns sounding angrily behind them. He hid behind a parked lorry and dived into a clothes shop, panting, his eyes darting around for Seekers. A young lady in a short red dress came over to him.

"Can I help you?" she asked in a posh voice.

"I'm being chased by bad guys and I stand out like a sore thumb in my uniform."

He took his rucksack off, threw his blazer on the floor and pulled a blue jumper on.

"That is far too big," she said, picking up his blazer and folding it.

"It's fine."

He put a trilby hat on.

"And that does not go with that jumper. Not at all."

"I'll take them." He saw Seekers running past the front of the shop. "Scarves?"

"Over there."

He ran to a stand and wrapped a bright yellow scarf around his neck, and put his rucksack back on.

"That should do it. How much?"

"Two hundred and thirty-five pounds."

"I only want to buy the clothes, not the shop."

She dropped his blazer on the floor and shrugged her shoulders.

"London prices, I'm afraid."

He realised he didn't have any money and gripped Amera's stone.

"I can have these free of charge."

"They are free. Thank you for your custom."

Pulling the scarf above his chin, he walked back onto Northumberland Avenue.

Trafalgar Square was full of people and pigeons, and he sat on a bench below the statue of a huge lion, trying to work out what to do next. His mobile rang and he took it out of his rucksack. He didn't recognise the number so he let it ring out.

Across the square, a man in a smart suit spotted his rucksack and took a picture of it with his phone and sent it off attached to a text. The reply was almost instant and Seekers appeared from everywhere to join him. Peter threw his rucksack over his shoulder and sprinted through a gap in the running men, dodging cars and taxis, to enter the Strand. He passed Charring Cross station with Seekers guarding its entrance and stopped. The road ahead was full of running men. Behind him, the Strand was full of Seekers, shouting out, pointing at him, speaking instructions into mobile phones. He felt sick and turned right into Villiers Street and ran down the hill, back towards the Embankment tube station.

"Oh, no."

This time he had no choice. Every other escape route was blocked and he entered the Victoria Embankment Gardens with the river Thames on his right. He called up.

"I'm getting hemmed in."

Grandpa's voice boomed out.

"Stay away from the river."

"But I'm by the river."

"Then go somewhere else."

"Thanks for nothing," whispered Peter.

"I heard that."

Peter dashed along a narrow, twisting path and passed an empty bandstand. Seekers came out of bushes to his left and walked forward to force him out of the gardens and closer to the river. He was nearly knocked down by a car as he darted over a zebra crossing and stood, gasping for air, below a tall Egyptian obelisk. A sign read –

Cleopatra's Needle.
Made for the pharaoh Thotmes the Third in 1460 BC

He stared up at the high finger of rock and the hieroglyphics carved upon it, and knew he was lost. The Seekers formed a half circle, trapping him beside the river. Hundreds of them, many rows deep. They fell to their knees and Peter turned to see a tower of bubbles rising up out of the Thames. He dropped his rucksack onto the ground and got ready to fight.

The dark waters by Cleopatra's Needle boiled. Angry waves radiated outwards and a cold wind blew down the embankment.

All the noises of the city melted away and Peter watched helplessly as the tower of bubbles rose up to dwarf the obelisk. Despite his terror and instinct to run, he couldn't take his eyes from the tower and the face that formed inside it. He had seen this face before, in a story, inside a waterfall. Its intense blue eyes flashed and Odin was there, in a dark blue suit, standing proud above his kneeling followers. He stared down at Peter from the top of the tower of bubbles, his voice like ice.

"Peter of the line of Donald, give me the stone."

His words cut deep into Peter's soul and he felt his hand open, Amera's stone for all to see on his upturned palm. It pulsed blood red.

"Give me the stone."

Peter walked forward to kneel beside the Thames, his head swimming, his body not his own anymore. Grandpa's voice boomed down.

"Fight him, Peter," but Peter did not hear his warning.

The tower of bubbles lowered Odin to stand face to face with the last Keeper.

"Give it to me."

Down river, in the Skepere office on Lower Level Five of the MI5 building, Holly Anderson watched Odin on live television pictures and put her phone to her ear.

"OK. Send the boys in."

Hundreds of police in riot gear ran out of the Victoria Embankment Gardens and charged the Seekers. Police vans raced from all directions, tyres screeching, lights flashing, more policemen ready to jump out. The kneeling men in suits leapt up to protect their master, and the Keepers and Seekers smashed together, fighting viciously, but no side gaining an advantage over the other. Grandpa's voice boomed down.

"Peter, listen to me."

Odin raised his outstretched arms to waist height and *Black Slugs* surfaced on either side of him, rocket launchers rising up from panels on their decks and locking onto Peter's body. Grandpa's voice fell on deaf ears again.

"He will kill you. Kill your family and Kylie. It won't be a story this time."

More police vans screamed along the Embankment and Odin waved a finger at Amera's stone. A red beam shot towards him and his flat hand deflected the beam at the vans. They burst into flames. Odin changed the angle of his palm and the death beam cut into the police who attacked his people. He smiled.

"My dear brother, your luck has finally run out."

***

Across the Thames, a huge bird perched on top of the Royal Festival Hall, its keen eyes watching every movement in the battle around the obelisk. Below him, on a flat part of the roof, the building began to shimmer, like moonlight on water, and Myroy rose up. The Ancient One pointed his staff at Odin and Gora opened his mighty wings.

***

Grandpa Donald rose up through the concrete and placed his big hand around Peter's hand, which held the brooch.

"Come on, laddie. We have got a job to do."

Peter stared at him through glazed eyes.

"Where are we?"

"Fighting a war. We must alter the beam."

They pushed their hands sideways and the beam, that Odin deflected onto the police, struck a *Slug*. The submarine glowed red and exploded. Odin's face changed and he willed the beam to return to his control. Peter and Duncan's hands shook as they defied the god's will, but fuelled by anger and greed, his power was too strong. The red line of light shot back to his palm and he angled it to strike Grandpa. Duncan's body glowed to become like fired, brittle glass and shattered into a thousand pieces.

Peter cried out.

"Grandpa!"

In that moment, the pictures of his family being blown up at the airport and hugging Kylie's bloody body on a concrete slipway, became crystal clear. His anger rose and he fought to regain control of the beam that jerked around in the sky, like a laser light-show. The Ancient One's blue eyes glared at him. Peter glared back, but his eyes caught a huge pair of wings behind the tower of bubbles.

***

Gora flapped hard to gain height then tucked his wings into his body and felt the freedom of the rushing air as he dived. Oh, how he had craved that feeling of freedom as a prisoner of the stone. He flexed his talons and calculated the distance to his target precisely. No eyes were on him, the enemy fought in battle, as he reopened his wings and skimmed above the water. He threw his head back, sank his talons into Odin's shoulders and screeched.

"I cannot kill you, but I can weaken you."

A second later, he dropped the god onto the land near Peter and flew away. Odin snarled and pointed his hand at the osprey.

"You die now."

But nothing happened and a look of fear shot across Odin's face. Peter ran at him and hit his face with the stone held in his fist. Odin flew back and crashed into Cleopatra's Needle, and staggered to his feet.

"Come to me, Valkyrie," he shouted.

Olaf Adanson and Thorgood Firebrand rose up out of the river, now holding swords and wearing Norse clothes, and stood in front of their master. Behind Peter, the Seekers beat off the last of the police and turned to attack him. Grandpa's voice boomed out.

"Use the story, Peter."

"I thought you were dead."

"I'm already dead."

A single phrase from Myroy's teachings leapt into Peter's mind and thumped around his brain like a loud heartbeat,

"Together we are stronger," he said.

He aimed the stone at the gardens across the road.

"Together we are stronger."

The grass glowed red. A deep rumbling noise came from the depths of the earth, like horses charging in battle, and the Seekers spun around. Peter gripped the stone as hard as he could and poured his anger into it.

"Together we are stronger."

Like an army appearing over the crest of a blood-stained hill, the tips of spears and the heads of Celtic warriors, rose up out of the red grass. Their bodies followed and then their Highlands. The line of horsemen walked forward onto the road to face the half circle of men in dark suits, who still surrounded Peter.

A single rider came forward and the wind lifted his long grey hair, beneath the crown he wore. Peter nodded at the king he had only ever seen in a story. The Younger smiled, unsheathed his claymore and the High Table of Scotland thundered forward.

Peter focused his mind onto the pain he had suffered and his grief when Kylie was killed by a single shot from a Computer Aided Rifle. It didn't matter that it hadn't been real. Odin would kill her if he let the Ancient One live. He shot a death beam at Odin who leapt aside, grabbing Peter's rucksack and diving off the embankment into the Thames. Olaf and Thorgood ran after him and Peter's beam missed them, but destroyed the last *Black Slug*.

Peter walked slowly to the side of the river and stared at the disappearing circle of bubbles, and listened to the screams of the wounded behind him. Across the river, on top of a high building, a giant osprey rose up effortlessly and flew north to become a mere speck in the distance. Malcolm the Younger came to stand beside him.

"It is done."

Peter felt numb and it was a while before he could speak.

316

"But it is not over."

They walked together, through the bloody bodies of the Seekers and policemen, and crossed the road. Malcolm mounted his stallion and called for his riders to join him.

"Will we fight together again?" asked Peter.

"I hope not. Keep the brooch hidden."

As the High Table descended into the glowing red grass, Peter looked at the brooch and, even though he knew the answer in his heart, he asked the stone a question.

"Will I be the last Keeper?"

The ruby pulsed once and Peter shivered with fear.

"So, I have to hunt Odin down and kill him."

***

The next day, Holly Anderson stood in front of the screen in the Skepere office in London. The traffic light beside the first agenda item, *Protection of the Keeper*, turned green. She smiled and spoke to the voice activation system.

"Location of the Seekers?"

The screen changed to become a map of the world. Hundreds of red dots were moving slowly towards Australia. Relief flooded through Holly's body and she whispered to herself.

"So, Odin looked in Peter's rucksack and read the false address, on the page from *Early Celtic Writings and their Meanings*."

She smiled and spoke excitedly.

"Seeker numbers in London?"

The screen went black and a number appeared in the centre.

41

"Seekers in close proximity to the Keeper?"

A map of the lower slopes of Pantekrator, on Corfu, appeared showing no Seekers on the island.

She picked up her phone.

"Hi, Bernard."

"Ah, Holly. Any news?"

"Our friends have read the page from an old book and believed every word. We should get some peace and quiet for a while."

"I am pleased to hear it. Someone told me there was some trouble by the Thames yesterday."

"I read about it in the papers. They all said that the filming of a new television drama got a bit out of hand."

"Oh, dear. And I understand that two needy families might need a free holiday. Would you make the arrangements for me?"

"I took the liberty. They are already there."

"That was kind of you. Where did you send them?

"Somewhere *very* special."

"I see."

Holly's voice changed.

"Bernard, we took a huge risk."

"We did."

"Anything I can help with?"

"No, not at the moment, but please keep me informed of any developments at work."

Holly turned off her phone.

"Screen up."

The screen rose to reveal a photo of the moon and she stared at it for a long time.

***

Peter and Kylie lay on sun-beds beside Bernard's pool.

"Are you going to tell me about the rest of the story you read in that book?" asked Kylie.

Peter smiled in the bright sunshine and sipped his pineapple juice.

"No. I'm on holiday."

"Oh, go on."

"I've had a busy weekend and, if you don't mind, I'd like to forget all that stuff for a while."

Bernard stepped out of the large patio doors and came to join them.

"Settling in OK?"

Peter slurped the last of his juice and Mrs Agnedes hurried across to give him a refill.

"I like it here."

"Me too," said Kylie. "When can we go to the Realm of the Dead?"

Bernard smiled.

"In a couple of days, there's no hurry."

"Any news from home?"

"I just spoke to Holly. Odin has bought the whole thing, hook, line and sinker. We could get years out of the deception."

"And Mum and Dad?" asked Kylie.

"Both your families are with The Twelve under Pantekrator. They will be having a fantastic time."

"So, they are all safe," said Peter.

"There was a real risk that Odin would find and kidnap them. But they *are* safe now."

"How did you cover up the battle by the Thames?" asked Peter.

"Normal thing. Television drama that got out of hand. MI5 cleaning up the rest of the mess."

Bernard left them and Peter smiled at Kylie.

"Fancy a swim?"

"Not until you tell me the rest of the story."

"No."

"Well, at least tell me about Prince Ranald's promise to Thorgood. I'm dying to know what he's up to."

"He's up to no good."

"I know that, but what did he say?"

Peter sighed.

"He promised Thorgood Margaret's hand in marriage. That means he will become King of Ireland in a single stroke and have his base to attack the Welsh people. Remember, he still

319

thinks Llewellyn has Amera's stone."

"And what does Ranald want?"

"To be king and win the help of the Norsemen in the coming civil war."

"So it isn't time yet for a new Long Peace."

"No. Not yet."

"Did Ranald promise him anything else?"

Peter went to stand beside the pool.

"Coming in?" he asked.

"When you answer."

"He said he would kill his father and give Thorgood Tain."

Peter dived in and felt the water cool his body. It was as if all his worries were being washed away. For the first time in a long time, he felt safe and free of the burden he carried. Kylie dived in beside Peter and, when they surfaced, she kissed him. They swam to the side of the pool, rested their elbows on the side and watched Mrs Agnedes pile home-made cakes onto the veranda table.

"I think the words of a shepherd apply, don't you?" said Kylie.

Peter kissed her again and said what had gone through both of their minds.

"There is no more worth having than this."

Dougie and Peter will return in their next thrilling adventure, *The Rise of the Red Empire.*

As Scotland descends into a bloody civil war, the High Table divides and clan fights against clan.

Prince Ranald fulfils his promise and Alistair of Cadbol turns to a friend, and an old enemy, to defend the Younger's legacy.

South of the land of the Gauls, a descendant of kings fights his way home and Myroy's prediction about the union of the royal houses, of Elder and Donald, begins to come true.

A new Long Peace is a while away yet, but the first seeds of hope take root.

In our time, Odin holds the stone and most of the planet kneels to his authority. His forces invade the free world and the Valkyrie enslave the peoples of Europe. Helped by a spy, a cuckoo in the nest, Peter, Bernard and the Winged Guardian lead the resistance in the Orange Band, but the very existence of the Keepers and the Realm of the Dead comes under threat.

Myroy watches helplessly, as the world he defended for centuries is torn apart. All of his fears become real and he tries to discover how to destroy the old magic, and free mankind from the curse of the Ancient Ones.

If you would like to read the start of the
next book then please visit –

www.myroybooks.com

TEACHERS

If you would like to invite Colin to your school for a book reading, please contact him at the following email address –

c.foreman123@btinternet.com

The normal size of group for a reading is 30 pupils and the best age range is 9 to 12 years.

We look forward to hearing from you.